UNDONE

VAMPIRE AWAKENINGS, BOOK 5

BRENDA K DAVIES

Copyright © 2015 Brenda K. Davies

ALSO FROM THE AUTHOR

BRENDA K. DAVIES PEN NAME:

The Vampire Awakenings Series

Awakened (Book 1)

Destined (Book 2)

Untamed (Book 3)

Enraptured (Book 4)

Undone (Book 5)

Fractured (Book 6)

Ravaged (Book 7)

Consumed (Book 8)

Unforeseen (Book 9)

Coming 2019

The Alliance Series

Vampire Awakenings Spinoff

Eternally Bound (Book 1)

Bound by Vengeance (Book 2)

Bound by Darkness (Book 3)

Bound by Passion (Book 4)

Coming 2019

The Road to Hell Series

Good Intentions (Book 1)

Carved (Book 2)

The Road (Book 3)

Into Hell (Book 4)

Hell on Earth Series

Road to Hell Spinoff

Hell on Earth (Book 1)

Into the Abyss (Book 2)

Kiss of Death (Book 3)

Coming 2019

Historical Romance

A Stolen Heart

ERICA STEVENS PEN NAME:

The Coven Series

Nightmares (Book 1)

The Maze (Book 2)

Dream Walker (Book 3)

Coming June 2019

The Captive Series

Captured (Book 1)

Renegade (Book 2)

Refugee (Book 3)

Salvation (Book 4)

Redemption (Book 5)

Broken (The Captive Series Prequel)

Vengeance (Book 6)

Unbound (Book 7)

The Kindred Series

Kindred (Book 1)

Ashes (Book 2)

Kindled (Book 3)

Inferno (Book 4)

Phoenix Rising (Book 5)

The Fire & Ice Series

Frost Burn (Book 1)

Arctic Fire (Book 2)

Scorched Ice (Book 3)

The Ravening Series

Ravenous (Book 1)

Taken Over (Book 2)

Reclamation (Book 3)

The Survivor Chronicles

Book 1: The Upheaval

Book 2: The Divide

Book 3: The Forsaken

Book 4: The Risen

CHAPTER ONE

Brian dropped the sleeping bag on the counter and grabbed a magazine from the holder next to the register. He ignored the disapproving look the old man behind the counter gave him as he flipped through a few pages of the *National Enquirer*.

He scanned an article about a sixty-year-old woman in Michigan who had given birth to her daughter's twins. *Interesting,* he thought, before skimming through an article on an alien sighting in Dubois. *The Men in Black would be all over that one.*

"Is this it?" the cashier asked and gave a pointed look at the magazine in his hand.

Brian flashed his teeth at him, causing the man to blanch and look hastily away. His fangs may not be bared, but he was aware of his effect on both humans and vamps. Most were unsure how to take him, and that was the way he liked it. It tended to make both species stay away from him, and there was nothing he liked more than being alone. He'd come to realize it was the simplest way to be.

"That's all of it," he replied, and slipped the magazine back into the rack.

The man maneuvered the sleeping bag around until he found the tag. The price gun in his hand beeped at the same time Brian's phone rang. The man's bushy gray eyebrows shot up at the *Fire and Rain* ringtone.

"Can't go wrong with James Taylor," Brian told him as he pulled his phone out of his pocket. He frowned at the unfamiliar number before silencing his phone and sliding it back into his jeans.

"Saw him in concert once," the man said, and moved the sleeping bag aside. Apparently, a shared appreciation for Taylor was enough for the man to forgive him for not purchasing the magazine and engage him in conversation. "He puts on a good show."

"He does," Brian agreed as the man rang up the lantern he was also purchasing. "I've seen him a couple of times myself."

His phone started to ring again. Pulling it out of his pocket, he glanced at the same unknown number before silencing it again and returning it to his pocket. If the person calling him wasn't in his contacts, he didn't want to talk to them, and if it was a telemarketer, he may hunt them down and kill them. Sometimes he much preferred the days before technology, no matter how convenient it was, it could also be a pain in the ass.

"Where are you planning to camp?" the old man asked.

Before Brian could answer, his phone rang again. He gritted his teeth when he saw the same number and sent it straight to voicemail. Hopefully, they'd finally get the point that he wasn't going to answer. "Going to do some hiking," he replied, "maybe climb Mount Washington."

"Nice trip, you'll need more supplies than this."

A human would; he didn't. "Got 'em in the back of the truck," he lied, and pointed at the pickup across the street.

The man hit the total button on the register as Brian's phone went off yet again. He didn't bother to look at it before hitting the silence button and handing the man some cash.

"Have a good trip," the man said as Brian gathered his supplies.

"Thanks."

He strode out the door and was halfway to his truck when his phone rang once more. He hit the straight to voicemail button as he tossed the sleeping bag into the back of the pickup next to his small bag of clothes. It had been years since he'd gotten a chance to do some camping. Not since his cabin in the Cascade Mountains had received an unplanned remodel five years ago, when he'd allowed his acquaintance, Ian Byrne, to use it as a hideout with his now wife, Paige.

He hadn't bothered to return to the cabin afterward and he never would now that other vampires had discovered its location. The vamps who had attacked Ian and Paige may be dead, but he hadn't survived nearly two hundred years by making stupid decisions. He was well aware there were many vampires out there who would prefer him dead and would love to feast on his power.

His cabin had been lost to him years ago, but that didn't mean he didn't miss the wilderness. Now, he planned to lose himself in the White Mountains of New Hampshire for a month or more. He glanced at his pocket in annoyance when his phone went off again. Pulling it out, he hit the green button as he flung the door of the black pickup open and slid inside.

"If someone's not dying, you will be. Who is this?"

"As rude as ever, I see!" a woman snapped back at him.

Brian's brows drew together as he tried to place the voice, but for the life of him he couldn't put a name to it. "Honey, I don't know who you are, so I don't think you can judge me. Plus, you're the one who has been calling me, nonstop. Now, since you don't seem to like me, and I'm not in the mood for belligerent females, I really don't see the point of this conversation."

"Maybe you don't remember me, but you know who I am, Brian Foley."

He'd been about to hang up and toss his phone out the window, but those words and something about the woman's voice intrigued him enough to stay his hand. Turning the key in the ignition, he started the truck. "I know I didn't knock you up."

"Gross. No, I have standards," the woman grumbled.

"This has been a pleasant conversation, and as much as I'd like to continue being insulted, I think I've had enough fun. Don't call me again."

"Wait!" Abby cried, terrified he would hang up on her and she would lose her chance at getting him to help her.

The frantic tone of the woman's voice halted him before he could toss the phone out his window. Something in his chest constricted as the frightened pitch of her voice called to him in an odd way.

With a sigh, he lifted the phone back to his ear. "Why?"

"I… I need your help," she blurted.

"I don't know who you are, and you clearly don't think much of me, so why would I help you?" he demanded.

"We met once before, about six years ago. My name is Abigail Byrne. I go by Abby."

Brian's hand squeezed around the phone, *another* Byrne. The Byrnes seemed to be everywhere, but then they were the largest vampire family he knew of in existence. He tried to recall this Abby, but the memory of which one she was in that clan eluded him.

"It was a brief meeting," she said, as if sensing his thoughts, "in a hotel room."

Realization hit with the force of a hammer between his eyes. "You're one of the twins."

"I am."

He dimly recalled seeing her in the hotel room where she'd nearly been slaughtered by vampires who had been hunting *him*. The twins had been merely children then. Children he'd barely paid attention to, but he did recall their pale hair and emerald green eyes. One of them had also possessed a brighter soul than the other, a soul that had shone through her fear while in that room. Listening to her now, he had a feeling Abby was the one who possessed that soul.

"Why are you calling me?" he asked.

He heard the rustling of her hair as she ran her fingers through it. The sound of her hair brushing against the phone caused his hand to tighten around it more. He didn't know what it was about this girl, but he found himself hanging onto every move and sound she made.

Pacing back and forth, Abby pondered his question as she debated how much to reveal to him, but she doubted withholding information would persuade him to help her. "My sister, Vicky, is missing."

That was the main reason she'd called him, but Abby couldn't deny she'd always known that one day she would reach out to him. It had been inevitable. Still, if it hadn't been for Vicky, that day would have been far in the future.

"And?" Brian prodded.

"And I need help finding her." *Desperately*, but she didn't say that.

"Your family could almost rival the Duggar's. I'm sure one of them can help you find her."

"They can't know about this!" she gushed out. "My parents would freak out, and they have my younger siblings to take care of. Ethan and Emma are expecting their first child, Ian and Paige are busy chasing their two boys, and Stefan and Isabelle just had a son."

He was aware of that. They may not send Christmas cards or talk on a monthly basis, but Stefan had started calling him every once in a while after he'd helped Ian and Paige find Paige's father. The conversations were often stilted and short, but Brian couldn't deny he liked seeing Stefan's name show up on his phone.

The friendship they'd once had was no more, and never would be again, but Stefan was the one who had known him best over the many years of his life. Fate had caused them to make different choices over the years, and they had gone their separate ways. Stefan was now married with two children, and he was still a mercenary who made his way through the world bringing death to those vampires deserving it.

He was glad Stefan had found so much happiness. He could never have that kind of happiness in his life and wouldn't waste his time looking for it. Any hope he'd had of a happy life had ended on the day his family was slaughtered and he'd been turned into one of the undead.

Every once in a while, Ian also picked up the phone to say hi to him, and he'd even spoken with Ethan once, but the one he spoke with the most out of the Byrne family was Aiden. The two of them had seen each other often over the past couple of months while Aiden was in training to work with Ronan's men. He liked the kid and would have helped more with his training, but he'd decided it was time for a vacation where no one could bother him. He'd been feeling burnt-out lately.

He should have known a Byrne would try to screw up his escape from it all.

"What about Aiden? Why can't he help you?" he inquired.

Abby emitted a disgruntled sound. "I tried calling him, but ever since he went to the training facility, he hasn't had his cell phone."

"They take it away," Brian said. "No outside distractions once you're in the training compound."

"I'm aware of that!" she shot back. "But when I tried calling to speak with him there, I was told, and I quote, 'Aiden doesn't have time for any ho's.' I didn't even get a chance to tell the guy I was Aiden's sister before he hung up on me."

"Sounds like Lucien," Brian said.

"Sounds like an asshole," she retorted, and he couldn't help but smile. "So, as you can see, I can't get in touch with him and all of my other siblings have yet to hit maturity and are only kids."

"So are you."

"I'm twenty-one, and I reached full maturity last year," she told him.

Abby paced to the other side of her dorm room and peered down on the dimly lit street as she tried to keep control of her swaying emotions. Just talking to him was causing her body to tense and her heartbeat to escalate. This could be the biggest mistake she'd ever made, but she had no other choice, and there was no going back now.

Watching the other students laugh as they strolled along the sidewalk in front of her dorm, she envied their lives of simplicity. As a born vampire, her life had never been simple; she'd had to learn at a young age to control her hunger if she were to fit in with the human world. When she'd finally gotten control of her vampire urges, she'd been allowed to go out amongst people, like her older siblings. She'd been enjoying attending school, going on dates, and having boyfriends until *he* had walked into her life six years ago.

Now, she'd managed to find a little peace and happiness here at college, and hated to think that she might not be returning to it. None of it would matter if she couldn't find Vicky. She tried to shake the possibility away, but it caused tears to swim in her eyes.

"Believe me, you were not the one I would have picked to call for this," she told him. "Ethan may not fully trust you, but some of my other siblings have started to, especially Aiden, and I've been told you can somehow find vampires and people who are missing or don't wish to be found. I need you to find Vicky for me. *Please*."

Her please caused his gut to clench. He rubbed at the bridge of his nose as he considered her words. "Why has she taken off?"

"I don't know. I haven't been able to find her or get in touch with her in five days, and I've looked everywhere and contacted everyone I can think of. We've never gone more than twelve hours without speaking to each other. She'd quit school and was seeing a new guy I hadn't really met yet, but she'd never go somewhere without at least telling me where she was going. Something is *not* right. She's my other half..." Her voice hitched. "I can't lose her. I have to find her. I'll do whatever it takes. I don't have much money, but I will find a way to pay you whatever you ask."

Brian glanced at the supplies in the back of his truck. He'd been really looking forward to one month alone in the mountains, hunting for his food.

On the other end, she sniffled. He was an asshole, he knew and freely admitted it, but that sniffle tugged at his heart.

"Oh hell," he muttered. "Where are you?"

"You'll help?"

The ecstatic sound of her voice had him kicking himself in the ass. At the same time, he couldn't help but smile. This girl had no idea what she'd invited into her life by asking for his help, but for some reason, he simply couldn't refuse her.

"If something goes wrong, it will be your fault when your brothers try to kill me," he told her.

"They'll never know you were involved, I promise," she vowed.

"Tell me where you are."

~

BRIAN DROVE down the dark streets of the campus toward the dorm building at the end of the road. The streetlights every hundred feet or so caused splashes of light to filter over the interior of the truck. It had only taken him two hours to arrive at Abby's college in Boston, but since hanging up the phone with her, he'd felt a driving sense of urgency to get to her and make sure she was safe.

"You're an idiot," he muttered. "This may end up being the thing that finally gets you killed."

Pulling over in front of the building Abby had told him she lived in, he put the truck in park and flung the door open. Lights blazed in most of the windows; he saw a few heads bent over desks as the students worked on whatever they were learning. Some girls were dancing and laughing together in one room, while in another, a couple was having sex against the glass pane.

The sight of the writhing bodies made the corner of his mouth quirk. It had been so long since he'd had sex, he barely recalled the feel of it, but he had to admit the couple made it look like fun. Maybe, when this was over, he'd find a woman before taking off into the mountains. He could endure the guilt for a little release; he had in the past.

As he continued to look around, the one thing he didn't see was Abby. She'd told him she would be ready and waiting for him. Worry gnawed at his gut as he glanced over the building again. Striding up the walkway to the main door, he dialed Abby's number.

"Where are you?" he demanded when she answered the phone.

Abby tried not to get irritated by his tone, he was helping her after all, but knowing he was so close had her completely on edge. "I'm finishing packing. My roommate... Never mind, I'll be down in five."

"What room are you in?"

"Men aren't supposed to be in here," she replied.

"That hasn't stopped one of your neighbors."

"Usually doesn't," she muttered.

"Besides, Ethan will try to break my neck for being here in the first place, so it doesn't matter where I'm supposed to be. Room number?"

The sound of her teeth grating together came through the phone before she spat out, "Thirty-five."

She hung up before he could reply. Opening the front door, he stepped into the well-lit hall and passingly took in the landscape paintings and old pictures of how the college had changed over the years.

It was all so foreign to him. Even when he'd been human, he'd been no scholar. Instead, he'd run through the streets of Boston, an urchin, trying to get by while his parents labored to make a living to support him and his four siblings.

There was an elevator to his right, but he opted for the stairs, taking them two at a time to the third floor. Laughter and music floated from the closed doors lining the hall as he walked toward Abby's room. The persistent beat of the human's hearts caused his fangs to tingle. He'd planned to feed on animals once he'd made it into the mountains, but those tempting pulses reminded him it had been two days since he'd last fed.

I could always have a little snack before going. He considered it as he eyed a long-legged brunette striding down the hall toward him. The smile she gave him, and the extra sway in her hips, told him he'd have no problem getting her to agree to let him in her room. He forced his gaze away from the vein pulsing in her neck and back to the room numbers.

Feeding could wait, first he had to locate Abby and get out of this place. He stopped outside door number thirty-five and knocked on it loudly. "Hold on," a muffled voice replied from inside.

Brian folded his arms over his chest and tapped his foot as he impatiently waited for her to answer the door. Almost a minute later, the door opened. He somehow managed to keep his jaw from dropping as his heart gave an erratic kick in his chest at the sight of the woman standing before him. Her sweet face and brilliant aura were the only things he could see as he hungrily drank her in.

One thing was for sure, Abigail was no longer a child.

CHAPTER TWO

ABBY COULDN'T TEAR her eyes away from the massive man standing in her doorway with his arms crossed over his chest and a look of annoyance on his chiseled face. His ice-blue eyes flickered with incredulity, and something more, when they landed on her. Her breath hitched in her chest and her pulse accelerated as his gaze raked her from head to toe. Those eyes running over her body left her more turned on than all of the many attempts she'd made to forget him with other men.

She vividly remembered him from their one encounter with each other—an encounter where he'd barely acknowledged her existence while she'd been trying not to gawk at him. He'd been so large, so handsome and powerful, and soooo off-limits.

He still is, she told herself, but she couldn't deny she itched to run her fingers through his white-blond hair and trace the angles of his face.

When she'd first seen him all those years ago, she'd believed him to be the ultimate bad boy. The type she'd never really chased after, not even as a helpless romantic, fifteen-year-old kid. However, as the years went by, she hadn't been able to block him from her thoughts and dreams.

She'd often speculated about what would happen if she ran into him again. She'd both dreaded and craved the answer, and now she would get it. Brian had plagued her thoughts for the last six years, but she had still tried to think of anything else she could do to find Vicky before she'd broken down and called him. Her family would *kill* her if they ever found out she'd done this instead of coming to them first, but she simply couldn't involve them, not yet anyway.

She forced herself to swallow in order to wet her suddenly parched throat as her gaze involuntarily traveled over his broad shoulders. The black T-shirt he wore hugged the carved muscles of his chest and flat stomach. She had the urge to tear his shirt off in order to see what the flesh beneath looked like; she imagined it would be as sculpted as the rest of him.

Her eyes wandered lower to his tapered waist and the obvious bulge in the front of his jeans. She fought against the heat creeping up her cheeks as she tore her gaze away from his powerful thighs to look back up at him.

That face! She had to fight against rising onto her toes and pressing her mouth to his full lips in order to finally taste him. He was better in person than she remembered. The impulse to touch him was more overwhelming than anything she'd ever experienced.

Over the years, she'd tried to replace her memory of him with other men, but every guy she'd dated after encountering him had paled in comparison. Those men had left her feeling hollow and unfulfilled while they were kissing and touching her. He was the reason she'd pulled away from all them before things went too far.

The frustration and resentment she'd felt over those encounters rushed back to her now. How could they all have left her feeling so cold, when one look at him had her half on the verge of pulling her clothes off?

She'd made a mistake calling him. He shouldn't be here; she

shouldn't be anywhere near him. He was dangerous. She'd been told he lived a brutal life, but none of that mattered when he was so tantalizingly close to her.

Those icy eyes bored into hers when she met them again. His platinum hair had been brushed back from his broad cheekbones and proud jaw. Darker blond stubble, the same color as his eyebrows, lined his jaw and made her itch to stroke it.

What steaming pile of crap had she stepped into by asking for his help? She suspected the answer to that, she had for years, but she didn't have time to acknowledge it or the implications behind it. Vicky was out there, somewhere, and if she didn't get to her soon, she had a feeling it would be too late.

If it wasn't already.

Taking a deep breath, she forced herself to step back and gestured for him to enter her room. Unlike her mother and her older sister, Isabelle, being a neat-freak had never been her thing. She wasn't an outright slob, but the clutter on her desk and now covering her bed would have driven Issy and her mom nuts. Looking for a distraction from him, she hurried over to her bed and finished tossing her things into her suitcase.

Brian couldn't tear his gaze away from Abby as she rushed over to finish packing the clothes sprawled across the bed. Her full breasts swayed in her loose-fitting shirt. His swelling shaft jumped in his jeans when he realized the young vamp wasn't wearing a bra, and she most certainly didn't have to. More than a handful but not overly large, her breasts were pert as they stood up, her nipples puckering beneath the material rubbing against them.

He wiped the back of his hand over his mouth as he resisted the impulse to feel those enticing buds under his hands. Then he would run his fingers down the front of her flat belly before dipping them between her quivering thighs…

He broke the image off as his cock jumped in his jeans again. This hunger for her was more than just lust pulsing to life within him, he realized. This was something else entirely, as he also longed to pull her into his arms and hold her there, to cradle her against him while she eased the loneliness of his soul, and for some reason, he believed she could be the one to do it.

He hadn't longed to hold a woman since his wife, Vivian, had been so ruthlessly torn away from him one hundred eighty-five years ago. He'd been with other women since her death, but none of them had stirred any tenderness within him. He'd simply been looking to slake the demands of his body with them before moving on.

Once done, he'd never returned to their bed. It had been nearly two centuries since Vivian had been murdered, but he still couldn't handle the guilt of betrayal he felt after only one encounter with another woman. He had no intention of finding out how he'd feel after two encounters with the same woman.

However, Abby and her enticing scent, was all he could focus on in this tiny room as she tossed her clothes into her suitcase. He didn't have to see her sister to know he'd been right; this was the one with the brighter soul. In all of his centuries, he'd never seen one so vivid before. It called to him almost as much as the woman herself did.

With most people and vampires, he turned his ability off. Walking around seeing souls all the time gave him a headache, but he found himself staring at hers in awe. He could feel the warmth of it brushing over his skin, and he couldn't bring himself to tamp it down, not yet anyway. It may become a distraction later, but for now, he basked in it.

It was even stronger now than when he'd first encountered her and would have let him know she'd attained maturity without her having already told him so. She was a fully matured, extremely sensual woman, and he desired her in a way he never had another, not even his Vivian.

"I'm almost ready," she muttered, and shoved a black lacy bra into her suitcase.

He almost leaned over and plucked it back out when she turned her head away. He much preferred her without a bra on, but he decided it was best to keep his hands to himself and to get control of his overreacting body. *Byrne*, he reminded himself firmly. He may get along better with the family now, but even Aiden would scream for his head if Brian added Abby to his list of one and done conquests.

"You're fully mature now," he murmured.

Her emerald eyes were wary when they lifted to his. In the glow of the lamp behind her, they sparkled like the gemstones they resembled. Her pale blonde hair had been cut to frame her oval face as it fell about her shoulders. Lips the color of a red rose parted, and his blood quickened when her tongue darted out to nervously lick her delectable mouth. He guessed her to be around five-six, about six inches shorter than he was.

"Yes, I told you that," she replied, and placed a pair of jeans into her suitcase.

"You did."

Abby glanced at him again, but she couldn't look at him for too long. She was afraid she would stop and gawk if she did. Instead, she turned away and grabbed the last of her underwear before dumping them into the suitcase and pulling the lid up. He was three feet away from her, but she could feel the heat of his body burning against hers.

This is not going to end well, she realized.

Her hand trembled when she tugged the zipper on her suitcase closed. Her gaze fell to her nails. They'd once been long and painted, something she did herself, and one of the few things she'd managed to keep up with since starting college and focusing on her studies. Now, the blue polish on them was chipped, and she'd bitten them down to nubs in her nervous concern over her sister. Never before had she bitten her nails, but since Vicky's disappearance, she couldn't seem to stop.

Taking a steadying breath, she turned to face Brian. Before she could speak, the door to her room flew inward, nearly catching Brian in the side. He scowled as he stepped away from the door and the angry woman who stormed into the room.

"You're really doing this!" the short girl with dyed black hair accused.

Abby lifted her suitcase and held it before her. "I'll be back soon, Jasmine." *Hopefully*, but she doubted her life would ever be the same again.

The young woman swung accusing brown eyes in his direction. Brian felt his upper lip curling in response to the hostility washing off her.

"You must be one fantastic lay!" she spat at him.

He lifted an eyebrow at her words. "Why yes, I am."

Heat burned through Abby's face as she walked across the room and grabbed hold of Brian's elbow. "I can assure you, I wouldn't know," she said to Jasmine. She tried to ignore the heat of his flesh burning into hers, but it took all she had not to rub against him like a cat. "He's going to help me find Vicky."

"I told you I would help you," Jasmine said.

Brian glowered back at the girl, his gaze shifting between her and Abby as he realized the real source of Jasmine's hostility. *Did Abby prefer the company of women to men?* For some reason, the possibility caused unreasonable jealousy to swell through him.

There was no reason to be envious; he was simply here to help this girl before moving on. There could never be anything between them, not with her family and his history; it was impossible. Even knowing all that, he couldn't stand the idea of this woman having had the chance to know Abby in a way he never would.

"You can't help with this, Jasmine. We have to go now," Abby said, and pulled him toward the door.

Brian glanced over his shoulder as he followed Abby into the hallway. Jasmine had tears in her eyes when she stepped into the doorway to watch them walk away. He didn't argue when Abby led him to the elevator and hit the button to close the doors. Taking the suitcase from her slender hands, he held it before him as the doors slid shut.

"She's in love with you," he said bluntly.

Abby laughed at the absurd notion. "No, she's not."

Brian turned to look at her as the elevator lurched into motion. "Yes, she is. If you're not as serious about the relationship"—she gawked at him—"you should end it."

"There is no relationship between me and Jasmine!" she cried, hating the blush creeping through her cheeks. "She's only a friend, and she became my roommate this year."

Relief filled him at her response. There was no reason for her to lie about it, and judging by the color of her skin and the stunned look on her face, she'd never realized her friend harbored deeper feelings for her.

"She does feel more for you," he told her. "It was obvious."

"No, Jasmine…" Her brow furrowed and her voice trailed off as the elevator doors slid open. "She had a boyfriend all last year."

"You can't help who you love," he said as he clasped her elbow and led her from the elevator. Her scent drifted to him when she stepped closer. She wore no perfume, but her natural scent reminded him of orange blossoms and cinnamon.

"I think you're wrong," she muttered, but didn't look completely convinced.

"I rarely am." He held the door open for her to step into the cooling October night. "Where did your sister disappear from?"

"From the city," she answered as he placed her suitcase in the bed of the truck. "We've been going to college together for the last three years. This was supposed to be our final year, or Vicky's at least. I plan to get my masters."

"In what?"

"Social work."

Of course she did. He barely managed to keep himself from smacking his forehead. He felt like he was dealing with the vampire version of Mother Teresa. "And what do you plan to do with that?" he asked.

"I'd like to try and work for an adoption agency or the foster care system in order to help find homes for children." He had a feeling she'd be trying to bring all those children home with her. "But first I plan to join the Peace Corp."

Brian blinked at her. She was a vampire; about the only thing she had to do was feed and keep their existence a secret, but this girl was talking about children and joining the Peace Corp. *Stay away. She's far too good for the likes of you. If you think the guilt is bad after sex with other women, try what you'll feel like if you cause her soul to diminish in some way.*

"I see," he said, but he didn't. He couldn't remember the last time he'd done anything altruistic.

He pulled open the passenger door of the truck and waited until she was settled inside before closing the door and hurrying over to climb into the driver's side. "You said it was supposed to be your final year together, what happened to change that?" he asked when he was settled.

He started the truck and drove onto the narrow streets of Boston. As a child, he'd run these streets, but over the years, the city had grown so much that the roads were often difficult to navigate if they were crowded with parked cars and other drivers.

"Vicky quit shortly before the semester started. We were supposed to room together, as we have for the last three years, but she decided she'd had enough of college. She was staying in an apartment with some friends from school who graduated last year."

Her eyes were haunted, shadows lined them when she turned toward him. "I tried to talk her out of it, but she said she was going to experience life. She'd started dating a guy recently, a vampire. She began staying with him a couple of weeks ago. With school and Vicky going out partying every night, I only saw him once, briefly. He was waiting on the corner for her to leave the place where we'd met for lunch. We didn't eat, of course, but we never turned down some day drinking."

She smiled at the memories. "I hadn't had the chance to really meet him or go to their place. We didn't see each other as much as we used to, but we still talked every day, and we did lunch four days a week. This isn't like her."

"Have you talked to the friends she was staying with before this guy?"

"Yes, they haven't seen or spoken with her in a week."

He pressed on the gas to avoid a yellow light as he drove past Fenway Park and toward the Mass Pike. With all the street lights, parked cars, and pedestrians, it would be a lot easier to concentrate on what she was saying on the highway rather than the busy city streets.

"What did your parents say about her quitting?" he asked as he merged onto the Pike.

The enticing way she nibbled her bottom lip made him briefly forget what they were talking about. "They don't know," she admitted. "I was trying to convince Vicky to tell them, but she kept putting it off. I had promised her I wouldn't say anything, but only if she did soon. Then, she vanished."

The tears in her eyes caused him to swerve the truck into the breakdown lane and park it. He turned toward her, draping his arm over the back of the seat as she wiped away her tears. "I'll find her," he vowed. He would have promised her almost anything to erase the melancholy look on her pretty face.

"What if we can't? What if something has happened to her and it's my fault for not doing something sooner to intervene?"

"Your sister makes her own choices; that's not your fault."

Abby bowed her head and nodded, but she knew he was wrong about this. If something happened to Vicky, it *would* be her fault. They were so much alike, but she was the more practical one, the levelheaded one who kept her crazier sister on track. She'd failed Vicky now.

"I was so mad at her for quitting and leaving me behind," she muttered. "For putting me in this position with our parents, but she's my sister, you know?"

"I do." His siblings and parents may have been dead for years now, but he recalled what it had been like to try and keep their secrets. Recalled the love he'd had for them.

When she lifted her head to look at him again, she brushed back the hair clinging to her flushed cheeks. "I'm the responsible one. I always looked out for her, and I failed. Now, I have no idea where she is, what she's doing, or if I can save her if we find her."

Unable to resist the tears in her eyes anymore, Brian wrapped his hand around her neck and pulled her close against him. A sigh of contentment escaped him when her head fell against his chest. He should push her away, shift into drive again, and find someplace where he could put some distance between them. Instead, he found his fingers sliding over her silken hair as he held her closer.

He waited for the inevitable guilt to slither through him as he tenderly stroked her. Vivian was dead, but she was still such an intricate part of him. She had given him their beautiful daughters; she had loved him and depended on him. She'd had such faith in him, and he'd failed to protect the three of them. He'd watched as they'd died.

Over his many years of wielding death to murderous rogue vampires, and unfortunately two human hunters who had been trying to kill him, he could barely see any difference between himself and the vampires who had changed him and stolen his family. He didn't intentionally hunt and kill humans, but sometimes he wondered if he could become a monster without crossing that line, or worse, if he already had become one.

He was completely undeserving of any kindness or love in his life, not like he wanted anything like that again, but he'd avoided any kind of contact like this with another for nearly two centuries. Sex was one thing, but to hold and comfort someone seemed more intimate. However, the much-expected guilt never came.

Reluctantly, he pulled away from Abby. He would only taint her if he stayed close to her. It was inevitable, as he tainted or destroyed everything he touched.

CHAPTER THREE

"Do you think she took off because she didn't want to tell your parents about quitting school?" he asked.

Abby missed the heat of his body against hers; her skin felt icy from the loss of contact. "No. She was dreading telling them, they were going to be mad at her for not telling them sooner, but they would get over it and she knew that. No matter what, she still wouldn't have taken off without telling *me*."

"Do you have something of Vicky's?" he asked.

He watched as she wiped at her eyes. Her sister, Isabelle, was striking in her beauty. Abby was far more delicate and innocent, more pretty than refined and elegant, but he could barely keep his eyes off her. She fascinated him in some odd way that had him fighting the urge to brush the hair away from her face so he could see her more clearly.

"Like what?" she asked as she twisted her hands in her lap.

"A picture, jewelry, clothing, anything." He could use Abby herself, but he was better off not touching her again if he could help it.

Abby dug into her purse in search of her wallet. She tugged it out and flipped through the pictures of her family and friends before coming to one of Vicky and her from the beginning of the summer. The picture was taken near their home in Maine. They were sitting on the rocks on the beach with the ocean crashing around them. Her sister-in-law, Paige, had taken the picture and planned to turn it into a painting, but she had given Abby and Vicky each a copy of the photo.

Their heads were bent close to each other, their hands draped over their knees in identical positions. It appeared as if they were the only two people on Earth, and Abby recalled not even realizing Paige was there as she'd sat with Vicky, talking and listening to the ocean waves.

"Here." She handed him the photo. She was about to point out which one was Vicky and which was her, when his thumb landed on Vicky. "That's her."

"I know," he murmured as he closed his eyes.

Her eyebrows shot up as she stared at him. Her own parents got them confused sometimes, but he had unflinchingly chosen Vicky in the photo. It had either been luck, or his gift of finding people that allowed him to pick Vicky out in the picture. That made sense, she decided. She sat back to watch the headlights playing over his masculine beauty as the cars drove by.

She longed to touch his cheek, but she dug her fingers into the cloth seat and forced herself to show some restraint. She had no idea what he was doing, but his shoulders hunched up and he shuddered. His eyes flew open, and then he handed the picture back to her and shifted the truck into drive.

"Do you know where she is?" she asked anxiously.

"I know where she was recently. She may be there now, or she may have moved on, but we'll find out when we get there."

"How do you know? What did you do?"

He smiled at her, but it looked strained and there was a hollowness in his ice-colored eyes that hadn't been there before. "I have my secrets, young Byrne."

"You won't tell me?"

"No."

Abby opened her mouth to question him further, but she clamped it shut again. He was helping her, who was she to demand answers when he wasn't willing to give them? "Did your ability tell you who Vicky was in this picture?" she inquired.

"No," he said, as he clicked on his blinker and exited the Pike.

He drove through the Easy Pass lane and back onto the crowded and convoluted streets of Boston. She'd lived here almost full-time for three years now and still managed to get lost every once in a while, but he drove with unflinching certainty as he navigated the roads.

"Then how did you know it was her?" she asked.

"You're very easy to tell apart."

Abby did a double take; she somehow kept herself from sputtering at his words. "*No* one has ever said that to me before, not even my parents."

He shrugged, but didn't look at her again as he drove into a part of the city she'd never been to before. It was less crowded here; homes lined the streets instead of skyscrapers and businesses. As they parked outside a white house that had been converted into an apartment building, Abby craned her head to take in the three story building next to her.

"Do you think she's here?" she asked eagerly.

"No," Brian said as he studied the home. A residual aura enshrouded the place. One that had been strong enough to draw him here, but it wasn't strong enough to indicate Vicky was still here now. Opening his door, he walked around the truck toward the passenger side. Before he could reach Abby's door, she opened it herself and began to step out onto the curb. He rushed to her side and grabbed hold of her elbow to help her out.

She gave him a startled look, one that had nothing on the surprise that jolted through him at the gesture. He wasn't a gentleman anymore; he didn't have any chivalry left in him. That part of him had died when his human life ended. However, he hadn't been able to stop himself from helping her.

You'd better start, a voice whispered in his head and he released her elbow.

"Thank you," she murmured.

"You're welcome. Stay close to me."

He led her to the back of the building and a set of stairs winding all the way to the third floor. Drawn onward, he climbed to the top with her close on his heels. The light on the top of the building did little to illuminate the night. His enhanced vision picked out more than enough details to know the place could use a good painting, and these stairs wouldn't last another five years as they creaked and groaned beneath their weight.

Opening the little gate on the back porch, he stepped inside and held the door open for Abby. The space was small, but a picnic table cluttered with ashtrays and beer bottles was set to the side. He didn't expect anyone to answer, but he still knocked on the door. Each rap of his knuckles caused flecks of paint to fall on his hand from the aging doorframe above.

He bent to peer through the glass into the gloomy apartment beyond. "What are you doing?" Abby hissed when his hand fell to the knob and he turned it.

The door swung open to reveal a surprisingly filthy kitchen. The kitchen was the least used room in any vampire's home. There was rarely ever a need to clean it, but this one had dirt and blood streaked over the linoleum and white cabinets. Half the cabinets were open; some of the others had no doors on them.

"Vicky would never stay in a place like this," Abby said from behind him.

He didn't look at her. "She was here."

Wrapping her hands around her middle, she hugged herself. "My sister is far from Mrs. Clean, but she wouldn't live in filth."

"A lot of this mess is new," he murmured, as his gaze lingered on the dry blood that couldn't be more than a day or two old, judging by the strength of the coppery scent. Inhaling deeply again, his fangs pricked and lengthened when he realized this was human blood.

"Do you think there was a fight? Do you think someone dragged her from here?"

"No," he replied. "This is human blood."

Beside him, Abby shuddered and hugged herself. Turning away, his eyes scanned the porch as he searched for something he could use to further guide him. Bending down, he peered beneath the picnic table. Spotting a jacket, he pulled it forward and grasped it in his hand. He allowed his mind to open to the residual pathways on the clothing from the person who owned it.

Finding a new soul to lock onto through the jacket, he tossed it aside and took hold of Abby's elbow. "Come."

"Did you see her?"

"No, but I did see the other vamp who is staying here."

Abby's mind spun as she glanced back at the trashed apartment before stepping out of the gate. Brian kept hold of her arm as he led her down the stairs and back to the truck. Opening her door, he helped her climb inside before walking around to the driver's side. Abby tried to keep the uneasiness gnawing her stomach at bay as he started the truck and pulled away from the curb.

Vicky would never take off without telling her. No matter how rebellious her sister had become, she never would have left without contacting her first. Abby had been trying to hang onto the small thread of hope that Vicky's phone was broken, or she had become so busy she had forgotten about the three lunch dates she'd missed since Abby last saw her.

Vicky had never forgotten their lunch dates before, but it wasn't entirely impossible. She loved Vicky, but responsibility and recalling times and dates had never been her strong suit. Abby was the one who had always handled remembering birthdays and getting presents for people. Vicky was attached to her phone, but she also went through a new one every three months. She was forever dropping them and destroying them. She'd even dropped one on the tracks of the T-line seconds before the train pulled into the station, but she'd still always found a way to contact Abby when something like that happened.

Now that hope was fading fast. Up to this point, she'd refused to give into her fear and admit to herself that something was terribly wrong. Now she could feel that fear threatening to take her over.

She was so focused on her misery, she didn't realize what her surroundings were at first. Her eyes widened as they drove through seedier and seedier sections of the city. Places she'd never been before and had never intended to go.

A sick feeling settled in the pit of her stomach as the row houses gave way to dilapidated and crumbling buildings. Plywood boarded some of the windows, graffiti streaked many walls, and more than a few looked as if they would collapse any second now. The main occupants of these forgotten structures were rats, stray animals, and lost souls.

"The people who can't tell you two apart don't know what to look for," Brian said randomly as he made a right-hand turn onto a dark roadway.

Abby pulled her attention away from the buildings and back to him, as he'd hoped when he'd spoken. He could sense her anguish and had been trying to think of a way to distract her from her morose thoughts.

"And what is that?" she asked around the lump in her throat.

"Life. It radiates from everyone differently, especially you."

What an odd statement for anyone to make, she thought. "But it was only a photo."

"Don't you know the camera steals a piece of your soul?" The wink he gave her tugged at her heart.

"That's true?" she blurted.

"Who knows?"

He was the most enigmatic, confusing, and complicated man she'd ever met. She found she actually kind of liked it.

CHAPTER FOUR

Abby hadn't realized he'd pulled to the side of the road until he put the truck in park. "Why do you think life radiates differently from me?" she asked.

He turned toward her, his hand only inches from her shoulder, but he didn't touch her again no matter how badly he wanted to. "That's the way it is with some," he replied. "This is it."

He pointed out the window behind her. Abby's gaze remained riveted on him for a minute more as she tried to bolster her courage before turning to look out the window. Her heart sank at the sight of the building he'd pointed to. Its roof sloped downward in the middle, as the process of falling in on itself was well underway.

Boards and plywood covered all the windows and the front door, which was partially ajar and sagged on its hinges. The Addams family would have run away screaming from this place, but *her* notoriously meticulous sister had been *here,* or was at least associated with someone who had been. Vicky could spend hours in front of a mirror doing her hair and trying to decide on an outfit. If there was a mirror in this place, it wasn't used for primping.

Before college, Abby had been much the same way as Vicky, but when school started, studies and friends had taken her focus instead of styled hair and a perfect tan. The same couldn't be said of her twin though. Vicky had always maintained her tan, never had a chip in her nail polish, her hair was perfectly styled, and her clothes were always immaculate. Abby berated herself for not paying closer attention to what was going on in her sister's life.

"Did Vicky ever come here?" she croaked out.

"I don't know," Brian said. "It could be someone else, a friend or an associate perhaps, who owned the jacket and came here. What did she say about her boyfriend?"

"Just that his name is Duke and he's a lot of fun to be around. It was full daylight the one time I saw him, so he wasn't a killer, and Vicky never would have dated him if he smelled like garbage the way other killer vampires do, like you did the first time we met…"

Brian winced at the reminder of what her first impression of him had been. At her tender age, she'd most likely believed him to be a monster. She might *still* believe him to be a monster. It had been years since he'd killed those human hunters, but he didn't know if the smell lingered on him or if it had faded away with time. Only born vampires like Abby could scent a vampire who killed humans. It was one of the many traits turned vampires didn't possess.

"But he wasn't right," she finished.

"Is anyone?"

"No," she admitted. "But I hated the way he stood on the curb across the street, waiting for her while we finished our drinks. She didn't go running out to him, Vicky doesn't run anywhere, but I could tell he expected her to drop everything to join him."

Brian studied Abby's delicate features as she stared at what could only be described as a crack house. Judging by the smells wafting from it, more than crack had been going on in there. He glanced around the quiet street. He didn't want to take Abby into that building, but leaving her in the truck wasn't exactly a great option either.

He scented the air. His ears strained to detect any hint of noise from somewhere, but the night remained eerily quiet, except for what was going on in that house. Leaving her here may just be the lesser of the two evils, he decided.

"Stay here," he said.

He climbed out of the truck but before he could shut his door, she was already out of the vehicle. He stalked around the front of the truck to join her. Taking hold of her elbow, he tried to steer her back into the truck, but she resisted him.

Abby thrust out her chin as she stubbornly dug her heels in. "If Vicky is in there, then I'm going inside and you can't stop me."

"She's not in there."

"If anyone she's ever met is in there, I'm going."

He stared down at her resolute expression before glancing at the dilapidated house once more. He cast a glance over his shoulder, noting the shadows coalescing over the street as the moon slipped out from behind the clouds. Nothing moved, but this wasn't a place where normal humans walked the family dog at night, at least not if they were expecting to live for long.

Turning back to her, he noted she was five shades paler than she had been. She took a step away from him, but he kept hold of her elbow, drawing her back against his side. "I'm going—"

"I know," he replied. "But you will be standing by my side as you do."

He gritted his teeth against his need to take her away from this place. If he did, she would only come back here the first chance she got, and she would leave his ass behind in order to do so. He could call Stefan and tell him what was going on. Her brother-in-law would come, drag her away, and Brian could continue his search for Vicky without the temptation of Abby and the risk to her life. She would be safe if he handed her over to her family, but she would likely hate him and would definitely turn against him.

What did it matter if she hated him?

It mattered; that was all he knew right now.

Taking a deep breath, he looked at her again. "You must be prepared for what we'll find in there."

"I know what we'll find," she said in a hushed voice. "I can smell too, maybe better than you."

"You purebreds, always so smug."

She forced a smile, but no color returned to her face. "We try."

He kept hold of her arm, staying slightly ahead of her as they walked up the cracked and broken sidewalk to the sagging wood stairs. The steps creaked beneath his weight but held firm enough for him to allow her to climb them too. He kept his senses attuned for anyone moving within the shadows. He doubted someone would be capable of attacking them here, but he wasn't about to take any chances with her.

He shoved aside the sagging front door. From within, he heard a sensual moan that stopped him in his tracks. Abby should *not* be in here. Seeming to guess at his thoughts, she planted her feet before he could spin her around and take her back outside. His hand twitched toward the phone in his pocket. He didn't know where her family's place was in Maine, but he knew it wouldn't take Stefan much time to get here if Brian told him what was up.

Her eyes followed the movement of his hand toward his pocket and narrowed on him. "Don't even think about it," she whispered.

"You don't know what I'm thinking."

"I'll be gone, and on the hunt for Vicky on my own, before any member of my family can show up to stop me."

Brian's jaw clenched as they stared at each other. If she got hurt because of him...

He broke the thought off. She wasn't his responsibility, and the only reason he was here was because of her and her sister. He may have led her to this place, but only because she'd asked him to. She was a full-grown, purebred vampire who was far more lethal than she appeared. Still, he couldn't shake his impulse to protect her.

Turning his attention back to the building, he studied the

shadows as the scents of urine, feces, body odor, and sex filled his nostrils. Beneath it all, he smelled the acrid aroma of some human drug that ate away at their souls as they eagerly dosed themselves with more.

"She never would have been here," Abby whispered. "She couldn't know someone who would be here."

"I may not always get the exact location, but I definitely get the general vicinity right. Someone from the apartment we just left is either here right now, or has been here recently."

Her hand shook when she brushed back a strand of pale hair from her eye. He glanced down at her plump breasts, swaying beneath her sweater. He may have no choice about bringing her in there, but he could at least make sure she had more clothes on when he did so.

"Come with me," he commanded briskly.

She didn't have a chance to respond before he was pulling her back out of the building. "I told you I'm not leaving!" she protested, and tried to jerk her arm free.

"We're not leaving," he told her. "I just have to get something before we can continue."

Abby reluctantly allowed him to lead her off the porch and back toward his truck. If he tried to force her to leave, she'd kick him in the balls so hard they'd never come back down again. Then, she'd go into that building by herself while he was still trying to figure out if he was now a female.

He didn't lead her to the cab of the truck but around to the back of it. After he released her, she watched as he grabbed a duffel bag and pulled it toward him. Jerking the bag open, he tugged out a windbreaker and returned to her. She frowned at the jacket when he held it out to her.

"I'm not cold," she muttered. He glanced pointedly down at her breasts before thrusting the jacket at her again.

With furrowed brows, she glanced down at her chest to where her nipples pressed against her shirt in the cool fall air. Heat blazed into her face as she snatched the jacket from him and slipped it on. She'd been in such a rush, and so annoyed with Jasmine for trying to get her to stay, she'd forgotten to put a bra on. The jacket nearly fell to her knees when she tugged it into place. She shoved the sleeves up to keep her hands free.

It's better than before, Brian decided before taking hold of her again and returning to the building.

Abby took a deep breath and walked beside him into the pit of despair. She'd never smelled anything as bad as this place in her life, and she'd grown up with a bunch of boys who considered disgusting smells great fun. Ian had proudly shoved his stinking, sweaty sneakers into her face more times than she cared to recall, and Aiden had thought it hilarious to put his younger siblings into a headlock after going for a twenty mile run.

She'd give anything for Ian's stinky feet right now.

Vicky wouldn't hang out with anyone associated with this place; she simply wouldn't have. Abby kept trying to deny it, but Brian's confident words kept ringing in her mind. Ian and Aiden called him a vampire GPS. Maybe his internal satellite, or whatever it was he used for navigation, had been blocked by the moon or something unexplainable this time and had brought him to the wrong place.

Her breath caught and her arm jerked in his grasp as they stepped into a sunken living room littered with people and vampires. She could instinctively pick her kind out in the crowd, but then it wouldn't have been difficult as three-quarters of them were feeding on the passed out humans sprawled around the room.

Bile rushed up Abby's throat. She took a step away before determinedly thrusting her shoulders back. She'd face this; she'd face anything if it meant finding Vicky. One of the vampires fell away from his food source. His eyes rolled back in ecstasy, and he wiped the blood from his mouth.

Abby was still trying to process what she was seeing when Brian gestured toward a set of stairs. Keeping her close to his side, he led her up them. At the top of the stairs, she heard the low sounds of someone having sex from a room at the end of the hall. After three years of living in a dorm, she knew those sounds well. She peered into the rooms as they passed each one, dreading and praying they would find Vicky inside. She didn't know how she would handle finding Vicky here, but at least she would have *found* her.

Brian kept Abby away from the room at the end, unwilling to have her see what he knew was going on inside. Peering into the room, he spotted the couple having sex. Neither one of them were the one who had drawn him here. Ducking back, he hooked his elbow through hers and pulled her back toward the stairs.

"She's not here," she whispered.

"She's not," he agreed as he led her down the stairs.

Her shoulders sagged, but whether it was from relief or despair, he didn't know. All he knew was he had to get her out of this place. He was beginning to wonder if he wanted her around her sister. Her twin had gotten herself mixed up in some pretty nasty shit if this was the type of vampire she'd become involved with.

Rumors about these new drug houses popping up in some cities were circulating amongst some of the seedier vampires he used as informants. They'd all laughed the rumors off at the time, but nothing about this place was cause for laughter. Most vampires knew these kind of places were not tolerated or allowed by their kind.

He was propelling Abby toward the front door when she abruptly broke away from him. "Abby!" he hissed when she turned a corner and stalked toward the back of the house.

"I'm not leaving until we've looked everywhere," she tossed over her shoulder.

He hurried to catch up with her as continued resolutely onward. "Abigail!"

She stopped at the edge of another room, her gaze scanning over the people and vampires gathered within. He arrived at her side just as a voice within the room murmured, "Vicky?"

Brian's head shot in the direction of the filthy vampire in the corner. He grabbed hold of Abby's arm when she started toward the vampire, tugging her back.

"Can't be you," the vampire slurred.

Abby jerked on her arm, but Brian held firmly onto it. "Let go of me!"

"You'll stay by my side," he commanded gruffly.

She glared at him, but relented when he started to lead her across the room toward the man. "It really is you," the vampire murmured when they stopped before him.

"My name is Abby; you know Vicky?"

"You're Vicky."

Brian kept hold of her arm when she knelt before the man. He'd have her jerked away from him and the vamp's throat in his hand before she could blink, if the bastard tried anything. Abby seized hold of the man's stubble-lined cheeks when his head lulled to the side. She ignored the filth covering him as she pulled his head toward her.

"Where's my sister?" she inquired. The vampire groaned and his lids drooped closed. "Hey! Wake up!"

"He said you were with them, Vicky," the vamp murmured. "No one comes back from where they go."

Heedless of the fact his clothes could stand on their own, Abby grabbed his slimy coat. "Who said that? Who is them?" she demanded with a sharp shake. "No one comes back from *where*?"

His head snapped back and forth with each of her jolting shakes, but he remained unconscious. "Wake up!" she yelled at him.

"Abby, it's useless." Brian rested his hand on her shoulder, determined to draw her away, but she fought against his hold on her.

She peered closer at the man, trying to see past the dirt and grime streaking his features but she didn't recognize him. Perhaps he'd been one of Duke's friends or even one of Vicky's new ones. She jerked away from Brian's grasp and pulled back her hand. The slap she delivered to the vampire's cheek reverberated in the room. Her hand stung from the impact, but he showed no reaction to it.

Brian's eyebrows shot up when she slapped the vamp. Mother Teresa wouldn't have done that. "Well now," he murmured.

Abby felt no remorse about hitting the unconscious man; she would do whatever it took to find Vicky. Pulling her hand back, she hit him once more. His fangs extended, but he didn't awaken. Before she could hit him again, Brian plucked her off the ground and swung her behind him so fast she didn't realize she'd moved until her feet hit the floor.

Brian's corded muscles rippled before her; his eyes blazed like the fires of Hell as he snatched the vamp by the throat and lifted him into the air. Abby gaped as he pulled the man back and slammed him into the wall.

The building vibrated around them. She glanced nervously at the ceiling as bits of dust and debris rained down on them. This place looked like the next breeze would blow it over, never mind an irritated vampire bashing another against its rotten walls. Around them, some of the people grunted and moved, but nobody ran away like any sane human or vampire would have done.

"I'd retract those fangs if you want to live," Brian snarled at the vamp in his grasp.

The man blinked at him blearily, and then his fangs retracted. "Now," Brian continued, his fingers digging into the vamp's throat deep enough to draw blood, "where is her sister?"

The vampire's bloodshot eyes swung toward her. "Vicky?" he croaked.

"Yes, where is Vicky?" she asked eagerly.

The vampire's eyelids sagged and fluttered back open when Brian smashed him into the wall again. Abby glanced nervously around as the floor beneath her feet vibrated. "You're right here," the man replied.

"No, I'm not Vicky."

"Yes, you are." Abby's heart sank. He was too far gone to understand she wasn't Vicky. "You went with them. No more. Gone away now."

Those words caused her heart to lurch in her chest. She took a step closer as the man started to ramble incoherent sentences. Brian's arm shot out to press against her chest and keep her held back. He gave a warning shake of his head at her. Abby sighed impatiently; she'd grown up in a home full of overbearing and overprotective men. She certainly didn't need it from him too, but experience had taught her it was best to pick her battles. Now was not the time nor the place for a battle of wills against Brian.

"I did leave," she said to the vampire in Brian's grasp, "but I decided to come back. Do you remember where I went?"

The vamp's head dropped before it shot back up. "Doncha ya know?" he slurred.

"No, I ah… I forgot."

He smiled as his head lulled forward once more. "Good times then."

Brian gave him a brisk shake, but the man's head remained on his shoulders. Without any remorse, Brian opened his hand and dropped the unconscious man to the floor. His lips curled in disgust when he glanced at his hand before wiping it on his jeans.

"Come." This time there would be no breaking free of his grip as his hand felt like a steel vise around her elbow.

"Shouldn't we bring him with us?" she demanded. "Maybe once he sobers up he'll be able to tell us more!"

"His mind won't be any clearer when he's sober. All he's going to care about then is finding his next meal and his next high."

CHAPTER FIVE

"What was that place?" she asked as Brian drove through the streets and back toward the highway. "I mean, I've heard of crack houses before, but vampire crack houses?"

"There have been rumors swirling around about them lately."

Abby turned to study his rugged profile. She couldn't shake the sick feeling in her stomach ever since he'd put her back into the truck and closed the door. "What kind of rumors?"

"That houses like that were beginning to spring up around the world again. The humans want their drugs, the vampires want their blood, and vampires tend to have a lot more money than humans, even the drug-addled vampires. It's a lot easier for a vamp to steal money and anything else without being caught. The vampires pay for the human's drugs and in return the vampires are allowed to feed from them, but the contaminated blood effects them too."

"I've seen my brothers drink a keg each and not be as messed up as those vamps in there were."

"Beer is one thing; drugs are something entirely different. Not to mention, your brothers allowed themselves to sober up after those kegs. These vamps aren't doing that. They're drinking drug-enhanced blood as often and as continuously as they can. It's building up in their systems and keeping them on a constant high. I saw something like it with the opium dens in the eighteen hundreds. Vampires were falling under the spell of drug-enhanced blood then too. Many of the vampires involved were slaughtered."

"Why?" Abby gasped.

"The knowledge of our existence can't ever get out to the humans. Drug-addicted vampires, who are under the influence of the blood containing that drug, often don't care about consequences and slip up. This sort of thing is not allowed amongst our kind. Not only do Ronan's men go after them, but so will other vampires in order to keep our existence a secret. Apparently these younger, imbecilic vamps never got the memo."

Abby's blood ran cold, and her mouth parted as her heart beat rapidly in her chest. "You're going to tell Ronan," she whispered.

She knew from her brothers that Brian sometimes worked with Ronan, the oldest pureblood of their kind. She'd never met the man, but she'd heard the stories of him from her family. If Ronan decided her sister was somehow a danger, or these drug-addicted vampires were, he wouldn't hesitate to kill them.

Vicky may know someone in that house, but she wouldn't be mixed up in the same thing as the vamps in there were. Her sister had changed a lot over this past month and half though. Maybe she was wrong and didn't know Vicky as well as she believed, at least not anymore.

No, Vicky is not messed up in this. There has to be something else going on.

Maybe she was in denial, but she'd call herself the queen of denial until she had definite confirmation of something different.

Brian glanced over at Abby, hating the horrified look on her pale face. He should tell Ronan about what they'd witnessed; it should be his first call when he got her somewhere safe. They risked exposure by allowing those vamps to continue with what they were doing, but he knew Ronan and his group would raze every vampire drug house they could find without a second's hesitation. It wouldn't matter who was inside, not even if it was Abby and Aiden's sister.

"I'm not going to tell him yet. We'll find your sister first," he assured her. *Lust has blinded you, you idiot, and it will get you killed. Go out tonight and find someone else to slake yourself on and come back to this tomorrow with a clear mind.*

Maybe that was all true, but when he glanced at Abby again, he knew he wouldn't be going out to ease himself between the thighs of the first woman who welcomed him. Desire for her may be clouding his decision making processes, but he wasn't going to leave her unprotected for one second while her sister remained missing. He had a feeling she wouldn't stay where he told her to, and he highly doubted he'd be satisfied with any other woman right now.

"If he finds out you didn't tell him and you knew—"

"He'll rip off my head," Brian informed her as nonchalantly as if he'd said it looked like it might rain.

The sick feeling in her stomach intensified. It was one thing that she'd involved him in this whole mess, it was an entirely different thing to put his life at risk. She couldn't stand the idea of anything bad happening to him because of her.

"I can do this on my own," she said. "You don't have to be involved anymore."

Those icy eyes flickered over her. "It's too late for that, young Byrne. I already know and haven't made the call to Ronan. If you try to do this on your own, I will find you and make the call."

Her eyes widened at the callous words and the flippant way he'd said them. "Don't threaten me—"

"I don't threaten. I make promises, and I keep them."

Abby glowered at him. Over the years, she'd eagerly drank in every word her family members had said about him. She'd raptly listened to their stories while ignoring the numerous times she'd heard them say he's cold, ruthless, indifferent, violent, yada, yada,

yada, but she had always believed there was so much more to this man who had captivated her six years ago. Her family had started to come around to him a little more after he'd helped them a couple of times, but they were still wary of him.

Out of all her siblings, Isabelle had been the only one who'd always believed Brian was, or could be, decent. Abby had never opened up to Issy about her strange feelings for him because Issy had left with Stefan shortly after they were married, and by the time she'd returned, Abby had been determined to get past her hang up on Brian.

Abby realized now that he could be kind and understanding, and he could be giving, but he was also very much the brutal man her family had spoken of.

Which side of him is the more dominant one? She had a feeling she'd find out the answer to that before this was over.

∽

"WHAT IS THIS PLACE?" she asked as they rode up the elevator past floor after floor.

"My apartment."

"You have an apartment in Boston?"

"Yes, for as long as I've been a vampire I've had numerous apartments in this city. I also have a beach house on Cape Cod."

"You must really love Boston to stay here for so many years."

He shrugged as he stared at the silver doors across from them with her suitcase in hand. "I was born here. The city is my home."

"I didn't know that."

"I'm sure there's much you don't know about me."

Abby glanced away from his probing stare. There had been a cool distance about him ever since they'd left that house behind and he'd told her he wouldn't call Ronan. "Are you and Ronan good friends?" she asked.

He snorted as he ran his fingers through his platinum hair. "I have no friends. Not anymore."

She winced at his words. "Not since Stefan?" The tick of a muscle in his jaw was the only indication she'd hit the nail on the head. "You two talk more now."

"We can never be friends again; our worlds are too different."

"Maybe so, but you're not a killer. I can't smell the rotten stench of death on you anymore."

Relief filled him when she revealed this to him; the last thing he wanted was to smell repulsive to this woman.

"How did you and Ronan meet?" she asked.

"He heard about Stefan and me, about how we were murdering vampires who killed humans and gaining power from drinking their blood. He warned us if we ever started destroying humans, he would come for us, but he left us be. After Stefan and I went our separate ways, he found me again and knew from my scent I had killed humans. When I explained I'd been attacked by hunters and had only been defending myself, he allowed me to live, but kept a closer eye on me. Over the last eight years, I've worked more and more often with him and his men, especially these last five years."

The elevator dinged and the doors slid open on the top floor. He made a sweeping gesture with his arm. She hesitated a moment; she was going to see where *Brian* lived. If someone had told her last week that this was where she'd be right now, she'd have laughed in their face.

Taking a breath, she stepped into the massive loft. She was fairly certain her eyes bugged out of her head as she gazed at the beautiful open space before her. The *entire* top floor of the building was his.

"Wow," she breathed. Her gaze latched onto the floor-to-ceiling windows across the way. "Amazing!"

She rushed across the floor and just barely managed to stop herself from flattening her hands and nose against the glass to stare out at the city laid out below her like a million twinkling stars. Cars moved through the streets; lights blazed from the buildings surrounding them. She spotted the Prudential building in the distance, rising high into the night sky.

Right then, she would have killed for Paige's artistic talent of being able to bring things to life with a pencil or brush as she gazed out at the sprawling city. Her sister-in-law would love to come up here and paint this view.

"It's beautiful," she said.

Brian stared at the city skyline then back at Abby's awed expression. He'd bought this place five years ago, but felt so out of place with all the luxury it offered that he rarely spent any time here. He'd been a street urchin for only ten years of his life, yet he'd never shaken his basic urge to be out in the open, in nature, and free to hunt. He'd only bought the apartment because he could, and it made for a good stopping place when he needed one while in town.

Looking at this place through her eyes, he realized it really was a spectacular view, even for one as old and jaded as he was. Seeing her reaction to the city skyline was almost as breathtaking as the view itself.

"Would you like a drink?" he asked to distract himself from the urge to touch her pale cheek still tinged with color from the fall air.

"Water is fine. My throat is dry."

"Are you hungry?"

"Not enough for it to be a concern," she replied with an absent wave of her hand.

Forcing himself to turn from her, he made his way over to the open kitchen with dark wood cabinets, black granite counters, and ultra-expensive appliances he would never use, except for the fridge. He pulled a bottle of whiskey from one of the cabinets and poured some into a tumbler.

"Come now, young Byrne, growing up in that household, I know your brothers and uncles introduced you to something better than water to drink over the years."

"They did," she replied, without looking back at him.

He removed a bottle of water from the fridge, stocked by the housekeeper he'd hired to come in once a month just to keep the place clean. He'd implanted it into the woman's mind that she never remembered anything about this place other than it was often tidy and unoccupied. She certainly never remembered the bags of blood in the fridge.

He walked over to rejoin her near the windows, handing her the glass of whiskey and the water. "One is for your throat, the other is for your nerves. I have blood in the fridge if you get hungrier."

"Thank you," Abby said and sipped at the water as she placed the whiskey on a glass table. "So if Ronan isn't your friend, what is he to you?"

"A necessary acquaintance," Brian replied as he turned and walked back to the kitchen area. Watching her swallow the liquid was testing his restraint more than anything else he'd encountered in all his long life. *That luscious mouth of hers wrapped around my cock—*

"What does that mean?" her question cut into his musings.

He turned subtly to adjust his growing erection so that she couldn't see his physical reaction to her doing nothing more than drinking a bottle of water. He had to pull it together if he was going to continue being around her for long enough to locate her sister.

"He pays me to handle jobs that require killing some of the turned vamps who murder humans when he and his men can't do it. Sometimes I help him locate problem vampires who are proving difficult to find. Other times, I help Ronan and his merry band when they have a large group to take down."

"So you're a mercenary of sorts."

"Not of sorts," he replied as he leaned a hip against the kitchen counter. "That is what I am. I enjoy destroying those of our kind who think it's acceptable to prey on the human race. No one should harm those weaker than they are. Those vampires deserve to die. If I make some money doing it, it's an added bonus."

Abby grabbed for the glass of whiskey. She hoped it really would help settle her nerves. "Do you think you'll ever stop?"

"When I'm dead."

For some reason, those last words caused her heart to turn over and she almost screamed the word *no*! She managed to bite it back before making a complete fool of herself, but her hand clenched around the glass so forcefully it cracked. His eyebrow rose as beads of liquid slid down the side and onto her hand.

He walked over to remove it from her claw-like grasp. "Guess you don't know your own strength yet, purebred."

"I... uh... I'm sorry," she managed to stammer as he tossed the glass into the trash and poured her another one.

"Try not to destroy this one, Hulk," he told her when he returned to hand her the new glass and a napkin.

"I won't," she muttered as she wiped the liquid from her hand.

He stood over her, his head tilted to the side as if in confusion while he watched her. Abby's pulse raced again, and heat flooded her body as those ice-colored eyes surveyed her from head to toe and back again. She felt like a child in his oversized jacket, but the hunger in his eyes said he didn't see her as one at all.

That *hunger*. It made her burn to do things to him she'd never done to any man before. He'd haunted every one of her fantasies for years. No human or vampire had ever been able to compare to the image of him in her mind.

She'd messed around with human men over the years, but only one vampire. A sophomore in college at the time, she'd been sure the hot vampire had been the answer to her problem, and she would *finally* feel something for someone else. It was another epic fail. She could still recall the clammy feel of the vamp's lips against hers and the way her stomach had turned over when his fangs scraped over her lip.

Would Brian's kisses do the same to me?

She felt the resounding answer to that question was a no. His lips and taste would only make her crave more and more of him. He would consume her, and she so desperately wanted to be consumed by something other than worry for her sister. Her family would have an absolute fit if they knew whom she was with, and what she was thinking about doing to him right now, but she didn't care.

Even Vicky, who had always been one for the bad boys and was certainly wilder than her, didn't like or trust this man. Abby had once tried to tell Vicky that something had happened to her when she'd first seen Brian in that hotel room, that she couldn't shake him from her mind, but the minute she'd brought up the whole 'so you remember that guy, Brian' conversation, Vicky had rolled her eyes.

She could still clearly recall her sister's words at the time. *"How could I forget? He's a killer who smells of death and nearly got us all killed. I hope we never see the bastard again."*

Those words had clamped Abby's mouth shut on any further conversation about him. It had been exhausting over the years to try to find someone else out there for her, instead of being so focused on the one vamp who her family would be completely against her dating. Before she'd met Brian, all she'd dreamed of was finding her mate. Afterward, she'd spent a lot of time hoping she hadn't just met him.

Her family may be against a relationship with him, but she longed to kiss him and ease her curiosity about this frightening, powerful, magnificent vampire. If it turned out he wasn't her mate, at least she would finally *know* it hadn't been him who had ruined her for other men; she was simply broken or off in some way.

If it did turn out he was her mate, her family would have no choice but to accept him. They well knew what it was like to discover a mate and the irrevocable bond it formed between vampires. They may not like it, but they wouldn't stand in the way of mates. They understood what would happen if the bond was denied or broken, and they loved her too much to have her endure the insanity and death that would result from that.

Brian couldn't tear his eyes away from her. The increased beat of her heart thrummed in his ears, and the enticing flush of her skin did nothing to slow the blood flooding to his cock. Her tiny tongue darted out to lick her lips, which was something he now realized she did when she was aroused.

It would be so easy to take the glass from her hand and wrap his arm around her waist. She wouldn't push him away if he pulled her against his chest, sank his hand into her hair, and took possession of those enticingly wet lips.

Her brothers will cut your dick off if you try.

That mental reminder had him stepping away from her. He never denied himself anything he wanted, he saw no reason to, but he couldn't have her. Abby was too good for the likes of him and deserved better than what he could offer her. He knew instinctively that one time with her wouldn't be enough but the guilt was bad enough when it was only once with a woman; what would it do to him if he was with Abby countless times?

Memories of Vivian and his children haunted him continuously. He should have died with them. Instead, he was still here, standing in a room with the first woman he'd truly desired in almost two hundred years. He downed his whiskey and walked over to pour himself another glass.

"Where do we look for Vicky next?"

Her husky voice sent shivers down his spine. "I'll need something else of hers, another picture maybe."

"I have nothing else," she whispered, "not on me now."

CHAPTER SIX

BRIAN GLANCED at her over his shoulder. He really didn't want to have to touch her again if he could help it, but he didn't have a choice. "I can try on you," he said. "You are a piece of her after all, and you look just like her."

"So I've been told," she replied with a wistful smile. She placed her glass on the table and tugged up the jacket that had slipped over her shoulder. "Whatever you have to do, do it."

He would have to touch her, which could be the same as opening Pandora's Box. In one gulp, he swallowed his fresh glass of whiskey before walking across the room to where she stood. She thrust out her rounded chin and tilted her head back to look him in the eyes. So proud, so determined, *so* alluring, yet he still couldn't bring himself to reach for her.

"I don't care if it hurts," she said.

"It won't." If it did, he never would have offered to do it. He wouldn't knowingly do anything to cause her pain, no matter how badly she wanted her sister back. "Remain absolutely still."

She nodded her understanding and stood stock-still. Taking a deep breath to brace himself, he took hold of her hand. Her skin was silken beneath his, the bones in her hands delicate to the touch. Her breath caught in her chest and her eyes searched his as he rubbed his thumb over the back of her hand.

The scent of her arousal filled his nostrils. He suppressed the growl rolling up his throat as he fought the urge to draw her against him. He'd love to know what those pert breasts felt like pressed against his chest. She wouldn't fight him if he tried to draw her closer; no, she'd eagerly meld her body to his.

He tried to block out his body's need for her as he closed his eyes and focused on the brilliant spark of her soul. He concentrated on finding the link she had to Vicky. Searching through the tangled, interconnected waves of her soul, he finally found the thread he sought.

Latching onto Abby's connection to her twin, the apartment fell away from his conscious mind when he was mentally pulled forward by the thread of Vicky's soul. Blinding white stars rushed past him in a blur as he was sucked down what felt like a tunnel toward somewhere else. The tunnel ended abruptly; he opened his eyes and found himself standing on a piece of land staring at a calm sea.

Turning, he realized he stood at the foot of a large statue. Tilting his head back, he stared at the towering woman before him with her torch raised proudly in the air. A smile curved his lips as he lifted his eyes to stare across the water. Millions of lights blazed from the buildings on the other side and reflected off the water.

Manhattan. This vision was probably as close as he would come to finding Vicky given the amount of people in the city. Locating her in Manhattan would be like trying to find the proverbial needle in a haystack, but he'd promised Abby he would find her sister, and he would find her.

Abby stared at Brian as his eyes closed and a blank expression came over his face. He still stood before her, yet she sensed he was a million miles away, completely unreachable. She had no idea where his mind had gone, but since she'd met him, this was the first time she'd seen him look almost peaceful.

She itched to brush back the strand of blond hair that had fallen against the corner of his closed eye when his head bowed forward, but she didn't dare disturb him right now. There was no way to know what would happen if she disrupted him while he was like this.

"Shit," he muttered and lifted his head. His blue eyes blazed into hers.

Abby's shoulders fell. "You couldn't find her."

"She's in Manhattan, but that's as close as I'm going to get to her. There are too many people there for me to pinpoint an exact location."

"But you found both those houses in the city tonight."

"They were both on the outskirts of the city so there were fewer people around either of them. It's not the same where she is now. Plus, I still only knew the general area of where those houses were located until I was closer to them. Trying to do that in Manhattan will be about as easy as pulling a star from the sky."

"We can still find her."

"It's going to be tricky."

"Doesn't matter. Manhattan it is. I'll get changed and—"

He tugged her wrist to stop her before she could start rushing around. "Tomorrow, we will go to New York. Tonight we both need some rest, and we have to feed. You may not be hungry, but I am, and I'm not up for a nearly four drive right now."

"But—"

"No buts, we're staying here tonight. Getting so exhausted you can't keep looking for her or you get yourself hurt won't do anyone any good. Vicky will still be there tomorrow."

"You can't know that."

"Then we will find her next location, and if she moves again, we will find the one after that. She can't run for long; she has a disadvantage we don't."

"And what's that?"

"She's going to be looking for places to feed that will satisfy her new appetites. It will slow her down."

"Vicky isn't like those vampires in that house. I know she's not."

He didn't know what her sister was messed up in, but after what they'd seen tonight, he wouldn't rule anything out. "Maybe you should consider staying here while I go," he said as he released her hand and took a step away from the wrath simmering in her eyes.

"I'm going."

"Suit yourself."

He tried to sound nonchalant, but that was the last thing he felt right now. The idea of taking her into more locations like tonight made him want to drive his fist through a wall. The vamps in those places may be mostly incapacitated, but they could still be a threat to her. Not to mention, any of those dens could be wiped out at any time by Ronan or some other vamp who discovered them and knew what a risk they were to the vampire race's existence.

There were also places he was going to have to go in order to find out more information. Places she shouldn't be in, but he knew she would insist on going with him. He needed more whiskey if he was going to get through this, and some blood, lots of blood.

"How did you discover your ability to find people like that?" she asked.

Walking back into the kitchen, Brian pulled the fridge open and removed two bags of blood. He didn't care what she said, he could see her exhaustion and hunger in the shadows under her eyes and the slump of her shoulders. She had to feed.

"It was always something I could do a little. Then, one day, I needed it for more than trying to find the best scraps when I was hungry. I had to find someone close to me when I was a child, and I did," he replied as he handed her the bag. He watched in fascination as she bit the corner of the bag and tore it open. Tilting her head back, she drained the blood in one gulp.

She wiped the corners of her mouth when she was done. "I was hungrier than I'd realized," she said.

He handed her the bag he'd meant for himself before returning to the fridge and removing another bag for himself.

"What about your parents? Didn't they feed you?" she asked.

"They took care of my siblings and I the best they could, but there were five of us to feed. My parents made the most of the little they were able to scrape together and I helped by bringing more food home. When I was twelve, they both died from influenza as well as three of my siblings. My youngest sister was only two at the time, and she was taken to an orphanage. I took off before they could lock me away too.

"My sister was the first person I ever went looking for. I had planned to rescue her from the orphanage when I found her, but she'd already been taken in by a loving family who could do more for her than I could. She deserved a better life than living on the streets and scavenging for food, so I left her with her new family and never saw her again."

Abby struggled against the tears burning her eyes. Her entire life had been sheltered; she couldn't deny it. When she was stable enough to control her hunger, she'd been let out into the world and allowed to go to school. She'd been given the chance to make friends and have a social life. Her large family was overprotective but also full of love and laughter. She'd never known adversity or loss, not like Brian did. She would have given anything to soothe the scars those losses must have left on his soul.

"You were so young," she murmured.

"There were many who were younger than me on the streets back then, believe me." He tore the top off his bag and drained the contents. He tossed the bag in the trash after he finished, then grabbed his whiskey glass.

"What did you do after you left her behind?"

"I survived, which was no small feat back then. If the starvation, diseases, and cold didn't kill you, then you'd better watch out for the others running the street with you, because they would. I had no friends then either."

No wonder he's so distant and harsh, she realized. *All he's ever known is violence, loss, and betrayal.*

"When I was fifteen, a blacksmith caught me trying to break in to steal some iron from his shop. Instead of handing me over to the law to have my hand lopped off, or beating me himself, he took pity on me and took me in. He set me up as his apprentice and taught me his trade. He and his wife didn't have any children and treated me as if I were their own. It was the first time in my life I went to bed with a full belly every night."

"That was wonderful of them."

Brian tapped his fingers on the counter. Those years with Simon and Martha had been bookmarked by so much misfortune on both ends of them, that he didn't like to think of the happy years he'd spent with the loving couple. It was sometimes more distressing to remember the happiness than it was to remember the sorrow.

"Simon and Martha Stover were their names," he told her. "I haven't thought of them in decades."

"What happened to them?"

"I hope they lived to be an old and happy couple before passing peacefully. It's what I've always chosen to believe for them anyway. After I was turned, I fled Boston and didn't return until twenty years later. They most likely would have passed on by then, but I didn't look for them. Seeing me again, untouched by age, probably would have killed them if they had been still alive."

Abby fought against tears. She knew he wouldn't appreciate them, and might stop talking if she did start to cry, but he painted such a lonely picture of his life. "How much time did you spend with Simon and Martha?"

"A little over fifteen years. As soon as I was old enough, and experienced enough, I went into business with Simon. He expanded his shop for me, and between the two of us, we were able to do a lot of work. Simon was in his fifties at this point, but still strong and healthy. He was looking to take it easier, so I did a lot of the work, but I was happy to do anything I could to help them. They'd saved my life at a time when it had still been worth saving."

Abby flinched at his words. She wrapped her arms around herself instead of around him like she would have preferred. The way he accepted what he said about himself made her ache for him. She ran her hands up and down her suddenly chilled skin.

Brian's fingers stilled on the counter as, for the millionth time, he realized it would have been better if Simon had handed him over to the authorities or left him to starve in the alleyways. The earth would be short one less bloodthirsty monster if he had.

"After I met Vivian, I stayed with Simon and Martha, happy to share the money though I could have made more on my own. They'd become like a mother and father to me by then."

"Who is Vivian?"

"She was my wife."

Abby felt as if she'd been kicked in the gut. The air rushed out of her; her hands stilled on her arms as ice and heat licked over her skin in a rush that left her stunned. She didn't understand the ferocity of her reaction to his last two words. He'd been *married!* He'd loved another, and judging by the sadness on his face now, he still loved her.

"You were married?" she croaked.

"I was."

Brian had no idea why he was telling her this. It was of no relevance to what they were both involved in now, but for some reason, he found the words spilling from his mouth. Perhaps, it was her bright, warm soul that had him revealing to her things only Stefan had known until now. Maybe it was because they didn't really know each other, or maybe it was because she was listening, and it had been so long since anyone had listened to him.

"Stefan never told you?" he asked. She closed her mouth and shook her head, but he didn't understand the flicker of distress in her eyes.

"No, he's never talked of his past or yours with me. Maybe he's told Isabelle these things, but not the rest of us. What happened to your wife?"

"She was killed, along with our two daughters."

Abby's eyes became the size of saucers as she gazed at him. "Daughters?"

"Two. Beatrice and Trudy."

She had to sit down before she fell down. She sank onto the leather sectional couch positioned against the windows. The life he'd led, the suffering he'd endured, she didn't know how he'd been able to continue living at all, never mind how he'd kept himself from turning into a blood-thirsty monster.

Then she realized why he hadn't given into his more malicious vampire urges. "They were killed by a vampire," she guessed. She lifted her head to look at him. He hadn't become a monster who preyed on innocents because he despised what and who those vampires were. Instead, he'd become a vampire who preyed on those he deemed worthy of death due to their actions. "The same one who turned you."

His gaze focused on the twinkling lights of the city beyond her. "There were two vampires that night. The male killed my family; the woman turned me." She pressed her knuckles against her mouth to hold back a sob. "Then they fled, leaving me there to endure the anguish of my family's death as my body was brutally assaulted by the vampire blood coursing through my veins."

"I've heard the change is excruciating."

"It's nothing compared to holding your daughter's hand while she bleeds out in an alleyway, while you are helpless to save her because you yourself have been drained of everything you are. It still haunts my nightmares."

"Do you have nightmares about it often?"

"Not as often as before," he muttered.

She was unable to stop the tear sliding down her face. He may be a better man than many judged him to be, but he was far more broken than she'd ever realized. There was no saving him, and she'd been a foolish girl to ever daydream about him. She didn't know if he could ever truly care for another again, if he could ever care for *her*.

What does it matter if he cares for you or not?

It mattered because she'd always been an undeniable romantic at heart, and a part of her had always believed he was her mate. She'd tried to deny it, tried to replace him with someone her family would find more acceptable, but it had been impossible. Brian had shaken every belief she'd had about what she thought she wanted from a mate when he'd stepped into that hotel room so long ago.

Prior to first seeing him, she'd always pictured a nice, calm mate, one who would love her family and who would be eagerly accepted by them for his kindness. She'd pictured a man who was a little more like Harry Potter with his massive heart for others, and a little less like Dexter the mindless killing machine.

She'd pictured her future mate with glasses and wavy brown hair. He'd be patient, would disdain killing, and would be content to curl up with her before a fire and read a book. This man was the exact opposite of what she'd dreamed. She didn't think he knew the meaning of relaxing and reading by a fire, but she couldn't deny the irresistible pull she felt to him.

She hadn't been ready for him at fifteen, and he'd barely known she was alive, but she'd been only a child at the time. If he had looked at her with romantic interest back then, she probably would have been skeeved out, and her family would have killed him. Now, she was a woman, and though he looked at her like a woman, it was clear he was still nursing a couple centuries old broken heart.

She couldn't compete with that, nor did she want to.

For the past year, ever since the day she'd woken up and realized she reached maturity and would never age another day again, she'd fought the urge to call him. She'd been curious what it would be like to see him again, to know if he could finally do what all the men since him had failed to do and make her desire to be touched by him.

Well, he could definitely do that, but that was all he would ever be able to do for her. He would never be the uncomplicated mate of her early daydreams.

"You loved your wife," she stated.

His eyes flickered; sadness crept over his weary features. He rubbed at the stubble lining his jaw. "Very much. I will always love her."

The little romantic in her was taking a big kick in the ass right now. If he was her mate, something she really hoped wasn't true, but had the sinking sensation it was, she'd be attached to someone who would forever be in love with a ghost. Just because they were fated to be together, or however the mate bond worked, didn't mean they had to love each other.

She couldn't live for an eternity without knowing love. She couldn't live with the knowledge that he would forever wish she were another. It would eat away at her soul until it destroyed her. No matter how badly she wanted to have him ease the clamoring urges of her body, she couldn't allow anything more to transpire between them. She could not take the chance of a bond forming between them.

This was a working relationship only; she had to keep it professional and stay away from him. It would be a lot easier if he didn't look so damn delicious and didn't incessantly pull at her heartstrings.

"What did you do after you were turned?" she asked, her curiosity winning out over her determination to distance herself from him. "I've heard it can be disorienting and that a newly turned vampire must feed right away. How did you survive?"

"When I came to in that alley, the loss of my family and the shock of everything that had happened nearly drove me mad. I fled from their bodies, unsure of where to go and hungrier than I'd ever been in my life. I fed on a stable of horses, which helped to calm some of my disorientation, but it took me years to figure out exactly what I was and what I was capable of doing. Somehow, I managed to stumble through all of the new sensations and abilities that came from being a vampire without being killed or killing any humans."

Stumble he had, badly, many times. "I decided early on to punish vampires like the ones who had killed my family, so I soon discovered that feeding from our own kind gave me more power. I'd vowed never to kill a human even before I knew their deaths strengthened and weakened us by making it so we couldn't go out in the sun and cross bodies of water. I broke that vow when those hunters attacked me and Stefan and I killed two of them."

Abby stared at him, willing him to look at her, but he remained steadfastly focused on the city beyond her. "That was self-defense."

"Doesn't matter. I became the one thing I'd sworn *never* to be that night."

Abby's fingers dug into her palms. Definitely not like Harry Potter at all, he wasn't like anything she'd ever encountered before. "But you haven't killed a human again since then. I would know."

"No, I haven't. I would put myself down before I became a killer of innocents like some of our kind. But make no mistake, I am a killer. It's what I enjoy most."

How was she supposed to respond to that? *Oh, I enjoy a strawberry margarita on the beach the most, but hey, we each have our preferences.* One thing was for sure, she had no idea how to handle this man. She wanted to run far away from him; at the same time, she wanted to throw her arms around him and ease his torment.

"It's time for some sleep now," he said abruptly.

She knew he wouldn't reveal any more tonight, something that was probably for the best for her. "Yes, of course," she murmured.

She swung her legs onto the couch and rolled to face the back of it. She'd never been so emotionally and physically exhausted in her life, but she had a feeling she wouldn't be getting any sleep tonight.

"What are you doing?" he inquired.

"Going to sleep," she muttered.

She never heard him move, but she felt the heat of him against her back before he touched her shoulder. Electricity sizzled through her body, which only made her feel like crying. If Vicky were here, she would know how to handle this, or at least listen to the whining tantrum Abby wanted to throw. Things had been tough for Isabelle and Stefan. Stefan had led a violent, brutal life like Brian, but his heart had at least been free to love.

She'd gotten a guy who was more closed off than Fort Knox.

And Vicky may be sitting in a crack house right now, feeding on drug addicts, so put on a helmet and suck it up, buttercup. It could still get a lot worse.

Taking a deep breath, she kept that reminder firmly in mind as she rolled over to face him. There were far more important things to concern herself with right now than the death of childish hopes. Vicky was her primary focus. There was a chance she'd been stuck with an emotionally unavailable mate, but she had a kick-ass twin she missed more than she would have missed her own arm.

"You can sleep in my bed. I'll take the couch," he offered.

"You don't have to—"

"I insist." He pointed to a set of stairs winding to the loft above. "Bed's up there along with another bathroom. There will be clean towels and bedding."

"Thank you," she murmured.

She moved away from his touch, rose to her feet, and trudged sluggishly toward the stairs. She was tempted to call Issy and talk to her about everything, but she couldn't put this on her sister, and she knew Issy wouldn't be able to stay away if she did. This was her dilemma to deal with.

She really hoped she was doing the right thing by keeping her family out of this right now. Vicky would be infuriated with her for calling them; they had their own lives and families to take care of now.

If she and Brian didn't find Vicky soon, she'd risk her sister's wrath and make the call, but for now, she would continue to keep them out of it.

CHAPTER SEVEN

Brian draped his arm over his head as he stared at the loft above him. Early morning sunlight filtered around the heavy drapes he'd pulled over the windows before crashing on the couch. He'd spent the last hour staring up there, willing her to wake up, praying she didn't, and trying to ignore his throbbing hard-on.

What kind of hold did this girl have over him? He'd dreamt of seeing her in that dorm room with no bra and her full breasts swaying beneath her shirt. He'd dreamt of her pale hair spilling around him as she'd moved over top of him while moaning in delight. Dreamt of taking one of those breasts into his hand and suckling upon her pert nipple before sinking his fangs into her tender flesh.

Now, the object of his tantalizing dreams was up there, in his bed. Had she slept in a nightgown, or had she been naked when she climbed between his sheets? He bit back a groan as he fought the urge to take hold of himself and ease some of his need.

What would she do if she woke to find him pleasuring himself? Would she blush and run away, or would she watch him in that rapt way she sometimes did? Would she offer to come down and do it for him? The mere thought of her small hand wrapping around him almost made him explode.

He could go up there and crawl into bed beside her. He'd seen the way she watched him; he didn't think she would turn him away. If he rose from this couch and walked up those stairs, he could be deep within her, pounding out his rampant arousal between her sweet thighs in minutes. However, he knew if he went to her, he'd be opening a can of worms he'd never be able to close again.

Throwing aside the blanket, he rose to his feet and walked over to the bathroom. He didn't think a cold shower was going to do much for him, but it was better than lying there torturing himself with thoughts of sinking into her welcoming flesh.

Abby was awake and moving around upstairs when he finished in the bathroom. He stalked toward the window. He was not at all eased by the half hour cold shower or the release he'd given himself while thinking of her. It had been centuries since he'd imagined another woman while stroking himself. Memories of Vivian were too painful to think about and imaginings of another were too much like a betrayal to his dead wife.

Pictures of Abby had flooded his mind though. He'd been unable to stop himself from picturing her as he'd worked his hand up and down his shaft. He shuddered at the memory of the powerful orgasm that had rocked him. He hadn't cum like that in years, and it was only to *thoughts* of her. What would being inside of her do to him? What would it be like?

He ran a hand through his damp hair as he pulled back the drapes to reveal the sun glinting off the thousands of windows within the city as it rose. The scent of Abby's freshly washed hair assailed him when she descended the stairs. He turned to watch her; his eyes raking over her curvy figure, admiring the sway of her hips and the movement of her breasts beneath her sweater. She had on a bra, but he found her chest impossible to look away from while he watched her walk.

She didn't look at him as she placed her suitcase by the elevator. "Did you sleep well?" he inquired.

"Well enough," she muttered, but it was a complete lie. She'd gotten maybe an hour in total with all the tossing, turning, and worrying she'd done. Not to mention the yearning that had spread through her body at the idea of him downstairs, so close and yet further away than he'd ever been before.

She finally forced herself to look at him; she couldn't avoid it forever. Her breath caught in her throat, and she almost fell over when she saw the sun cascading over him as he stood before the window. She'd give anything to be one of the rays embracing his body so intimately as they slid over his pale flesh.

He hadn't dressed after his shower but simply wrapped a towel around his tapered waist. The muscles in his powerful forearms and biceps flexed when he folded his arms over his chest. His abs weren't just chiseled, they were carved from marble and more like a twelve-pack than a six. She could spend hours running her fingers over him, committing every detail of his magnificent form to memory.

His chest was speckled with blond hair, but as her gaze slid lower, she noticed the trail of hair from his belly button down to where it disappeared beneath the towel was darker in color. She found herself glaring at the towel, fighting the urge to tear it from his hips and reveal the rest of him to her voracious gaze. Her hand trembled when she lifted it to make sure she wasn't drooling before she abruptly turned away from him again.

Why did he have to be so irresistible?

"You're ready then?" His voice came out gruffer than he'd intended, but the way she'd been looking at him had his shaft surging with blood again and straining against the towel.

"As I'll ever be," she muttered.

She wasn't ready for anything right now; she felt testier than a cat in a bath. She didn't know why, but the sudden urge to punch him in the face was almost overwhelming. That gorgeous face had haunted what little sleep she'd managed to get last night.

"I'll get dressed," he said.

Please don't—I mean do! She thought as she kept her gaze focused on the granite counter. She couldn't stop herself from looking anymore when she heard his feet on the stairs. Maybe the towel would fall away... She found herself breathlessly hoping for this.

In love with his dead wife! The reminder was the slap in the face she needed. She turned away from him and walked over to stare out the windows as she listened to him open and close doors upstairs. When she did find Vicky, she was going to choke her sister, then hug her and choke her all over again for forcing her to turn to Brian for help in the first place.

He returned wearing a black, button-down shirt, and a pair of jeans. The clothes were something she'd seen on thousands of other men over the years, yet he somehow made them sexier than she'd ever believed possible. "Aren't you bringing anything?" she asked grouchily.

"I was planning on going camping for at least a month when you called. I have clothes in the back of my truck."

"Oh," she muttered. "Sorry I ruined your plans."

"I'll just go when this is over." He grabbed his keys from the counter and snagged her suitcase off the floor.

Abby didn't respond as she followed him over to the elevator. He pressed the button and the doors slid open. Stepping inside, she kept her gaze focused straight ahead while he hit the button to take them to the garage. Maybe if she didn't talk to him, it would make all of this easier. Not speaking to him was a good way of trying to distance herself from him. It would certainly help to keep her from learning anymore staggering and heartrending revelations about his life.

The only problem was she could feel the heat of his body so close to hers, and she wanted so badly to feel his flesh beneath her fingers. Her foot tapped and every breath she took felt strained as the seconds stretched endlessly onward before the doors slid open with a ding. Abby almost bolted out of the elevator; she was kept from doing so when he took hold of her elbow and guided her out to the garage.

The smell of motor oil and gas tickled her nostrils as their footsteps echoed throughout the concrete confines. Brian hit the alarm button on his keychain; it beeped twice as they approached his truck. They were almost there when she saw movement in the shadows and caught the rancid scent of garbage.

She stiffened as she recognized the scent of vampires who killed humans nearby. Before she could say something about it, Brian pulled her behind him and tossed her suitcase to the side. "There's someone—"

His warning died off as three vampires emerged from the shadows. "Brian," one of them greeted with a malicious gleam in his red eyes.

Brian's muscles rippled before her, his shoulders hunching up as his gaze traveled over each one of them. "Children," he replied. "I'm guessing you have a death wish."

The largest of the three, a brute at least six foot eight, cracked his knuckles and leered at the two of them. "The only death we wish is yours."

"If you didn't learn it as a child, you're going to learn now that wishes don't come true."

One of the others shot a nervous glance at the brute. Abby's mind continued to spin as she desperately looked around for some kind of weapon. The idea of carrying anything that could kill her or someone else had never sat well with her, but now she was defenseless, and these assholes were looking to kill Brian. She'd tear them apart with her bare hands if it became necessary, she decided as her fangs slid down behind her lips.

Brian smiled at the largest man when he stepped forward. He

would have preferred this not to happen in front of Abby, but there was no way to suppress his excitement at the anticipation of the kill. "You first then, big boy," he taunted. "You'd be better off coming at me all at once. It would at least be faster and easier for me to kill you all that way, but it's your funeral, so we'll play this your way."

Abby's eyes flew back to Brian. Why was he antagonizing these guys?

Brian raised his hands and waved at the hulk of a guy to come at him when he hesitated. Over the years, he'd discovered confidence was half the battle when it came to a fight. Not over-confidence, that would get someone slaughtered in seconds, but enough confidence to unnerve his attackers, like now.

They'd been brash and assured when they'd stepped from the shadows; now two of them looked as if they were debating running, while the largest one realized he'd committed already and would have to see it through. Abby's warm body pressed against his back as he kept her in between him and the pickup. He wouldn't take the chance of any of these vampires being able to get at her.

The bloodlust in him rose at the notion of any one harming her. He'd make them pay dearly for daring to attack him while she was in his care. "You picked the wrong day for this, boys," he growled.

Before any of them could react, he lunged to the side and caught the smallest one by his throat. Lifting him over his head, Brian slammed him onto the concrete floor with enough force to break his back. The vampire squealed in pain; his fingers scrabbled at the concrete as he tried to crawl away. Brian spun when the next two lunged at him as he'd hoped they would.

His punch connected with the underside of the big guy's jaw. Hulk's head shot back as he flipped over onto his back, his hands and feet kicking in the air like a turtle as he squirmed backward to get out of the way. The other one tried to lunge around Brian to get at Abby, probably hoping to use her as leverage or protection against Brian. It was the biggest mistake he'd ever committed in his life.

With a ferocious snarl, Brian snagged hold of his arm before his grasping fingers could so much as touch her. Driving down with his other hand, he broke the man's arm with enough force to drive his bones through his skin. A howl erupted from the vamp's throat, but Brian abruptly cut it off with an elbow to his larynx.

The man gagged and sputtered. His good hand fluttered to his crushed throat as Brian drove his fist into his chest and wrapped his hand around the vampire's heart. He tore it free and tossed it aside before turning his attention to the one whose back he'd broken. Grabbing hold of the vamp's head, he twisted it to the side and tore it from his body.

The biggest one had regained his feet and was running through the parked cars toward the main entrance. The sunlight would have him smoking in a matter of seconds if he ran into its direct rays, but apparently he didn't care right now. Brian did though; they couldn't take the risk of mortals seeing him burning beneath the rays of the sun.

"Stay here!" he barked at Abby before taking off after him.

Abby couldn't get her mouth to close again as she gazed at the carnage surrounding her. The hotel room had been the only other time she'd ever seen anything like this. Now she had a head lying next to her feet with its unseeing eyes staring up at her. She tore her gaze away from the decapitated body and fought the urge to kick the head as far away from her as she could get it.

None of the carnage mattered while Brian was still pursuing the remaining, biggest vampire. She spotted him instantly as he raced through the shadows of the garage in a near blur of speed. The brute's feet slapped against the concrete floor and echoed throughout the garage, but Brian's step was eerily soundless as he pursued his prey. Turning in between cars, Brian leapt over the top of two of them before crashing into the back of the remaining vamp and dragging him down beneath him.

Abby rushed forward when he vanished from view behind a red

Lamborghini. The distinct thuds of a fist hitting flesh reached her seconds before a sickening, cracking, wet noise resounded through the garage. She now recognized that sound as someone's head being torn from their body.

Not Brian, please not him, she pleaded as she skidded around the front of the red sports car.

Brian was rising to his feet with the brute's head still in hand when she finally saw him. The revulsion and fear coursing through her vanished when her eyes latched onto him. Her gaze ran rapidly over him, but though he'd just taken on three vampires, she didn't see any cuts or scratches on him as he bent to grab hold of the brute's arm.

"I told you to stay by the truck," he said as he looked over at her.

"I had to make sure you were okay," she replied.

"You shouldn't be seeing this."

Brian tore his gaze away from her pale face as he dragged the body from between the cars. Abby fell back, her lower lip quivering while she watched him. He could kick himself for her having witnessed this. However, maybe this had been a good thing; maybe letting her see what kind of man he truly was would make her quit looking at him with such longing in her eyes.

"I've seen it before," she murmured.

He sent her a sharp glance over his shoulder. "When?"

"The hotel room."

"Shit," he muttered. Shaking his head, he tossed the big guy's body into the back of his pickup and threw the head on top of it. She'd witnessed only a little of the evil in the world during her life, and he'd played a starring role each time. "Both times with me."

He didn't realize he'd said the words aloud until her hand fell on his arm. He glanced down at the small hand heating his flesh. The urge to grab hold of it and pull her against him seized him, but he pulled his arm away from her and turned to pick up the next body. He'd destroy her if he got too close. His world was not a place where she belonged, and he was the last creature on Earth who deserved any kind of solace or peace.

"Did you know these guys?" she inquired as she fought against the disappointment filling her over the loss of physical contact with him.

"Nope." The third body thumped against the bed when he dumped it into the truck. He pulled a tarp over the three bodies.

"Why did they attack you then?"

"Because that's my life. I kill their kind, and they try to come after me for it. It would be a huge coup and a lot of power for one of them, if they were ever successful in taking me down and drinking my blood. They must have discovered I had a place here."

Abby pressed her hand against her mouth as concern for him coiled in her belly. "They come after you often?"

"Only the dumb ones. Many have tried to kill me, all have failed. Their attempts aren't as frequent as they used to be."

That did nothing to ease her concern for him. He appeared completely unfazed by what had occurred as he pulled a towel from the silver toolbox on the back of the truck. He wiped his face and hands on it before tossing it back inside and closing the lid. He retrieved her suitcase and threw it into the backseat of the truck before walking toward her.

He didn't look like someone who had just slaughtered three vampires who had been trying to kill him. He hadn't broken a sweat, there wasn't a mark on him, and the only blood she could see was a couple of specks on his right cheek that he'd missed with the towel. She had no idea what to make of this man who could make her body ache and her heart beat faster, all while her brain was telling her to run for the hills.

"You have some..." Without thinking, she brushed away the blood on his cheek.

Before she could wipe her fingers onto her jeans, he grabbed hold of her wrist. "You shouldn't be touching that," he said as he tenderly wiped her fingers off with his own.

"I've dealt with blood my whole life," she said with a smile, hoping to coax one from him too. His expression remained unreadable and distant.

"Not death though," he replied after a little bit. "And you shouldn't have to deal with it at all. Maybe—"

"I'm not going anywhere," she insisted before he could suggest it, as she knew he was going to.

His eyes were like chips of ice when they met hers. "I'm not someone you should be around, Abigail."

Her fingers wrapped around his hand as he continued to hold her. She shouldn't be around him, vampires everywhere hunted him, he was beyond hazardous to her heart, but she couldn't walk away from him.

"Maybe not," she replied honestly, "but I'm here and I'm not going anywhere."

His eyes searched her face before he released her hand and stepped away from her. Taking hold of her elbow, he walked her to the passenger side door and opened it for her. He helped her climb into the tall vehicle. She immediately missed his touch when he released her elbow and closed the door.

Fool. Keep your distance. However, the loneliness she sensed in him, the need for something more than death and violence in his life, called to her. She so badly wanted to make his life about more than fights in a garage and fending off those trying to kill him.

"What about cameras?" she asked when he started the truck and pulled out of the parking spot. In a building this upscale, there had to be a security system.

"I'm sure those guys took them out before they came after me, but just in case…" his voice trailed off as he stopped outside the guard's office. Abby hastily turned away from the blood-splattered walls and windows of the small office near the exit of the garage.

Brian gritted his teeth at the realization he was once again exposing her to more death and violence, but he had to make sure there was no taped evidence of what had transpired. Opening the door, he jumped out of the truck. "Stay here," he told her.

"I will."

He stared at her for a minute, but she kept her gaze focused on her hands folded in her lap. Closing the door, he walked over to the room. He stepped over the two mutilated bodies of the guards as he headed for the monitors set up on a desk. All of the screens were blank, including the ones that would have shown the inner halls and elevators of the building. At least those three morons had been smart enough to cover their tracks before coming after him.

Walking out of the small room, he stopped when he saw Abby still intently focused on her lap rather than the massacre in the room. He didn't like her exposed to these things but he had to make sure she stayed protected throughout her hunt for her sister, and he didn't trust anyone else to keep her safer than he could. He had vamps hunting him, yes, but due to his age and the power he'd harvested from the countless vamps he'd killed over the years, he was a lot stronger and more lethal than most. He also had a lot of extremely powerful allies. Right now, by his side was the safest place he could think of for her.

Her family was strong, but he would happily destroy any vamp who tried to hurt her, and he had more experience at it than the Byrnes did. Hurrying back to the truck, he pulled open the door and jumped inside.

"I'm glad those vampires are dead," she whispered.

"So am I," he told her as he shifted into drive.

"Will you come back here?"

"No. If they managed to find out I was living here, others will too. It's time to sell and move on. It isn't the first time, won't be the last."

Tears burned her eyes for him and for the poor humans who had only been doing their jobs when their lives had been torn away from them. "Where are you going to put the bodies?" she asked.

"There's a quarry nearby I've used before."

Abby refrained from asking how many times he'd used that location. She probably wouldn't like the answer, and it really didn't matter in the grand scheme of things. They didn't speak as he drove to the quarry, tied some rocks to the bodies, and tossed them over the side into the water below. She cringed at the sound their bodies made when they splashed into the water before soundlessly sinking to the bottom.

CHAPTER EIGHT

Abby barely noticed the streets and buildings they passed as he drove through the city and toward the highway. She took a steadying breath as her thoughts turned to her sister. What was Vicky doing? What had she gotten herself mixed up in?

Before this, the brazen and wild things Vicky had done had always been more free-spirited and fun. Like when she had streaked across the football field on prom night or stolen five pigs from a local farm and put them in the principal's office. She'd always enjoyed a good party but had always disdained the use of drugs before. Her sister could be wild and sometimes reckless, but none of this was like her. Abby rubbed at her temples as she tried to ease the headache forming there.

"Are you okay?" Brian inquired.

"Yeah," she murmured and sat up in her seat. She'd vowed she wouldn't ask him anymore about himself, but she'd happily take any distraction from thoughts of Vicky right now. "Why are you able to locate people and vampires?"

"Why are some humans able to see the future, commune with the dead, or bend things with their minds? They are simply born differently, and just as my strength and power has grown over my years as a vampire, so has my ability to locate others."

"Interesting."

"That it is," he replied and glanced over at the rigid set of her shoulders.

Her chin was thrust forward, her eyes now fastened on the scenery. She was steadfastly avoiding looking at him, which irritated him far more than he would have believed possible. His hands tightened on the wheel. Was it because of what had occurred in the garage? Was she afraid of him now or repulsed by him?

What does it matter? It shouldn't, but it did. He missed her attention even though he wanted her to keep her distance.

"I used to be able to find things my mother misplaced when I was only three," he said, trying to draw her attention, but she still wouldn't look at him. "Vivian" —her fingers twitched at the name. *Interesting*— "was always losing things and coming to me to find them. I can't locate things from long distances, but I can still uncover them if they're within a few miles of me by following the traces of the person they belong to. The vampires who attacked my family and me that night were the only ones I couldn't find right away."

"Why not?"

"They fled the country shortly after turning me. I didn't realize that at the time, and my ability hadn't developed enough for me to be able to locate them. It took over a hundred years for that to happen, and the minute it did, I went after them."

His voice came out a gravelly rumble, and his knuckles were white on the steering wheel. "And then you helped Stefan find the vampire who turned him?"

"That took more time. I'd known what my attackers looked like; they were a part of me. Stefan described the woman who had turned him, but it wasn't enough, and he's not much of an artist. I do a lot better when I have a clear image of someone in my head."

"And then what happens?"

He smiled at her and leaned back in his seat. "Not so fast, young Byrne," he replied. "Some things are for me to know."

"You've told me almost all of it, why keep this from me?" she asked in frustration. She was foolishly still eager to learn every detail she could about him.

"Perhaps some things are too unknown to explain."

"I see," she said, although she didn't.

She lapsed into silence once more; her emerald gaze fixated on the roadway as the tires spun over the asphalt. He turned on the radio, but he found not even Creedence Clearwater Revival could soothe his irritation over the distance he sensed in her. She didn't speak again for another hour.

"How old were you when you were turned?" she inquired.

"Thirty."

"How old are you now?"

"Two hundred and fifteen in vamp and human years. I was born in eighteen o'one."

Abby managed to keep her jaw from dropping. He wasn't as old as Stefan, but he'd definitely been around the block a few times. *What things has he done in two hundred and fifteen years? How many women has he been with?*

Never mind. She really didn't want the answer to that question. She took in his handsome countenance with his broad cheekbones and the chiseled jaw he'd removed the stubble from this morning. Lines crinkled the corners of his eyes. She doubted they were laugh lines, but more lines earned from when he'd still been human, dealing with human tribulations and standing over a forge while he learned to become a blacksmith. She had a feeling that when he'd been human, he still hadn't laughed much. She was dying to know what his laughter would sound like.

"In all that time, what is the craziest thing you've done?" she asked.

"I think you're too young for the answer to that question."

"I'm not a child."

No, she most certainly wasn't a child anymore. He couldn't keep his gaze from the form-fitting black sweater snugged over her breasts. Blood flooded into his cock, hardening it in his jeans.

The heated look that came into his eyes when they latched onto her breasts stole her breath. "Eyes on the road," she murmured when the truck drifted into the other lane.

He glanced away from her, his hands clenching on the wheel once more. He couldn't get away from the pressure of his erection against the front of his jeans. The sweet scent of her hair and the aroma of her blood called to him in a way it never had with any other before her.

He'd fed on many vampires over the years, taking their power, absorbing more and more until he'd teetered on the edge of becoming like one of the monsters he was determined to hunt and destroy. Never had he longed to sink his fangs into someone as badly as he wanted to sink them into her and experience the connection it would bring.

Her blood would be sweet, like her, potent and delectable. A purebred's blood, he'd never tasted it before, and his fangs throbbed with the urge to do so now.

Shifting uncomfortably, he adjusted his jeans as he focused on the road again. They may both be immortal, but the last thing he felt like doing was crashing into something at eighty miles an hour or being launched from the vehicle because he was paying more attention to her than the road. He'd gone through a windshield once before in the sixties. Sliding down the road on his stomach had been an experience he'd never forget. It had taken two days for his skin to heal and to get out all of the glass.

"I've done many crazy things over the years," he finally said. "Almost two hundred years as an immortal tends to get a little boring. I'm always looking for something new and different to try."

"Is that why you agreed to help me?"

No, your voice, it ensnared me. I couldn't say no. "Perhaps," he lied, knowing he could never acknowledge his growing desire for her. Her mouth pursed, and she turned away from him once more. Unwilling to have her stop speaking to him again, he decided to give her some of the less violent details of his life.

"I climbed to the top of the Sphinx, and had dinner with Lucky Luciano. I've been to the running of the bulls, camped in the wilds of Alaska, kissed Marilyn Monroe, and ran around with Billy the Kid for a month. By the way, Pat Garrett didn't shoot him."

Abby couldn't stop the delighted laugh that escaped her. "Really?"

"Truly," he replied with a wink. "Or at least, that's what I believe. I simply can't see the man I knew killing his friend."

Abby turned toward him, eager to learn more. "Did you know Wyatt Earp?"

"I had a brief encounter with him."

"What happened?"

"He tried to arrest me for stealing a horse. I, of course, escaped."

"Oh, of course," she said with a laugh. "What else?"

"I went to Woodstock. I've been to every country there is on the planet, many of them multiple times. I've met kings and queens and tsars."

"Sounds amazing," she said.

"Some of it was," he admitted. "And a lot of it was brutal." She drew her legs up and hugged them against her chest. "A lot of it was death, vengeance, and feasting on the blood of those we slaughtered in order to gain power."

Abby's fingers fiddled with her jeans as she watched the merriment fade from his face and the harsh, distant side of him once again emerged. "We all do what we must to survive."

His eyes flashed red as he glanced at her. "And what about you, Abigail, what have you done to survive?"

"I must drink blood, too."

"Have you ever killed? Have you ever fed from a human?"

"I've never killed, but I have fed from a man before."

He almost tore the wheel from the truck at the idea of her sinking her fangs into another's neck. He knew well how intimate the exchange could be, how *arousing*. He took a deep breath, fighting against the shudder wracking him. Had the mortal been inside of her while she'd been feeding from him? Had that man heard her cries of ecstasy as she rode him?

He barely suppressed the impulse to pull to the side of the road, draw her head back, and sink his fangs into her neck while he caressed one of the breasts that had haunted his dreams last night.

Easy, he counseled himself. He hadn't felt this out of control and savage since he'd found the two who had murdered his family. That had been a bloodbath the likes of which he'd never unleashed before or since. However, if the boy she'd fed from had been standing in front of him right now, it would have been another bloodbath.

"And you enjoyed it?" he grated through his teeth.

"It wasn't great, wasn't horrible; it was just different. I was used to blood bags at the time, but my curiosity about what it would be like to drink straight from the vein finally got the best of me."

"I see."

Her eyes were unreadable as they studied him. "Do you think I was wrong to do it? Did you expect I was like Issy and Ethan and shunned all things human? You have met Ian and Aiden before, right? They dove headfirst into the human world, and I must admit, it fascinates me too."

"Hence college and the social work degree?"

She smiled and leaned closer to him. Her citrus smell assaulted his senses. The beat of her heart fascinated him as his own heart raced faster to beat in rhythm with hers. Perhaps her family would never have to know that he and Abby had any kind of an encounter, and they could both go their separate ways after? Yeah, and pigs flew to the moon every night at ten.

"Yes," she said. "Humans know they face death every day, yet they bravely go out into the world. They smile, laugh, and love all while knowing it could be over in the next instant. We're immortal and yet they're a far more resilient species. I mean, how is it possible to live so much while knowing death is the only end they will have?"

Brian stared at the roadway as he recalled his days as a mortal. He could clearly remember the first time he'd seen Vivian standing in the crowd, her auburn hair shimmering in the sun as she inspected some cloth. Her hair had been what drew him to her first; it had been a burst of color in a drab crowd.

"That's *why* they live so much. They know death is their only escape," he replied.

"Did you live more as a human than a vampire?"

"Yes. Once I became a vampire, my existence became focused only on death, revenge, and increasing my power."

"I like to think I'm focused on the good things, but sometimes…"

"What?" he inquired when her voice trailed away.

"Sometimes I wonder if humans are luckier, if immortality isn't more of a curse that weighs heavily upon the souls who face an eternity alone."

"And you think you face immortality alone?"

"You've met my family, right? And they keep growing. No, I'm not alone, but many immortals are. There are times I'm lonely, even with all of my family and Vicky by my side. My older sibling's lives are far different than mine now. Aiden is involved in something few of us know anything about."

"He'll be fine."

"I know he will, but you know more about what he's doing than any of his family members. It's a strange thing to realize when we've all been so close over the years."

"I suppose it is."

She leaned her head against the seat as she watched him. "Your wife, how did you meet her?" Call her a glutton for punishment, but she had to know more about him.

A muscle in his jaw twitched. "It was at a street fair."

"What did she look like?"

"She had auburn hair and freckles all over her face. Her eyes were brown. I found her beautiful, though many probably wouldn't have."

"Love at first sight?"

He glanced at her; there was something behind her words, a wistfulness or sadness perhaps. "No. I was curious about her. She intrigued me with her coloring and gentle demeanor. Love came later."

Jealousy speared Abby so fiercely that she sucked in a breath as her fingers dug into her legs. Why on earth had she started on this line of conversation? She'd already lost his heart to an intriguing ghost, why was she punishing herself like this?

"Vivian was vibrant, but refined like the women of those days were. I courted her for a year before we were married," he continued.

"How old were you?"

"I was twenty-three. She was nineteen."

"So young."

"In those days, I was almost an old man by then," he replied with a smile.

"I suppose you were." She turned to stare at the roadway again, absently noting the 'Welcome to New York' sign they passed on the highway.

"Beatrice was born two years later," he murmured, drawing her attention back to him. She held her breath, scared to make a sound or else he might stop talking. "And Trudy came two years after her. Beatrice's hair was blonde, like mine, but Trudy inherited her mother's auburn tresses. They were both so beautiful."

"They sound like it," she whispered. Unable to resist, she rested her hand comfortably on his bicep. "I'm sorry for your loss."

He shook his head as if tearing himself from a reverie. "It was years ago."

"That doesn't mean the hurt stops."

Brian glanced at her, noting the strain on her face and the sorrow in her eyes. He hated that look from her. "I don't want your pity."

She recoiled from the sneering tone of his voice and tore her hand away from his arm. "I don't pity you."

"I've come to terms with their loss over the years." He was acutely aware of the lack of heat from her touch as he watched the buildings around them beginning to crop up more and more. "Life is cruel."

"It's also amazing."

"And that is where we disagree, young Byrne."

Abby's teeth clamped together when he called her that again. She recognized it as a way for him to distance himself from her by looking at her as if she were still a child. Turning, she plopped her feet on the floor, having had enough of this conversation with him. He could pretend he'd accepted the loss of his family, but they both knew the truth.

CHAPTER NINE

Abby had just finished drying her hair when she heard the knock on the door. Placing the dryer down, she hurried through the large, elaborate hotel room he'd rented for her. She'd tried to pay for her room, but he'd taken her credit card away from her and handed it back. The censuring look he'd shot her when she'd started to protest had silenced her.

She threw the locks on the door and pulled it open.

"Did you check to see who was standing out here first?" Brian demanded.

"I knew it was you," she replied as she turned away.

"And how did you know that?"

"I just did."

He insisted on keeping his secrets, so she wasn't about to tell him that she'd become attuned to his scent and the beat of his heart. Let him try to puzzle out how she knew it was him standing on the other side of her door.

She felt the heat of his gaze as it slid over her, but she didn't turn around. She'd packed only sensible clothes for this trip—sweaters, jeans, and T-shirts to sleep in. However, when he'd told her they'd be going to a club tonight to speak with some vamps he knew in the city, she'd gone down to one of the stores along the street and found something more suitable for club wear. Something entirely *un*-childlike.

"You packed that?" he inquired, his voice hoarser than normal.

"I purchased it," she replied as she brushed her hair out and set the brush on the bureau.

"When?"

"While you were in the shower. I can walk around in public you know."

"Not alone."

"You're right, my mom and dad have still been holding my hand all these years."

He folded his arms over his chest, his scowl deepening as he raked her from head to toe and back again. Her breath caught when the ice color of his eyes deepened to a softer blue. She spotted the growing bulge behind the zipper of his black pants and almost hiked up her barely-there skirt to hop on him and wrap her legs around his waist.

What she wouldn't give to feel the rigid length of him sliding over her, within her. Wetness spread between her legs and her nipples hardened at the prospect of sex with this man. His gaze latched onto her bellybutton ring with the chain running around her exposed midriff. A mewl of desire almost escaped her when the light of the room glinted off one of his fangs, but she managed to keep it suppressed.

"Your family would have my head for allowing you to walk around in public like that," he said.

"First off, no one *allows* me to do anything. I'm a full-grown woman who is perfectly capable of running my own life and more than capable of defending myself, especially against a human. Second, my family has seen me go out to the clubs before. It's not like Ian and Aiden were monks for crying out loud."

Anger and lust roared within him as his eyes ran over her again. The black skirt she wore shouldn't be considered a skirt at all; it was more like a stretch of material barely covering her firm ass. An ass he wanted to grip as she rode up and down his shaft. Her top wasn't much better, exposing her flat belly and accentuating her rounded hips and plump breasts with every step she took.

Once again, she was without a bra, which was okay as her breasts didn't need a bra to keep them firm and high. With the off-the-shoulder style of her top, straps would have been visible. Her black boots came over the top of her knees, the heels on them making her legs look longer and shapelier.

Then there was that belly button ring… What he wouldn't give to run his tongue over it and tug on the chain with his teeth. He decided she'd be the death of him when she bent over, causing the belly chain to slide up her back.

"Maybe you should stay here," he suggested. If she walked into a vampire club looking like this, he'd be beating the men and women off her.

The tilt of her chin and the fire in her eyes let him know that wasn't going to be an option even before she spoke. "Not a chance in Hell."

"You'll freeze," he said.

"Good thing I'm immortal then," she replied, and grabbed a knee-length, black coat from where it hung on the back of the desk chair. "I have to fit in at a club. No one is going to give us info on Vicky if I'm looking like a preppy narc."

"You don't look like a narc because you're wearing *clothes*."

"I'm in *clothes*," she retorted, her eyes narrowing on him. "What is your problem?"

Everyone is going to be looking at what I so desperately want and can never have. "I hate to see a woman flaunting herself," he said instead.

Red blazed through her eyes as she strode across the room

toward him. Her hips swayed in a way that had him gritting his teeth against the urge to throw her onto the bed and strip those barely-there clothes from her. Stopping before him, her eyes were green again when she tilted her head back to look at him, but fury radiated from every inch of her sinful body.

"Then it's a good thing you won't have to see me anymore after we find Vicky. You'll never have to watch me *flaunt* myself again."

"So eager to get rid of me then?"

"I can't wait for it," she lied, but damn if she wasn't contemplating driving the toe of her boot into his nuts right now. That flaunting herself comment had her fingers itching to claw his eyes out.

"You should change."

"No, I shouldn't."

He had no idea how to handle this woman. She had him harder than he'd ever been in his life, yet, at the same time, he was considering throttling her. He was tempted to rip the risqué clothes from her body and force her to wear something that wouldn't make every male in the club want her as badly as he did.

Vivian would have done as he had asked without hesitation. She'd been a good woman, but she'd also been a meek product of her time and upbringing when it came to a man's will. He hadn't given one rat's ass what all the other women he'd encountered over the years wore or their safety. He'd sought his release then moved on. Now, he was acutely aware of what this woman was wearing, and her safety was his number one concern, right above the men who would be panting after her.

The look in Abby's eyes said, if he attempted to force her into something more modest, she'd try to claw the eyes from his head. He had to admit he did want to see her in this outfit, many times, but only for *him*. He'd give anything to watch her strutting back and forth in these clothes, with her hips swaying and her breasts bouncing as she walked to him before falling to her knees and taking him into her mouth.

Shit, if she didn't kill him, his fantasies of her would.

"We had better get going then," he replied through gritted teeth as he fought against the blood still rushing to his groin. "The sooner we're able to part ways, the better."

"My thoughts exactly." Abby buried the hurt his words had caused; she'd been saying the same thing to him after all.

He held the door open for her, and she stepped into the hallway. She ignored the startled look of the woman passing by and the lecherous look of the man walking by her side, as his gaze ran over her body.

She pulled her coat on and tugged it closer around herself. She ignored Brian's pointed look when she tied the belt around her waist. Truth be told, she'd never dressed this provocatively before, but she hadn't been able to resist the skirt and shirt or having Brian seeing her in them. Getting closer to each other would be a very bad idea, but she'd been dying to see how he would react and hoped he would stop thinking of her as a child.

She hadn't expected him to go all Neanderthal on her, but he had been born in the eighteen hundreds when things were much different. Women had been kept at home and had worn enough clothing to cover them from head to toe. She'd never be that woman, and though she'd hated his words, she'd still thrilled at the heat in his ravenous gaze as he'd watched her.

He looked so unbelievably tantalizing tonight. The deep blue shirt he wore emphasized the color of his eyes and the flex of his powerful muscles as he moved. The black pants hugged his taut ass and powerful thighs. Not to mention, they emphasized the massive size of the erection that had blazed to life when he'd seen her.

Either she gave into her body's clamoring hunger for this man and had her heart broken, or she continued to stay far away from him. The idea of spending an eternity never knowing what it was like to have a man inside her was a bleak and depressing prospect. So was having a broken heart for an eternity.

Maybe she'd never own his heart, but she desperately wanted to possess his body. No one else would ever satisfy her; she'd had enough failed attempts with other men to know that was true. And maybe, just maybe, he'd leave her cold like the others too. *Yeah and maybe Hell has Slurpees.*

She could worry about all of that at another time. Now she had to focus on trying to find her sister in this massive city. She huddled deeper into her black coat as Brian hit the button for the elevator.

"Cold?" he inquired.

It wasn't said in a gloating manner but more of a concerned one. "Just thinking about Vicky."

"We'll find her."

The doors slid open and she stepped into the elevator with him beside her. The music flowing from the speakers did little to calm her anxiety as the floors flashed by on the panel over the doors. He took hold of her elbow when the elevator stopped and led her across the marble entryway to the golden doors the doorman pulled open for them.

Brian stepped back to allow her to pass through the door first before walking to the curb to hail a cab. The cold air blew over her skin and caused her hair to tickle against her face as she watched the cars moving by. People hustled up and down the sidewalk, talking and laughing. Other people walked by with their heads down in determination.

An energy she'd never quite experienced before sizzled through the air. She could see why it was called the 'City That Never Sleeps.' All around her she sensed an aura of excitement drawing her into the city itself. Laughter filled the air; everywhere she looked there were lights and billboards for shows. She loved Boston, but she felt as if she could get lost here forever.

Vicky. Had her sister felt the same way? Had she been caught up in the same energy? Had she been swept away by the feeling of being able to do anything this city allowed? Had whoever she'd left Boston with brought her here because they had known she would enjoy it?

"Abigail."

She turned to find Brian holding the back door to a taxi open for her. She had no idea how long he'd been calling her name; she'd been too focused on everything around her.

"Ready?" he inquired.

She hurried toward him. When she reached his side, he clasped hold of her elbow to help her into the vehicle before following behind her. Once he was settled, he gave the address of the club to the cabby, then tucked her close to his side as the driver pulled away from the curb.

"This city is so *alive*," she murmured as she eagerly drank in the sights surrounding them.

"It is," he agreed, however he knew he didn't look anywhere near as starry-eyed as she did right now.

He found himself watching her every expression instead of their surroundings as they drove down the streets. Her eyes sparkled with merriment; a smile tugged at her mouth as her gaze darted from one side of the street to the other and back again. It had been years since he'd seen so much joy in anyone, and he thrived on watching it come from her.

Without thinking, he placed his hand on her bare knee. Her eyes flew to his, and her breath sucked in as his fingers slid over her supple flesh. *She's going to push me away, tell me to stop.* Instead, that fascinated gaze had become riveted on him as his hand slid closer to the top of her thigh. If he slid it up only a few more inches, he would feel her underwear and the delicious warmth just beneath. Would her underwear be lacy or silken like her?

He could push them aside and dip his fingers into the heated flesh he longed to touch. He had a feeling he would find her already wet with wanting for him. His cock jumped in his pants, drawing her attention to it. Yearning flared over her face as she stared at it. His hand tightened on her thigh, and he pulled it firmly against his leg.

Her riveted gaze never left his as his hand slid further up and his fingers brushed over her center, answering his question; they were as silken and soft as she was. A small breath escaped her, and her eyelids became heavy as he stroked her again. As he'd suspected, she was already wet for him.

He desperately wanted to sate the need he sensed pouring from her as she lifted her hips invitingly toward his finger. Taking hold of her hand, he held her gaze as he placed it against his thigh and ran it up toward his aching dick. Her tongue slid out to lick her lips. He held his breath as he waited eagerly to finally feel her hand against him.

She was only inches from where he wanted her when the cabby spoke. "We're here."

The urge to break the man's neck shot through him when Abby jerked her hand away and pulled her coat closed. He'd been so wrapped up in her that he hadn't realized the taxi was now stopped. Reluctantly, he pulled his hand from under her skirt and threw the man a twenty. He surreptitiously tucked his erection into the band of his pants before sliding from the car.

He took hold of Abby's hand, helping her from the vehicle. Red marked her fair cheeks and she wouldn't meet his gaze as she adjusted her skirt and coat. He took hold of her hand once more, sliding her arm through his and locking it against his side as he led her toward the line winding down to the underground club.

"Dracul," Abby said when she spotted the red sign on the front of the building.

She kept her gaze on the sign instead of him as she tried to suppress the waves of embarrassment still flooding her from their car ride. She'd been so wrapped up in him and the way he could make her feel, that she'd completely forgotten they weren't alone in the cab. Maybe the driver hadn't gotten a total eye full of the activities taking place in his backseat.

"As in Dracula. This club is owned by a vampire," Brian said.

Her eyes shot to him. "Kind of flaunting what he is, isn't he?"

"She," he replied.

"What?"

"The owner is a she, Karina."

"Oh."

Abby made a move for the back of the line, but Brian guided her straight toward the mountain of a vampire standing outside the front door. The bouncer didn't smell off when they stepped before him, but she instinctively recognized one of her own kind.

"Karina is expecting us," he said to the bouncer.

The bouncer pulled back a red chain blocking them from going down the stairs. *How well does he know this Karina?* She wasn't sure she wanted the answer to that question. There were already too many women in his life as far as she was concerned. His desire for her was obvious, no matter how much he tried to distance himself from her, but she wanted more than just his desire.

Why? It's not like you love him. You could be mates and still never come to love him.

Sometimes her little inner voice made good points, even if they were bleak and depressing.

At the bottom of the stairs, the door opened to reveal a hallway that was dark as night beyond. If she'd been human, she wasn't sure she'd be able to see the walls surrounding her as they made their way down it. Music thumped in the distance, it was a melody that didn't suit the enthusiastic dancing she'd always seen in clubs before. This melody brought to mind X-rated porn, and she hoped they weren't walking into some kind of vampire/human orgy.

The hall opened into a small room. Brian stopped at the coat check and took hold of the shoulders of her coat to help her remove it. Her fingers momentarily clenched on it before she let it go. It had been one thing to strut around brazenly in front of him in her scant outfit, but it would be an entirely different thing to do it in front of a group of strangers.

He couldn't know she didn't dress like this every time she went out though, and she refused to give him the satisfaction of seeing her balk now. With a confidence she didn't feel, she shrugged free of the coat. Hunger blazed to life in his eyes again, his gaze remained locked on her as he leaned over her to hand it to the coat check girl.

The movement caused his chest to press against hers. His thick muscles rippled beneath his body-hugging shirt when he came into contact with her. Of their own volition, Abby's hands came up to rest against his chest. She inhaled his evergreen scent, and her eyes closed as pleasure slid over her body.

Vicky! She forcefully had to remind herself of her sister and their current mission in order to get her legs to step back from him. As she moved further away, his gaze reminded her of a lion stalking his prey.

He took hold of her arm again, leading her down another dim hallway to the room beyond. Abby gawked when the hallway opened to reveal a large, black-and-red-painted room. Cages hung from the ceiling, men and women, wearing far less than she was, danced within them. Bite marks on their necks, wrists, and inner thighs marred their pale skin.

"They have bites on them," she whispered.

"All part of the show, or at least that's what the humans believe," he replied as he studied the room.

The musky smell of sex permeated the air as many of the occupants didn't wait to get home, but went into the back rooms Karina had established. The more acrid scent of drugs was beneath the aroma of arousal and gratification. Karina didn't allow drugs to be peddled in her club, but people still smuggled them in or took them before arriving.

Red lights swirled over the dance floor, not in a pulse-pounding fashion, but in a sensual one. Humans and vampires ground eagerly against each other. He pulled Abby closer against his side, wrapping his arm protectively around her waist as he shot a look at an overeager human coming toward her. The murderous look had the human slinking back into the crowd. A woman tried to touch his chest, but he grabbed hold of her hand and thrust it away from him.

"Is it open season in here?" Abby inquired.

"I told you not to wear that."

She stomped on his foot. It had been childish, but she hated the, *I told you so.* He scowled at her, but she refused to back down from him. "I think I could be wearing a burka and these people would still be leering at me."

"At least with a burka there would be something left to the imagination," he snapped back, irritated by the lecherous stares following her through the crowd.

He could practically see the images bursting through the men's heads as they gazed at her and adjusted themselves. He was certain many of those same images had run through his mind since meeting her again. These men would have her bent over the closest table if she gave them any indication she would let them.

"You're a dick," she grumbled.

"I hope you're not just realizing that," he muttered and pushed back a human who bounded up to her.

"No, I've known," she replied flippantly. She thrust her shoulders back and tried to maneuver away from him, but he refused to release her.

"Would you like to dance?" the human asked as his eyes ran over her.

Brian stepped toward the man who stumbled away from them. "Back off!" he spat.

The human turned and fled through the crowd. "You can't do that!" she protested, though she couldn't deny she enjoyed his protective manner. Still, he had no right to try to control anything in her life. "You're not my family, and you're not my boyfriend or husband! You have no say in my life."

He could never be any of those things to her, could never be any of those things to *any*one again, but he'd enjoy tearing the heads off every oversexed man in this place. She was fresh, delectable meat and they were the salivating wolves looking for a chance to pounce.

"If you would like to see someone die tonight, then by all means, dance with them," he growled. Her delectable mouth parted as she gazed at him. "I may not be any of those things to you, but as long as you're with me and under my protection, I'm not going to allow any man to molest you."

Unless it's me, but he kept those words to himself.

"Dancing isn't molesting," she replied.

"It is in this place."

He stiff-armed his way through the rest of the crowd with her warm body snugged close against his side. The feel of her did nothing to ease his lust for her, but at least the urge to kill one of these men was making his erection go away. At the other end of the room, behind the massive bar, was a set of roped off stairs. Another vampire stood at the bottom of the steps with his arms folded firmly over his barrel chest.

"No one goes up," the man told him in a high-pitched, squeaky voice completely out of place with his massive size.

"Karina is expecting me," Brian replied.

The man's brown eyes skimmed over him before his attention shifted to Abby. A small flicker ran over his face, the man's only outward reaction, but Brian sensed his interest in her. Brian wrapped his other arm around her, ignoring the fact her hands went between them to try and push him away.

"Get her," Brian commanded the bouncer with far more antagonism than he normally would have used to deal with this situation.

"I don't take orders from you," the man replied.

"Easy, Ruben," a voice purred from the shadows behind him. "Allow them up."

Brian glanced at Abby. Her gaze was riveted on the dance floor as the music changed beat and the occupants pushed closer and ground more determinedly against each other. The coppery scent of blood permeated the air as a vampire in the corner fed from a man whose mind she'd taken control of. He couldn't tell if Abby was fascinated or repulsed as she wore both emotions on her expressive face.

"It's going to be worse up there," he said quietly to her.

Her attention came back to him. The lights of the club danced over her face, giving her an ethereal quality he found enchanting. Her lips pursed before she gave a brief nod. Brian didn't bother to look at Ruben again as he removed one of his arms from her and led her past the bouncer. He kept his other arm around her waist to make it clear to everyone above that she was under his protection and off limits.

CHAPTER TEN

ABBY COULDN'T CONTROL the frantic beat of her heart as Brian led her up the stairs. She couldn't get the image of what was happening below out of her mind. She'd been to clubs with her brothers and plenty more with her college friends. Never had she seen anything like this place.

Part of her wanted to run from here as fast as her boots would take her; the other part was completely fascinated by their freedom with their sexuality. What would it be like to be on that dance floor with Brian? Maybe not in a corner like some of the others, but to be dancing with him, in his arms, feeling his body grinding against hers as he fed from her.

She shuddered at the prospect, her fingers curling into his shirt. His eyes deepened in color when he glanced down at her. Images of his hand sliding over her thigh and rubbing against her core in the cab assailed her. She ached to feel those fingers moving inside of her.

"Well now, aren't you a sight for sore eyes," a woman said in a raspy voice.

Abby's gaze was torn away from Brian when a sultry woman

glided toward them. The woman moved with the confidence of someone who knew she could have anyone she chose. Her hips swayed in a way that screamed sex, and her black hair shone with blue highlights in the dim red lanterns hanging from the walls.

Abby recognized the voice of the woman who had spoken to the bouncer from the shadows of the stairwell. She also recognized a woman she'd like to punch in the face as she stopped before Brian and ran her hand sensually down the front of his shirt. Her fingers fiddled with one of his buttons as her hand paused in the center of his chest.

"I thought you'd forgotten all about us, Brian," she pouted.

"I could never forget about you, Karina," he replied smoothly and winked.

Abby's hands fisted as she fought the urge to hit them both. Karina smiled and batted her sweeping black lashes as she pressed closer, not at all caring Abby was standing *right there.* This simpering, overt bitch was really pissing her off, and Brian was lapping it up like a dog getting a belly rub.

Her teeth ground together as a barely clad Karina purred low in her throat and all but licked him under his chin. Would they screw right here or at least have the decency to go into a back room? She might kill him if he did, and she'd definitely kill Karina.

Brian's arm tensed around Abby's waist when she trembled beside him. Her eyes shimmered with red as she stared at Karina with a look meant to kill. He was afraid she would leap on Karina and ruin any chances they had of getting her to cooperate with them.

He couldn't deny her anger toward Karina amused and pleased him. There were many who wished to share his bed, it was nothing new in his life, but this possessiveness was new for him, and he liked that he wasn't the only one of them who felt it.

Bending low, he nuzzled her silken hair with his lips and murmured in her ear. "I told you it would be worse up here, behave."

If looks could kill, she would have had him buried six feet under in a concrete tomb right then. He suppressed a chuckle, knowing it might send her over the edge, and as a purebred, she was a force to be reckoned with, even if she didn't know the full extent of her abilities yet. She was young, but she could still do a lot of damage, especially if pushed. As she aged, she'd become one of the most powerful beings to walk this earth.

"Perhaps I should leave you two," she replied.

She moved to spin out of his arms, but he jerked her back, securing her against him. Her head tipped back and her eyes narrowed, but he kept her pinned. She may be powerful, but he was more so, and she would learn his will was stronger than hers.

"And who is this?" Karina inquired with a sly edge to her tone.

"She's mine, Karina. Off limits to everyone here," he told her as he tore his attention away from an irate Abby to focus on the stunning woman across from him.

"Too bad," Karina murmured as her gaze raked hungrily over Abby. "She's got an innocence about her that would drive the men here crazy. Perhaps you would consider not being selfish and sharing her, Brian?"

"No."

"Oh well, come along," Karina replied with a flick of her black nails and a brush of her raven locks over her shoulder.

Abby walked with him past the vampires and humans gathered within the booths. Her fangs pricked and tingled when she spotted the vamps openly feeding from the humans in one booth. Blissful sighs escaped the humans as their heads tilted back and the vamps bit deeper.

She'd fed from a human boy before, but he'd had no idea what she was doing at the time, and she'd taken the memory from him afterward. He may have enjoyed it, but he certainly hadn't reveled in it like these humans were. She also hadn't been having sex with the boy like half of those gathered in here were.

Heat burned her face when she spotted the couples going at it. She wasn't a prude, but she'd never seen anything like this place, and she had no idea how to react to it.

Is that what it's like to feed from someone who knows what's happening, and wants it? She'd never wanted to be fed from before, but if it caused that same look on her own face, she'd happily do it, especially if it was Brian feasting on her blood and pleasuring her body.

She hastily looked away before her thirst was aroused too much. Some of the vampires watched them as they passed, and a few men slid to the end of their booths to get a better look at her. Brian growled at one who leaned too close to her. The man slid back when Brian flashed his fangs at him.

"I'll castrate you before you can blink," he snarled and pulled her away from the questing hand of another male vampire.

He'd be lucky if he made it out of here tonight without killing one of them. Her hands dug into his shirt as they continued onward. A woman walked toward him, but he never even glanced in her direction as he kept shooting lethal glares at the men ogling Abby.

They entered a long hallway lined with doors. As they passed each door, she could hear the sensual sounds of couples, and sometimes more than a couple, having sex. Brian's fingers caressed the flesh of her exposed midriff. It had been a gesture meant to relax her, but instead it only enhanced her conflicting urges to either run from here or press herself closer against him.

"Here we are," Karina said, and swung open a door at the end of the hall.

Brian hurried Abby through the door of Karina's office and waited until she closed it behind them. Abby's growing distress and arousal beat against him, making it difficult for him to concentrate on anything when all he could think about was dragging her into one of those side rooms and sinking every hard inch of him into her.

Her family would kill him, but right now, he'd happily embrace death to ease the need of both of their bodies. Karina's brown eyes slid back and forth between them. Abby grasped his shirt tighter and kept her head bowed so her pale hair shielded her delicate features.

It didn't matter what she said, or how much she fought him on it, he was never going to bring her into a place like this again. She didn't know what to make of it or how to handle it. Yes, she was in college and had older siblings, but she was still very innocent in so many ways. She was mostly unaware of what their kind was capable of.

Karina lifted a sleek, black eyebrow when he wrapped his hand around Abby's head to shelter her further by cradling it against his chest. He ran his hand over her hair comfortingly, letting the strands slide through his fingers.

"What can I do for you, Brian?" Karina inquired.

"You know a lot of what goes on in this city," he said.

Karina grinned at him as she perched on the corner of her desk. Her dress rode up to reveal the edge of her lacy black underwear, a move she'd made on purpose. He'd never slept with Karina, not for a lack of trying on her part, but simply because he knew it would be a tangled web he refused to get ensnared in.

Though striking, Karina was also manipulative, cold, and would run her own mother over to get what she wanted. There was actually a rumor that she had killed her mother after being turned into a vampire.

"I know *every*thing that goes on in this city," she replied, and slid further back on her desk to reveal almost all of her lacy panties that did nothing to shield her sex from view.

Abby lifted her head from his chest. He felt the ripple of shock that went through her before her eyes turned the color of rubies. Karina chuckled and leaned forward to expose some of her ample cleavage.

"Enough!" he barked at Karina. He pushed Abby a little behind him as he turned to face Karina. "You can play with every other person in this place, leave her be."

"Or what?" She nonchalantly studied her nails, which she had filed into lethally sharp talons.

"You're a hundred years old, Karina. You know how I got my power. You are no match for me, and I will drain you dry if you so much as look at her again."

Dead silence followed his statement. Karina's eyes shot up from her nails, her mouth parted and her eyes widened. Abby's breath froze as she gazed between the two of them, waiting to see what would happen. She didn't think Karina was one who took being threatened lightly, no matter who was doing the threatening.

Karina spun suddenly, lunging for something at the front of her desk. Abby hadn't seen Brian move, yet he was grabbing hold of Karina's wrist and slamming it onto her desk. Karina cried out and a stake tumbled from her grasp to land a few feet away from her. Abby jumped forward and snagged the weapon off the ground.

Brian leaned over the top of Karina, using his size to keep her pinned against the desk. Within one of his hands, he held both her wrists down as he fought to control his bloodlust. He'd come here with no intention of fighting, but Karina had dared to pull a weapon with *Abby* in the room. He relied on Karina's help too often to be able to kill her, but it was taking everything he had to keep himself restrained from doing so.

"Don't *fuck* with me on this, Karina," he warned. "I don't want to kill you, but I will."

"Then let me go!" she cried.

"Brian—" Abby started as Karina's breasts heaved with her rapid inhalations.

"Tell me what you know about the drug dens popping up again," Brian said, over the top of Abby.

"What drug dens?" Karina replied, her lower lip quivering as she thrust it out.

Abby's grip on the stake tightened as she fought the impulse to stake the woman for that contrived, pathetic look.

"Don't play stupid with me," he told Karina.

Karina's expression became one of boredom as she realized the lower lip wasn't going to get her anywhere. "Fine, I've heard rumors of them cropping up all over the city, but I don't think they're true."

"Why not?"

"Because no one is going to be stupid enough to get mixed up in that again. I mean, everyone knows Ronan and his group destroyed every vampire who was mixed up with it all those years ago. I'm sure some idiotic vamps have been secretly feeding on drugged humans over the years, but *no* one would flaunt it in the way the rumors say they are."

"Have you heard where these places are located?"

A crease ran across her forehead; she glanced between him and Abby. He moved to keep Abby blocked from her view. "I've heard they move about. Few know where the next location is going to be. Another reason to assume it's nothing but a rumor."

"Who knows where they are?"

"No one I know. That's not something I'm willing to get mixed up with, Brian."

He believed her on that. Releasing her wrists, he took a step away from her and straightened his shirt. She sat up, pulling her dress down over her thighs as she rubbed at her wrists and pouted prettily at him. "You hurt my feelings," she murmured.

"What feelings?"

She flashed a grin as she leapt off the desk and ran her fingers over the front of his shirt again, her hurt feelings already forgotten. "When you're done with virginal princess, you know where to find me."

Abby's fingers flicked over the grains of the wooden stake. Would anyone really be upset if she staked this bitch or Brian if he kept letting her touch him like that? Lucky for him, he grabbed hold of Karina's hand and pulled it away from his chest.

"Keep an ear out for anything unusual or for someone who knows where those parties are," he told Karina.

Karina leaned against the desk once more. "Did Ronan put you up to this?"

"This is my own mission, for now."

"I don't want any trouble, Brian. You know Ronan and I don't have the best history. He'd happily shut this place down on me."

Brian reached into his pocket and pulled out a wad of cash. "I promise nothing will come back on you." Grabbing hold of her hand, he shoved the money into her palm. "Call me if you hear anything."

Her eyes lit hungrily at seeing the hundreds in her hand. The only thing Karina loved more than sex and blood was money. "Whatever you want, gorgeous. Are you going to stay up here and enjoy the place for a bit?"

"I think it's best if we return downstairs," he said, and stepped back to take hold of Abby's hand.

Abby's head had been bouncing back and forth between them during the exchange. Her mind spun from how swiftly it had gone from a life-and-death situation, to a stay-and-have-drinks one. She'd been born a vampire, but some of her species truly confounded her, Brian being the number one leader in that category.

"Free bottle of champagne to loosen things up a little," Karina offered with a suggestive waggle of her eyebrows at Abby.

Yep, she officially hated this woman.

"Another time," Brian said, and tugged Abby in front of him, using his body to shield her as he moved her toward the door. He pulled the door open and removed the stake from her hand. Turning, he tossed it to Karina. "Next time you pull one of those on me, be prepared to have it driven through your heart."

Karina caught the stake and placed it on the desk. "Next time, the only plan I have for the two of us is zero clothes and hours of carnality."

Abby shot a look over her shoulder. She was contemplating going back to beat the woman to death when Brian closed the door. He rested his palm in the small of her back as he propelled her forward.

"Is she going to stab us in the back or have her guys jump us?" Abby inquired.

"Karina may be a lot of things, but she's far from stupid. None of her men are enough to take me on, she knows that, and she knows it would mean her death if she had them try anything."

"Did you ever date her?" she demanded as he led her down the hall.

"No."

"Did you ever have sex with her?"

An amused smile actually quirked the corners of his full mouth when he glanced at her. Abby's nails dug into her palms. "No. Would it bother you if I had?"

Abby snorted and forced herself to relax her hands. "Of course not," she lied with far more ease than she'd believed possible. "But it's good to know you have some standards."

He laughed, actually *laughed* as they stepped into the main part of the upstairs again. All of her annoyance with him vanished as that deep, baritone laugh rumbled out of his chest and his eyes sparkled with amusement. His laugh was better than she'd imagined it would be, and she decided then and there that she would try to make him laugh as often as she could.

She couldn't help but smile as he slid his arm around her waist again. She was so focused on him that she didn't notice the vamps and humans in the room when they passed through this time.

"I do have some standards, but they are few and far between," he told her as he led her down the stairs.

The massive bouncer at the bottom stepped out of their way.

"Now what do we do?" Abby asked as her delight over his laugh vanished and she realized they were no closer to finding Vicky than they had been before coming here.

"Now, I'm going to talk to some of the people and vamps here before we go. There may be someone who knows something."

CHAPTER ELEVEN

ABBY'S FEET were screaming to be free of her boots by the time they returned to the hotel. She was going to burn the boots and her clothes as soon as possible, but first she was going to scrub herself clean of club Dracul.

Her fascination with the club had waned the more time they spent in it. By the time they were ready to go, she'd never felt dirtier in her life. It was a world she'd never known existed, never could have imagined. She was glad she knew of it now, but she never wanted to see anything like it again.

Unfortunately, she had a feeling they'd only encounter worse if they didn't find Vicky soon. Brian kept his arm around her waist, his eyes shooting daggers at the man who turned to watch her pass. He'd spent the better part of the past two hours scaring off any man or woman who came too close to her, his mood had worsened with every would-be pursuer he chased off.

He hadn't spoken to her since they'd left the club, and she was okay with that. She was too tired, dirty, and disheartened to have to deal with him on top of everything else. In the elevator, he released her and took a step away to hit the button. He stood, his platinum hair falling forward against one of his chiseled cheeks as he stared at the buttons.

The set of his shoulders made him look as if he were carrying the weight of the world. Her fingers twitched with the impulse to soothe some of the tension from him, but she kept them at her side.

Turning away, she watched the floors light up until they arrived on the twentieth. The doors slid open with a ding, but she found herself reluctant to step out of this elevator and go to her room, alone. Loneliness, like she'd never known before, assailed her. The urge to cry hit her so fiercely that tears burned her eyes.

I'm just overtired and stressed. She tried to convince herself of this, but she knew it was more. Gripping her coat around her, she forced herself to step from the elevator. Brian hesitated before following her into the hallway. Bronze sconces lined the hall, and lights danced from behind their glass casings as she walked toward her room and pulled her keycard from her coat pocket.

Abby's fingers trembled when she slid the card into the slot. She held the door partially open as she turned to face him. "Thank you for your help tonight."

His locked jaw jutted out as he ran a hand through his hair, watching her. The wooden step he took toward her indicated he'd been fighting against the action. He rested his hand beside her head on the door jam, and his chest brushed against hers when he leaned forward. The feel of his body so close to hers made her sigh with longing.

"Anytime," he murmured, his head bending closer to hers.

Her gaze latched onto his full lips, her body thrummed with the need to feel those lips against hers, to taste him, to *know* if he would leave her cold like the others, or if he would set her body ablaze. There was nothing cold anymore about his usually icy blue eyes as they burned into hers.

She didn't dare move, didn't dare breathe, as he remained looming over her. His head bent closer to hers, and his breath warmed her cheek before she felt the heat of it against her lips. Then, his arm dropped and he took an abrupt step back.

That awful urge to cry rushed over her again, but she lifted her chin to stare at him. Confusion flitted over his face as he tugged at his hair.

"Goodnight, Abigail," he murmured before turning and walking to the door next to hers.

Unable to stand there and watch him enter his room, she shoved into hers and hurriedly closed and locked the door before leaning against it. Her chest heaved as she struggled to keep her tears suppressed. She failed as one trickled down her cheek to drip off her chin.

"Pathetic," she cursed herself as she wiped the tear away and stalked toward the bed. She tugged her coat off and threw it over the desk chair before jerking off the now-hated boots. "Idiot!"

She kept her voice low so he wouldn't hear her, but she fought the urge to scream and kick and rant as she destroyed this room and everything around her. Instead, she yanked off her clothes, pulled free the chain around her waist, and stormed toward the bathroom.

"Keep it strictly business, Abby," she muttered as she turned on the water in the shower.

She stepped beneath the stinging drops when steam began to swirl around the room. Standing under the punishing waves of water, she was torn between sobbing in misery and screaming in anger. It didn't help that she was still aroused by the mere thought of what his lips against hers would feel like.

∽

BRIAN STOOD in the hallway for a minute after Abby had closed her door. He took a step toward it, his hand resting against the wood as he fought the overwhelming impulse to knock on it and kiss her like he should have.

She's too good for you.

It was no longer thoughts of her family keeping him from her; it was his own thoughts and fears that kept him away from her now. He wasn't much in the mood for taking on the Byrne clan, but he could deal with them if he had to. He wasn't good enough for her though. He wasn't a man; he was a monster who relished delivering death to those who deserved it. The souls of many stained his hands, so many he'd lost count of the numerous lives he'd taken over the endless years.

There were too many out there who wanted him dead, too many who wouldn't hesitate to use her against him if they thought they could. They'd be right too; they would be able to use her against him. Little had passed between them, and already he felt more protective of her than anyone else he'd encountered since becoming a vampire.

Abby had stared around the club in curiosity, but also with a burgeoning disgust that had darkened her striking eyes and had her pulling away from any who came near her. If that club disquieted her, what would his past do to her?

She already knew much of who he was and what he did. She knew he'd killed humans, knew he was a mercenary for hire, knew he destroyed their own kind in order to gain power. Granted, they were the evil ones of their kind, but he still happily took their lives and hadn't any intention of stopping. She deserved so much better than someone like him. The thrill of the kill and the power that came with it were all he had in his life.

He banged his fist against the wall before turning and entering his room. He listened to the sound of running water next door, his shoulders heaving at the image of her in that shower with the water sliding over her silken, bare flesh. To follow those beads of water with his tongue would be heaven. He'd nudge her thighs apart, his hand dipping between her legs to ready her for him, before he followed his fingers with his shaft.

His erection throbbed in his pants as he took a step toward the door dividing their rooms. She was on the other side of the door, nude, and oh-so willing. *Too good for you.*

It occurred to him that Issy had accepted Stefan knowing his past. Stefan had managed to keep her safe and protected from those who may also be hunting him. Maybe Abby could do the same for him, and he could keep her safe from those hunting him while she was with him; for he knew one time inside of her would never be enough for him. No, he'd take her repeatedly until he was branded on her inside and out, until every vampire in a hundred-mile radius knew to whom she belonged.

Shaking his head, he rested his hand against the door separating their rooms. He was thinking like a mated vampire, and he most certainly was *not* mated. They'd never kissed before; they couldn't possibly be mated. Besides, from what he'd heard, there was an instantaneous pull toward a vampire's mate when they encountered each other.

Yes, he'd barely been able to tear his eyes away from her since she'd opened her dorm room door to him. However, he'd seen her in that hotel years ago and felt no such pull. Yet, when she'd called him, her voice alone had kept him fascinated enough to continue talking with her. All he'd wanted was to help her, to ease her distress.

Still, he'd seen her before, they'd *met* before now, if only briefly. Wouldn't he have felt something then if she were supposed to be his mate?

His fingers dug into the wood of the door. *She was a child then.* A fifteen-year-old vampire who'd not yet matured when he'd first met her. She hadn't been a woman who radiated innocence and sensuality in a way no other woman he'd ever encountered could. Vivian's hair had drawn him in the day they'd first met; *everything* about Abby drew him to her and had him on the edge of breaking down this door in order to get at her and claim her.

He knew how the mated thing worked, but perhaps it was

different with pureblood vampires, maybe they couldn't be mated until they were older. He may not know the answer to that, but he knew someone he could trust who would. Forcing himself to step away from the door before he broke it down, he pulled his phone from his pocket and called Declan.

"Little late, don't ya think?" Declan inquired, though he didn't sound as if he'd been sleeping.

"New York never sleeps," he replied.

"Thought you were going to play Mountain Man or some shit."

"Change of plans."

"Interesting. Woman?"

"How did you know?" Brian inquired.

"Only a woman could make a man go from the mountains to the city in a day."

"If I ask you something, will it stay between us?"

"Do you have to ask that?"

"I do."

"You know I don't divulge secrets."

No, that Declan didn't do, and he carried more secrets than anyone Brian knew. Out of all of Ronan's men, Declan was the one with the most baggage, and not just his own baggage, but also the baggage of others who had come and gone throughout his life.

"How does the mate bond work with purebreds?" Brian asked.

"Same as with you turned vamps," Declan replied with a laugh. "Once you're caught in the trap, it's impossible to break free, or so I've been told. I've been lucky enough to dodge that bullet these six hundred years. Do you think you've been shot?"

What an accurate way of describing it. "The recognition of a pureblood mate is instantaneous?"

"The attraction is, yes, but that doesn't mean love will follow it or ever come from the pairing. It only means fate thinks you'll be a good match," Declan replied slowly. "What's going on?"

"Let's just say, hypothetically—"

"Oh, of course."

Brian continued as if Declan hadn't spoken. "The first time two mates encountered each other, one is a purebred who is only a child and isn't fully matured yet. Would there be an instantaneous connection then?"

Declan didn't answer right away, but Brian heard the squeak of a chair as he settled in. "Are you attracted to children?"

"Of course not!" Brian snapped.

"Then no, there would be no recognition. Not to mention, she would be too young and unable to bear children. Purebred female vamps cannot get pregnant until they hit maturity."

"I didn't know that," Brian muttered as he ran a hand through his hair.

"Few do. Don't forget, most of you are turned and human women are different than our own, even after they become one of us."

"So, the mate bond is to produce offspring?"

Declan chuckled, his boots thudding when he propped them on something, most likely his desk. "Perhaps that's what nature intended it as, but few vamps choose to have offspring, so a lot of times it doesn't end up quite working out that way. The mate bond may be a biological drive that recognizes another as being well suited to reproduce with, or it could simply be lust, or perhaps love at first sight. Like I said, I've been lucky enough to dodge the bullet, and I'm not looking for someone with a gun."

He hadn't gone looking for someone with a gun either. He'd never envisioned another woman in his life—someone he could lose and who could shatter his heart yet again. And children... The idea of more children made his heart stutter.

Not one day went by that he didn't think of Beatrice and Trudy and still grieve their loss. Their deaths had left a hole in his heart that could never be filled. Never had he considered having another child. He'd endured the loss of his children once, he wouldn't do so again, and Abby was a Byrne, she would want children.

"What happens if the bond is never sealed?" Brian asked. "If no steps are ever taken to complete the mating?"

"How many licks does it take to get to the center of a Tootsie Pop?"

"Declan—"

"The world may never know as it's never been done before, as far as I know. From what I understand, it's an irresistible draw that only grows stronger until the bond is completed. If you're asking these questions, I'm guessing you're thinking you've been shot. It hasn't even been two days since you left us, and you're already calling me about this mystery woman possibly being your mate. That tells me there's a definite connection. It's not going to get easier. Do yourself a favor, get laid and enjoy the ride. It's sure been long enough since you got yourself some."

"That's not going to happen," he grated through his teeth, more annoyed Declan had talked so flippantly about Abby than the knowledge Declan already believed him defeated.

"By the way, when *was* the last time you had sex?"

Brian walked over to the bed and back toward the door as he mulled Declan's question. He barely recalled the woman or the encounter, but it had been before he'd gone to Stefan for help, before he'd seen Abby in that hotel room. His breath rushed out of him when he realized it had been nearly seven years.

He'd often gone for extended periods without sex over the years. He hated the guilty feeling of having betrayed Vivian that always accompanied the act. He'd put it off for as long as he could until his body was consumed with the demand to feel a woman once more. When the sex was over, he would be filled with a sense of betrayal strong enough that he would go for years without it again before he turned to another once more.

It had been a constant cycle of self-hatred and desperation, but he'd never gone *seven years* before. Often he went three or four, once he'd gone five, but he hadn't even realized that seven years had passed since the last time. He may have felt no instantaneous connection with Abby in that hotel room, but if she was his mate, something in him had recognized something in her as such. All signs were beginning to point in the direction of the two of them being linked in some way.

His lengthy periods of abstinence were something he kept hidden from others, even Stefan hadn't realized that many of the women who had thrown themselves at him over the years had never made it to his bed. He'd never wanted anyone to know about this lingering, emotional hang-up. It wasn't something someone could exploit, but he'd always seen it as a personal weakness, and weakness had no place in his line of work.

He should have known Declan would have figured it out or at least sensed something off about the way he was with women.

"Fuck," he hissed.

"I already suggested that," Declan replied with a laugh.

Brian's teeth grated at his casual response. "Did you suspect I had somehow found my mate before this call?"

"I suspect many things and know nothing for certain."

So true and extremely frustrating for Declan to have to go through life like that, Brian realized. "This can't happen, not with her."

"And who is she?"

"No one you know." It wasn't a lie. Declan and Aiden had met, but he'd never seen Abigail. "If she is my mate, I will not allow the bond between us to be sealed."

"This will be interesting. Make sure to call me with updates on your progressing insanity. I'll be eagerly awaiting the news."

"Asshole."

Brian hung up the phone on Declan's laughter. On the other side of the door, he heard the shower turn off. Drawn irresistibly back toward the door, he rested his hand against it and inhaled the scent of her shampoo on the air. A low groan escaped him when he also caught the musky and compelling scent of her arousal.

What he wouldn't give to be the one to ease her.

He forced himself away from the door and over to the bed. Sinking onto the mattress, he scrubbed at his face with his hands as he contemplated Declan's words. Maybe no one had resisted the bond before, but he would, he had to. If he didn't, he would only end up destroying them both.

CHAPTER TWELVE

FIVE DAYS LATER, Abby was beginning to realize two things. One, Brian was a *super* dick, and two, they may never find her sister. Neither one of those things made her feel good at all about where she was now. She'd thrown herself into the search for Vicky, but every new lead smacked into a dead end. Her self-confidence was taking a pounding as Brian grew more and more distant and she continued to dream of him. She woke every night on the verge of tears as her body clamored for someone who didn't want it.

Now, sitting on the park bench and absently throwing birdseed to the ducks, she felt as if she'd been run over by a truck, then backed over and parked on. Her eyes were heavy with sleep; her shoulders hunched forward as she tried to think of some other way to find Vicky and get Brian out of her life. One of those two things had to happen soon, before she completely fell apart.

A shadow fell over her, blocking the warm afternoon sun creeping toward the horizon. She didn't have to look up to know who it was; her skin prickled at his closeness and her awareness of his body. Shading her eyes against the halo of illumination surrounding Brian, she tilted her head back to look at him as he towered over her.

The scowl on his face would have made a mortal piss themselves and a vamp run; she glared back at him. She was as annoyed with him for interrupting her time here as he was with her for whatever new reason he had.

"What are you doing?" he demanded.

She glanced at the bird food in her hand. "Planting magic seeds in the hopes of finding the golden egg," she retorted.

A muscle near his right eye twitched as he folded his arms over his chest and braced his feet further apart. "You never should have left the hotel without telling me you were going," he shot back.

"I'm sorry, I didn't realize I needed permission to walk about. Are women not allowed to do such things?"

The thunderous expression on his face caused a man walking his dog to steer five feet off the path away from them. One of the ducks walked up and took some of the seed from her palm, not at all deterred by the six-foot vampire standing before her. She tossed another handful to the ground before focusing on the lake across from her. The sunlight shone on its blue surface as the mellow breeze caused ripples to skim across the water.

"It's not safe for you to be out here alone," he said.

"Yeah, it's the attack of the killer ducks," she muttered and tossed another handful of feed to them.

"I'm not talking about ducks! There are plenty of other risks out here."

"I am perfectly capable of defending myself against a human."

"There are worse things in this world than humans," he said, stepping closer to her but not close enough to touch. He hadn't touched her since he'd almost kissed her the other night. He made her feel like the kid on the playground with cooties, and she hated him for it.

"No vampire, who is a killer, is going to be out in the daylight. In case you forgot, they can't tolerate the sun."

"I know exactly what kind of an impact the sun has on a vampire who has killed humans. It has been years since I killed those two human hunters, and the sun still burns my skin faster than before. I feel it to this day. I am also a murderer, but I walk about in the day."

She crumpled the empty bag of bird feed and sat back on the bench. She fought against the annoying part of her that insisted on believing he was a good man and not an overbearing ass. However, he'd plucked at her sympathy when he'd admitted he still felt the effects of the sun's rays.

"The vampires who have killed more humans than you and who do it for enjoyment and sport wouldn't be able to be here right now," she reasoned.

"Or they could just be getting started in their career as a killer, and you would be one appealing prize. You're not to be on your own."

"You're not to command me! How did you find me anyway?"

"Have you forgotten the reason you contacted me in the first place?" he inquired.

"I thought you couldn't pinpoint someone in a city so big."

"You're different."

Just one more reason for me to believe you are something more to me. Something I can never have, he realized as her eyes blazed with red fire.

"And why is that?" she demanded.

"I don't know." *Liar.* "I followed your scent. We're not far from the hotel." *Bullshit.* He may have been able to follow her scent here, but her soul had been a powerful beacon, drawing him in from the second he'd realized she'd left the hotel.

"Oh," she muttered.

Had disappointment fluttered across her face, or was he just hoping it had? He took a step away from her, needing to put some distance between them. She didn't appear to notice as her gaze drifted back to the lake and the ducks waddling toward it. Wiping her hands on her jeans, she rose to her feet.

It hadn't mattered where they'd gone over the past few nights, she'd worn jeans and a sweater. Somehow, even in the absence of seeing her belly button ring, he now found her more modest clothing more enticing than her skimpy outfit and boots from the night they'd visited Dracul.

She didn't look at him as she strolled across the park, her blonde hair blowing back from her face as she walked. A male nearly walked into a light post when he turned to watch her go by. Brian shot the man a fulminating look as he hurried to catch up with her. No, Abby may not be as perfectly beautiful as her older sister and mother were, but there was something entirely captivating about her round face, curvaceous figure, and emerald eyes.

He wanted to tear the head off every guy who lusted after her. He'd only killed two humans in his life, but by the time he was finally able to free himself from this woman, he may slaughter dozens more. The man hurried away as Brian caught up to walk by her side.

He couldn't trust himself to grab her elbow and jerk her to a halt. Touching her again may push him over the edge, and he'd end up dragging her back to his room to stake his claim on her.

"Where are you going?" he demanded.

She waved her hand at him as if he were an annoying fly she was trying to slap away. "For a walk."

He thought his teeth might shatter when he clamped them together. "Not on your own."

"I didn't ask for your company."

"I don't care what you asked for!"

She whirled on him and thrust her finger in his face. "And I don't care that you've appointed yourself my stand-in brother. I already have five of them, I don't need another one!"

Some people turned to stare at them when he stepped closer to her, trying to force her to take a step back, but she resiliently held her ground. "I am going to keep you safe."

All of her frustration, resentment, terror, and exhaustion since Vicky had taken off and Brian had been thrust into the center of her life boiled to the surface. "Oh, screw you!"

She saw the unraveling within him at the same time the vast wave of power he emitted shot through the air and blasted against her skin. He grabbed hold of her finger. It didn't matter his hand tightened around it, or that fury radiated from him, a shiver of relief went through her at the feel of his skin against hers.

Finally, she breathed inwardly and immediately hated herself for it.

His eyes flickered from blue to red and back again as he stepped into her and backed her against a tree. Abby's heart hammered in her chest, her breath came in shallow pants as she labored to get air into her lungs. She tugged her finger free of his grasp, but when she went to turn away from him, he set his hands on her hips and jerked her back.

"Believe me," he grated as his body leaned into hers. "There is nothing familial in my thoughts about you."

A whimper escaped her when he rubbed the hard length of his erection against her to prove his point. His fingers slid over her hips, skimming up to the bottom of her sweater as his eyes continued to flicker between red and blue.

"If you had any common sense, you'd run screaming, Abigail."

Run screaming? All she wanted was to unbutton his jeans and run her fingers over the hard length pressing against her. Her head fell back when his fingers found the bare flesh of her stomach and slid over her skin to rest against her back.

"If your brothers had any idea about what I dream of doing to you, they'd kill me." His eyes fastened on her breasts. "How I think of tasting you, savoring your body..."

His words trailed off as his hand slid down to cup her ass and draw her more firmly against him. He'd maneuvered himself so he now pushed tantalizingly against her core, that place where she ached for him most. Heat spread between her legs, and wetness grew as he rubbed against her again and squeezed her ass.

"To sink myself deep within you and make you forget every other man before me."

She opened her mouth to tell him there were no other men, but all that came out was a low moan as liquid lightening sizzled through her body when he ground against her again.

His breath tickled her cheek and ear as he continued to speak. "To sink my fangs into your neck as I thrust inside of you."

Her fingers dug into the bark of the tree as her heaving breaths brought her chest into contact with his. She wanted to grab hold of him, but she forced herself not to do it. She may be a panting mess right now, but at least she wasn't attacking him physically.

His eyes burned into hers as he watched her. Like a teenage boy feeling up his first girl, he was close to spilling in his pants right now. Close to tearing her jeans off and sinking himself into her in the middle of this park. "Would you let me fuck you, Abby?" he inquired.

Yes! Words failed her when his lips brushed over her neck in a heated caress that had bits of bark breaking off beneath her fingers. When he pulled away from her, his eyes glistened with fire and his fangs peaked out from beneath his upper lip. Those fangs only served to arouse her further, something she hadn't believed possible.

His fingers slid over her cheek to clasp her neck. Her breath froze, and she couldn't tear her eyes away from his lips when they dipped toward hers. If he pulled away from her again, she might kill him. If he pulled away again, she would forever hate herself for this weakness she had for him.

Tilting her head, she stared at him as his eyes searched her face with an anguished expression. She should step away from him. She should be the one to turn him away this time, not to get back at him for how discarded he'd made her feel the other night, but because she obviously confused and distressed him. The last thing she wanted was to bring anymore torment into his life.

Releasing the tree, she rested her fingers against his cheek. The bristly stubble lining his jaw tickled her fingers. He was all she wanted, but she didn't think it would ever be possible. Her hand slipped down his cheek and toward her side. He snatched hold of it and pressed it against his face once more. His distress had slipped away to be replaced with a look of resolution and yearning that robbed her of her breath.

Before she could pull away from him, he jerked her against him, threaded his fingers through her hair, and pulled her head back. Abby gasped when his mouth slanted over hers in a demanding, claiming way that seared into her soul. Her legs nearly gave out, and her hips bucked against his. He growled low in his throat when the movement caused her to grind against him in a way that sent a firestorm of pleasure shooting through her.

The heady, sweet taste of her enveloped all of his senses. He didn't care he'd vowed to keep his distance from her, didn't care if he would destroy her or bring danger to her life. He'd denied himself this for too long. He had to taste her, to feel and devour her. Her lips were a brand against his.

She was liquid heat and honey all rolled into one, and he knew he would never forget the taste of her. Her lips opened beneath his probing tongue; her breath filled his mouth as he slid his tongue in to taste her. He kissed her so deeply he didn't know if it was her breath or his flowing into his lungs. His fingers clenched in her hair, drawing her head further back as he rubbed against her again.

Her arms wrapped around his back, drawing him closer as her fingers dug into his flesh. He lifted her against him, thrusting her against his aching shaft.

She quivered in his arms and ground against him. The musky scent of her arousal drew him in like a bee to the sweetest nectar, driving him toward a snapping point. He couldn't take her now, she may let him, but they were standing in the middle of a park, and no one would see her body again, except for him.

He could have her back at the hotel in less than a minute, naked and screaming beneath him in ten. He pulled her away from the tree, unwilling to break the kiss. Reality would descend if he did, and reality would tell him he was making a mistake. If they did this, he could be binding them together in an irrevocable way.

Recalling that was like dumping a bucket of ice over him. He was a ruined man and she was a vibrant young woman who made heads turn everywhere she went, including his. He broke away from her, his head falling into the hollow of her neck. Her tantalizing, citrus scent filled his nostrils as he inhaled it deeply.

Tremors shook her as he held her. His fingers stroked her nape; she was so fragile, so small in his arms, and she belonged to him. He knew it with unfailing certainty, but the best thing for her was to let her go, and that was exactly what he intended to do.

He'd done many difficult things in his life; the toughest one was releasing her and stepping away. She gazed at him, her lips still swollen and wet from his kisses. She was young, but she was an alluring woman with a body made for bedding. He knew her body was the only one that would ever be able to ease his again, but still he forced himself to move further away from her.

Abby's fingers slid to her mouth. She could still taste him on her tongue and feel his lips burning into hers, as he'd robbed her of her breath and reason. Every other kiss she'd ever experienced had left her cold and empty. They'd all felt wrong no matter how much she'd tried to make them feel right.

This kiss had *only* been right. She'd worried his kiss would pale in comparison to her childhood daydreams and her adult fantasies. There had never been any reason to worry, because it was better than she'd ever expected. It had made her come alive in a way she'd never known possible. Like a drug, she craved more of him, but he was already taking another step away from her. His eyes became guarded once more as he watched her.

She was addicted, and he was already replacing the wall between them that she'd come to hate. This time she didn't get angry or feel the hot wash of tears burning her eyes; there was nothing left in her for that. Turning, she walked away from him before he could do it to her. She didn't look at him again as he walked beside her to the hotel.

CHAPTER THIRTEEN

ABBY STARED AROUND THE CLUB, her body instinctively swaying to the brisk beat of the music. This was a human club, the kind she was used to, but there were far more vampires here than she was accustomed to in Boston. Between the thrilling vibe of the city and the easy prey found in the bars and clubs, New York was a draw for vamps.

Beside her, Brian scanned the crowd, searching for someone he might know or someone who could be useful. She'd resorted to not speaking to him, as it was easier that way. For the past five days, they'd been snippy and irritated with each other. After what had happened in the park today, she found she had no snippiness left in her. She didn't have much of anything left in her anymore.

Her heart ached for her sister. Every day, she debated calling her family then decided against it, but if they didn't find Vicky in the next couple of days, she would be calling Isabelle. At this point, she didn't have much of a choice. Vicky would be pissed at her for involving their family, but she was running out of options.

What had Vicky become mixed up in, and why couldn't they find her? The vampire in that drug house in Boston had said no one comes back from where they go. Had it just been the drugs talking or had he actually meant something by that? And where do they go and who are *they*? Had Vicky gone with them willingly or had they taken her? And why would anyone take her sister? Every day brought more and more questions but no answers.

She tried to maintain calm about it all, but sometimes she couldn't help but wonder if her sister had become mixed up in drugs and taken off. If maybe no one came back from where they went because they didn't want to.

Not Vicky, she decided firmly. This unending search for her sister was rattling her resolve a little, but she knew Vicky wouldn't be mixed up in drugs, and she never would have taken off, at least not without calling her first. She may have quit school and been partying more, but Vicky would never abandon her in such a way.

Brian glanced at Abby by his side. He disliked the pallor of her skin and the firm set of her lips as she surveyed the crowd. Her fingers were pulled into the sleeves of her V-neck, form-fitting black sweater. The color of the sweater enhanced the paleness of her hair and the vibrant green of her eyes.

He could stare at her for hours and never get bored as she wore her emotions on her face, and he loved to watch them playing across her delicate features. She frowned in consternation when someone danced too close to her, then smiled when the song switched to one she began swaying along to. It was all noise to him but she enjoyed it.

He'd thought he'd welcome her silence as a buffer between the two of them, but he found he resented it. He'd hated the bickering between them these past five days; he'd gladly welcome it back, if she would only talk to him again.

Be grateful. This is for the best. He couldn't be grateful when all he wanted to do was take her back to the hotel and finish what they'd started in the park. He recalled Declan's words about his progressing insanity. That was exactly the way he'd begun to feel, like he was unraveling a little bit at a time until there would be nothing left but this maddening urge to possess her in every way.

Then what would happen? Would he give into this insanity, take her by force, or succeed in pulling away from her? None of those options was any good, but he felt like he was losing his mind.

That kiss today was the first time he hadn't felt guilt over kissing a woman since Vivian's death. Granted, it had only been a kiss, but he desired her more than he had desired anyone else before her, including the wife he'd loved so much. Such a realization would have had guilt eating away at his insides with any other woman, but with Abby he only wanted more.

He rubbed his hand over his face, scratching at the stubble shadowing his jaw. Abby stepped onto the dance floor and wound her way through the crowd. He watched the sway of her hips with a burgeoning hard-on before striding forward to catch up with her. He pushed aside anyone who dared to get too close to her. She didn't notice, or at least she never acknowledged *him,* as she made her way to the bar and settled onto a stool.

The bartender hurried to her, drawn by her inherent vampire ability to lure others in and her amazing vitality. Life didn't radiate from her right now as vibrantly as it normally did. Exhaustion, stress, and fear were beating her down, but she was still surrounded by an aura of warmth. An aura that had him reaching out to brush her hair aside before he could stop himself as he sought to soothe her in some way.

Abby shied away from his touch. She was so unbelievably tired of this back and forth game they played. A game that was gradually shredding away pieces of her soul. "Don't."

His hand fell away as frustration and anger warred within him. He turned toward the bartender and barked out a drink order before resuming his search of the crowd. She'd shrank away from his touch, told him not to touch her. He should be happy; instead, he found himself fighting against tearing everyone in this room to shreds.

Turning back to her, he almost seized hold of her shoulders and dragged her against him. Who was she to deny him what was rightfully his? And if they were mates, then she was *his*. That possessive impulse swelled in his chest, causing him to step closer to her while she glared at him as if he was the worst form of life. He could feel the madness slithering through his mind, the insanity swelling forth as he fought against taking possession of her.

"I'm not playing this game with you anymore," she spat. "Back away from me, *now*."

"I'm not playing games, Abby."

"But you are," she replied, and smiled at the bartender when he handed her the Rum Runner she'd ordered.

She grabbed hold of her straw and took a sip of her drink, refusing to acknowledge the seething vampire standing at her side. She understood his frustration, understood the draw between the two of them, but she refused to give into it again when he was acting like a thirteen-year-old girl who couldn't decide which outfit to wear when it came to her. There was no way she was going to be tried on and tossed aside again by Mr. Can't-Make-Up-His-Mind because he had commitment issues.

Because he's committed to his dead *wife*. Yep, that reminder made her resolve settle more firmly into place. Grabbing her drink, she spun to face the crowd. "Do you see anyone you know?" she asked him.

She could feel his eyes boring into her, but she didn't look at him again. Finally, he focused on the crowd, and after a few minutes, he nodded. "I do."

"Maybe you should see what he knows."

Brian wasn't used to being dismissed or ordered around. "This isn't done, Abby."

She glanced at him from under the sweeping fringe of her blonde lashes. "But it is."

He banged his fist onto the bar before spinning away and storming into the crowd. The people eagerly parted to allow him to pass.

"It's none of my business, miss, but are you okay?"

She turned and smiled at the human male who had eagerly slid into Brian's empty spot. "Fine," she assured him. "Thank you."

His eyes latched onto her mouth when she took hold of her straw again. *Ugh.* Just what she needed, an oversexed human who believed her to be vulnerable at the moment, or maybe he assumed she was in an abusive relationship and he could rescue her. Who knew what the human was thinking, and she didn't care to find out, as she was perfectly capable of rescuing herself.

She watched Brian as he stopped before a young woman with brown hair dangling against her waist. *Not a he and not a vampire,* Abby realized.

A stab of jealousy hit her so fiercely she nearly crushed the glass in her hand when the woman squealed and threw her arms around his neck. Abby's fangs sprang free, her teeth gritted as she fought the killing impulse trying to take her over.

She'd never felt this way before, never been so close to this very treacherous precipice of losing all control as the woman leaned back to smile at him. Her arms remained wrapped around his neck; his arm was around her waist as they swayed to the music. Their movements were extremely far off the rapid beat filling the room as they moved slowly back and forth, laughing and talking.

The woman was stunning, so dark compared to his lightness. They made such a striking couple, and he wasn't pushing the woman away, wasn't jerking her this way then that way, as he constantly did with her. A lump lodged in her throat as the glass in her hand cracked.

"Apparently he's found someone new," the human commented as he leaned closer to her.

Abby shot him a look, and her eyes fell to the vein in his neck as she fought the impulse to lean over the bar and sink her fangs into him, to tear his throat out and ease some of the jealousy festering within her like an infected cut. The human's heartbeat picked up, but he didn't move away from her.

This idiot didn't realize how close he was to death, but if she didn't get away from him, he would. She placed her leaking glass on the bar with far more calm than she felt. Another glance at Brian and the woman revealed they were still deep in conversation as they danced close together. She wouldn't be able to get a slip of paper between their bodies, she realized in disgust.

The woman stood on her tiptoes, her breasts flattening against his chest. Brian's head bent so that her lips rested against his ear. He smiled as she spoke.

That was it, the final straw.

Abby leapt from her chair. The human grabbed her arm, but she waved him away as she fought against the impulse to take him into a back corner and feed on him. She had to do something to help curb the bloodlust growing within her, and she had a feeling that even though Brian was occupied with the human, it would piss him off to find her feeding on someone else. She would love to piss him off right now, but with the way she was feeling, she may end up accidentally killing the human if she did feed from him.

Throwing back her shoulders, she slipped into the crowd and made her way toward the door. She had to get out of here, had to get away from Brian before he drove her to kill someone, something she'd vowed never to do. She'd never be able to live with herself if she killed an innocent, could never live with the shame of her family knowing what she'd done, and they would know. There was no way to mask the scent of a vampire who had killed from any of her siblings.

Shame jolted through her. Her sister was missing, and she was falling apart. Vicky was counting on her. *Vicky's not counting on you. Vicky left you behind, you idiot. She doesn't want to be found.*

Tears burned her eyes as she studiously avoided going within a fifty-foot radius of Brian and the woman. She tried to tell herself that Vicky hadn't left her behind, something had to be wrong, but she was feeling like a kicked puppy right now.

Finally making it to the front of the club, she grabbed her coat from the coat check girl and fled into the bright lights of the city that had dazzled her before. Now all she felt was hollow as she hurried to the curb and flagged down the first cab she saw. Before she could rethink what she was doing, she flung open the door, slid inside, and closed it behind her.

"Where to?" the cabby inquired.

Abby contemplated that for a second. Where was she supposed to go now? She'd fled the only vampire she knew in this city, and she hoped never to see him again. Shuddering, she wrapped her arms around her stomach as she fought the urge to start sobbing and never stop. The cabby looked at her like he regretted pulling over for her and was contemplating tossing her back onto the street.

Before he could do that, Abby gave him the name of the hotel where she was staying, and he pulled away from the curb. She should leave this city, return to her life, and let Vicky do whatever she chose to do. Her sister was an adult; she was capable of making her own decisions, but the idea of not knowing what happened to her twin caused something inside her to wither and die.

Vicky may not want her, but Abby wanted her sister. Maybe it was selfish, but she wasn't ready to give up, not yet. She had to get away from Brian though. She couldn't do this anymore with him. Every day their constant push and pull was destroying her a little more. He loved a dead woman; she was an idiot. It didn't matter if they actually were mates or not, all that mattered was she was losing herself in this mess, and she couldn't allow that to happen.

Abby threw the cabby some cash and leapt out of the car when he stopped at the hotel. She wouldn't have much time before Brian realized she'd left. If he chose to come after her, she had to be far from here by then. He may have followed her scent to the park, but he wouldn't be able to trail her through an entire city filled with scents and people.

~

Marissa played with the hair at his neck as she swayed against him. Brian gritted his teeth against the feel of the woman. At one time, he may have contemplated bedding her, it had been seven years after all, but now he found himself repulsed by the feel of her. He forced himself to smile as Marissa chattered on about her ex-boyfriend's drug connections.

"Then the asshole actually tried to get me to do some, can you believe that?" she inquired.

"Fool," Brian said.

He glanced at Abby as a young man leaned toward her. Brian's eyes narrowed on them, but Abby remained as aloof with the human as she'd been with him. She believed he was playing games; he believed he was playing with fire. At this point, he'd welcome being seared by her heat if it meant finally having some kind of release from this unending torment.

"Have you heard anything about some underground clubs and raves that are moving about, ones involving the vampire world?" Brian asked Marissa.

Marissa was a Feeder, a human who knew of their existence and allowed vampires to feed from her in the hopes of one day being turned by one. She kept the secret of their existence in exchange for the possibility of immortality. Also, the first vamp who had brought her into their fold had planted it in her mind that she could never reveal their existence to a human without excruciating pain followed by certain death.

Marissa nodded in response to his question as she rubbed her breasts against his chest. The erection Abby could so easily bring to life softened with Marissa. He couldn't wait to be free of her.

"I have," she whispered in his ear. "But I've been told not to talk about it."

His curiosity was piqued as he turned his head into her ear. "You're not to talk of it with humans or with vamps?" he inquired.

"With *any*one else."

"Was this implanted in your head by a vamp?"

She leaned back. "Yes."

Shit! Just as she could never reveal their existence without death, she'd never be able to tell him anything. "I'm sorry," she whispered. True regret shimmered in her hazel eyes.

He may be able to get into her mind to undo the command, but it would take a while and a lot of patience. There was also a chance his probing may trigger something in her mind that could kill her anyway.

"Would I be able to talk to your ex about this?" Brian inquired.

Her mouth pursed as she deliberated her next words. "If you would like to talk to Garth, I can always give you his number." Her breath froze, she braced herself for intense pain but after a minute, her shoulders sagged and a smile spread across her mouth when she remained the same. "Let me see your phone."

He handed his phone over to her and watched as her fingers flew across it. "There's both of his numbers," she said.

Stepping against him again, she slid the phone into his pocket. Her hand brushed against his shaft as she maneuvered the phone in his pants. His dick shrank away from her touch as surely as it would shrink in the Arctic Ocean. She didn't notice as she gave him an inviting smile and pressed her hips against his.

"I could make you happy," she murmured, and batted her lashes invitingly.

He grabbed hold of her hand when she tried to stroke him and pulled it away. "'Fraid not tonight."

She pouted prettily, but it only made his revulsion increase when she ground her hips against him again. He managed to keep himself from throwing her hand away. She'd risked her life to help them, and he couldn't repay her with callousness now. He also may need her help in the future, and a pissed off woman was one who tended not to be so willing to talk.

"Come on," she purred. "It looks like your date has left anyway."

Brian stiffened as his eyes flew to the bar and Abby's now-empty seat. He blinked once before his gaze flew around the crowd surrounding him. He didn't see her anywhere amid the dancing couples, didn't feel the pulse of her aura within the confines of the club. She wouldn't have been so reckless as to leave here on her own; she couldn't have left *him*.

He stalked through the crowd, shoving people and vamps out of his way to arrive at the bar in mere seconds. His gaze fell on the puddle of liquid spreading beneath her nearly empty, cracked glass. His heart sank and his gut twisted as he spun toward the human who had been talking with her.

"Where did she go?" he snarled.

"If she was smart, far from you," the human replied. When Brian took a step toward him, the human blanched and moved closer to a group of humans behind him.

Running a hand through his hair, Brian tugged at it as he spun to face the crowd. Panic threatened to engulf him when he scanned the crowd once more. *Easy. You can find her. Remain calm.*

He could find her, but would it be too late? There were so many dangers out there. Abby was strong, but so were the vampires who killed and fed on others. A pureblood vampire, with her looks and vitality, would be a prime target for someone seeking to increase their power, much like he had increased his power on the blood of others. If any of his enemies had seen the two of them together over the past week, they would eagerly drain her dry.

Brian forced himself to take a calming breath. *Tune into her and find her. She's the most vibrant soul you've ever encountered; it won't be difficult to locate her.*

His heart sank when he realized she'd gotten farther from the bar than he'd thought possible in the short time since he'd last seen her.

CHAPTER FOURTEEN

Abby had tossed her clothes into her suitcase and left the hotel she'd been staying in with Brian. She'd briefly considered grabbing another cab, but decided the best way to disguise her scent was to lose herself within a crush of people. She'd hurried to the subway and hastily descended the steps. Standing in a group of people, she'd kept her teeth clenched against her body's growing demand to feed as she allowed them to bump and jostle against her in order to throw off her scent further.

She'd ridden in a subway car for three blocks before deciding to reemerge on the surface. She walked for five blocks before finally grabbing a cab and arriving at her newest hotel. It wasn't as elaborate as the one she'd been staying in, but it was far from a dump, and it wouldn't make her credit card scream. She could have gotten the room for free by using her vampire abilities and changing the mind of the desk attendant, but she'd made the decision to play by the rules of humans when she'd gone to college and joined their world.

Now, she pushed open the door to her new room and stepped inside. She stood watching the shadows playing over the walls before turning the light switch on. The lamps beside the beds flickered on to reveal a decent-sized room with red comforters and a crème-colored carpet. A small sitting room with a flat screen TV, sofa, and recliner was off to her left.

Despite the clean, inviting colors and spicy scent of potpourri, she'd never felt more alone in her life. Before arriving here, she'd had a mission, a goal to get away from Brian and find somewhere else to stay. Now that she'd attained her goal, she felt as flat as roadkill when she placed her suitcase on one of the queen beds and sank onto the other one.

Her head fell forward as her fingers dug into her thighs. Grief overtook her, and her body was wracked with waves of misery. She took her phone out of her pocket. On her way here, she'd decided it was time to call her family, but she hesitated before she could hit Isabelle's number.

Her older sister would be the easiest one to deal with right now; she would get her brothers to calm down before they descended on this city and *her*. However, she wasn't much in the mood for talking to anyone right now, and she knew if she called Isabelle, she'd turn into a crying, blubbering mess the second she heard Issy's voice.

She could always call The Stooges. Her adopted uncles may be the best way to go with this. They'd be here in a heartbeat. Jack would probably choke her and yell at her for an hour. Mike and David would take control and form a plan. Doug would stand by with his calming presence, and right now, she could really go for one of his awesome bear hugs.

But again, she knew she would turn into a blubbering mess the minute one of them asked how she was doing, and she wasn't ready to unleash her despair on anyone, much less her unsuspecting uncles. Her mom? Her finger hesitated over her mom's phone number. Suddenly, all she wanted was to hear her mother's voice. She'd be so mad Abby had kept Vicky's disappearance from them, but she'd come here. She would hug her and she would understand.

She wouldn't tell any of them about Brian. She'd promised him they would never know he was involved, and she would keep it that way. He was her private misfortune to deal with. She would bare the rejection and loss of him for as long as she existed, and what a lonely existence it would be.

She finally had her answer about him. Before, when she'd tried to make herself feel something for others, a small part of her had believed she'd one day find someone who would affect her as he had. Now, she knew she never would. He'd irrevocably changed her life the minute he'd stepped into it six years ago, and there would be no going back.

She could now look forward to a lonely life of never knowing the touch of a man, an eternity of always pondering where he was and what he was up to. She dropped her head into her hands; a sob escaped her, but no tears slipped free. There were no tears to be shed, not anymore.

She would find Vicky, she would leave this city behind, and she would finish her degree. She'd spend the rest of her life traveling the world, discovering things, meeting new people, and trying to help them in whatever way she could. It wouldn't be so lonely if she was doing good in the world, and there was much good to be done on this planet.

Maybe one day any reminder of him wouldn't hurt so badly. Time healed all wounds and all that nonsense.

She tried to convince herself of this as she tossed her phone onto the other bed. She'd call someone tomorrow, when she'd gotten some rest and fed. Thirst burned through her veins and caused her fangs to feel heavy with the urge to descend. As much as she didn't like it, she would have to find a human to feed from. Her stomach turned at the idea, but she couldn't wander around in a city full of people while an emotional mess and famished. That was a recipe for disaster.

Room service could bring her a Coke and someone to feed from she decided as she rolled to her side. She was grabbing for the phone on the nightstand when a forceful knock sounded against her door. Abby jumped and held her breath as she waited for the visitor to identify themselves. Had room service gotten the wrong room? But didn't they announce who it was when they knocked?

She shoved herself to her feet and trudged toward the door. If it was room service, she may have just had her meal delivered to her. "Who is it?" she inquired.

Silence met her question. Uneasiness churned in her gut, and she hesitated as a growing certainty built within her. It couldn't be him. There was *no* way he could have tracked her scent through the convoluted, human-filled pathways she'd taken.

If it wasn't him, then why was her body becoming electrified and her heart racing faster when she hadn't even reached the door?

Taking a deep breath, Abby rested her hands against the door and rose onto her toes to peer out the peephole. Brian's red-filled eyes burned into hers as he stared at the door. His shoulders were hunched forward; the muscles bulged in his arms as he grabbed the doorframe.

She ducked back, biting on her lip as her mind spun. How had he possibly been able to track her here?

"Open the door, Abigail," he commanded gruffly from the other side.

"I don't want to see you!"

What an awful lie. She'd never been happier to see anyone in her life. However, she'd just managed to break free from him and resigned herself to a life of loneliness. Now he was here disrupting all her plans. She prayed he would go away at the same time she prayed he'd never leave.

"I don't care," he replied.

"No, you don't, do you!"

The low growl emanating from the other side caused the hair on her arms to stand on end. "Open the door or I'm going to break it down, witnesses be damned!"

"You wouldn't dare."

The knob rattled at the same time his hand smashed against the door, causing a splintering sound to echo through the room. He was only showing her he wasn't playing around. If he chose to be in this room, he would be, and there was no way this door was going to keep him out. When the police showed up, he'd simply convince them that everything was all right and to move along.

"Stop it!" she yelled at him.

"Then open the *fucking* door!"

Knowing he wouldn't stop, she threw the locks and pulled the door open. His ruby eyes blazed down at her, and his shoulders heaved as a vein in his forehead pulsed to life. She'd never seen him look so angry and rattled, but she was pretty pissed off herself.

She stepped into the doorway in an attempt to block him from entering when he stepped forward and wrapped his hand around the door she held. "You're not welcome here," she told him.

Madness, insanity, he could feel it slithering through his mind, creeping closer as she tried to deny him entrance to her room. *Keep it together. Don't hurt her.* He kept telling himself this, but it took all he had not to pick her up, throw her on the bed, and bury himself in her. He would show her who was in control here, teach her she was *his,* and there was nothing she could do about it.

"You should have bought a house if you planned to keep me out," he grated through his teeth.

Abby refused to relinquish the door to him. "What do you want?" she demanded.

He wrenched the door from her grasp, forcing her back when he stepped further into the room and slammed the door behind him. The mirror over the bureau rattled, and the glasses hanging above the mini-bar clinked together from the force of the closing door. Abby backed further into the room as he stalked toward her, looking every inch the lethal vampire he was.

"You left me," he accused.

Her chin tilted up, and she planted her feet as she refused to relinquish another inch to him. "So?"

"So?" he snarled. She never saw him move before his hands were gripping her arms. He lifted her off the ground as he drew her forward. His fangs glistened when his upper lip curled back to reveal them. "So!"

She tried to break free of his grasp, but found herself trapped by his overwhelming strength and power. "You were busy and I thought you'd like some privacy with that woman. Now let me go!"

She hadn't expected him to release her, but he dropped her like a stone onto her feet again. Trying to maintain her dignity, Abby straightened her sweater as she defiantly stared at him. "Wasn't much fun for her, I'm guessing, if you're here already," she said haughtily. "Ever hear of a minute man?"

Brian couldn't stop shaking. His fingernails tore into his palms as he fought the urge to grab her again. He was afraid he'd do something he could never take back if he touched her right now. The edge he teetered on had him close to snapping; if he snapped, if the insanity won, he'd take her, and he would hurt her.

He'd hate himself forever if he did, but she'd *left* him. The desolate and incensed feelings that had engulfed him when he'd found her things gone from her room in their hotel still rattled him. He hadn't felt either of those emotions so strongly since he'd lost his family.

Abby had taken her things and fled, thinking he wouldn't be able to find her, hoping to lose him in the city. She had tried hard to lose him too. He'd caught her scent in a convoluted trail that may have thrown him off if her soul hadn't been blazing so bright, showing him the way to her. Now he'd found her, she was safe, and she was telling him to *leave*.

He couldn't take it, couldn't handle it anymore. She was his and she was trying to kick him out of her life. He longed to cut her as deeply as she'd sliced into him.

"I've never left a woman unsatisfied," he replied, his mouth curving in a malicious smile.

Distress flickered across her face before her eyes blazed with the fires of Hell. "Get. *Out*," she bit out crisply.

"You're not in charge here, Abigail."

"And you are?"

"Goddamn right I am."

Her nostrils flared, and for a second, he believed she was going to swing at him. Instead, she did some kind of Karate Kid move that had him dodging the first foot she kicked at him. Her second foot managed to land a glancing blow against his nuts. Grabbing himself, he doubled over as pain lanced through his body.

Abby scooted back, pride blazing over her features as she smirked at him. "Goddamn wrong, boy-o!" she retorted.

Brian lunged for her, but she spun away from him, leaping onto one of the beds to glare down at him.

Like an avenging angel, one who belongs to me, he realized.

"You have to leave," she said.

"Or what?" he inquired as he stalked her. She danced back on the bed, the bounce causing her breasts to sway invitingly. As much as he'd like to get his hands on her, he had to admit he enjoyed watching her like this.

"Or I'll tell my family all about this."

"Will you now?" he murmured as her nipples hardened.

"Yes!" she cried.

Abby's desperation mounted. What made it worse was the ravenous way he watched her as she moved. She'd kicked him in the nuts, but instead of yelling at her or trying to make her pay for it, he was staring at her as if she were the most delectable thing in the world, one he was going to devour, and she so badly wanted to be devoured by him.

"I don't think you will," he said. "I think you want me as badly as I want you."

"You're wrong!" she shouted at him before jumping for the other bed.

Brian leapt forward. Snagging hold of her wrist, he jerked her back in mid-jump. She cried out as air rushed up to meet her, but he caught her easily in his arms. He spun her around, pinning her on the bed she had jumped from and jerking her wrists above her head. Her luscious breasts pressed against his chest with every breath she took, and her lips quivered, but her eyes remained the color of rubies.

"I don't want you!" she yelled.

"Don't lie."

She cried out in frustration and tried to draw her feet up to kick at him, but he was situated firmly between her thighs, and when he thrust forward to grind his erection against her aching center, a moan escaped her. Her feet fell back to the bed, and her legs trembled as he thrust again, the friction of his arousal causing heat waves to spiral up from her core.

Her head fell to the side, and she panted for breath as he moved over her again. A low groan escaped him when he pushed against her again. Her body ached with the need to feel him deep within her. Her wrists jerked in his grasp as he kept them pinned above her head.

She nearly screamed when he used his other hand to pull her sweater up and his large hand flattened against her stomach. His palm burned into her skin as his fingers caressed her flesh in small circles. She wiggled beneath him, desperate to escape, yet eager for more of his touch.

Stop this. It will only end badly.

I don't care how it ends as long as it's with him inside of me.

Her mind warred with her body as she undulated beneath him, impatient to feel him moving over her again. He gladly gave her what she desperately sought as the delicious friction of his body sliding over hers sent spirals of desire throughout her entire being. His head bent to her right breast. Through her sweater and bra, she could feel the alluring heat of his mouth against her flesh as his tongue ran over her and liquid heat pooled between her thighs.

She jerked at her wrists, eager to be free of his grasp so she could touch him too. Releasing her hands, he sat back on his heels. His eyes were a deeper shade of blue as he stared at her before pulling his shirt over his head. Abby's eyes bulged as she drank in every chiseled inch of him.

Pale, smooth flesh pulled tautly over his hard pecs and the carved ridges of his abs. A trail of darker blond hair dipped enticingly toward the band of his pants, and her fingers itched to follow its path. His broad shoulders blocked out the room behind him, but then all she could see right now was him.

Before she could form words, much less touch him, he reached down and tore open the front of her sweater. She went to grab at the ruined material when air brushed over her bare skin, but he grasped her wrists and jerked them above her head once more.

His eyes were deadly, his face harsh. The warmth of his bare flesh against hers seared her skin and branded her soul. His hand settled over her breast, rubbing her taut nipple through the lacy material of her black bra until it hardened beneath his ministrations. She bucked against him, unable to stop herself from crying out at the delicious sensations he so easily aroused in her. He bent his head until his mouth was just over her breast, his eyes latched onto hers as his tongue swirled over her nipple.

"Now tell me you don't want me," he said as he nipped at her.

She tried to deny his words, but she was fighting a losing battle. Why not give in? She'd been accepting of a lonely life, without the touch of a man, before he'd arrived here. If he left her after this, or it simply wasn't to be between them, at least she would have the memories of his body against hers, of tasting and savoring him as he drove in and out of her.

She was still trying to process it all when the sound of more cloth being ripped reached her. The button of her jeans hit the far wall when he yanked them open. He managed to turn himself in such a way that he was able to pull her jeans off while keeping her wrists pinned above her head.

Sitting back once more, Brian drank in the vision of her beneath him. Her sweater was torn open to reveal her black bra and heaving breasts, her nipples pert against the material and eager for more of his touch. He ran the back of his knuckles down her side toward the lacy black underwear that did little to shield her golden curls from him. That belly button ring...

Bending his head, he ran his tongue around it, pulling gently on it with his teeth before running his tongue over her skin once more. He'd believed it impossible, but the salty, sweet taste of her flesh caused his eager cock to thicken further.

He moved further down her body toward the lacy panties hanging low on her hips. His hand slid over her underwear to cup her mound; he growled when he found her already wet for him. She squirmed beneath him once more and ground herself against his palm.

The drive to take her clamored within him, but he found himself slowing his touch. He wanted her begging for him. Wanted her as desperate for him as he was for her. He pulled his hand away, smiling in satisfaction when she whimpered a protest that turned into a sigh of pleasure when he lowered himself over her to thrust against her once more. She jerked against the hand binding her wrists above her head, but he refused to relinquish his hold on her.

"Magnificent," he murmured as he ran his free hand over her pale flesh toward her quivering breasts.

His mind spun as conflicting emotions battered against him. She was too good for him, but she was *his*. She deserved better than him, but if this continued, he would never be able to set her free to live the life she dreamed of. The idea of setting her free caused the madness, which had eased at the touch of her, to race to the forefront again.

His grip on her wrists tightened as his mind and body screamed with the urge to possess her.

The smell of her blood on the air pierced through his insanity and passion infused haze. He lifted his head from her breasts to see a bead of blood forming where she'd bitten her bottom lip. She whimpered when his eyes latched onto it, and his own fangs slid free in eager response. Bending, his mouth hovered centimeters above hers as his tongue flickered out to take in that single bead.

He'd consumed blood from many vampires over the years, but none of them compared to the potent, powerful taste of her pure blood. Her fingers brushed against his hand as she watched him. He trailed his tongue over her lips one more time before leaning away from her.

"You deserve better than me," he bit out, but he was unable to resist the lure of her puckered nipple as he ran his thumb over it. He found the clasp for her bra in the center of her chest and flicked it open. His breath failed him when her luscious breasts sprang free.

"You're the only one I've wanted for years," she murmured. "There is no one better, not for me. Since I first saw you, it's only been you."

He froze at her words, and his head lifted as he stared down at the temptress before him. "What do you mean?"

Abby hadn't meant to reveal that to him, but she couldn't stand the idea of him thinking she was too good for him, that he was somehow less than she was. He had to know there was *no* one else. "You've haunted me since the first day we met."

CHAPTER FIFTEEN

CONFLICTING EMOTIONS FLITTED across his face as he stared at her. "You were only fifteen when we first met."

"I *did* notice boys and men at that age."

He released his grasp on her wrists, but kept his body over hers, refusing to allow her up. "You have had sex with a man before."

Abby fought against the blush trying to creep up her cheeks as he continued to stare at her. Why did he sound so confounded by her? Why did they have to have this conversation in the first place?

"I tried to have sex with other men," she admitted in a whisper. "I *really* tried to feel something for them in order to be free of the pull I felt toward you, but no matter how much I tried, my encounters with them always left me feeling cold and lacking. You have no idea what it's like to long to be free of something and not be able to shake it."

"Oh, but I do, Abigail," he grated out. "Ever since I picked up the phone and heard your voice, I've known what it's like to not be able to shake the thought of someone."

Feeling a little too exposed for this conversation, Abby tried to cover her breasts.

He grabbed her hands, pulling them away to drink in the sight of her again. Despite his growing exasperation, he couldn't tear himself away from her. She'd felt an instant connection to him, yet she'd never said a word to him about it.

"Would you have ever contacted me if Vicky hadn't taken off?" he demanded.

"Probably not for years," she admitted. "You've haunted my dreams, but you also terrify me. You are a killer, your world is volatile, but I've always believed you were good. What if I'd been wrong in that belief? What if I'd built you up in my head, and you rejected me? What if I met you and kissed you, and you left me feeling as emotionless as all those other men have over the years?"

His eyes flickered with red at the mention of other men, but she kept talking. "Before I saw you in that hotel room, I'd had boyfriends. I'd gone on dates and been as normal of a teenager as possible, considering I'm a vampire, but after I saw you, I was never the same. There was always an emptiness within me. If I'd met you again and the emptiness continued, I don't know if I could have survived it. As long as there was still the dream of you, then I could pretend that maybe one day I would feel normal again."

Brian's head spun as her words sank in.

"I also knew you felt nothing for me when we first saw each other," she continued. "So what if I'd found you again and you laughed at me or walked away?"

"You were only fifteen," he muttered.

"I know how old I was!"

"Your family would have killed me if I'd responded to you in *any* way back then. They still might."

She would have been a little disturbed if he'd shown any interest in her at that age too, and overwhelmed. She may have enjoyed dating before she'd met him, but they'd all been human *boys*. Back then, she never would have been able to deal with a vampire, who was clearly no boy, showing an interest in her. She was a woman now and she still had no idea how to deal with him most of the time.

"So when you called me, you knew there was a chance a deeper bond could form between us?" he inquired. "That there was a possibility we are mates."

She sucked in a breath as he said the words she'd refused to say out loud over the years. He felt enough of a draw to her that he suspected it too. However, something about his words caused her hackles to rise.

"I wasn't trying to *trap* you, Brian. You were not number one on my speed dial. I had to do a surprise visit home and steal Stefan's phone in order to get your number. I was happy before I met you! I never thought to be tied to anyone at *this* age, never mind fifteen! I planned to travel and try to do some good in the world. I want to experience other cultures and visit other countries. I want to feel something for someone other than *you*!"

She placed her hands against his massive chest and shoved him, but he barely budged. His muscles and facial expression became as rigid as stone.

"Do you think I wanted to be irrevocably tied to someone? Do I strike you as that kind of man?" he demanded. "I live my life day to day. I do what I want, when I want. I have no use for a woman in my life."

"You've made that clear repeatedly!" she shouted at him. "Yet tonight you looked very happy to have a woman in your life on that dance floor!" She tried to gather the tattered edges of her sweater and pull them together, but he grabbed hold of her wrists again, pulling her hands away. "Stop it!"

"Let me see you."

"No!"

She jerked her wrists free, and this time he didn't stop her from tugging her ruined sweater together. She had no idea how this had all gone so horribly wrong. One minute she'd been so freaking aroused she'd thought she would orgasm just from the feel of him against her, and now she was contemplating punching him in his arrogant face.

"You should go back to her," she told him.

He grabbed hold of her wrists, pulling her toward him until their noses were almost touching. "Nothing happened between Marissa and me."

"But it has before?"

"Not with Marissa, but yes, Abby, I have had sex before."

The tone of his voice made it sound as if he were talking to a child. "Get off me!"

A burst of strength shot out of her, and this time when she hit him in the chest, he rocked backward far enough that she was able to jerk her legs out from under him. He grabbed for her, but she rolled away too fast and shot to her feet before he could get his hands on her. She kept her sweater closed and her chin thrust out as she backed away from him. Keeping her shoulders back, she tried to muster as much dignity as she could in her panties and ruined clothes.

She tried not to ogle his muscular frame as he rose before her, but she couldn't keep her gaze from his broad shoulders and carved abs as he followed her every move like a predator hunting his prey.

"I'd much prefer to get you off," he said as he moved toward her.

Abby's jaw fell open at his brazen and tantalizing words. She tried to hide the flush of need that went through her as she backed around the sofa, placing the piece of furniture squarely between them.

"Has a man ever made you orgasm before?" he inquired as they circled around the sofa.

"You're a pig." Yet she couldn't deny the stirring between her legs caused by his words. He could do it; she knew it with absolute certainty, and she so badly wanted him to do it.

"It's a simple question. Answer it, and I won't heave this sofa through the wall to get at you," he said.

"Someone will call the police if you do."

"Let them. I'll change their memories and have them walking out of here whistling Dixie."

He grabbed hold of the arm of the couch. "Don't!"

"Then answer the question."

"This room is on my card; they'll charge me for any damages."

"I'll pay you back."

The muscles in his arm bulged as he lifted the couch effortlessly into the air. "No!" she cried. "No man has ever brought me to completion before."

His eyes glittered, and the couch thumped when he set it back to the floor. "How many did you allow to try?"

She knew exactly how a deer felt against a coyote right now. Cornered, unable to escape, and stalked by something far more lethal. "Enough to know it wouldn't work."

"How many, Abigail?" he demanded.

"How many women have you been with, Brian?"

"Do you really want the answer to that?"

No. "Yes."

"More than thirty, less than forty."

She really shouldn't have insisted on knowing as a knife sliced through her chest, but she kept her face impassive as they continued to circle the sofa. It could have been worse, she realized. If he'd had one woman for every year he was a vampire, it still would have been nearly two hundred. That number wouldn't include his human experiences, and that would have been if he'd had *only* one a year. Many vampires had far more partners than one a year. Still, she'd known no other man, but he had dozens of women to compare her to.

"So you were like Stefan at the end and started having relationships with women instead of bouncing from one to the other like Ian used to?" she inquired in a hoarse voice.

He stopped circling, and she halted on the opposite side of the couch from him. "I don't do relationships. I would go years before seeking the company of a woman, and when I had spent myself between her legs, I never went back."

"Why?" she whispered.

"Because I felt I was betraying Vivian when I was with another. She may be dead, but she was my wife."

If she'd thought his number of women had cut her deep, those words sliced her open until her insides were exposed and broken.

"You're the only one I've never felt guilt with. Somehow, I can touch you and lose myself in you, and it doesn't tear me apart inside. I haven't been with a woman in seven years. I've gone for five years once before, but never seven. I hadn't even realized it until recently. I think we both know the reason why I haven't sought out a woman in so long."

Hope and something more rose within her. Maybe it wouldn't be love between them, but it could be something else. He could be an ass, but she liked him, and he obviously wanted her, could that be enough for them? It was better than years of loneliness and remorse. She couldn't tear her gaze away from him as he watched her from the other side of the couch.

"Now, Abigail, how many men failed to satisfy you?"

She swallowed nervously. "Ten." A muscle ticked in his cheek, but that was the only reaction he gave her.

Ten had failed; he would not. He started moving around the couch again, but she continued to keep it between them as they walked in a slow circle. "So you've never experienced an orgasm before?"

"I didn't say that."

His body thrummed at the implication of her words. The idea of her touching herself, fondling those beautiful breasts as she brought herself to completion made his heart race and his mouth water.

Abby's eyes widened at the ravenous look in his hooded eyes. She was in trouble, deep trouble. "Brian..."

Her voice trailed off when he grabbed the arm of the sofa and lifted it to stand on end without so much as breaking a sweat. She backed away from him until her heel connected with the wall. "Stay away," she warned. What he'd said to her had brought her optimism, but she wasn't sure she was ready for him when he had that look in his eyes.

He advanced on her until he was standing toe-to-toe with her. "Tonight you'll know what it's like to have another make you scream in ecstasy," he declared.

She thrust her chin out and tugged her sweater closer together. "How do you know you'll be able to do that?"

A sensual, smug smile curved the corner of his mouth as he rested his hands on the wall beside her head and leaned closer. "Now, Abby, we both know I can."

Before she could respond, he dropped his hands on her waist and plucked her easily off the ground. He started carrying her toward the bed. "No, Brian, wait."

"I'll stop if you tell me to, but don't deny yourself this. Let me show you what it feels like to have another's touch drive you mad. Tonight, it will only be about you, not me."

She wiggled in his arms, wanting to be free of him as badly as she wanted to have him deliver on his promise. Years of frustration warred with common sense inside her. Before she could gather a protest, he bent his head and nuzzled her neck. His fangs scraped over her sensitized flesh, and she almost screamed aloud at the feel of his heated mouth against her.

He laid her on the bed again and tugged the edges of her ruined sweater apart once more. She gave into his touch with barely a protest. Cool air brushed over her exposed skin as he stepped back to stare down at her. His massive length strained against his pants, but he didn't reach for the button as his hungry gaze ran over her. The heat of his stare was enough to make her squirm.

Mine. He realized as he stared at her splendid body spread out before him. He slid his fingers over her legs, and she tried to clamp her thighs together, but he gently nudged them apart to trail his fingers leisurely down them. Her emerald eyes darkened with passion while she watched his every move.

"Who did you think of, Abby? When your fingers were in you as you sought release, whose fingers did you imagine they were?"

Her breath hitched and redness spread over her cheeks before her eyes darted away. She quaked when he dipped his hand down to rub against her heated center. "Was it me?" he pressed when she lifted her hips to him. "Was it my touch?"

His eyes fell to her quivering breasts with their dusky nipples. It took everything he had to pull his hand away from her. She moaned her discontent over the loss of contact. He had to know her answer though. "Tell me, was it my touch you fantasized about?"

Again his fingers dipped teasingly toward her center and stilled as he waited for her response.

"Yes!" she blurted, unable to stand his teasing any longer. "Yes, it was your face in my mind every time. It was always you!"

He was pretty sure he was going to burst out of his jeans as she confirmed what he'd suspected. Had he really told her tonight would only be about her? Jesus, he wouldn't be able to walk if this kept up; yet he found himself determined to give her a taste of what she'd been missing, to make sure she felt treasured even if it meant denying himself.

As he pulled off her panties, his hungry eyes latched onto her wet, golden curls. Kneeling between her legs, he nudged her thighs further apart and slid his thumb over her swollen clit. Her head fell back, thrusting her breasts up in such an inviting way that he was unable to resist them.

Bending forward, he took one of the taut buds into his mouth and swirled his tongue around the tip. He nipped at it before scraping his fangs over the soft flesh of her breast. Her fingers threaded through his hair, drawing him closer as his hand stroked over her center once more. Her delicious cries of excitement drove him onward as he dipped a finger into her wet entrance.

He groaned when her hot, wet recesses clenched around his finger. What he wouldn't give to have her gripping his shaft in such a way. Lifting his mouth from her breast, he took hold of her lips, catching her cry as she rubbed against his palm more demandingly.

Her nails dug into his shoulders as he pulled away to leave a trail of heated kisses down her neck to her collarbone. His tongue slid slowly over her sweet flesh as he moved steadily lower. Grabbing her thighs, he lifted them over his shoulders and grabbed hold of her ass, drawing her closer to him. He may not be taking her tonight, but he would taste her.

She gasped when his tongue dipped into her belly button and licked over the small silver hoop clasped there. She couldn't tear her gaze away as she watched him work his way down her body. Each scrape from his fangs was followed by a warm, wet wash of his tongue as he tenderly licked the spot where his fangs had been.

Everything about this experience was different than it ever had been before. If this had been any other man, she would be pushing him away by now, but with Brian, she couldn't get close enough and felt no embarrassment about being so exposed. All she wanted was to draw him closer, but he was moving further down her body and away from her touch. His mouth seared across her thighs toward where she ached for him most.

Her legs spread further as the heat of his mouth settled over her. Never in her life had she experienced such exquisite decadence as his tongue working against her clit. She'd often imagined this with him, longed for it even, and it was far better than her dreams had ever been.

Her hands twisted in the sheets, tearing them from the bed when his tongue drove into her in deep, penetrating thrusts. She couldn't breathe, she was certain her heart was going to explode from her chest, but she never wanted it to stop. Something within her began to build; she recognized the feeling of impending release, but this was more intense than she'd ever felt before.

His thumb rubbed her clit as his tongue greedily thrust in and out of her, and he pushed her over the edge. She cried out, her back rising off the bed as waves of ecstasy crashed over her. She'd never experienced anything like this before as the orgasm continued to rock through her body.

"That's it, Abigail," he murmured as he settled over the top of her.

The heat of his chest seared into her hypersensitive skin. She fell back as aftershocks of pleasure continued to roll through her body, making her limbs deliciously limp. He slid his fingers into her again as he reclaimed possession of her mouth. His tongue entwined lazily with hers as he thrust into her relentlessly, pushing her back over the edge once more.

CHAPTER SIXTEEN

THE SOUND of footfalls reverberated off the walls of the surrounding buildings as they walked through the alley. Beatrice's hand was warm in his as she talked about the lessons her mother had taught her that day. She was learning her numbers now and was doing exceptionally well with them. He smiled as he listened to her eagerly prattle on; he didn't think he'd ever get tired of hearing how excited she got about things.

Trudy yawned and nestled closer against him as she dropped her head onto his shoulder. Her breath tickled his neck as she breathed in and out. Dinner at their pastor's house had gone longer than normal tonight, but Brian had been eager to see and discuss the plans for the new church building the pastor had recently drawn up. They were hoping to break ground on the larger facility next week.

Vivian smiled when Beatrice took hold of her hand too. They were almost to the end of the alley when a man and woman entered from the other end. He didn't pay the couple any attention.

"Swing me," Beatrice said, and he and Vivian lifted her off the ground so she could swing out and back.

Vivian smiled and corrected the bonnet on her head when it fell back. A small laugh drew his attention to the couple again as they continued toward them. The woman was wearing a form-fitting dress that revealed more of her breasts and legs than he was used to seeing. A feeling of discomfort filled him at the idea of his family seeing a woman so exposed. The woman's chestnut hair flowed freely down her back instead of being tied back and covered, as it should have been.

A working woman? He wondered as the slit in her dress revealed her entire thigh and lack of undergarments. Vivian ducked her head as a blush crept up her pale cheeks. Beatrice stopped swinging as she too noticed the strange couple. He wanted to cover her eyes, but he didn't have time to adjust Trudy in his arms before the man and woman were stopping before them.

"How sweet," the woman purred, and the man moved to block Vivian from continuing onward.

"Let us pass," Brian said coldly to the man. He had his knife strapped to his side, but it had been years since he'd had to pull it on someone. He didn't like the idea of having to do so in front of his children, but he would.

The couple snickered behind their hands. Vivian pushed Beatrice against his side as she stepped closer to him. He could feel his daughter's fright in the tremor of her body against his. He had no idea who this couple was, but he'd kill them both before he would ever let them hurt his family. Switching his hold on Trudy, he wrapped his hand around the handle of the foot-long knife he'd forged himself.

As a child fighting over scraps in an alley, he'd stabbed someone once. The older boy had pulled a knife on him first and had been looking to kill him. Brian had sliced his arm, leaving him alive, but wary of Brian afterward. He'd gained some respect amongst the street kids that day; he'd never had to use a weapon on anyone since. He had a feeling that was about to change.

"Not tonight, friend," the man replied.

"I am not your friend," Brian hissed through his teeth.

Beatrice shivered against his leg. "Daddy," she whispered.

"Shush, honey," Vivian said.

Trudy released a small snore and cuddled closer against his neck. Brian thought he saw a flash of red in the woman's eyes, but it was hard to be sure in the dim light of the moon. The lanterns lining the streets only ten feet away did little to illuminate the dark alleyway in which they stood.

Can't be, he said to himself seconds before the woman leapt at him with fangs extended.

He clung to Trudy and pushed Beatrice behind him to fight against the monsters attacking them. Unable to understand fully what was going on, shock jolted through him when fangs sank deep into his neck. He thrashed against the woman, kicking and swinging his knife as he continued to try to fend them off. Trudy screamed as her arms tightened around his neck to the point of cutting off his air before she was ripped from his arms.

Limp and weakened from the blood loss, his legs finally gave out, and he fell to the ground. Vivian was already lying there, her eyes open and unseeing as the last of her blood dripped into the earth. Anguish twisted through him, he wanted to get to his wife, but he had no strength to move. She was already gone, and he knew he would be joining her in Heaven soon.

A hand grabbed hold of his hair and yanked his head backward; something cool was shoved against his lips. He thrashed against the hand entangled in his hair as a warm liquid trickled into his mouth and down the back of his throat. He swallowed to keep from choking on the foul-tasting liquid.

Laughter rang in his ears as his head was released abruptly. His forehead banged against the ground, causing the soft skin to split apart; his blood spilled from the open wound, but he barely noticed as a renewed strength flooded his battered body.

He crawled toward his daughters and wife and slid his hand into

Beatrice's when she called for him. He wrapped his hand around hers as the burst of strength faded away, and he fell to the ground. Darkness surged up to claim him.

⁓

BRIAN JOLTED AWAKE; his heart hammered in his chest as memories of that unbearable night replayed in his mind. He lay quietly, quaking as he fought against the bloodlust and loss that always came with the nightmare—a nightmare he'd had countless times over the nearly two centuries that had passed since the murder of his family.

Sweat beaded on his brow and slid down his cheek. In the beginning, he would wake crying in the night before the rage took over, but after the first fifty years, the tears had dried and stopped falling. The sorrow remained lodged in his throat; he could clearly recall the feel of Beatrice's small hand in his, and Trudy's warm breath against his neck. He could live a thousand years and never forget either of those things.

His fangs slid free, and his hands tore into the sheets beneath him as the urge to kill overwhelmed him. He rolled over to leap out of bed and go in search of some vampire who deserved a good ass-kicking followed by a brutal death. It didn't matter that the sun was shining; he'd find a vampire to kill somewhere.

He froze when his eyes landed on Abby, curled on her side with her blonde hair tumbling about her bare shoulders. Some of his wrath faded as he watched her sleeping peacefully, her breathing slow and even as she trustingly lay by his side, so unaware of the monster she'd allowed into her bed. Her lips were still swollen from his kisses.

If she had any idea what was going on inside him right now, she'd run screaming.

If he left her alone and unprotected while he went out and found his release, she would be vulnerable to attack. He couldn't do that to her. He'd already failed those he cared about once before; he would not fail her.

She was the first thing in centuries that felt right and good. The first thing that had made life bearable for him again. When he was with her, he wasn't consumed by a thirst for revenge and murder. He wasn't constantly looking for a way to ease the rage that had been consuming him since he'd been turned into a vamp all those years ago.

With her, he could almost believe he might have a chance to be happy again. He didn't dare get his hopes up. He knew how cruel and unpredictable life could be, but she'd brought peace and solace to him when he'd never thought to feel either of those two things again.

Rising to his feet, he paced over to the door. The warm air of the room drifted across his bare flesh as he moved. He rested his hands against the door as he struggled to shake the lingering images of the nightmare from his head. When he'd first been turned, he'd had the nightmare every night. Over the years, it had dwindled down to only a couple times a month. He hadn't had it at all since Abby had called him, but he should have known it was only a matter of time before it returned.

Walking back into the bedroom, he stopped to stare at her again. He kept waiting for the guilt to set in, but it hadn't come yet.

Maybe it was because they hadn't had sex yet, but they would. He had no doubt in his mind about that. No, the reason the guilt hadn't come was because she was different from any of the other women he'd ever been with, but then they both already knew that. The guilt would not come with her, because she belonged to *him*.

He'd failed his family all those years ago. He deserved to relive it over and over again; he didn't deserve the peace Abby gave to him. Even so, he was never going to let her go. He'd do whatever he could to keep her protected.

Walking over to the sofa, he pulled it down from where he'd set it on its side earlier. He couldn't bring himself to crawl into bed with her again when he was still so geared up for the kill. He didn't want her to see this side of him. He feared she'd take one look at him in his current state and know what he truly was, a coldhearted murderer.

CHAPTER SEVENTEEN

THE SUN WAS BARELY FILTERING around the edges of the drapes when Abby woke late the next day. She'd never felt so exhausted and happy in her life. Brian enveloped her, his massive arms locking her against his chest. His powerful hands slid over her as he languidly explored her body. There wasn't one inch of her he hadn't seen or tasted last night before she'd surrendered to exhaustion. This morning, he still seemed fascinated by her.

Brian had crawled back into bed with her an hour ago, when he'd finally managed to shake most of his bloodlust. The minute his arms had slid around her, any of his remaining fury had vanished. He should have come back to her sooner, but he hadn't wanted to be eased. Now, he couldn't imagine being anywhere else.

"I think," he murmured against her ear, "it's safe to say that I can make you cum."

The smug tone of his voice and the satisfied smile she felt against her cheek should have pissed her off; instead she found herself laughing at his statement. He rolled her over, his arrogant smile firmly in place as his fingers trailed over her face and toward the hollow of her neck.

"Was it as good as you'd imagined?" he whispered as he bent to kiss her earlobe.

"Better," she admitted.

His eyes danced when he pulled back from her. A lock of hair fell across his face and against the corner of his eye in a youthful way that warmed her heart. He didn't look cold and distant when he smiled at her like that.

"And it's only going to get better," he vowed.

Abby's smile slipped away. "You know what it could mean if this progresses between us."

He propped his head on his hand as he stared down at her. His other hand stilled its movement on her collarbone when he sensed a hesitation in her. "I know what it *will* mean," he said. She was going to understand he would have her.

She didn't know how to respond to that. Her heart swelled with joy at the same time something within her shriveled. All of the old problems were still there. His life, her family, his dead wife and sealed off heart, his commanding nature, and her dreams. She couldn't picture him traipsing around behind her as she traveled the world and worked with those in need, and there was no way was she going to give up her dreams.

It may not matter; she wouldn't be going anywhere if she didn't find Vicky. She had to make sure her sister was safe before she ever considered leaving the country.

His smile vanished as he studied her. She wore her every emotion on her face, and right now, he could see her hesitance and fear. "Abby—"

"I've always planned to help others," she whispered. "It's all I've ever dreamed about, besides you."

Brian realized she may have dreamed of him for years, but for those years, she'd also fought against what she'd suspected. He could have had a whole year of this with her before her sister had taken off.

"You should have come to me when you hit maturity," he told her.

"Why? You didn't want this, you admitted that yourself. I always thought, if I stumbled across you again, so be it, but I wouldn't search you out. We do have an eternity after all, and sex was not my number-one concern in life."

He grinned at her as he trailed a finger over her swollen bottom lip. "Wait until I have my way with you, then let's see if you feel the same way about sex."

Apparently, numerous orgasms had rattled her brain, because instead of elbowing him for his conceited statement, she melted beneath his touch. "Or I could realize that I really wasn't missing anything after all," she teased.

She never saw him move, but she found herself pinned beneath him as his naked body settled over hers. He hadn't entered her last night, but she'd eventually gotten his jeans off to reveal the splendid, massive part of him she'd longed to touch. He'd taught her how to satisfy him with her hand by taking it and stroking it up and down his rigid length. She hadn't been able to get enough of how hard and soft he was, how he throbbed beneath her hand, and the groans he emitted when she brought him to release.

"We could find out right now," he said as he slid the silken head of his shaft against her thigh.

Abby gasped and goose bumps broke out on her flesh as his phone began to ring. "Ignore it," he commanded when her head turned toward the nightstand where it sat.

She'd happily do that, she decided as he bent his head to kiss her. Just minutes ago, she'd been worried about problems between them; now she could barely remember her name as his fingers skimmed over her body. The phone went off again, the vibrations carrying it to the end of the nightstand.

"It could be important," she murmured against his mouth.

"Don't care," he replied as he nibbled on her lip.

His phone rang again, the force of the vibrations causing it to tumble off the edge and onto the floor. Brian released a volatile curse and rolled off her. He snatched the vibrating phone from the ground and brought it to his ear. "What?" he barked into it.

The greeting was nicer than when he'd answered her call, but he seriously needed to learn some phone etiquette. She rolled onto her side, propped her head in her hands, and stared at his sculpted back. Her nails had left marks upon his flesh. They were fading away, but she enjoyed seeing them on him. He was hers, and she would happily mark him so that every woman in a thousand-mile radius knew it.

Brian rested his head in his hand and listened as Karina spoke. "Did you talk to Marissa yesterday?"

"I did," he confirmed.

"She's dead."

He shot to his feet and paced away from the bed. Behind him, Abby sat up and pulled the blanket against her chest. "How?" he demanded.

"Murdered, by vampires. And not in a pleasant way," Karina replied. He knew how unpleasant a vampire could make another's death. "What did you ask her, Brian?"

"The same questions I asked you," he muttered as he rubbed at the stubble lining his jaw.

"Did you mention my name to her?" Karina's voice held a note of panic; he heard the bolt on a door slide closed from her end of the line.

"No."

"Good. I think it's best if you stay away from my club until this is all settled."

"I will."

Karina hung up. He turned back to Abby. She looked so sweet and innocent as she sat on the bed with her hair tumbling around her shoulders. There were vampires out there who knew he was looking for them. If they discovered she was with him, they would go for her too. Stronger than many vampires, she would be able to put up a descent fight, but not enough of one as far as he was concerned.

He'd planned to leave the hotel they'd been staying at behind soon, he realized now it may have been for the best that she'd already done so. His clothes and truck would stay where he'd left them, he wouldn't take the chance of returning for them now.

"What's wrong?" she asked.

"Marissa is dead."

Her mouth parted as she gazed at him. "How? Why?"

"Vampires. They know I'm asking about whatever is going on, and they're trying to take care of anyone who might have any idea about it. That will include me and whoever is with me."

She'd dragged him into this. She'd called him, and he hadn't been able to refuse because of some mystical bond between them. "I never should have called you."

Brian placed his phone on the dresser and stood before her in all of his naked glory, not seeming the least bit embarrassed by it. Nor should he be, he was magnificent, and he was now at risk because of her.

"Yes, you should have," he said. "Now, it's time to call your family. They may also try to kill me, but we'll deal with that when they get here."

"They won't," she murmured, but she wasn't convinced of that either.

"Tell them you'll be going home—"

"What?" she blurted.

"You're going home until I know it's safe for you."

"No, I'm not."

"Yes, Abigail, you are."

She kept the sheet against her chest as she rose to her knees before him. He may feel comfortable facing off in the nude, but she didn't, and the sheet gave her a false sense of security. "No, Brian, I'm not."

His eyes flashed red. His fangs gleamed in the fading light filtering over him. "I won't have you in this city when vampires could be hunting for you. They could be on their way here right now."

"Let them come!" she retorted. "And I'll show them what happens when they tangle with a pissed off pureblood."

"You're not strong enough to tangle with these vamps."

"I know a pureblood can be capable of just about anything when necessary."

"True, but you're not *cruel* enough to fight against them. You want to save the world, not tear the throat out of a vampire trying to kill you."

"I want to save my sister more than anything else right now."

"*I* will find Vicky, and you will do as I say."

"Do as you say!" she nearly screeched. "I'm not five, and I'm not leaving my sister and possible mate behind!"

His nostrils flared as he exhaled sharply. "*Possible* mate?"

She stared back at him unflinchingly. "The bond isn't complete yet. I've lived this long without you in my life, I can do it again."

She *might* be able to live without him, maybe. She was in it a whole lot deeper with him now than she had been for the past six years, but she wasn't going to spend the rest of her life having him order her around whenever he felt like it.

"Do you think to try and leave me again?" His voice was deceptively calm given the mounting strain in his body.

"I'm not going to let you order me around. This isn't the eighteen hundreds anymore. In case you missed it, women now have the right to vote, get a loan, buy a house, and you'll be amazed to know we can even think and talk for ourselves! Most importantly, we can do it all *without* a man!"

Brian took a deep breath to keep himself from leaping on the bed and claiming her completely. He had to put a stop to any idea she might have of escaping whatever this was between them. Abby didn't back away when he took a step closer to her, but rather rose higher on the bed in preparation for a battle.

"You will listen to me on this," he grated. "Once this bond is completed between us, our lives will be bound together, and it *will* be completed no matter what you think."

He may not have been looking for a woman in his life, but he knew he wouldn't be walking away from her. She'd fled three blocks from him by the time she was done traversing her convoluted route, and he'd nearly lost his mind.

If she left him for good…

If he had to live without her, he'd destroy everything and everyone he got his hands on. He would become the one thing he'd hated most. The thing he'd battled against becoming after he'd killed those two humans. No, she would *not* be walking out of his life. They may not love each other, but there was something else pulling them together, and he was going to do everything in his power to keep her with him.

"The bond won't be completed if you force me to leave here without Vicky. You don't always get what you want," she told him.

She kept the sheet pulled against her as she crept backward on the bed. His eyes were the color of blood, and the muscles in his arms and legs stood out. He looked tensed to spring on her. She was half-afraid she may have pushed him over the edge, and he would force her to complete the bond.

To be honest though, she'd cave faster to his touch than a house of cards in a tornado if he got his hands on her again. She had to get some distance between them before he could grab her, or else she feared there would never be any separating them again. Rising, she pulled the sheet from the bed and wrapped it around herself.

"I'll never forgive myself if you get killed because I allowed you to stay," he said in a voice hoarse with emotion.

Those damn traitorous heartstrings of hers tugged again, but she couldn't cave on this. He would think it was okay to continue to order her about for the rest of their lives if she gave in now. "And what if you die because you forced me away?"

"That won't happen."

"Your arrogance will get you killed one day."

"Most likely."

"So, I'm supposed to give myself over to you and complete this bond when you freely admit your behavior will likely get you killed?"

"Abigail—"

"If this bond is completed, your death would mean my death. Doesn't that bother you? What if we have children? Your actions would orphan them."

"There will be no children."

Abby recoiled from him as if he'd slapped her. Grief twisted her heart and caused her fingers on the sheet to tremble. He'd accepted there was a bond between them, that their lives would forever be interwoven together, but he would never love her, and he would never want children with her.

Fine. I don't need love or children anyway.

She could tell herself that all day, but she did need love, and she did want children. She thrived on love and happiness, thrived on the laughter of her family. She'd always dreamed of her children knowing such love as she'd grown up knowing. They'd know joy while running around with their many cousins and aunts and uncles.

Instead, she would watch her nieces and nephews grow while never knowing what it would feel like to have a child of her own.

Fate had thrown her either a sexless, lonely life, or a life of sex and loneliness with a man who would push her away for the rest of their lives. She didn't know which was worse, but it didn't matter. She had to stay focused on finding Vicky, and in order to do that, she had to stay in this city.

"If they killed Marissa, it's because they realize you're getting closer to finding Vicky or discovering what is going on," she said. "I'm not leaving here without my sister."

She didn't wait for him to respond before she spun away and stalked into the bathroom. She barely refrained from slamming the door shut behind her.

Brian ran a hand through his hair as he stared at the closed door. She'd been unable to hide her despair when he'd told her there would be no children. He'd known she would want children, but she had no idea what it was like to lose one, and being born a vampire was no guarantee their children couldn't be killed.

He'd barely survived it before; he wouldn't survive it again if he lost another child. His gaze fell to the hand Beatrice had held as she'd regaled him with her day. She'd been so trusting, so young, and he'd been her hero until he'd become her biggest disappointment.

No, there would be no more children for him. Abby would come to see it was for the best, just as she would come to understand leaving here now was the best for her as well. She would get over her anger at him eventually; she had far too many years ahead of her to carry a grudge for long.

Like you've gotten over your anger and moved on from the loss of your family?

They were entirely different situations. He told himself she would get over it, but what if she never did and her resentment toward him only grew as the years went by? Did he want to take the chance she might hate him for eternity?

If it meant keeping her alive, it was a risk he was willing to take.

CHAPTER EIGHTEEN

A*BBY WAS BACK* to not speaking to him as she stood by his side with her hands folded demurely before her. The only sign of her inner storm was the fire that blazed to life in her eyes the minute she'd emerged from the bathroom, and he'd informed her he'd called Stefan to let him know what was going on. She had clamped her mouth shut when he'd told her some of her family would be arriving soon.

The words he'd left unspoken had hung heavily in the air between them. *And at least one of them will be taking you home.*

He hated the idea of being apart from her and despised making her unhappy, but this was for the best. She had no idea how horrific the nefarious side of the vampire world could be. She'd gotten a glimpse of it in Karina's club and in that drug house they'd been in, but she hadn't even touched the tip of the iceberg.

She'll forgive me. She has to. Although, deep down, he knew she didn't have to forgive him and might not. Being mated to someone didn't guarantee happiness, and he'd driven two rather large wedges between them by first declaring no children, and then seeing to her removal from this situation.

Now she stood, her eyes back to their emerald color though he could see a hint of red in them as she stared at the elevator doors. He wouldn't have brought her into public right now, but they both had to feed. He could have called for room service, but he never would have been able to tolerate the idea of her feeding from another in front of him. Right now, he didn't think she'd be willing to accept the idea of feeding from him, so he'd had no choice but to bring her with him to secure blood from the nearest hospital.

The elevator doors opened with a ding and she stepped out. She held herself so stiffly, he half-believed she'd break apart as she strode forward. He went to take hold of her elbow, but she sidestepped him with ease. "Abby!" he hissed.

"Screw you."

Abby didn't look at him when he huffed out an irritated breath and dropped his hand back to his side. She'd been planning to call her family last night to get their help, but she'd intended to stay here when they arrived. Now, she had no doubt they'd be trying to drag her away from the city. They would see no reason for her to stay any longer. Brian could fill them in on everything and get them more leads.

Before, she probably could have convinced them she would be needed to help find Vicky. At the very least, she would have convinced them that she may be the only one who could get Vicky to leave willingly if she wanted to stay, but she had no hope of that now. They would be infuriated she hadn't been the one to call them; they would drag her away from here kicking and screaming if necessary, and they would do the same to Vicky, if and when they found her.

They may never forgive her for keeping this from them, and she may never forgive Brian for not giving her the chance to speak with them first. He'd gone behind her back to force her to do his bidding. She'd had plenty of overprotective alpha men in her life. She didn't need or want another one.

"You'll forgive me," he insisted when they stepped outside and onto the busy sidewalk as dusk descended on the city.

"You keep telling yourself that, see how far it gets you."

When he went to grab her arm again, she moved four more steps to the side, allowing the crush of people to flow between them. She contemplated fleeing down the city streets, but he would find her before she made it to the nearest subway station. He'd taken away her freedom, her choices; she'd never been so angry in her life.

She was also hungry; she didn't think she'd ever been this hungry before. She never should have come out in public feeling like she did, but she couldn't remain in the hotel room. He surprisingly hadn't argued with her when she'd put on her coat and low-heeled boots to join him.

She kept the people between them, but she found her gaze going more and more toward the pulse in their necks. Unwittingly, she licked her lips as one man brushed entirely too close to her. The man had been trying to get a cheap feel; he nearly got her fangs in his throat.

Brian was suddenly beside her. Taking hold of her elbow, he steered her toward an alley lit only by the lights they'd left behind on the sidewalk. "Stop it!" she protested.

"It's either you feed from me or on one of the passersby, right now," he replied. "You're staring at them like they're meals on legs."

"They are meals on legs," she muttered, then shook her head in annoyance at herself. She was hungrier than she'd realized if that was her attitude about humans at the moment. "I didn't mean that."

"When was the last time you fed?"

"I don't know, a few days ago. I was going to call for room service last night, but you interrupted me before I could."

A jolt went through Brian at her words. "You will *not* be feeding directly from humans any more. It will either be blood bags or me."

"Oh, you managed to go almost a half an hour without bossing me around. It must be a new record."

"Abigail—"

"I bet it's perfectly fine for you to continue to feast on humans though, and I'm sure you prefer females."

He had no idea how it had all gone so bad so fast. Last night she'd been moaning and writhing beneath him; now she was pricklier than a cactus. He was beginning to realize it was only going to get worse if something wasn't done to stop this downward, angry spiral between them.

"I will provide for you," he told her.

"You won't be providing shit for me." The truth was she actually didn't care for feeding from humans. She'd been scared she was going to hurt the human boy she'd fed from. It had been too stressful to be fulfilling, but Brian's words had infuriated her all over again. "Not until you can treat me like an equal."

She glowered at him before bowing her head to focus on the alley and her boots as she walked. She rubbed at her neck, hating the tension there. His hand slid up to replace hers; his strong fingers kneading her flesh eased the tightness in her muscles.

She melted beneath his touch before coming back to herself and slapping his hand away. "Stop that."

She didn't find his arrogant smile cute anymore. He pulled her to a stop and moved her backward to press her against the brick wall of a building. "What are you doing?" she demanded.

"You must feed. We have no choice but to go back into public before we reach the hospital. You have one alternative to grabbing a human and draining them dry, and that's me."

"I'll starve, thank you."

He blocked her when she tried to squeeze around him. "You won't starve, you'll snap."

"I am perfectly capable of restraining myself, unlike you."

His hand rested against her hip, drawing her up against the bulge in his pants. She squirmed away from him, refusing to let him melt her in any way.

"I'm being very restrained right now, just as I was last night. But I won't let my mate go hungry," he stated.

"The bond is not complete. I am *not* your mate."

He grabbed hold of her chin, forcing her to look at him. "It's as good as sealed, Abigail. You may be pissed at me, but you better get that realization through your head."

She rested her hands against his chest, looking to force him away from her, but her fingers curled into his shirt. She despised this need she had for him.

Her fangs slid free, pricking her bottom lip when he leaned closer to her and turned his head to expose more of his throat. She inhaled his enticing scent; it reminded her of pine trees and the forest around her home in Maine. She wanted his blood, nearly as badly as she wanted to feel him inside of her, but she couldn't give into him.

"It's not giving in, Abby. It's simply fulfilling a need."

He seemed to have read her mind by uttering those words. Words she tried to shake off, but he was right, wasn't he? It didn't matter, her head spun with thirst as his blood rushed through his veins in a mouthwatering rhythm; she felt her heart slowing to match. She was far weaker than she'd ever thought herself as she leaned into him, her fangs resting against his flesh.

"That's it, dove," he whispered.

She shivered at the endearment, something she'd never expected from him. His hand wrapped around the back of her head, keeping her locked in place. As the vein pulsed beneath her lips, saliva filled her mouth and a whimper escaped her. She was helpless to resist the lure of his blood.

His body jerked against hers when she sank her fangs into him. The hot wash of his blood in her mouth was the most delectable thing she'd ever tasted as it filled her in pulsing waves. His lust pounded against her as he grabbed hold of her ass and thrust her against him. What had been a bulge before, was now a full erection he ground against her in his growing frenzy.

"More," he commanded.

Helpless to resist, she bit deeper. His hand smashed against the wall beside her head; she scarcely noticed the bits of debris and brick falling around them. Her body quivered as she became swept up in all of his tumultuous feelings for her and his gratification over what was happening between them now.

Wetness spread between her legs as she lifted them and wrapped them around his waist. She rode him up and down with reckless abandon. Through his blood, she could sense he was barely keeping himself restrained from tearing her jeans from her and sinking himself deep into her.

She was so far gone on the taste and power of his blood right now, she wouldn't stop him from taking her virginity in an alley that smelled of things she tried not to think about. His hips thrust demandingly against her, causing her body to splinter apart as an orgasm ripped through her.

Her cry of pleasure was muffled by his throat; her nails raked down his back. His body gave a heaving shudder as his satisfaction and frustration flowed through his blood and into her as he found his release, but not inside of her.

"Will have you," he whispered against her neck.

His fangs pressed against her, but he didn't bite down. She wanted to scream at him to do it, but kept herself restrained.

Releasing her bite on his neck, she rested her head on his shoulder and turned to watch as the humans strolled up and down the busy city street with no awareness of what had just transpired fifty feet away from them. The humans were all so close, yet she'd never felt further removed from their world before. She was losing everything that had ever meant anything to her—her freedom, friends, dreams, and most importantly, her family.

Brian ran his hand over her hair. His fangs ached from their need to be buried within her, but he was far more concerned about seeing her fed than he was with leaving his mark on her. Her need for blood didn't beat against him anymore as he cradled her closer. However, he could sense her euphoria fading away to be replaced with misery once more.

He didn't know what to do to ease those feelings in her. She melted at his touch, but he couldn't keep her in bed for the rest of their lives, no matter how inviting the prospect was. Besides, she would probably be leaving tomorrow, and he didn't know when he'd get the chance to see her again. Her anger and resentment would only grow during their separation. When he finally did see her again, she wouldn't run to him with open arms.

The scent of her arousal and climax drifted to him, causing him to become hard again. He'd ejaculated in his own pants; a feat he'd managed to avoid his entire life, but she managed to make all of his control and restraint become completely undone whenever he touched her. She made him forget about everything except for pleasing her. She made him forget what a monster he had been.

What a monster he still was, especially with her. He didn't like upsetting her, but he wasn't used to someone fighting him every step of the way. Well, not every step. She was fairly easy going until he decided she was going to do something she didn't want to do.

An eternity of driving wedges between them would only equate to an eternity of unhappiness for them both. There would be no divorce, no until death do they part. No, there would only be unhappiness and arguments. He rested his lips against her temple. Her hands flattened against his chest to push him away as her legs unwrapped from his waist.

Their brief moment was over; they would soon return to fighting. They couldn't do this forever. It would be best for her if she left here, but it would be worse for them in the long run, and truth be told, he didn't want to part from her, not even for a day.

"You can stay," he murmured against her hair. "I won't force you to leave before we find Vicky."

Abby's hands jerked on his shirt. She tilted her head back to look at him, uncertain if she'd heard him right, but he didn't appear to be joking. His blue eyes were a deeper, sea blue as he watched her with an unreadable expression.

"Really?" she asked.

"Yes, but you are to stay out of it, for the most part. If I tell you it's too dangerous for you, you have to listen to me. Promise me you will do as I say, and I will keep your family from taking you home."

"I promise!"

"I mean it, Abby. If you fight me on anything, I will personally drag you out of here, and that won't do any good for Vicky."

"I mean it," she said. "I promise, but why did you change your mind?"

His thumbs rubbed over her cheekbones as he studied her beautiful emerald eyes. *Because there isn't anything I wouldn't do to make you happy.* "I guess I'm getting soft in my old age," he said, instead of the truth.

Her elated laughter filled the air as she flung her arms around his neck. She rained kisses across his cheeks and mouth. He would agree to almost anything, if it meant making her this happy again.

CHAPTER NINETEEN

"What were you thinking, Abby?" Ethan ran a hand through his black hair as he paced back and forth before her, shooting her disapproving looks every chance he got.

She folded her arms over her chest and glared back at her older brother. "I was thinking Vicky wouldn't want you involved, and neither did I."

"You could have gotten the both of you killed."

"I'm as capable of defending myself as you are."

"You're a newly matured vampire. You're not sure what you're capable of yet."

"And neither are you. I believed I could find her on my own."

"But you called *him*!" Ethan exploded and thrust a finger at Brian.

"So did you when you needed help!"

Ethan stopped walking to scowl at her before resuming his pacing.

"What leads do you have?" Stefan asked. "Brian?"

Stefan's prodding caused Brian to break away from following Ethan's every move. He was seriously considering beating her brother if he didn't watch what he said to her. His attention turned to Stefan, the man he'd once considered his best friend. Time had torn them apart, but to this day, Stefan was the only man he'd ever counted on as much as himself. Stefan was one of the few who had understood his compulsion to avenge the death of his family and had helped him to do so.

Stefan's onyx eyes burned into his as he waited for an answer. Behind Stefan, Abby's adopted uncle, David sat sprawled out on the sofa, his long legs spread before him. Her brother, Ian leaned against the wall beside David. Ian's sky-colored eyes flitted curiously between Brian and Abby as Brian remained standing protectively in front of her.

If Ethan was mad now, he was about to hit a whole new level of pissed off when Brian staked his claim on Abby. He didn't care if he had to take all of them on at the same time. No one was going to take her from him.

"Not many leads so far," he replied to Stefan's question. "However, I found out this morning that a girl named Marissa, a Feeder I questioned last night, was killed shortly after we spoke. She knew more than she could tell me due to compulsion, but someone didn't like her talking to me enough to kill her for it. She gave me the name of her ex, Garth, and some numbers. I planned to follow up on him tonight."

"Fine," Ethan said. "We'll get in touch with this guy tonight. David has agreed to take Abby home."

"I'm not leaving," she said firmly.

Ethan spun to face her, looking as if he might grab her and shake her. A warning growl emanated from Brian as he nudged her back with his shoulder. He knew her brother wouldn't hurt her, but he wouldn't let him upset her any more either. The gesture caused eyebrows to shoot up all over the room.

"She's not going anywhere," Brian said firmly.

Ethan's green eyes, so similar in color to Abby's, narrowed on him. "She's not staying here. Our parents are expecting her, and it's too risky for her here. These vamps are killing off the people you're talking to; they can't know she's connected in any way."

"Tell your parents she's not coming back until she's ready. We have more to worry about than Abby's connection to me or her safety from those vamps. If Ronan finds out about any of this, he'll kill everyone involved, including Vicky. He may kill me for not telling him sooner." Abby's breath hissed in behind him. "But I will deal with that after we find your sister. Until then, Abby stays."

"You have no say in this. It's a family matter," Ethan replied.

"I have every say in this if you think you're taking her anywhere she doesn't agree to go. You are *not* taking her away from me."

Ethan did a double take at Brian's words. His jaw dropped open when Abby stepped forward and wrapped her hand around Brian's arm. Tilting her head back, she stared defiantly at her brother.

"You've got to be fucking kidding me!" Ethan blurted.

"Ethan—" Abby started.

"Is he your mate?"

Abby thrust her shoulders back. "He is."

The amount of pride in her voice caused something to pull at Brian's heart as he watched her unflinchingly stand up to her powerful sibling. Ethan turned away from her to glower at Brian. The muscles in his body tensed as he prepared for Ethan to attack him, but her brother remained where he was.

"You know what that means, Ethan," Abby said.

"I know what it means," he grated.

"You can't separate us."

Ethan's face softened as he looked at her. "I wouldn't dream of trying, Abby. I'd never knowingly cause you to suffer."

The tension in Brian's muscles eased at Ethan's words. His love for his sister would keep him from fighting this, but Ethan didn't have to say he'd hoped for better for his sister. Brian saw the truth of it in the sadness filling his eyes as he watched her.

"I'm not leaving without Vicky," she said to Ethan.

"I know," he said to her before focusing on Brian. "But I think you're putting her in danger by allowing her stay."

Brian felt a vein throbbing to life in his forehead. "I do too, but I compromised."

Stefan's loud burst of laughter drew lethal looks from everyone in the room. "This is kind of perfect," Stefan said in between his laughs, "and more than a little shocking. You've seen each other before."

"According to one of Ronan's men, Declan, if she hadn't matured yet, there would have been no connection. At least not on my part," Brian replied. He didn't think they need to hear that their teenage sister had affected him enough that he hadn't had sex in seven years.

Their gazes all went to Abby. "What?" she demanded. "I don't tell you guys *every*thing. I didn't even tell Vicky about him, and it's not as if I knew for certain he was my mate at fifteen. I knew he was different from other men, but that was it."

"We get the point," Ethan assured her.

"Well, it looks like the family has grown some more." Ian walked over to slap Brian's shoulder. "Welcome."

Brian wasn't so sure about that. He'd barely come to terms with having Abby as his mate, never mind the entire Byrne clan as his extended family. He'd been flying solo for years; solitary was the way he liked things, and he couldn't deal with the idea of losing another family. He kept those thoughts to himself; he'd already wounded Abby with his declaration of no more children. He wouldn't turn away from her family.

"Thanks," he muttered.

"Does Aiden know about this?" David asked.

"You're the first ones to know," Abby said. "I tried calling Aiden for help before I called Brian, but Ronan's man at the training facility wouldn't let me talk to him."

Ethan glanced between them once more before rubbing his

temples and turning away. Stefan's face was turning red from trying not to laugh again. He finally lost the battle.

∼

BRIAN DIDN'T ACKNOWLEDGE Ethan as he stepped outside and onto the relatively tranquil sidewalk. In the distance, he could hear horns blowing and the thump of music, but here there was also laughter and the murmur of conversations as the distinct scent of pizza and Italian food wafted through the air. Ethan tugged his jacket closer around him and folded his arms over his chest as he studied Brian.

"Is this going to be the protective big brother conversation?" Brian asked as he pulled his phone from his pocket. "Because I am not in the mood."

"No, I think you know what you stepped into with our family. You know what will happen to you if you hurt her."

"That's not going to happen."

Ethan's head tilted to the side as he surveyed him. "Out of all of my siblings, Abby is the most tenderhearted and the dreamer. You're not what I pictured for her."

"And what did you picture for her?"

"A good man, a patient and loving man who wouldn't crush her spirit as I believe you will."

Brian almost crunched his phone in his hand. "I have no intention of *crushing* her spirit," he bit out.

Ethan held up a hand. "Maybe you won't mean to do it, but she's... fragile."

Brian laughed at that assessment. "I don't think you know your sister as well as you think you do. Yes, she is the most loving and caring woman I've ever met. No, she's not vicious, manipulative, or cruel, but she's far from fragile."

"She won't take well to being pushed around—"

Brian released a harsh bark of laughter. "No shit," he interrupted. "She kicked me in the nuts."

The prideful grin spreading over Ethan's face had him contemplating punching the younger vamp. "Really? Never saw that one coming from Abby."

"She's stronger than you're giving her credit for."

"She's always tried to make everyone else happy, and I don't want her to be buried by someone who has a stronger will than her," he said with a pointed look at Brian.

Irritation pricked at Brian's skin. "You really should reevaluate your sister, or at least get to know her better. Do you honestly believe I wanted her involved in this still? The main reason I called Stefan was to get her out of here, but she was so mad and unhappy when she realized what I'd done."

"So you agreed to let her stay?"

Brian contemplated how to respond to that; in the end, he went with the truth. "I'd agree to almost anything to make her happy. I may not like her being here, but I can keep her protected. I'll destroy anyone who tries to harm her."

Ethan's head bowed before he met Brian's gaze again. "Maybe I'm wrong."

"You are." Brian turned away and focused on his phone as he punched Garth's number into it. "Is this Garth?" he asked when a man picked up the phone.

"No."

The line went dead. Brian stared at the phone before turning to look into the restaurant where Abby sat with her family. They may not be eating the pizza cooking in the ovens behind them, but it was a much more comfortable environment than being crammed into her hotel room.

"He's not going to talk to me," he muttered.

Ethan followed his gaze to Abby. "I don't want my sister talking to him."

"Do you think I want that?" Brian retorted. "But the only way she's leaving here is if we find Vicky."

He might kill Vicky himself when they found her. If she was mixed up with drugs, Abby could be chasing her for the rest of her days or at least until Vicky was finally killed by Ronan, or some other vamp looking to put an end to the risk of exposure she represented. Abby would repeatedly put herself in danger to rescue her sister.

"What was Vicky thinking to get involved in this mess?" Ethan muttered.

"I don't know," Brian said. "But the sooner we find her, the happier Abby will be."

Ethan's eyes bored into him as Brian lifted his hand to wave Abby over to where they stood. Brian ignored him. He was aware of how powerful a pureblood vampire could be, and Ethan was larger than him, but he would take Ethan down if he tried to intervene in his relationship with Abby.

She frowned but rose to walk over to them with Stefan close behind her. Brian grabbed hold of the door and pulled it open for her. He ignored the startled look on Ethan's face and the smirk on Stefan's.

"What is it?" Abby inquired.

"Garth isn't going to talk to me," Brian told her. "I don't know if it's because he's been advised not to talk to any men he doesn't already know, or if he's always been paranoid, but a woman might be able to get through to him."

"You want *me* to call him?"

"I do."

She pulled her phone from her pocket as Brian counted to ten to keep from tearing it out of her hand. He was nearly to fifty before he felt calm enough to give her the phone number of the vamp who may have killed Marissa, a woman who had only been trying to help him in the hopes of immortality. Thousands of souls stained his hands; he didn't like adding Marissa to the few he felt bad about.

"The number?" Abby asked for the third time.

Brian bit the number out from between his gritted teeth and thrust his phone at Stefan before he crushed it. Stefan looked as if he were about to start laughing again but wisely refrained from doing so. Abby turned and walked away from them as she waited for her call to be answered. Garth could do nothing to her through the phone, yet Brian hurried to catch up with her.

He hovered over her shoulder when she tried to wave him away. She glared at him, and he glared right back. "Hello," a tired male voice greeted.

Abby's mind spun, she hadn't considered what she was going to say if the phone call was answered. Going on instinct, she blurted out the first words that came to her. "I'm looking for the party tonight."

"We're all looking for the party, sweets, but only the chosen few get in. What's your name?"

"Vicky."

Brian's face turned red and his teeth clenched so hard she thought they might shatter. He was holding himself held back, but he wouldn't let her talk for much longer. Through the line she heard some shuffling and then what sounded like boots hitting the floor. She strained to hear anything else, but Garth's movements were the only ones she detected.

"Ahhh, Vicky, back so soon. You know the deal, no pic, no deets."

Abby glanced at Brian before pushing him back a step. His hand grabbed for her phone before falling back to his side and fisting there. Turning her phone around, Abby held it far away from her and tried to stay as much in the shadows as possible. No one outside of her family, and apparently Brian, could ever tell her and Vicky apart, and her family sometimes still confused them. However, she had no idea what Vicky had been through and what kind of toll it may have taken on her; maybe she'd cut her hair, dyed it black, or gotten yellow contacts.

Taking the picture, Abby clicked a few buttons and sent it to Garth. She could *feel* Brian seething beside her.

"Pretty as ever, I see," Garth said a few seconds later. "I'll send you the locale. The party is already going."

Did one thank their drug-dealing connection before the call ended? Fortunately, that was a question she was spared from having to answer as he hung up before she could stammer out a response.

A few seconds later, her phone beeped. She was rewarded with an address and one word, Bubblegum.

CHAPTER TWENTY

"There is no way Vicky is in there," Ethan said.

Abby stared across the street at the sagging warehouse with boarded windows and the faint sound of music playing within. The solid steel door on the front of the building was completely out of place with the rest of the crumbling, brick structure. She'd seen tombs more inviting than this place, but a couple of humans were practically skipping as they approached the door.

"A couple weeks ago, I would have agreed with you," she replied. "Now, I'm not so sure."

Brian stood beside her, his arms folded over his chest as he scowled at the building. "You're not going in there alone."

"I'm not," she said. "David has agreed to come with me."

"*I* am going with you," Brian insisted with a menacing look at David. If he'd considered protesting Brian's words, he wisely decided not to.

"You can't go in; they know who you are, and I'm not about to orphan any of my nieces and nephews if something goes wrong, so you three are out," she said with a wave at the others.

Brian's eyes turned red at the possibility of something going wrong. Abby geared herself up for a big argument from all of the men hovering around her. This was not going to be easy, but she wasn't about to back down.

"What if Vicky is already in there?" Brian demanded. "What if she had contacted him before you, and Garth was only setting you up to try and draw you into whatever she's mixed up in? Did you think of that?"

She had thought of that, but there was only one answer for it. "It doesn't matter. She's my sister, if there's the smallest chance she's in there, I'm going."

"So am I," Ian said.

"No, the three of you have children and mates, or you're soon to have children. If something goes wrong, I'm sure David and I will figure out some way of letting you know." Her attention turned to Brian when he stepped closer to her. "Please don't make me break my promise to you. This is *Vicky*. I can't... You don't know how much she means to me. It would be devastating to me if something were to happen to her."

There went his plans for throttling her sister, but he still didn't like the idea of her going into that building with only one other vamp. He ran a hand through his hair, tugging at the ends of it as he wrestled to keep himself under control.

"Abby, you're not keeping us from going inside," Ethan said.

Abby turned to face him. "If you die, so will Emma. Maybe she'll be able to last until your child is born, but she would follow shortly after." Ethan flinched at her words as his eyes flickered red. "Besides, I'm sure it will be a lot easier for me and David to get in there without an entourage of large male vamps following us."

Ethan, Ian, and Stefan looked completely torn, but she'd struck on the one thing none of them could ever sacrifice, the life of their mate.

"And what about me?" Brian inquired. "If something happens to you in there, what happens to me?"

Abby winced, her heart twisting as tears burned her eyes. "I won't let anything happen to me."

"Abigail—"

"I won't," she insisted. "If I think there's any threat to my safety, you will come first. I'll leave immediately, but David can't get in there without me, and if we all go storming in there, it could get someone killed; it could get Vicky killed. This is the safest way, and if I wasn't your mate, you would happily use me as an option."

"But you are my mate."

"And I am still the best option."

Brian's breath exploded out of him as he swung away from her and paced toward the corner of the building. She hated the stress she could feel radiating from him, but she couldn't back down. Spinning away from the building, he stalked back toward her. She braced herself for him to toss her over his shoulder and carry her away from here. Her brothers wouldn't protest the action; they'd probably happily follow along, smiling at her the whole time.

Abby shifted her stance as she prepared to punch him and run for the warehouse. He stopped before her, stress radiating from the lines etched around his eyes, but an amused quirk lifted his mouth as he took in her fighting stance. "Can you wait an hour?" he asked.

She folded her arms over her chest as she tried to figure out what his ploy was. "I'm not going to change my mind."

"I don't expect you to. I'm just going to get you more help."

"Who?"

"Aiden."

"They wouldn't let me talk to him before."

"They'll let me."

"Where he is?"

"They have a training facility outside of the city. He can be here in no time. Either that, or I will take your brother's side in this, and I will remove you from here. If you're willing to break your promise, so am I. I compromised, it's your turn."

Abby felt the body heat from her brothers and Stefan as they closed in around her. She barely managed to keep herself from rolling her eyes, *men*.

It was only a little longer before Aiden could be here, and she had to admit she'd feel a lot better having someone else to go into that building with her and David. If Brian could compromise, she could too.

"Call him," she said.

~

AIDEN ARRIVED LESS than an hour after Brian called him. They'd waited until he joined them before filling him in on the rest of the details of what was going on.

"Will you get in trouble for being here?" Abby asked anxiously as she embraced her brother.

Aiden's strong arms wrapped around her, and he pulled her close. "Family comes first, always."

"What did you tell them in order to get out?" Ethan asked.

"I was meeting my brothers for some drinks, so you have to buy me a few rounds when this is over. I can't be a liar."

"Deal," Ian said.

"They let you out for that?" Abby asked.

"The complete lockdown portion of my training is over." Aiden's gaze turned to the run-down building across the street. "There is no way Vicky is in there."

"We've already established it's a possibility," Abby said as she stepped from her brother's embrace.

She couldn't believe how much he'd changed in the past six months. He'd always been muscular, but now he was solid muscle and broader through the chest and shoulders. His black hair had been shaved into a buzz cut; his leaf green eyes were assessing as he studied the building. He looked like he'd joined the Marines, but then she supposed Ronan's men were the vampire equivalent of the military.

"There's no way they're going to believe you're an addict," she said to him. "You look far too healthy."

"Hate to break it to you, Abs, but you're not looking like shit tonight either."

"That might be the nicest thing you've ever said to me," she muttered.

Wrapping his arm around her neck, he pulled her close to give her a noogie. "Won't happen again," he assured her.

"Cut it out," she said and shoved against him. Though she had to admit there was something comforting in the familiar torment of her older brother.

He chuckled as he released her. Abby gave him a death stare while she straightened her matted hair. Brian had taken a step closer to them when Aiden grabbed her. She reached out to take hold of his hand before thinking better of it and letting her hand fall back to her side. She'd been more intimate with him than anyone else in her life, but their relationship wasn't an openly affectionate one.

They were mates, she didn't deny it, but public displays of affection weren't exactly their way. The members of her family, who were mated, were always touching and kissing each other, but they were also in love, and she didn't kid herself into believing Brian felt that way about her. She didn't know how she felt about him either, so at least they were even on that front.

"Weapons?" Brian asked.

Aiden pulled back his ankle-length, black coat to reveal the stakes tucked discreetly inside and the small crossbow strapped against the side of his chest. Brian nodded before turning to her and handing her a couple of stakes. After they'd been attacked in the hotel room, Stefan had taken it upon himself to teach all the members of the family self-defense and how to kill another vamp; she'd always hated handling the weapons.

David tapped the two stakes tucked into his waistband before pulling his jacket over them. "We should get going."

Brian grabbed hold of her wrist, tugging her back when she set the hood of her coat over her head. He grabbed the edges of the hood; his eyes burned into hers as he fought to keep himself from changing his mind.

"If anything goes wrong in there, you run. No matter what," he told her.

"I will," she promised.

He pulled her back when she went to step away again. The torn expression on his face caused her to wrap her hands around his. He'd already experienced so much loss in his life; she didn't know if he could take another blow if something were to happen to her. She hated that she was putting him through this, but she had to find her sister.

"This is a promise I will keep. I will run out of there, for you, if anything goes wrong," she assured him.

"I'll throw her over my shoulder and drag her ass out of there if it becomes necessary," Aiden vowed. "We're already down one sister, I won't let it be two."

Abby smiled tremulously at Brian as she squeezed his hands. "See, and Aiden is a pureblood with some kind of vamp military training. David is in his fifties, and I'm a pureblood, so we have a lot of power behind us."

She tried to move away, but Brian kept his hands firmly on her hood, holding her in place. His reddened eyes searched her face. "Brian—"

Before she could finish, he jerked her close and took hold of her lips in a possessive kiss that had her melting as the world lurched beneath her feet. Unable to resist, her mouth opened to the tender probing of his tongue as he tasted her in deep, penetrating waves. So much for her opinion on his views about PDA. Dazed, she swayed toward him when he broke off the kiss.

Brian rested his forehead against hers. "Any longer than fifteen minutes, and I'm coming in after you."

"Got it," she said, still trying to regain control of her quaking body.

He reluctantly released her hood. Abby fought the urge to touch her lips as she took a hesitant step away. Turning, she noticed her brothers had become extremely focused on the façade of the building.

"Let's go," she murmured.

David and Aiden stepped out from the building with her and hurried across the potholed street to the building across the way. Shadows danced across the asphalt as the street lights illuminated the quiet city street. She fought against looking back at Brian, but lost the battle. His eyes were a fiery red in the night as he watched her. Stefan's hand rested on his shoulder, holding him back from following after her. She could feel the battle he waged with himself to let her go, a battle that had her debating running back to him and throwing her arms around him. He'd probably never let her go if she did. She forced herself to turn away before she did exactly that.

Please let Vicky be in here. She needed this to end, for her sanity as well as Brian's.

Stepping up to the front door, she kept her face impassive as a large vampire with skin the color of chocolate and eyes to match stepped from the shadows. Beside her, Aiden stiffened as the putrid scent of a landfill washed off the man. She'd never smelled a vampire so rotten before.

Abby fought the urge to wrinkle her nose and press her finger under it to block the sickening stench. She suspected most who entered this building couldn't smell the man, and those who did, showed no reaction to it. David, unable to smell it, still eyed the man like he was a bug he was contemplating squishing.

"What do you want?" the vamp demanded.

"We're here for the party." Abby decided to go with something close to what she'd said to Garth. The guard's eyes narrowed on her. Before he could say something more, Abby blurted, "Bubblegum."

He glanced at Aiden and David. "They're my friends. You can trust them," she hurriedly assured him.

"Can I now?" the man murmured, but he stepped aside to let them pass.

Abby elbowed Aiden in the ribs when he stared the man down as they entered the old warehouse. Her brother didn't flinch, but he tore his eyes away from the guard. Instead of stepping into a large center room like she'd expected, they entered into a dimly lit hallway. Goose bumps broke out on her arms. The full-on creeps took her over when she accidentally brushed against the walls while they moved down the hall. She kept her arms forward and her shoulders hunched to avoid touching the germy, critter-covered walls again.

"If Vicky's in here, I might kill her myself," Aiden muttered. "Ronan has to know about this place."

"He destroys the vampires mixed up in this," Abby protested. "If we don't find her here, he could find her before us."

"There's a reason they're killed, Abby. You smelled that guy at the door. That wasn't a one or two humans killed scent like Ethan and Brian had. That was a full-on 'I've killed more people than cancer' stench."

Abby huddled deeper into her coat. "What about Vicky?"

"Have you considered there may be no saving her?"

"Aiden," David said in a warning tone from behind her when she gasped and shook her head fiercely back and forth.

Aiden held his hands up in a gesture of peace. "I'm only saying it's a possibility she may not want to be saved. After encountering that guy back there, it may be a very good one if she's mixed up in the same stuff as him. I love her too, and I'd do anything to save her, but I've seen a lot more since joining Ronan's group. Some of us can't be saved, no matter how badly we'd like to try to help them. Sometimes it's kindest to let them go, for all involved."

Abby struggled against the tears burning her throat and the constriction in her chest. "No," she said. "I've never considered it, and I won't."

She forced her attention away from her brother as more light filtered into the hall. The walls fell away from her as she followed Aiden into a room the likes of which she'd never thought to see in her life. Aiden's muscles tensed and a tremor ran through him. His eyes blazed a fiery red color as he gazed at the debauchery before them.

"Aiden." She rested her hand on his arm, uncertain if she was trying to hold him back from killing everyone in this room or from joining in with them. Would she lose two siblings to this place? The possibility sent a cold chill of terror down her spine. She'd never once considered that something could happen to Aiden in here too. He'd always been so strong and confident that it had seemed impossible. Now, she wasn't so sure.

Aiden shook his head, but his fangs remained elongated, and his eyes continued to glisten like rubies. David stared at him over the top of her head; his face tensed as her brother took a step back.

Ian had told her the purebred males of their species experienced maturation differently than the females. Often a hunger for different things would arise in them that they grappled to control until they found their mates. He'd said some of the women purebloods experienced it on a smaller level, but for the males, it became a nearly all-consuming impulse that drove them every day.

She tried to recall his exact words. *Ronan told us some of us crave pain, others copious amounts of blood, some cannot have enough sex, some lock themselves away from humans to resist the temptation, and others give in and kill in order to make it stop. Some experience all of those things.*

She hadn't asked Ian what it had been like for him. She'd seen the vast amount of women who had come and gone from his life before Paige, and he'd tried to keep that part of his life hidden from her. Ethan had withdrawn with Issy; however, there had always been a darker side to him, but what of Aiden?

Aiden had always been easygoing, quick to smile and laugh. He'd never had a parade of women like Ian, never been distant or as overprotective as Ethan. He'd screamed and cried when he'd broken his arm, years ago, finding no enjoyment in the pain. She had no idea what had taken hold of Aiden after hitting maturity, but it didn't matter; all aspects of those things were somehow incorporated into this room.

In the corners, and in the middle of the floor, couples and groups were having sex. To her right was a human male tied to a post while a woman sliced open his skin and drank the blood trickling from the lacerations. Others were screaming in agony from another hallway on the opposite side of the room. Everywhere she looked, vampires were feeding. The room stank of blood and the potent smell of refuse as the killing vampires drank greedily from their drugged prey.

Lights flashed above them, illuminating the room in strobes like a haunted house. The slurping sounds and cries of pleasure and torment made her long to slap her hands over her ears and block it all out. She'd known her species could be sadistic and brutal. She'd almost been killed when she was fifteen by vampires looking to feed, but this was worse than anything she could have ever imagined.

Why did the humans come here? There was a pile of their remains in the corner. Were they that desperate for drugs, or had they also been promised a chance at immortality to lure them in? She had a feeling it was a combination of both.

Not Vicky. Not here.

Aiden shuddered beside her and his eyes closed as his hands fisted.

"We should go." The words croaked from her throat. Her entire body screamed against leaving here without searching for her sister. This was the closest they'd ever been. However, Aiden looked to be unraveling before her eyes, and she'd be damned if she lost another sibling to this atrocious lifestyle.

"Yes," David said. He grabbed hold of Aiden's shoulder, but Aiden waved him off. "Aiden, we have to go."

"We'll search for Vicky first," he said in a voice so hoarse it sounded as if he'd been chewing on glass.

"Aiden—" she started.

"I'm fine, Abs. I can control it. It's what I've been working on."

But is he ready? There was only one way they were going to get the answer to that question as he stepped away from her and further into the macabre room.

She cast David a frightened look. "He'll be fine," David said, but he didn't sound convinced of it.

CHAPTER TWENTY-ONE

Brian paced anxiously back and forth beside the building, tugging at his hair with one hand as he glanced at his watch for the hundredth time since they'd gone inside. Only two minutes had passed, but it felt like an eternity.

"I should have gone with her," he muttered as he pulled at his hair again. "We could have slaughtered every vamp in there."

"There could be a hundred in there," Stefan replied.

"You're not helping!" Brian pulled back his arm and punched the warehouse beside them, shattering the brick. He barely acknowledged his broken and bloody knuckles. They would heal. He would not if something were to happen to her. He spun back toward where Abby had disappeared and took a step after her.

"Talk to her through the bond. It will help keep you calm and assured of her safety," Stefan said.

"I can't," Brian muttered. "The bond's not completed."

"Shit," Ian muttered.

Stefan stepped forward. "You can still sense her, believe me, I know. I sensed Issy was in danger before our bond was completed. You can do it too. Focus on her. She's fed from you." Brian hadn't bothered to cover the bite mark on his neck. There was no need to; she was his, and everyone would know it. "That will help you to connect with her."

Brian stopped pacing and turned to face the warehouse again as three more humans hurried up the stairs to the massive vamp standing outside the door. He mentally searched the building and himself for any hint of distress from Abby. The minute she was out of there, with or without her sister, he was taking her someplace private and completing the bond. He'd never be shut off from her again.

After what had transpired between them in the alley, he'd intended to seal the bond as soon as they'd returned to her hotel room. However, by the time he'd been able to secure blood from the hospital and they'd returned to the hotel, her family had only been an hour away, and there was no way his first time with her was going to be a quickie. No, he would savor her body for hours, days if he could. Once at the hotel, he'd settled for another cold shower, but he regretted that choice now. Not knowing what was going on in there was going to drive him mad.

He could feel her in there, but he got no other impressions from her. "Nothing," he muttered.

"That's not a bad thing," Stefan replied. "It simply means she's safe. You'll know if she's not."

"I hope so," he replied as he resumed his pacing. He glanced at his watch again, three minutes. He didn't think he could take another twelve minutes of this. "I might kill your sister for putting Abby through this," he shot at her brothers.

"You might have to get in line," Ethan replied, his eyes focused on the building. "Especially if they don't come back out."

Beside him, Ian nodded in agreement. "We may have just sacrificed three more to save one," he murmured.

What was I thinking to agree to this? Keeping her happy was one thing, keeping her alive was far more important. Brian swore as he started toward the warehouse. Stefan grabbed hold of his arm, pulling him back before he could storm across the street and unleash Hell upon everyone in there.

"You told her fifteen minutes," Stefan reminded him.

"I lied," he snarled at him.

He jerked his arm free of Stefan's hold and stepped off the curb toward the warehouse when he caught a new scent on the wind. Turning to face them, he spotted the red eyes of at least a dozen vampires approaching from behind Stefan and the others. They must have caught the scent of them too as their heads turned to look behind them.

Trap! His mind screamed at him. *Abby! They'd set her up, and now they had her.*

His gaze shot to the warehouse Abby had entered; bloodlust surged through him as the vampires pounced.

~

ABBY STEPPED over the body of a human who was as close to death as one could be while still breathing. As the breath passed in and out from between the human's blue lips, it sounded worse than a baby's rattle. *Look away. There's nothing you can do for her right now.*

She forced her attention away from the dying woman and back to the writhing, screwing, keening crowd around her. What were they doing here? Maybe Vicky really didn't want to be found. She obviously had something to do with this life, if Garth so easily recognized her face and name.

But why, and what is she doing involved in this mess?

They'd had a wonderful life growing up; they'd never known anything but love. No one had ever abused or mistreated them, and if someone had tried, they would have faced the full wrath of their family. Vicky had always been outgoing, popular, and happy. She hadn't liked school as much as Abby, but she'd done well enough to get by. She'd always been invited to more parties than Abby, had more friends, and been the center of attention.

Had those numerous parties been her undoing? Had what Abby assumed was good fun been masking a deeper need? Abby didn't want to believe it, but she didn't know what to believe in this chaotic and messed up world surrounding her.

A single tear slid down her cheek, but she didn't know if she was crying for the sad souls surrounding her, the brother who was battling against his demons beside her, or the sister she missed so desperately. A sister who may, or may not, have abandoned her and their family for this sort of lifestyle without so much as a good-bye.

A clearly intoxicated human woman stumbled into their path, nearly colliding with Aiden who bared his fangs at her. Instead of being put off by the display of promised violence, the woman smiled and batted her lashes invitingly at him. Abby's stomach twisted at the sight of her black and rotten teeth.

"Get away from me!" Aiden spat at the woman, his eyes blazing a ferocious shade of red and his muscles rippling. The woman grimaced before scurrying into the shadows.

Beads of sweat dotted Aiden's brow as he focused on the hallway across from them again. Finally breaking free of the crowd, they slipped into another hall. Screams and cries reverberated against the walls surrounding them. Never had she longed for Brian as badly as she did right now. His arms may be the only thing that could help erase the hideousness of all she was seeing and hearing.

Aiden reached into his coat and tugged his crossbow free. "We're going to have to start opening doors to see if she's in one of these rooms."

"Wait," Abby said and pointed down the hall toward a set of stairs enshrouded in the gloom at the end. "We should probably check up there before we start alerting everyone that we're not exactly here for the party."

He nodded his agreement, and they walked down the hall to the stairs. Abby's heart hammered as every step up they took creaked beneath their weight. When they reached the top, Aiden pressed his ear against the closed door. His brow furrowed as he listened to whatever was happening on the other side.

"I don't hear anything but stay behind me," he said to Abby.

She pulled one of her stakes free. Turning the knob, Aiden pushed the door open to reveal a large space the same size as the downstairs. The two vampires closest to the door whimpered before scuttling into the shadows where they huddled against the wall. Their chains clattered against the wooden floor, they shook as they drew their knees against their chests.

The smell of terror oozed from the vampires as their frightened eyes followed them into the room. "What the fuck?" Aiden murmured.

Abby's gaze fell on a woman about her height, but she weighed a good thirty pounds less than she did. The woman's collarbone stood out against her dirt-streaked, pale flesh. Abby could count every rib on the woman's hundred-pound frame due to the fact she was wearing nothing but a bra. Abby didn't catch the rancid scent of drugs or death on her, only the sour stench of never-ending fear.

Beneath the layers of dirt, Abby realized the woman was covered in bite marks. Aiden hissed beside her, and David cursed as he took a step toward the woman who immediately scooted away from his approach.

"No more," the woman whimpered in a pitiful voice that broke Abby's heart.

"Jesus," Aiden said. "What is going on here?"

"Aiden?" the weak voice came from the shadows at the back of the room.

Abby's heart leapt into her throat at the sound of that voice. Without thinking, she shoved past her brother and raced by the other vampires in the room who scampered away from her.

"Abby, wait!" Aiden commanded from behind her.

She wasn't waiting for anyone though as she continued onward. Then, through the darkness, she spotted someone at the end of the building. Instead of scurrying into the shadows, Vicky surged forward, tears streaming down her face as she strained against the chains binding her.

"Abby!" she cried.

Abby fell before her, unaware that tears streaked her own face until they fell upon her sister and left clear trails in the dirt covering her. She'd never felt so relieved or happy in her life. "Vicky!"

She threw her arms around her twin, pulling her close against her and sobbing openly as Vicky's emaciated body quaked against hers. Beneath the layers of sweat and dirt, the scent of garbage wafted from her sister. Shock rippled through Abby, but what had caused that scent was something they could deal with at another time. They had to get Vicky free of these bindings and out of here first.

Pulling away, she grabbed at the steel cuffs secured around Vicky's thin wrists. Blood and bruises marred Vicky's chaffed skin from straining against her bonds.

"They don't break," Vicky whispered. "I've tried everything, but they won't give out. I don't know what they're made of, but they're designed to keep a pureblood restrained."

Vicky lifted her head to look at Abby. Her identical green eyes shimmered with tears when they met Abby's. "You have to go, Abby. They'll be coming soon, and you can't be here when they do."

"Not without you," Abby promised as she yanked at the cuffs again.

Aiden fell to his knees beside her. "What have you gotten yourself into now?" he asked Vicky as he pushed Abby's hands aside to grab at one of the metal cuffs. He'd be able to break it; Abby was certain of that, but as Aiden tugged at the metal, it refused to give. "What the—?"

"They're designed specifically to keep a pureblood restrained," Vicky told him.

Aiden released the cuff and leaned back to study the chain going to the large bolts in the wall behind Vicky. The chain ran through the manacles at her wrists, allowing for about three inches of space between Vicky's wrists. Standing, Aiden grabbed hold of the chain and gave it a violent yank, but it remained secured to the wall.

"You *have* to go," Vicky said again. Her gaze darted toward the door. "They'll be here soon. Abby, go."

"Who will be here soon?" Abby demanded.

"The vampires who imprisoned us." Vicky pushed against her. "Go."

"No."

She rose to her feet. Behind Aiden, she grabbed hold of the chain with both hands. They both planted their feet against the wall and pulled back as hard as they could on the bolts holding it in place. Her arms strained as sweat beaded across her brow and slid down her cheeks. She might tear her arms from their sockets, but she wasn't going to give up until Vicky was freed.

David grabbed the rest of the chain behind her, adding his strength as they pulled against the bolt in the wall. A low screeching sound filled the air before the chain gave way with a pop. The abrupt release caused Abby to fall backward. She tripped over David's feet, taking them both down. She found herself sprawled on top of him on the floor. Aiden fell on top of her, his elbow jabbing her in the gut. The breath exploded out of her, and she instinctively curled in on herself.

Her pain vanished when she realized they'd managed to pull Vicky free. Her sister lifted her hands and laughed as she brought her wrists before her face. Around them, the other chained vampires crept forward, their eyes wide and hopeful. Vicky threw herself forward, wrapping her arms around her three rescuers who were still on the floor where they had landed.

Abby eagerly hugged her back as she tried to free herself from her brother's weight. "We have to go," Aiden said as he rose to his feet. "Now."

"We have to set *her* free first," David said as he extricated himself from the bottom of the pile.

Vicky kept her arms around Abby as she lifted her head to look around the room. "We can't leave them," Vicky whispered. "They're purebloods, like us."

"All of them?" Abby asked as she gazed at the six vampires peering at them from the shadows.

There were only a little over a hundred purebloods in existence. As far as she knew, the highest concentration of them was her family. Then there were Ronan's men, though she had no idea how many of them there were. The number of purebloods could have grown over the years, but how had they gotten so many purebloods in this room, and why were they all chained to the walls?

"All of them," Vicky confirmed.

"This way," David said and jerked his head toward the front of the room.

He hurried back to the first woman Abby had seen cowering in the shadows. The woman crept a little closer to them as they walked down to join David. Abby cringed when she spotted those raw bite marks again. A glance at her sister's neck confirmed she also had bite marks on her. She didn't know about elsewhere as Vicky was still wearing a dirty, red sweater that hugged a frame much thinner since Abby had seen her last.

Abby reluctantly released her sister to take hold of the chain behind David. "How did you find me?" Vicky asked as she grabbed the chain beside Abby.

"Brian helped me," she whispered.

Vicky did a double take; her startled green eyes appeared larger and brighter due to her weight loss and the dark circles under them. "He must really hate our family. We're always dragging him into shit."

Aiden snorted. "There's at least one in our family he likes," he said with a pointed look at Abby.

Abby pretended not to notice her sister's questioning gaze as she braced her leg against the wall and gave a forceful heave. They all teetered as the bolt worked its way out before releasing with another pop. This time, Abby managed to keep herself from falling as she danced out of the way of the others.

"Thank you," the woman murmured. Tears streaked her face when she threw herself into David's arms. David seemed to have no idea what to do with the crying stranger; he patted her back awkwardly while she clung to him.

"Us too?" the vampire beside her whispered.

His chains rattled when he stretched his thin arms toward them. Abby's stomach curdled when she realized he couldn't be much older than thirteen. Sorrow twisted in her chest at the sight of his bruised and battered body.

"What is going on here?" Abby demanded.

"Hell is going on here," Vicky replied as she hurried toward the boy.

Abby glanced at her watch. Her heart sank when she realized they only had three minutes left and five more vampires to release before Brian and her brothers came in here. They would never be able to free them all in time. Pulling her phone from her pocket, she hastily typed him a text.

We're fine. Be out soon. Won't be coming out the front door. Have Vicky. Stay outside.

She had no idea how they would be getting out of here with all these vamps, but they could figure that out once they were all freed. Grabbing hold of the boy's chain, she planted her foot again and gave a mighty jerk.

The chain had just clattered free when a baritone voice spoke from the doorway, "Look at what we have here."

Abby froze and a chill ran down her spine when Vicky trembled violently beside her. The woman who had thrown herself into David's arms pulled away to slink into the shadows. A low whimper came from her as she sat on the floor and drew her legs against her chest once more. Abby released the boy's chain, letting it fall to the floor as she braced herself to face whomever had joined them.

Turning, her heart sank when she spotted the numerous vampires standing in the doorway with their eyes glistening the color of blood.

CHAPTER TWENTY-TWO

Brian hit the first vampire who lunged at him. The vampire's nose broke beneath the force of his blow, but the six-ten, four-hundred-and-fifty-pound beast kept coming at him. Brian dodged to the side, and the vamp's fingers slid down his back, tearing his shirt and skin open. A grunt of anger escaped him when he scented his own blood on the air, but he spun around and slammed his fist straight into the throat of the next vamp lunging at him.

Skin and cartilage gave way beneath the punch. The vamp tried to howl, but only gurgling sounds escaped his mutilated windpipe. Brian lifted his foot and drove it straight into the vamp's stomach, sending him flying backward as the sumo-wrestler-sized vampire wrapped his arms around him from behind.

The crack of one of his ribs reverberated in the air. He gritted his teeth against the discomfort and swung his head back, bashing it off of Sumo's forehead. The impact caused stars to dance before his eyes, but he managed to retain consciousness. The vampire took a staggering step back. Before he could recover, Brian banged the back of his head off his nose again.

Sumo's grip on him lessened enough that Brian was able to get his arms up between them to break his hold. To his right, Stefan staggered back as two vamps leapt at him with their fangs extended. Ian and Ethan had their backs to each other as they fended off five more vamps. Both of them had taken on the reddish black hue that tinged the skin of a pureblood in a rage.

Ian grabbed one of the vamps and sank his fangs into his neck. The vampire howled as he beat at Ian's face, but Ian tore his fangs away before twisting the vamp's head all the way around. The vamp staggered back before falling to the ground.

Brian tugged his stake free and drove it into the chest of the one whose throat he'd ruined. Before the vampire finished twitching in death, Brian turned and leapt onto the back of Sumo vamp. Wrapping his arms around Sumo's neck, he jerked his head back and sank his fangs into the hefty vamp's throat.

Warm blood spurted into his mouth, but whereas before he'd thrived on the rush of power that came from a vampire's blood and the thrill of the kill—especially one such as this vamp, whose blood told him he'd done his fair share of killing both human and vampires in his day—now it was a means to an end.

He grabbed hold of the bastard's throat, biting deeper as he tore his flesh away in an attempt to bleed him out faster. The vamp staggered backward, crushing Brian against the warehouse behind him. Releasing his bite, he held on as the vamp leaned forward then bashed him into the wall again.

More of his ribs cracked, but he refused to give into the pain. Grabbing Sumo's head, he wrenched his neck to the side before the large vamp could turn him into a pancake. Bone cracked and gave way beneath Brian's hand. Weakened by blood loss and the severing of his spine, the massive vamp finally fell to the ground. Brian drove his stake through his back before leaping off him. He stood over Sumo's corpse, his shoulders heaving as he spun to face the next threat.

Ethan and Ian were dispatching the last of their vampires. Both of them resembled some of the paintings of Satan he'd seen over the years. Their skin was mottled red and black in color, their shoulders heaving as blood dripped from their lips, but they were still in control of themselves as they wiped the blood from their mouths.

Stefan yanked a stake from the back of another. He rested his hands on his thighs as he turned to stare at them. "I'm going in," Brian said.

Nothing was going to stop him from going after Abby now. He still didn't sense any distress from her, but he wasn't going to take any chances, not after what had just occurred. He'd only taken one step when his phone vibrated in his pocket. He almost ignored it, but this was Abby's only way of communicating with him right now. If it was her and he ignored her message...

He pulled his phone free to see Abby's message. "Who is it?" Ian demanded, his skin already returning to its tanned hue when he stepped beside Brian.

Brian held the phone toward him as he studied the warehouse. What if he went in there and got her hurt?

∽

ABBY PUSHED her battered sister behind her as Aiden stepped before them both. "Twins," one of the vampires murmured and had the nerve to lick his lips.

David moved toward the woman they'd freed when she released a low whimper. The boy scuttled through the shadows behind Aiden and further past her and Vicky. Abby had no idea what was going on here, but she'd never been more terrified in her life. She could actually taste the sour fear radiating from the chained and battered vampires surrounding them.

Sweat beaded across her brow and slid down her back, sticking her sweater to her flesh. Her heart beat so fast, she was certain she would have had a heart attack if she'd been human. Her gaze slid to the boarded over windows. From the outside, it looked as if they were covered by wood, but she now realized the windows were covered by a sheet of steel. There would be no busting out the boards and leaping from the windows. More vampires came up the stairs and fanned out behind the first one.

"What do we do?" Vicky whispered.

"We fight through them," Aiden replied. "It's the only option we have."

It wasn't the greatest of options, considering most of their allies were chained to the walls. The woman was too weak to fight and the boy and Vicky both looked like they were going to drop at any second. However, fighting against them was far better than being chained to a wall too, something she knew these vamps had every intention of doing if they got their hands on them.

"Take them alive, until we know if they're pure or not," the ugly, lead vamp instructed.

Abby slid her hand into her coat and pulled out a stake. She would fight to the death before she ever let them slap those chains around her. *Brian*. Her text to him may have bought her some time, but if she didn't leave this building soon, he would come in after her. When he did, they'd kill him, just like she believed they'd kill David if they realized he wasn't a pureblood. Her heart turned over at the thought, and her hand tightened around the stake as she shifted her stance.

She couldn't let them take any more of the people she loved. Aiden tugged his crossbow free and pointed it at the first vampire. "You think you're going to kill me with that?" the vamp inquired.

"No, I think I'm going to kill you with my bare hands. This is to give you a little tickle," Aiden replied.

Abby gulped. Before she knew what was happening, Aiden fired the crossbow and leapt forward. She wasn't a fighter, had always been more of a 'stick her nose in a book' kind of girl. Now she wished she'd paid a little more attention to Stefan when he'd been trying to teach them self-defense.

Aiden smashed his shoulder into the first vamp, driving the bolt from his crossbow deeper into the man's arm. David rushed in behind him, his fists flying as he pummeled one of the vampires before another kicked his legs out from under him. One of the vampires punched Aiden in the face, causing blood to spill from his broken nose. The sight of that blood caused fury to burst hotly through Abby.

No one hurt her siblings, and these bastards had chained Vicky to a wall and done God only knew what to her, and now they'd caused Aiden to bleed. Without thinking, she leapt onto the back of the first, ugly vamp Aiden had been fighting. Going on instinct alone, she yanked his head back and sank her fangs into his throat. Hot blood rushed into her mouth, but unlike Brian's blood, this guy tasted horribly bitter.

Pulling her head back, she spat out the offensive blood. The vamp reached behind him and landed a blow against the side of her cheek. Stars burst before her eyes, and her hands slipped on his shoulders. Aiden swung his arm out and slammed his stake deep into the vampire's heart. With his other hand, he grabbed Abby's arm and yanked her away from the vamp crumbling beneath her.

The fall of their leader didn't deter the other vampires as they slashed their way forward. David jumped out of the way in time to avoid a blow that would have eviscerated him. Aiden spun her to the side when someone swung a stake at her. The stake that would have plunged into the center of her chest embedded in his upper shoulder.

Aiden grunted and threw his other arm back, seizing the vamp by the throat and heaving him across the room. The vampire crashed into the wall, shaking the building on its foundation with enough force that Abby worried it might collapse when dust and debris rained down on them from the rafters. David edged toward them to press his back against hers.

Abby adjusted her hold on the stake as the remaining fourteen vamps encircled them. They barely flicked a glance at the three who had been freed from the wall and Abby understood why. The beaten-down, freed vampires would be easy enough for them to recapture and would offer little fight now.

Chum in the water. That's what they were and these bastards were the sharks circling them.

"At least the girl is pure," one of them said and flicked his fingers at Abby.

"Make that two," Aiden stated, drawing the vampire's attention to him.

Aiden smiled back at him and gave a 'come on' wiggle of his fingers. Abby gulped again. She knew her brothers could be a little crazy, but she was beginning to think Aiden might be certifiable.

The vampire grinned back at him. "I'm going to enjoy chaining you down."

"If you bring a whip, I might enjoy it too," Aiden shot back.

Yep, he's insane.

David moved to position himself so he was in front of the freed woman too. Through the wall of vamps, she caught a glimpse of Vicky leading the young boy toward the door. The vampires encircling them had left the exit exposed, but there was no way Abby, David and Aiden were going to make it through them and to that door with the woman.

Abby hoped her sister followed the boy out of here and didn't look back, but Vicky pushed the boy toward the stairs and spun back into the room. She kept her chain in hand, silencing it as she circled behind the vamps.

Run, Vicky, she inwardly pleaded. There was no reason for all of them to be trapped here, and if Vicky got to Brian and the others, she could tell them what was going on so they could bring back help.

As one, and without any indication it would happen, the vampires pounced on them. Abby swung out wildly, hoping to connect with a punch against one of these monsters as they grabbed at her. She bit her lip to keep from crying out when a hand wrapped into her hair and jerked her forward.

Torn off her feet, her legs kicked in the air as she fought to land a blow against the monster holding her. It was impossible as he held her in the air before him to avoid her kicks. Her hair had to give out eventually, didn't it? But no, it remained attached to her skull. Pain radiated out from her roots and tears involuntarily burned her eyes as the man carried her from the center of the fray.

"Abby!" Aiden bellowed.

He leapt toward her, but four vampires fell on him, pushing him back as they landed blow after punishing blow on him. Agony exploded through her head when some of her hair gave way. She lashed out and finally succeeded in kicking her attacker dead center in the crotch.

He grunted and bent over to grasp himself, but he didn't release his hold on her. Vicky ran forward. Swinging her chain out, she smashed it against the man's shins. He grunted from the force of the impact and staggered to the side, but when Vicky swung at him again, he caught the chain and dragged her against him.

"Bitch!" he spat before bashing his hand against the side of Vicky's head.

"No!" Abby screamed when her sister crumpled to the ground.

Her kicking and punching intensified, but the man held her away from him, shaking her head back and forth like a rag doll. The bellow that ripped through the air shook the building and caused the man holding her to stop his incessant shaking. Abby tried to get her bearings, but she didn't have enough time before a blur crashed into the man's side.

She and the vampire were thrown back from the force of the impact. The man tumbled to the ground, slamming Abby down with him. The snap of her rib and its sharp edge digging into her right side caused her to cry out. She attempted to roll away, but the bastard still had her hair wrapped around his hand.

She grabbed hold of his hand to try to free his hold on her as the sound of fists hitting flesh filled her ears. A bone cracked loudly. She had no idea which bone it was, but it caused the man's hand to tighten its hold in her hair. She would gladly rip all of her hair out if it meant being free of him as he jerked with each blow he received and yanked on her as he tried to fend off his attacker. She hadn't seen him yet, but she knew it had to be Brian pulverizing this bastard.

Pulling her head down, she winced and bit on her lip as more of her hair gave way, but she was finally able to free herself from his punishing hold. Rolling to the side, she leapt to her feet and stumbled back. She whimpered when the movement caused her broken rib to dig into her again.

Disbelief filled her when her gaze fell upon Brian on top of the vamp. Blood coated him from head to toe. She realized most of it hadn't been from the man he was beating. The man's face now resembled ground beef, but there was far too much blood on Brian for it to have come from this one guy.

So much blood caked his hair that she could no longer tell what color it was. Red obscured his features and turned his clothes maroon. Berserkers would have run screaming from him, she realized as he punched his hand through the man's chest and tore his heart free. All she wanted was to run *to* him.

He tossed the still-beating organ aside with a flick of his wrist. His head rose, and his eyes burned ruby fire from his blood-streaked face as they ran over her. Abby didn't care that he was covered in blood and appeared on the verge of losing complete control; she ran forward and flung herself at him. He wrapped his arms around her waist, drawing her close against his chest.

"Abby," he breathed in her ear, his blood-coated hands smoothing the hair back from her face.

He jerked suddenly to the side, pulling her beneath him as he rolled rapidly across the floor. Behind them, the entire building quaked as something crashed into the floor. Brian came up against the wall, his hand clasping her head as she looked back at the vampire who had torn a beam from the ceiling and smashed it down where they'd just been.

She gawked at the splintered hole in the floor the beam had created. It seemed the vampires no longer cared about keeping any of them alive, but had decided to do anything necessary to keep witnesses from leaving this place. Brian kept her against him as he leapt to his feet. Behind the vampire who had broken the floor, Ethan rose up. His skin was a mottled red and black color as he broke the vamp's neck.

She glimpsed Ian and Stefan behind him. All of them were caked in blood too, but they were nowhere near as bad as Brian was. She took a step forward, but Brian pushed her back as two more vampires lunged at them. Abby tugged her remaining stake free and stepped to the side as one of the vamps landed a staggering blow against the side of Brian's face.

Her fury over seeing Aiden bleed was nothing compared to the wrath engulfing her at seeing Brian's blood. A scream tore from her as she swung her arm out, driving the stake into the neck of the one who had hit Brian. The vamp's hands flew to the wound in a useless attempt to staunch the blood flow. Abby yanked the stake free of his neck when he stepped back to reveal his chest.

Blood sprayed from his neck as Abby swung the stake forward, plunging it into the man's heart. The other vampire crumpled at Brian's feet, another stake protruding from where Brian had speared him in the chest. Abby heaved in gulping breaths of air as the last vampire in the room fell before David.

Brian spun toward her, his eyes crazed as they ran over her. His fingers traced her face, as he seemed to be reassuring himself she was still here.

"I'm fine," she murmured.

"You're bruised," he said as his hand stilled on her cheek.

"It will fade, the hair will grow back, and my rib is already healing," she told him with a smile. "Really, I'm fine."

Some of the tension finally eased from his face as he cradled her cheek in his palm. A smile curved his mouth as his eyes ran over her blood-splattered frame. His fingers wound into her hair, but when she winced from the soreness of her scalp, he moved his hand down to her nape. Bending his head to hers, his lips brushed tantalizingly over her mouth in a teasing caress that left her yearning for more when he pulled away.

Brian inhaled her sweet scent. The warmth of her body and her bright aura soothed some of the murderous impulses still beating against him. He'd been out of control as he'd carved his way through this warehouse, convinced he was going to lose her, as he'd lost Vivian. Then he'd seen that vampire with his hands on her, *abusing* her, and he'd lost all sense of reason. He'd been enraged and broken after losing his family, but he'd never been as out of control as he'd been tonight.

"It was too close," he murmured against her lips as he resisted his growing impulse to claim her. *Not now, not here. Not like* this!

With those words lodged in his mind, he forced himself to move away from her a little. There were few regrets in his lengthy life, but taking her now, in this place, feeling as volatile as he did, would be near the top of the list. It would sit right alongside of not being able to save his family. He gazed down at her as she watched him, so unaware of the urges pulsing through him, so innocent and trusting of him. He wouldn't do anything to risk that trust.

The blood caked on him had rubbed off against the front of her clothes, her cheeks, and mouth. He reached up to wipe it away but pulled his hands away when another drop of blood fell from his fingertips. "I've tainted you," he murmured.

"Don't," she said when she sensed the distance swelling up within him again. "I am well aware of who and what you are, Brian.

I always have been. You can't change it, and I don't want you to. There's a fair amount of blood staining my hands right now too, and I am just as capable of violence as you are."

Abby didn't wait to hear what else he had to say; she rested her hand against his cheek and rose on her toes to press a tender kiss against his lips. Although she would have preferred to be in his arms, she turned away before he could come up with some protest that would have her contemplating hitting him.

Ian was kneeling at Vicky's side when Abby walked over to join him. "Is she okay?" Abby demanded as she took in her sister's unconscious form.

Ian brushed Vicky's dirt-streaked, stringy hair away from her face to reveal the purple bruises on her skin. His fingers shook as he answered. "She will be."

"What is this place?" Ethan asked.

"We can figure that out later," Aiden replied. "For now, we have to free the rest of these vamps, take care of any survivors or witnesses, and get out of here."

Abby wasn't going to argue with him. She rested her fingers briefly against Vicky's cheek before rising to her feet and hurrying to help the others tear the rest of the chains from the walls.

CHAPTER TWENTY-THREE

ABBY STIRRED, her head coming up when a small whimper woke her from sleep. She'd been fighting to stay awake for the past twelve hours, but at some point, she'd lost the battle and begun to doze. Another whimper drew her eyes to Vicky lying on the massive bed. Abby had cleaned her up the best she could with a washcloth and water as her sister remained unconscious, but her hair was still dirty, and there would be no scrubbing away the faint scent of garbage emanating from her sister's skin.

"What happened to you?" Abby whispered when Vicky stilled again. Leaning forward, she brushed her sister's hair back from her forehead.

The door to the room creaked open, and Brian stepped inside. He'd scrubbed the blood from himself shortly after they'd arrived at the training facility where Aiden was staying. He was paler than normal, and the stubble lining his face was thicker than she'd ever seen it before. The haggard air surrounding him caused a twinge in her heart. She supposed they were all haggard and beaten though; trying to clean up the mess at the warehouse had drained them all.

She'd seen a lot more of what Brian was capable of when they'd reentered the bottom floor of the warehouse. There had been dead vampires and body parts everywhere she'd looked in the warehouse. She understood now the vast quantity of blood coating him and suspected that more of the massacred vampires had fallen at his hand than at any of the others.

The humans had all still been trapped in the warehouse either by the lack of blood in their bodies, their extreme inebriation, or the massive beam that one of her own had thrown in front of the door to keep them from fleeing.

It had taken nearly an hour to change the memories of all the humans. Any surviving vampires had been slaughtered while she remained in the hallway with Vicky's still form in her lap and the other prisoners huddling around her as screams resonated through the hall. Those battered vampires had shaken against her, their whimpers causing grief to rise in her chest as she tried to block out the screams of the dying. She'd felt no sympathy for the vampires who were killed, but she wanted it over. They had to get the prisoners away from whatever torment they'd been forced to endure.

When it was finished and no vampires remained, Brian, Stefan, and Ethan had voted to set the building on fire and burn the remaining humans inside. Aiden had been straddling the fence on the idea, but she, David, and Ian had been adamant on changing their memories instead.

"It may not be killing them by draining their blood, but what if it still makes it so we all smell like a landfill and can't go out in the sunlight anymore?" Abby had reasoned about burning the humans.

"Those are sacrifices I'm willing to make," Brian replied.

Knowing he wouldn't back down, she'd turned to Ethan and Stefan. "Maybe you're willing to make the same sacrifices, but what of your children? What will you tell them when they're old enough to realize what that smell means, or why you can't join them at our annual end of the summer bash? Oh, you know, Daddy decided to torch a warehouse of innocent humans?"

"They're not innocent," Ethan had stated.

"Their fangs weren't sinking into Vicky's flesh. Your children will know that."

"You win," Stefan had muttered.

Ethan had stared at her for a minute before finally bowing his head in consent. "Fine, we'll change their memories."

Outnumbered, Brian had reluctantly agreed to help with the process, but even with all of them working together, they'd walked away beaten and exhausted from the drain on their abilities. The vamps they'd freed from their chains in the warehouse had been brought here with them. They had nowhere else to take them that would be big enough to house them all and keep them safe.

David had flagged down a bus to take them out of the city. With some coercion, the bus driver gave over control of the bus to them with a dazed look in his eyes. Brian and Aiden had insisted the rest of them be blindfolded for the journey. Abby had hated not being able to see anything as Aiden drove, especially after the events that had just unfolded, but she didn't protest when Brian tied a band of cloth around her head. He'd settled in beside her and held her close throughout the trip.

There had also been another reason for bringing all the prisoners here. Brian hoped Aiden's trainer, Lucien, would be able to find a way to remove the chains. So far, they'd had no luck with it, but she could hear the dull ringing of a hammer hitting metal from somewhere in the massive house.

"Did you speak with Ronan?" she inquired of Brian when he came closer. Apprehension clawed at her heart, and her body tensed as she awaited his answer. What if Ronan decided Brian wasn't worth the effort of keeping around and killed him for not telling him about what he'd discovered sooner? What if he decided to punish them both by keeping them apart?

She'd rather die, she realized, and she'd do so by going after Ronan herself. It didn't matter he would likely destroy her; she would make him regret that decision before her life ended.

"I did," Brian said.

"Was he mad?"

"Infuriated. I will be made to pay."

Her heart leapt into her throat, and her hand stilled on her sister's forehead as he walked over to her. "How?"

He rested his hands on her shoulders. "I'll have to do some free missions for a while, but he's not going to kill or imprison me."

"You intend to keep working for him?" She didn't know what he'd envisioned doing after this was over and done. Didn't know if he expected her to go back to her family while he stopped by when he could, or if he expected her to stay somewhere else. She hadn't thought about what she would do either now that she had Vicky back. He rubbed at her shoulders, but his touch did nothing to ease her anxiety.

"This has been my life for a long time. Even if I wanted to walk away, I have no choice right now. I either do this, or he *will* kill me."

"No," she breathed. "I will do it. I will work for him. I dragged you into this, so I will suffer the consequences for it. It shouldn't have to be you. I can kill. I did it last night." She'd hated it, hated the blood on her hands, but this should be her punishment, and she would gladly endure it, for him.

Brian's hands froze on her shoulders. "No, you will not. I agreed to help you with this and kept quiet on what we discovered all while knowing what the consequences could be. This way of life is nothing new for me. I simply won't be earning money from it for a time, but I have plenty of that."

"But—"

"No buts," he said forcefully. "I will *not* have you mixed up in this. I have bent on so many things with you, but not this. You nearly died because I went against my better judgement in the warehouse—"

"I'm fine!" she blurted.

The thunderous look on his face and the muscle that twitched to life next to his eye clamped her mouth shut. She sensed that what had happened in the warehouse had pushed him to a snapping point. *Pick your battles*, she reminded herself, and this was not a battle she would win.

"I will not give way on this, Abigail. There will be no further discussion of you trying to take my place. Besides, it is my ability Ronan wants the most; you will be of no use to him on that front."

Abby blinked back the tears filling her eyes. "I understand. Doesn't mean I have to like it. You could die because of me."

"No, I could die because of who I am and always have been. Besides, with the amount of trouble your family gets into, you could get yourself killed too."

"Ha ha," she whispered as she took hold of Vicky's hand. "I'm sorry I put you in this position."

He knelt before her. Seizing hold of her chin, he turned her head toward him. He hated the tears in her eyes. "I'm not and I never will be sorry. Having you makes it all worth it, dove. This will not last long. Ronan is mad now, but he will get over it."

Abby bit her lip to keep from sobbing at his tender words. He didn't want children with her and could never open his heart enough again to love her, but he did care for her. She could be happy with that, for now. She didn't know how she would ever rid herself of her dreams for children, but she would have to find a way.

Brian released her chin and leaned forward to lift her from the chair. She wrapped her arms around his neck as he settled himself into the chair with her on his lap. Snuggling against him, she rested her hand on his chest as she listened to the solid, reassuring thump of his heart.

"Have any of the other purebred vampires who were chained in that room said anything?" she asked.

"A few of them are talking, most are too traumatized," he replied. "Apparently, the vampires who had imprisoned them were capturing purebreds and using them to feed on. They were also auctioning them off to those who would pay a lot of money for a chance to feed from them."

"But why?"

Brian brushed the hair back from her sweet, intriguing face. He basked in the warmth of her soul; he had yet to block it off as he did with everyone else he encountered. His cock swelled when her full breasts pressed enticingly against his chest.

She's too tired and far too upset for that, he told himself firmly. However, he couldn't stop himself from reacting to her. His hand wrapped around her neck as he drew her closer.

"Purebloods are rare. Their blood is powerful," he said. "Those vamps could have just fed from and killed them in order to gain their power, but they figured out a way to make money while being able to continuously get the blood they wanted from them."

She shivered against him. Anger slithered through him as he embraced her. It could have been Abby in that room, and until they found the vampire mastermind behind this whole thing, she and her family were still in danger. He'd gladly serve Ronan for free the rest of his life, if it meant getting the chance to destroy anyone who would harm her.

"That's horrible," she murmured as her gaze fell on her sister again. What had they done to her over the nearly two weeks she'd been missing? The answers tumbling through her mind made her want to sob and tear the room apart, but she remained where she was. If Vicky woke to find her on a rampage, it would only upset her more.

"Ronan and his men will make sure they destroy every vampire involved in it. They can't let it get around that a purebred's blood is desirable to other vampires."

She leaned back to gaze at him in alarm. "We're far too outnumbered."

"*No* one will be coming near you, Abby. I'll destroy anyone who tries to hurt you."

"The bond hasn't been completed. You might be able to break free of me. Maybe, if we—"

"No!" he hissed.

"But—"

"I said no," he snarled, his eyes turning red as he spoke. "You're *mine*. No one is going to change that or take you from me, not even you. The bond will be completed, soon."

Her heart beat faster at his words, alarm and desire mingled within her. She wanted so badly to be possessed by this man, but if they sealed their bond, he'd never be able to break free of her and the risk she might pose to him.

"I could drag you down with me if they come for me and my family," she said.

"Then I will happily go down beside you. Don't mention it again, Abigail. I mean it; it is *not* an option."

She opened her mouth to protest but clamped it shut again when he gave her a blistering look.

"The more you speak of not completing our bond, the closer you push me to losing total control and taking you in a way no one should experience for their first time," he told her.

Those words should have terrified her, but instead they thrilled her. "I won't mention it again."

The tension eased from his powerful muscles. Her fingers slid over his black shirt and across the buttons as his scent drew her closer to him. Vicky's moan brought Abby's head around as she spun toward her sister. Vicky's eyes fluttered behind her lids, but she remained unconscious.

"Rest," Brian said and kissed her temple. "I'll watch over her."

Abby settled her head into the hollow of his neck. She had no intention of sleeping, but it felt wonderful to be held so close to his warmth.

~

A GENTLE NUDGE caused Abby to stir sometime later. She didn't recall falling asleep, but apparently she had. "She's awake," Brian murmured in her ear.

Abby bolted up so fast she would have toppled from his arms if he hadn't tightened his hold on her. "Vicky!" she gasped when her sister's eyes met hers.

Vicky smiled wanly and stretched her hand out. She winced when the movement caused her chains to rattle. Disgust and hatred twisted her features as she glared at the metal still clamped around her wrists.

"Now that you're awake, we can get them off," Brian assured her. "Lucien has discovered a way."

Abby glanced questioningly at him. "Aiden came in to inform me they had found a way while you were sleeping," he explained.

She must have really been out of it if she hadn't heard her brother enter. Vicky's eyes zipped back and forth between her and Brian as Abby pulled herself from his arms and settled onto the bed beside her. "What is going on with you two?" Vicky asked.

"I think I should be asking what's going on with you," Abby said.

"Yeah, but my story sucks. Yours looks like it might be kind of entertaining."

Brian watched the sisters. Their mannerisms were so similar, their features identical, yet even without Vicky's thinner weight and chains, he would have been able to tell them apart instantly. He didn't know if it was because Abby was meant for him, or if it was just her, but the vibrancy of her soul made him yearn to touch and hold her once more. There had also been a shifting of Vicky's soul, which he recognized amongst those who had killed before.

Rising to his feet, he took a deep breath to steady his need for her. She had to be with her sister now. Bending, he kissed her head before pulling away. "I'll get Lucien while you two talk."

Abby's eyes followed him to the door and watched as he slipped outside.

"He is delicious," Vicky murmured and licked her lips.

"Hands off." Abby's voice came out sharper than she'd anticipated, but the ravenous look in Vicky's eyes caused the fiery burn of jealousy to spear through her.

Vicky's eyebrows shot up. "Hands way off," she promised. "Now, tell me about you two."

"You tell me what happened with you first."

Vicky frowned, her mouth curved into a pout, but Abby wasn't going to back down to her sister's wishes as she normally did. "Not much to tell. You saw the guy I was dating—"

"I did," Abby interrupted, "and I ran into what I'm pretty sure was one of his friends in a crack house in Boston. He was higher than a kite and assumed I was you."

"Duke had a lot of friends, but I never knew any of them to be like that," she muttered, her mouth pursing at his name and her eyes flickering with red.

"What were you doing with a guy like him, Vicky?"

"He was *really* cute and a lot of fun in bed. I'm sure you know what that's like," she said with a conspiring smile and an elbow to Abby's, thankfully, healed ribs.

Abby didn't smile back. "No, I don't."

Vicky's brow furrowed, and her smile slid away. "You were practically purring like a cat in his arms, and you two haven't done it yet?"

"No."

"With that red-eyed jealousy you just exhibited, I'd thought maybe he was your mate."

"He is," Abby admitted, "but we've been busy trying to find you." *And fighting each other and the way we feel.* She didn't say that to Vicky; her sister had been through enough without that info dump.

"There's always time for sex, Abs," Vicky teased, but there was no laughter in her troubled eyes.

"Back to Duke," she said in a no-nonsense tone. "Why didn't you tell me he was involved in drugs or whatever he's involved with?"

"Why didn't you tell me about your feelings for Brian?"

"Brian and I weren't exactly hanging out together before you disappeared."

Vicky's eyes narrowed shrewdly. "Maybe not, but with the way you've held yourself back from men over the years, I'm willing to bet he was the reason."

"I dated!" she retorted.

"No, you sampled. You tried one on and tossed them aside faster than I toss aside last year's wardrobe. You haven't been excited about any guy, or eager to go on a date, and you haven't gushed about someone in years..." Her voice trailed off as her eyes raked Abby from head to toe and back again. "You knew in the hotel, when we first saw him."

Her accusing tone caused Abby to wince before she threw back her shoulders. "I didn't *know*."

"But you suspected!"

"I felt a connection to him I've never felt to another, but he didn't react to me at all. I was determined to try and find it somewhere else too."

"Why didn't you tell me?"

"I tried to talk to you about him once. You said he was a killer who smelled of death, nearly got us all killed and you hoped we never saw the bastard again. How was I supposed to explain what I was feeling to you after that? I couldn't even explain it to myself."

"You still should have tried."

"I did. You wouldn't listen. Now, you're not going to get me off topic that easy. Spill!"

Vicky folded her arms over her chest, scowling at the chains when they rattled again. "Duke and I were dating for about a month. He was fun. He liked to go clubbing and dancing, and he had a wild side."

"And he was into some pretty sketchy things."

Vicky brushed back a strand of her hair. "I didn't know that while we were dating."

"When did you find out?"

Vicky glanced away, and though her sister had been trying to act tough and talk as if it hadn't mattered, tears burned her eyes when she spoke. "When those vampires showed up at Duke's apartment to take me. They hit me with a Taser that must have been built for an elephant because it knocked me on my ass, but I was still conscious when they gave Duke a suitcase full of money. Then they hauled me out of there and into a waiting car. They slapped these chains on me and took me to that warehouse. I've been there ever since. Every day I feared they would bring you in too. Duke knew you were my sister and where you went to school."

Abby shuddered at the thought. "Does he know about our family?"

"He knows I have siblings but I never told him how many or where they are. You were the only one he knew more about."

"That's good. So the parties moved around, but you didn't," Abby murmured as she rested her hands on Vicky's. "You're safe now."

Vicky wouldn't look at her as she kept her gaze focused on the far wall. Abby tried not to stare at the bite marks marring her flesh, but her eyes were repeatedly drawn to them. She couldn't imagine what Vicky had endured.

"Vicky." Her sister's watery gaze finally came back to her. Abby crawled further up the bed and settled beside her. She wrapped her arm around Vicky's shoulders, drawing her close. Vicky hesitated for a minute before resting her head on Abby's chest. The stiff set of her shoulders relaxed, but her hands twisted in Abby's shirt. The last of her 'I'm fine' façade crumpled away when she started to openly sob.

CHAPTER TWENTY-FOUR

"They didn't feed us much," Vicky whispered. Her head was on Abby's shoulder, and her fingers traced Abby's hand in a circular pattern as she spoke. It was something Vicky did often when they would huddle together and talk late into the night. "When they came to feed from us, they would pin us down, and then sometimes five or six of them at a time would feast on us."

Abby kissed the top of Vicky's head as her sister became still once more. She swallowed heavily, she didn't know how to ask her next question. "Did they… did they rape you?"

She braced herself for Vicky's answer. She'd kill every last one of them. She planned to help do that as it was, but she'd also make them eat their balls before she delivered the death blow. Tears slid down her face, wetting Abby's shirt.

"No, they were more focused on our blood, but I felt so violated, so helpless, and it hurt so bad…" Her voice broke off as she sobbed again.

"It's okay," Abby whispered as she brushed Vicky's hair away from her face. She couldn't imagine what it must have been like to be so helpless, afraid, and abused. Vicky's anguish tore her heart to pieces.

She grabbed Vicky's hand and squeezed it. Those hideous chains rattled before falling silent. Her gaze fell to the bruises and bite marks marring her sister's pale flesh. She may make them eat their nuts anyway by the time she was done with them.

A knock on the door drew her head up. "It's Brian," she said to Vicky when she scented him on the other side.

"Let him in," Vicky said as she wiped away her tears.

"Come in!" Abby called.

Brian opened the door and poked his head in before stepping inside. Vicky threw back her shoulders as she sat up to welcome the group hovering on the other side of the door. Their brothers stepped aside to allow a tall, muscular vampire entrance to the room. Abby stared at the man she assumed was Lucien. He had sandy blond hair and eyes the color of raven's wings. He carried himself with the confidence of one who knew their power and owned it.

Stopping beside the bed, he gazed between the two of them before setting a bag on the floor by his feet. "Let's get these things off," he said to Vicky.

"Those are the sweetest words I've heard in weeks," Vicky replied.

Abby slid from the bed as Vicky scooted to the edge, dragging her chains with her. She was back to acting blithely as she smiled at the handsome, heavily muscled vamp and thrust her wrists forward. Lucien bent and pulled a vacuum flask from his bag before pulling on a pair of thick, rubber gloves. Brian stepped forward and rested his hands on Abby's shoulders when she shot him a troubled glance.

"It will be fine," he murmured near her ear.

She watched as Lucien pulled out another set of gloves and slipped them onto Vicky's hands before placing a piece of thick plastic above the cuff on her wrists. Vicky's smile faded away. "Are you going to cut my hands off?" she asked with a nervous laugh.

"No, this is to keep your skin as protected as possible," Lucien replied.

Not the most reassuring words, Abby thought as she watched him. He pulled out a bucket and uncapped the flask. Mist or something drifted from the flask before he turned and poured it into the bucket. More of that strange mist flowed upward as he poured.

"What is that?" Vicky asked. When she leaned forward to get a better look, Lucien nudged her back.

"Liquid nitrogen." Uneasiness turned in Abby's gut, and Vicky's playful demeanor vanished. "You're going to stick your hands in the bucket for two minutes. The gloves will protect you, as will the plastic, but if any does get on your skin, it's going to hurt. You'll heal, but you'll also have to take the pain and not pull your hands out."

"I can take it," she assured him.

He gave her a doubtful look she returned with a haughty expression and a raise of her chin.

"After these past couple of weeks, I can take it."

Abby bit her lip at her sister's words. She wanted to turn away but felt helpless to watch as Vicky placed her hands in the bucket. Her sister's face remained impassive, but a twinge in her cheek alerted Abby that some had gotten onto her. Lucien kept an eye on his watch. After a little bit, he bent and pulled an iron mallet from his bag.

He tapped his foot as he watched the seconds tick by on his watch. Abby was certain far more than two minutes passed before he gestured for Vicky to pull her hands free of the bucket. He grabbed hold of the chains, moving them to the nightstand and resting them against it before raising the mallet and smashing it down on the bolts holding the cuffs together.

Abby bit back a cry when Vicky winced but remained mute. The first cuff shattered beneath the impact. Another loud thud and the second cuff fell away with a clatter of metal onto the ground. Vicky eagerly pulled the gloves off and dropped them on the floor. She rubbed at the bloody flesh hidden beneath the cuffs—from jerking against the bonds, her skin had pulled back to reveal her muscle.

Lucien gathered his supplies and dumped them into his bag. "Are the others who were with me all free too?" Vicky inquired of him.

"Yes. We've sent the ones who have family home, with the understanding they have to relocate, preferably to somewhere in another country until all of this is settled. The rest we're relocating ourselves."

"What about our family?"

"They've already been spoken with, but you were not taken from your home as some of the others were. We see no reason to relocate them right now, but that could change in the future," he replied.

"Why did they only take one member of those families and not all of them?" Abby inquired.

"A whole family vanishing is a lot more noticeable than one wayward child," Lucien said. "The families notice of course, but they believed them to be runaways or away at college. Because of this, they didn't contact others and decided to deal with it on their own. The ones you removed from that room and brought here were all young. Some hadn't even hit maturity yet.

"From now on, when a purebred goes missing, it will be reported immediately. I'm sure it's already gotten out amongst the vampires that our blood is stronger. Many had probably assumed it anyway, given our vampire births, but they weren't foolish enough to try something like this. The punishment for this will be swift and merciless. Vampires who speak of this retribution will shake with terror over it for centuries to come."

"Good," Abby muttered.

"I want to be involved when it happens," Vicky said.

"It's going to be ugly," Lucien replied as he lifted the bucket from the floor.

"I don't care. I am going to find Duke," Vicky said. Abby almost told her that Brian could help find him, but she bit the words back.

She'd already put his life at risk once; she wouldn't drag him into this if he preferred not to be involved. "I'll go after him alone if I have to."

"You won't be on your own," Abby assured her.

Vicky smiled at her before focusing on Lucien. "That's two purebreds—"

"Three," Aiden said.

"We will also go with them," Ethan said.

"You're going home," Vicky replied. "I'd never forgive myself if you missed the birth of your child, or if something happened to you. The same with you two," she said with pointed looks at Ian and Stefan.

"We're not going to let you do this alone," Ethan told her.

"Not alone," Abby reminded him.

Brian's hands tightened on her shoulders, but he didn't protest, and he didn't tell her she couldn't help her sister. He had to know it would only result in a fight. However, she had a feeling there would be a lot of rules and demands placed on her before she was allowed to leave this place again. She may actually follow some of these rules. She was in no rush to die, and the warehouse had been too close of a call for her liking.

Brian gritted his teeth against the urge to argue with her, but he knew it would be pointless. She would make sure everyone who had mistreated her sister ceased to exist, and do anything to protect her twin. And he would do anything to protect her.

∼

AN HOUR LATER, Abby sat on the bed with Vicky again, her arm draped around her sister's shoulders. The fresh rain scent of the shampoo and soap from Vicky's recent shower still couldn't mask the odor of refuse wafting from her.

It had taken a lot of convincing, but eventually Ethan, Ian, and

Stefan had agreed to leave in the morning. In the end, it had been the chance of someone stumbling across their home and taking one of their younger siblings or children while they were away, that convinced them to return.

Vicky had just finished telling them about her capture and subsequent imprisonment. She didn't cry again, but her voice broke when she spoke briefly of the abuse she'd endured. Ethan rose and paced away. He ran his hand through his hair as he muttered curses and threats. Ian sat on the other side of Vicky. He took hold of her hand while David and Aiden remained unmoving at the foot of the bed. Brian sat in the chair beside Abby, his hands clasped before him and his elbows on his knees.

"Death was too good for those vampires," Ethan said.

Another question formed on the tip of Abby's tongue, but she really didn't know how to ask why or whom Vicky had killed. The others must have felt the same way as none of them uttered the question, yet she knew her siblings would all be able to smell it too.

"For the first week and a half, I wasn't given any blood," Vicky said. Her grip on Abby's hand became bruising, but Abby didn't pull it away from her. "I hadn't fed for a few days before they took me, so the hunger... I'd never been so hungry before. The burning, the *need,* it was so intense. Maybe it wouldn't have been so bad under normal circumstances, but they kept draining us and not giving us anything back. It was horrible..."

Vicky's voice broke, and Abby was sure the bones in her hand were going to crack as Vicky continued. "Then, one day, they threw a human in with us. She ran screaming from the others as they lunged at her from the shadows, but I remained hidden, too weak to make a move toward her. She never saw me until she was falling before me. They'd... they'd cut slices across her wrists and neck. The scent of her blood..." Vicky shuddered as her voice broke off.

"You don't have to," Abby whispered.

"It was all I could smell," Vicky continued. "It invaded all of my senses and made me burn with thirst. I had no control over myself when I fell on her. She never had a chance. She..."

Vicky broke off and abruptly released Abby's hand. "I need some rest," she said.

The others remained unmoving as her words sank in. Ravenous, drained, and beaten, Vicky had attacked the girl, and the girl hadn't walked away. Brian may not have been able to smell the death on Vicky, but he didn't give the impression he was surprised by this admission, as his face remained expressionless. David's mouth parted, but he refrained from saying anything.

Brian kept his hands clasped as Vicky revealed what he'd already known upon seeing her again. The slight shift in her soul hadn't been there when he'd seen her in the hotel, or in the picture of her and Abby. He'd seen the same kind of shift when Stefan had been forced to kill a human. Ethan had also experienced the shifting, and he was sure he had too.

It wasn't so much a dimming of the soul, but more of a new knowledge or a heaviness that vampires who refrained from killing humans didn't carry. Those who killed for pleasure did so without regret, and those who refrained from killing had no idea about the weight of another's soul on their hands.

He would have to let Lucien and Ronan know what had occurred with Vicky. Lucien already knew she'd killed by smelling her, so there would be no way to hide it. They would overlook this, unless Vicky decided she would prefer to be a killer. Then they would put her down without hesitation or regret.

"We'll let you rest then," Ethan said and jerked his head toward the door.

"Would you like me to stay?" Abby asked anxiously. She didn't want to leave her sister, not yet.

Vicky glanced at Brian before replying. "No, I want to be alone right now."

"Do you need anything?"

"No, go on. Stop worrying about me, Abs. I'm going to be fine."

She said the words, and Vicky was resilient, but Abby knew her sister would never be the same again. How could she be after what she'd endured and been forced to do? Leaning over, Abby kissed Vicky's temple.

"It wasn't your fault," she whispered.

Vicky smiled tremulously at her, but she wouldn't meet her gaze.

"Come," Brian said. Rising, he extended his hand to her. After a moment's hesitation, Abby took hold of it and allowed him to pull her to her feet.

"If you need me, for anything, call or send for me," she said to Vicky.

Vicky settled back in the thick mound of pillows. She grabbed the remote for the TV they'd pulled from storage in the basement off the nightstand. "I'll be fine. I've got TV and these pillows, what more could a girl ask for?"

Ian and the others all hugged her before they reluctantly shuffled toward the door. Abby had to fight the impulse to bolt back into the room when the door clicked shut behind them. *She wants to be alone.* Abby stood staring at the wood before forcing herself to step away from the door.

She waited until they were far enough away that Vicky wouldn't hear her before she gave into her overwhelming urge to cry.

Brian swept her into his arms as sobs wracked her body. He didn't look back at the others as he strode purposely away from them and toward their room. Running his hands over her hair, he didn't bother to try to hush her; there was no stemming this flow.

CHAPTER TWENTY-FIVE

ABBY BLINKED HER EYES OPEN. She had no idea what time it was as Brian had closed the thick, metal shutters over the windows last night with a click of a button. Her eyes felt grainy, but then she had cried herself to sleep in his arms last night, arms that were now noticeably absent.

Frowning, she turned to search the room for him, but it remained empty. She bolted up in the king-size bed and scooted to the edge of it. The thick red curtains draped over the canopy swayed with her movements. She caught her reflection in the floor-length mirror across from her. Her hair stood up in places, her eyes were swollen, and she realized she'd fallen asleep in her rumpled clothes.

The armoire she passed on her way to the door was large enough to hold three wardrobes and looked as if it had come from the seventeen hundreds. It was a masculine room, but she didn't get the impression anyone stayed here, as all she could smell in the room was she and Brian.

Before she made it to the door, it opened and he stepped inside with a tray in hand. His ice blue eyes lit up when he smiled at her.

His face was freshly shaven, and he looked more rested than he had yesterday.

"Good afternoon, Sleeping Beauty," he greeted and nudged the door shut with his heel. The scent of blood wafted to her from the decanters he had on the tray. "I thought you might be hungry," he said as he walked by her and set the tray on the table.

She started to say starving but bit back the word. After Vicky's words last night, she realized she had no idea what starvation was. "I am," she admitted as she followed him to the table in the corner of the room.

The table was old with ornate, swirling designs carved into the legs, and on the tabletop. She may have no idea where they were located in New York, but she pictured the home as more of a castle, due to the elaborately fine furnishings she'd seen in the small sections of the house she'd been through already.

He pulled the top off the decanter and poured some blood into a glass before handing it to her. He poured himself his own glass and leaned against the wall, watching her as she sipped at the liquid. "Do you know if Vicky is awake?" she asked.

"She's with Aiden in the gym, beating the stuffing out of a punching bag."

"I didn't think Vicky knew what a punching bag was." And if she had known, she would have avoided it like the plague before all of this, because it would have damaged her nails.

"She does now and Aiden doesn't seem at all pleased with being the one holding it for her."

Abby took another sip. "She's got a lot of anger to get out."

"She does."

"What about the rest of my family?"

"Stefan, Ethan, and Ian left early this morning. They told me to say good-bye to you and to have you call as soon as you could. David has decided to stay a little longer."

A twinge of regret tugged at her. "I had hoped to say good-bye."

"They were eager to get home."

"Understandable." She waved her hand around the room. "So what is this place? Is it a castle or something?"

He chuckled as he shook his head. "No, it's not that big, but it's close. The new recruits come here to train for battle. Aiden has been under Lucien's supervision, but only because the last training instructor lost control and started killing humans. They're still hunting for him. Lucien normally isn't here, and I'm sure he's eager to get back to Ronan and the others."

"Where are they?"

"I don't know the answer to that. I could find them if I chose to, but they'd kill me if they ever found out I'd located them. My relationship with Ronan is based on the understanding I will never try to locate their main residence. Only pureblood vampires who complete the training ever learn the location of it."

Abby set the empty glass down and went to grab the decanter, but Brian lifted it before she could. He poured her a glass and settled into the chair across from her. "So once Aiden completes the training, he'll know where they are."

"Yes, *if* he completes it. Few do. It's a year of Hell from what I've been told."

"Aiden will make it."

Brian smiled at her and leaned forward to brush back a strand of hair that fell over her face. "So sure," he murmured as his fingers lingered on her cheek.

"I am. How many other recruits are here with him?"

"To be a member of Ronan's order, he's the only one."

Abby almost choked on her blood. "Really?"

"There aren't that many purebloods in existence," he reminded her. "Aiden is their first new recruit in fifty years."

"So he and Lucien are kicking around this massive place all by themselves?"

"No, there are others here too," Brian replied. "There are some turned vamps who are also here to train to fight and kill vampires, and there is a staff to help run the place, but none of them will make it into the inner circle. Every vamp here gets their own security code. When they leave, the code is erased and never used again. Only vamps with the code are allowed to know where this place is, and if they ever try to come back again, they will be killed. My code has never been changed, but if I became a killer, it would be, and I would be hunted to the ends of the earth."

"They have a lot of faith in you not to betray them."

"I could have done so many times. I'm one of the few who could probably get the drop on them and kill at least one of them. We have a symbiotic relationship that neither of us is willing to risk."

"But you risked it when you helped me."

Brian shrugged. "I had faith in Ronan to keep his temper about that."

"Did you train here?"

He scoffed as he leaned back in his seat and smiled smugly at her. "No, I taught myself everything there is to know. I've been here to watch some of the training, and I've been brought in to help with it a few times."

Abby couldn't help but smile back at him. He appeared more relaxed and casual than she'd ever seen him. "What did they have you teach them?"

"How to fight dirty. There's certainly no fighting fair when it comes to survival, which is something you have to remember."

"I will," she assured him and placed her empty glass on the table. He went to lift the decanter for her, but she waved his hand away. "I'm full." He returned it to the tray and leaned back to watch her again. "Will you tell me now how you're able to locate others?"

"I'm not sure how to tell it," he replied. Her face fell, and her eyes darted away. He hated the brief hurt that flashed across her face before she covered it. "But I'll try."

When her eyes flew back to his and a smile lit her face, he knew he'd do anything to keep that smile in place, even reveal the one thing he'd never told another living soul. "If it stays between us," he said. "The air of mystery has served me well over the years, and though no one else can do it, as far as I know, I'd prefer to keep everyone in the dark about it."

"I'll never reveal it to another soul," she vowed solemnly.

He didn't doubt her for an instant. "It's not so much that I find *them*. It's more their souls find *me* and lure me toward them. If they're in a crowded location, I cannot see exactly where they are, but I can see enough to figure out where in the world they are. With Vicky I saw the Statue of Liberty."

"What did you see with Paige's father?" she inquired. He'd also helped her sister-in-law locate the man who had been trying to kill her since she was a teenager.

"The 'Welcome to Las Vegas' sign."

Her head tilted to the side as she studied him. "But if it's souls calling to you, then how do you find them from a picture, drawing, or their things?"

He folded his hands behind his head and crossed his legs before him. "I only need some kind of connection with them, as in knowing what they looked like, a picture or something they once held. It's almost like their souls leave a residue or perhaps an imprint behind on their things, and the soul draws me in from there. Even though I knew what Vicky looked like I still needed a stronger connection with her in order to locate her. Sometimes it takes more than others."

"It kind of sounds like their ghosts coming to haunt you or something, and it's their ectoplasm that they've left behind."

"I've thought of it like that a time or two myself," he admitted and relished her laughter.

"What do the souls look like?"

"Every soul is different. Some glow more while others are sallow and weak. Some change."

"Change how?" she asked.

"They shift in a way. I can still find them, but sometimes things happen to them that make them different than the way they once were."

"Vicky's is different now," she guessed.

"Hers is now, and so is Ethan's and Stefan's. I'm sure mine shifted after I killed those humans."

"Is it only death that causes the shift?"

"Murdering a human does," he replied, "not death."

"It's not murder if you're defending yourself or starving to death," she retorted. "And I don't care what anyone else says about that!"

He smiled at how fierce and protective she was of those she loved. "You have the brightest soul of anyone I've ever encountered. I remember being surprised by it the first time I saw you all those years ago," he admitted. "It has only grown over the years, radiating from you in waves of warmth and love. Maybe it's because you're my mate that I find it so vivid, but I think it's also who you are."

A lump swelled up Abby's throat at his words and the look of awe he gave her. "Vicky's soul was different than mine before the shift?"

He dropped his hands and leaned toward her. "Very different." Taking hold of a strand of her hair, he rubbed it between his fingers. "Yours calls to me in a way no other's ever has. I could find you anywhere, Abigail Byrne."

"*That's* how you found me in the park and the hotel room. You didn't follow my scent!" she guessed.

"I could have followed your scent, but your soul is far more enticing to me."

"Fascinating," she murmured, her eyes wandering to his full lips as desire shimmered in his eyes. Anxiety and anticipation roared to life within her. She'd wanted him for so long now, but what if she was bad at this? She should also be with her sister right now, not thinking about jumping her delectable mate. "I need a shower."

He released her hair as she leapt to her feet and hurried toward a bathroom the size of her dorm room. Tugging off her rumpled clothes, she tossed them onto the floor and turned the water on. Steam was rising from the shower when she stepped into it and tugged the curtain closed.

It had just settled into place when it was pulled open again. A sputtering noise stammered from her when Brian unabashedly stepped into the shower with her. Those protesting sounds died when her gaze fell on the shaft jutting out from his nest of dark blond curls. Semi-hard it was still massive.

A new fear churned in her stomach as it swelled in front of her eyes. How was that *ever* going to fit in her? Though it caused uneasiness to grow within her, the sight of it jutting out from his body also aroused a fervent need in her. She was desperate to know what it felt like to have him stretching her, filling her as he moved within her.

Her eyes flew to his as he stepped forward. The spray of water beat down on his massive chest and slid over his pale skin. Unable to stop them, her hands rose to press against his chest. Heat flared up from her palms at the contact with his flesh, so soft and yet so hard and unyielding beneath her touch.

The warmth of the water spilling over her had nothing on the fire he so easily stoked to life within her. His hands slid down to her ass, cupping it within his grasp as he pulled her against him.

"I'm going to have you, Abby," he murmured as his tongue ran over her ear. "I'm going to make it so everyone knows you're mine. No more waiting."

Her heart thundered at his words, and her nipples puckered in anticipation of his promise. Bending his head, he claimed one of those nipples, running his tongue over the rigid bud. She nearly screamed when he nipped at it. His fangs scraped against her sensitized flesh before he drew it into his mouth and sucked upon it. Her fingers threaded through his wet hair, drawing him closer as her hips instinctively bucked toward him.

Easy, Brian cautioned himself as he nipped at her again. He'd seen the look of panic that had crossed her face before she'd fled the bedroom. She would flee again if reason returned, not because she didn't want him, but because she was uncertain of what was to come.

He had to keep her here, with him. He'd waited long enough to make her his, too long. The urge to possess her clamored through his veins, compelling him to sink his fangs into her throat and his cock into her tight, wet sheath.

He had to fight it, had to make sure she was prepared for him when he took her. Her eager cries and enthusiastic movements didn't help him to keep his restraint as she rubbed her heated center invitingly against him before crying out in delight at the friction the motion created.

He groaned when her hand slid down to grasp the throbbing length of him like he'd taught her. Her thumb rubbed over the head, spreading the drop of moisture that had beaded there in anticipation of her. He was supposed to be the one seducing her, but he found himself falling apart as her hand stroked him again with far more confidence.

He gritted his teeth against his need to cum as he ran his hands over her luscious breasts and leaned back to study them. They were so inviting and delectable as he dragged his thumbs over the nipples. Slowly, he released them and slid his hands down her sides. His eyes latched onto the beads of water sliding down her smooth, pale flesh.

Bending his head to her again, he trailed those beads with his tongue, licking them from her as he slipped his hand between her legs. His fingers slid through her wet blonde curls, her head fell back when he dipped one into her. He couldn't tear his gaze away from the rapture playing over her face as he slid his finger more demandingly in and out of her.

Gently, he stretched her further to slide his other finger into her in preparation to take his shaft. He wrapped his other arm around her waist, keeping her against him as her hips thrust faster and her muscles contracted deliciously around his fingers, greedily pulling at him. He bit his lip, drawing blood as he fought the urge to pull his fingers away and drive himself into her in order to feel those muscles clenching around him.

She cried out, her muscles constricting around his fingers as she climaxed against his hand. Not giving her time to come back to earth, he reached around her to shut the water off before wrapping his arm around her waist, lifting her up and climbing from the tub. He kept his fingers inside her as her hips moved languidly with his touch once more. Carrying her over to the bed, he placed her onto the thick mattress.

He nudged her thighs apart as he settled himself between her legs, which fell invitingly open to him when he slid his fingers from within her. She looked so enticingly beautiful with her swollen lips, pale hair fanned out around her, and her lush body sprawled so invitingly beneath him. Her eyes deepened to a forest green, and her breaths came in quick pants when he skimmed his fingers over her thighs. Her hips lifted as he dipped teasingly low before sliding his hands back up her smooth flesh again.

"Brian!" she gasped when he moved forward to rub the tip of his sensitive head against her wet entrance. Gritting his teeth, he grabbed hold of his shaft to guide it into her.

Abby's hands entwined in his hair when he bent to take possession of her mouth again. His lips moved sensually over hers as his tongue flickered against her lips before she opened her mouth to his invasion.

Her tongue hungrily entwined with his as he moved inch by excruciatingly slow inch into her, so as not to hurt or frighten her. His body clamored for release and to seal this bond, but he was determined to make it pleasurable for her too.

He paused when he was halfway in, allowing her to become accustomed to his size. Her hips rolled invitingly up, begging for more. He seized hold of them, pushing her back into the mattress.

"Still," he managed to grate out. "I can't control myself if you move."

Abby panted beneath him as she fought against thrusting her hips up and feeling him fill her completely. However, she sensed his unraveling restraint in the quivering muscles of his arms and the sweat beading across his brow. She remained still beneath him as he bent his head to kiss her again. Unable to resist, Abby nipped at his lip, drawing blood and causing her body to roll upward as she sucked on the wound she'd created.

Brian barely held himself back from thrusting into her when she slid her tongue over her bite again. He released his grip on her hips and planted his hands on either side of her head. Her hands fell onto his ass. She grabbed it but kept herself unmoving beneath him as he leaned over her.

Finally, he moved within her again. The full feeling of him inside of her, stretching her, was like nothing she'd ever experienced before. Pleasure and pain swirled and mingled together as a feeling of rightness stole through her. His hot, water-slickened body sliding over hers was driving her mad.

He hesitated again before plunging forward and driving himself into her with a groan of bliss. Pain burst through her, but she was too far gone to care; she wanted more of him. She pressed her knees against his sides and lifted her hips to him. This time, he didn't hold her back as he withdrew and thrust into her again. The discomfort ebbed further as his rocking hips and demanding body doused the lingering pain and roused her to heights of ecstasy she'd never thought capable of achieving.

She grabbed at him, needing more, demanding it as he took complete possession of her body. His chiseled chest against her sensitive nipples caused ripples of pleasure to swirl out from her aching breasts. Her head fell into the hollow of his shoulder. The scent of him and the pulse of his blood engulfed her senses, causing her fangs to lengthen as a new hunger burst to life within her.

Reacting on instinct and unable to stop herself, she sank her fangs into his neck. Her fingers dug into his back as the hot wash of his blood filled her mouth.

A guttural shout escaped him as his hands slid under her ass and he lifted her from the bed. Abby moaned as he thrust more demandingly within her, grinding his hips against her as he pumped relentlessly in and out of her, stoking the fire ever higher. Tension built within her body, spiraling out from her core to clench at her belly as he pushed her closer and closer to the brink. Lifting her hips, he slid her up and down him, as he rubbed her clit against his body and sent her careening over the edge.

Brian's fingers dug into her hips when she screamed against his throat and her back arched up to rub her breasts against his chest as another orgasm tore through her. He groaned when he finally got to experience the rapture of her tight muscles clenching around his cock, nearly wrenching his seed from him.

He managed to keep himself from spilling as he sank his fangs into her shoulder. A shudder racked him as the ambrosia of her blood filled his mouth and her sheath continued to constrict around him. He could feel the bond between them intensifying, solidifying as he moved within her and gorged himself on her blood.

Her satisfaction beat against him as pathways in their minds opened between them. He could feel her elation and pleasure, feel her thirst for more as she bit deeper and another orgasm caused her nails to tear into his back. He'd meant to pull out, to not spill his seed within her, but when she came again, he found himself pulled helplessly over the edge with her.

He released his hold on her shoulder, and his back bowed as a shout of possession bellowed from him. Semen rushed hotly from him, filling her and marking her as his. His body shook as the stream seemed to go on endlessly. He'd never experienced such ecstasy before, never known something could be this all-consuming and intense.

She trembled within his arms, her body limp against his, her head on his shoulder as her fangs retracted. He missed the connection immediately. Pulling her closer, he was amazed to feel himself hardening within her again as her heavy breasts rubbed deliciously against his chest.

Gritting his teeth against his arousal, he withdrew from her and pulled her to the side. A feeling of contentment stole through him as he cradled her against him. She fit perfectly against his side, her supple body yielding against his hard edges.

The citrus scent of her had now become mingled with his own scent as it drifted up to fill his nostrils. He pulled her closer, unable to suppress a growl of possession as he held her. Her mouth curved into a smile against his side, and her fingers slid over his chest as her lashes brushed over his flesh. The air brushing over him cooled his heated skin but did nothing to douse his growing arousal.

He never should have spilled within her, not when his fate with Ronan was still so uncertain, but he hadn't been able to stop himself. With others, there had always been some control, with Abby, there was none. He had no idea how long Ronan would expect him to work for him before he was finally freed, but he couldn't have a babe during that time.

During that time? Was he actually considering the possibility of another child in his life? He'd sworn never again, had been steadfastly careful with every one of his brief encounters to ensure against spilling within a woman. He doubted human birth control worked for vampire women, but condoms did, and even with the condom, he'd always made sure to pull out before release. He should have pulled out now. In truth, he hadn't wanted to.

Another child never would or could replace Trudy or Beatrice, but it wouldn't be replacing. This child would be his and *Abby's*. To his utter amazement, he found he wanted that more than anything else in nearly two centuries. He couldn't replace Vivian either, but Abby and Vivian were so completely different from each other.

They'd both been loving and protective, but that was where their similarities ended.

Abby was defiant, proud, and willful in her determination. She didn't back down from anything. Vivian had been meek and subdued. She'd never stood up to him, never argued with him. She'd been raised to believe the man was right, it was his home, and she had accepted this. Brian had never thought about the arrangement at the time, there had been no reason to. That was the way things were. However, things weren't like that anymore, and he liked Abby's fiery personality and ability to stand up for herself. It was something he'd never believed he'd enjoy, but he found it refreshing.

What if they had a babe and he failed to protect his family again? That possibility doused some of his longing for a child. Abby, and any child he had with her, would be stronger than his human family had been, but they could still be killed. They would be bigger targets than his human family because of their pure blood and the fact they would be *his*. Many out there would love nothing more than to make him suffer.

He was stronger now though, he had powerful allies at his back and a whole family of purebloods who would happily kill any who threatened a member of their family. He wasn't ready to thrust himself into the Byrne existence, but knowing they would be there to help if anything went wrong was reassuring.

For the first time since he'd become a vampire, he allowed himself to contemplate an existence that didn't revolve around blood, death, and destruction. Allowed himself to ponder a life revolving around family and peace once more. He didn't think he could handle living on Byrne land, but they could live near Boston and visit her family as often as she liked. Perhaps, maybe one day, he could even have a child again. He would not fail them this time, no matter what it took.

Kissing Abby's temple, he nuzzled her hair as he inhaled the scent of his blood flowing within her. The bond was completed now, unbreakable. Every vampire who came near her would know she was *his*. There would be no turning back now, and he didn't want to. There was no guilt with this woman, no despair and self-hatred; there was only peace and fulfillment.

Abby's heavy lids slid closed. She'd never felt so connected to someone in her life. Ripples of pleasure continued to run through her body. His blood was still potent on her tongue and strengthening as it flowed through her. Years of killing their own kind in order to gain his revenge and further his quest had made his blood stronger than anything she'd ever tasted before.

There had been no proclamations of love, but she hadn't expected any, not from him. His heart belonged to another. Closing her eyes, she tried to cling to the happiness that had suffused her only seconds ago. They got along well enough when he wasn't being an overbearing ass, and he was at least willing to work with her on certain things. They could have a good life together; it should be enough, but it wasn't.

She wanted the love too, especially when her feelings for him were growing more and more every day. *Don't lose your heart, Abby; it will only lead to misery.* The problem was she had a feeling it was already too late for her to keep her distance or her heart.

She pressed her hips against the stiff evidence of his arousal when he turned her to face him. "Did I hurt you?" he asked as his fingers traced her face.

"Only for a moment," she replied.

Brian also thoroughly enjoyed her honesty. It was unique in his world where betrayal, backstabbing, murder, and death were often the ways vampires moved ahead. Subterfuge had been his way of life for so many years, he'd forgotten how freeing it felt simply to *be* with another.

His lips brushed over her swollen mouth; his cock jumped in expectation, but he gritted his teeth and pulled away. He'd taken her virginity far too roughly, but she'd been so eager and receptive beneath him, another difference between her and Vivian.

Abby enthusiastically enjoyed sex; Vivian had believed a woman shouldn't enjoy the act. It had taken him a long time to get her to loosen up enough that she actually found some pleasure in it instead of considering it her wifely duty.

Stop comparing them, he told himself sternly. *Vivian is gone. She loved you and would want you to be happy; Abby is here before you, with her face aglow from sex, and her soul brighter than ever.*

Wrapping a strand of her hair around his finger, he drew her closer to kiss her lips. Her leg moved enticingly between his, but he shook his head at her. "Rest."

"I got plenty of rest last night," she murmured, and before he knew what she intended, she rolled so she was on top of him. Her smile was wicked when she rested her palms on his chest and rose to sit above him. His erection pulsed with the blood flooding it. He fought against the hunger coursing back to life within him, but he knew he was done for when her hands traced over his chest and she bent to follow their path with her tongue.

CHAPTER TWENTY-SIX

Rolling over, Abby's hand fell on the empty place where Brian had been only hours before. The bed was still warm, the pillow indented where his head had been. She froze as she felt eyes boring into her back. A chill crept up her spine and the hair on her nape rose as the predatory nature of that stare caused her survival instincts to kick in.

Flipping over, her eyes searched the shadows enshrouding the room. What little light there was in the room glistened off Brian's eyes, making their color appear even icier in the dark. There was a ruthless air to him as he watched her; it was so different from the relaxed and contented man she'd fallen asleep next to earlier.

She didn't speak, barely breathed, as he lifted a glass of blood to his mouth. His eyes never left hers over the rim of the goblet as he drank deeply. Something about him caused her heart to thunder in her chest. She'd seen him beat someone to death, but she'd never seen him look this savage before, and she didn't know what had caused it.

"Is everything okay?" she inquired as she tugged the sheet against her chest and sat up in the bed. A muscle ticked in his jaw and his elegant fingers drummed on the surface of the table as he took another sip of blood. "Brian, what is it? Has Ronan changed his mind about something?"

"No."

The single word was clipped out at her. She scrambled to try and understand what could have happened between the time she'd fallen asleep in his arms and now. "Did you have a nightmare?"

That muscle ticked more fiercely in his jaw and his eyes bled to red as he turned his gaze to the wall. Abby realized she'd hit the nail on the head. He'd told her once before he still dreamed of his family, of the night they'd been slaughtered, but she'd never seen him after one of those dreams. He looked every inch the lethal vampire he was.

She had no idea how to handle him, but she instinctively knew he needed her. A murderous air surrounded him when she released the sheet and scooted to the edge of the bed. His eyes followed her and flared redder when they latched onto her breasts. Rising to her feet, she'd barely made it three feet before he was across the room and standing before her.

She gasped at the speed with which he'd moved before his hands fell to her waist and his fingers bit into her flesh. He would never harm her, but she had to fight the instinctive urge to pull away from the savagery he radiated.

"Mine," he growled.

"Yes," she whispered and laid her hand against his cheek as she tried to comfort him. "And I'm not going anywhere."

Those words did nothing to relax him as he released her and stalked across the room toward the door. For a second, she thought he was going to fling the door open and storm out naked, but he spun and came back toward her. Through the bond connecting them, she could feel the swinging pendulum of his emotions. The urge to kill, to rend something apart with his bare hands, simmered within him, as did his mounting lust for her and his need to forget.

Her gaze was drawn downward as he hardened with every step

he took. Despite her uncertainty, her mouth watered, and her breasts tingled with her rising desire. That part of his body was magnificent as it pulsed beneath her gaze and grew longer and thicker to stand straight out from his body.

She tore her gaze away from his erection when he stopped ten feet away from her and walked over to sit in the chair again. "Brian—"

"Come here," he commanded.

At any other time, such a command would have had her hackles up, but now she felt compelled to go to him. He needed her in a way she'd never seen before, and she couldn't refuse him if there was something she could to do to ease that need. She walked slowly toward where he sat in the chair with his long legs spread out before him and his shaft standing proudly in the air. The ravenous way he watched her every step had her aroused and aching before she reached him.

"No one will take you from me," he murmured.

"No one," she vowed, though he'd been saying the words more to himself than he'd been saying them to her.

The haunted air surrounding him when he lifted his hand and scrubbed at his face tore at her heart. To relive the death of his loved ones repeatedly like this was something she couldn't imagine. His hand snaked out and wrapped around her wrist, and he tugged her forward another step so she stood between his spread thighs.

Brian couldn't tear his gaze away from her. The fading images of the nightmare haunted him, but all he wanted was to lose himself in her. He couldn't shake the certainty he would lose her too, that she would be torn away from him.

Had he actually been contemplating children with her earlier? It couldn't happen. The nightmare tonight had been a reminder of that. Vivian hadn't been in it this time; it had only been Beatrice's hand lying so trustingly in his as the life slipped from her eyes. He couldn't risk that loss with Abby; he'd never allow her to know such anguish. There could never be children, but his need for her now was bordering on the edge of insanity.

"You should run from me," he told her.

"Never," she whispered.

"I made a mistake tonight. I never should have spilled in you, but you make me come completely undone when I'm with you. I won't let it happen again." He hated the sadness that lit her eyes at his words, but it couldn't be helped. "What I want to do to you now should be done to no woman. Will you run from me now?" he demanded in a harsh whisper.

He didn't know if he could let her go if she tried. Would he hunt her through these halls until he was inside of her again and seeking the escape from his existence only she could bring to him as he lost himself within her once more? If she tried to run, he was greatly afraid he would.

Sorrow twisted like a blade in her heart at his words. He was raw right now with the reopened wounds of his loss. If she turned from him, he would fall deeper into his grief, and she couldn't leave him to that. He'd hurt her, but it was because the suffering that had been inflicted on him all those years ago was far deeper than anything she could ever imagine or had ever endured in her life.

"No. I will never run from you. Never," she promised.

He tugged her a step closer until her hands rested on his chest. "Will you get on your knees for me, Abigail?"

Abby drew her bottom lip into her mouth as she considered his words. "I've never... I don't know how."

"I'll teach you."

She swallowed nervously as the wetness between her legs grew. How badly she wanted to know the taste of him, to experience him in such a way, but could she do it? Her gaze slid to that temptingly rigid part of him. Without realizing it, she licked her lips as a bead of moisture formed on the head of him.

His hands dug into the flesh of her waist when her tongue flicked over her lips and a rapacious gleam lit her eyes. He fought the impulse to guide her downward, but no matter how badly he longed for this, no matter how out of control he felt right now, he'd never force her to do something she didn't like.

Stepping a little back from him, she lowered herself to her knees before him. Her breasts brushed against his shaft as she settled herself between them. The feel of her hardened nipples against his flesh caused him to suck in a breath, and his cock jumped in anticipation.

"Wrap your hand around it," he said, his voice hoarse. "Yes," he breathed when her small hand enclosed around his thickness. "Now—"

His breath hissed in as her tongue slid out to lick over his head before he could instruct her further. His body bucked at the sensation of her heated, wet tongue working over his shaft, tasting him. He should have known she'd require no instruction; his Abby was an extremely fast learner and just as eager to please him as he was to please her.

Abby shivered at the salty taste of him on her tongue. His hands gripped the bottom of his chair as his fevered eyes watched her every movement. She realized she held him in the palm of her hand in more ways than one. This massive, formidable man was hers, and he was watching her with rapt attention.

Leaning over further, she took him deeper into her mouth, swirling her tongue around him as she worked her mouth over him. When he groaned and bits of chair broke away beneath his hands, she knew he enjoyed it. Fascinated by his reaction to her, the taste of him, and the growing feeling of power over having such a man as this completely out of control for her, made her bolder as she moved over him.

He rested his hand on the back of her head; he didn't push her down on him, but simply held her as she worked up and down his shaft. The blood pulsed more hotly through it, and he could feel his semen rising to the top, desperate for release, but he didn't want this to stop, ever. His hips surged up and down with her movements. He was completely out of control, lost to the thrill of her heated mouth.

"Look at me," he commanded gruffly. Her emerald eyes flew open and up to his. His blood thundered through him as she kept hold of his gaze while her hand and mouth drove him to madness.

He leaned forward and grabbed her waist. A mewl of disappointment escaped her when he lifted her up and away from him. It died away when he lowered her into his lap and guided himself into her. Abby nearly screamed as he stretched and filled her. Her nails dug into his shoulders as he thrust himself up and into her.

"You were enjoying that," he murmured against her ear as he lifted her and slid her back down again.

"Yes!"

His hand entangled in her hair, and he tugged it back to expose her neck. Striking with the speed of lightening, his fangs sank into her vein. A scream tore from her as she rode him with reckless abandon while he pumped eagerly in and out of her. Releasing his hold on her throat, he licked the blood from her pale flesh as her sheath clenched around him and her body shook with the force of the orgasm rocking through her.

So close, he was so close…

With a guttural shout, he somehow managed to tear himself free from her before he came. Wave after wave of semen spilled between their bodies as he clung desperately to her slender back. Despite the magnitude of his release and the calming balm her body was to his soul, a sense of incompletion filled him at not having lost himself completely within her.

It's for the best, for both of you, he told himself, but when he was holding her like this, he couldn't be so sure it was for the best. Earlier he'd allowed himself to consider having children again; now he would do anything he could to keep her with him and to shelter her from knowing what it was like to lose a child.

Abby turned her head on his shoulder to stare at the wall. Her body continued to be wracked by tremors of pleasure but a hollowness filled the pit of her stomach. She didn't want children now, she was too young, but she couldn't shake the sense of loss his pulling out had left in her. Even after everything they'd experienced tonight, it felt as if he were pulling away from her in more ways than one.

Rising, he carried her into the bathroom and turned the shower on. He kept her in his arms as he stepped beneath the spray. His expression remained almost clinical as he washed her body off, but a muscle jumped in his jaw and his shaft swelled between them. Despite the heat of the water washing over her, Abby shivered.

When he was done, he wrapped her in a towel and returned her to the bed. Abby watched as he pulled the towels away and climbed into the bed beside her.

Brian drew her closer to him and rested her mouth against his throat. "You must feed."

Abby tried to resist, but she craved the connection between them. Dropping her head to the hollow of his throat, she licked the water from his flesh before she bit deep. The heady flow of his blood filled her mouth. Through the bond connecting them, his confusion, anguish, and need beat against her. The horror and unspeakable loss of the night he'd become a vampire slipped through the bond before he shut it off, but she'd seen enough to feel the magnitude of his grief as if it were her own.

Tears welled in her eyes, and her fingers slid into his hair as she held him closer, needing to comfort him. She sensed the way she eased him, the desperation he had for her. Before her, he would have gone out to kill after the nightmare; now he stayed because his need to keep her safe was stronger than his impulse to destroy.

She kept her hurt over his pulling out of her locked away from him, just as she knew he kept pieces of himself locked away from her.

CHAPTER TWENTY-SEVEN

Over the next week, Abby worked with Brian, Aiden, Lucien, and Vicky to learn as much about fighting and defending herself as she could. She often did well; she was fast and strong for someone so young. The only time she got tripped up or planted on her ass was when Brian would whisper deliciously distracting thoughts into her mind while they were sparring with each other.

At first, she'd been so thrown off by the bond between them and that they could communicate in such a way, that she'd found herself flat on her back, pinned beneath him more often than not. His arrogant grin had done nothing to douse the yearning his promises awoke in her mind. Over the week, she'd come to learn how to give as good as she got though. Two could play that game, and she'd learned to play it as well as he did.

Now, they were alone in the gym as they circled each other on the mats placed on the floor. She distracted him with the thought of flicking her tongue over the tip of his head and swept his legs out from under him with her foot. She pounced when he fell on his back with a grunt. Landing on top of him, she grinned proudly down at him as she straddled him.

"I meant for that to happen," he said and rolled his hips beneath her.

Abby's breath exploded out of her when his growing arousal rubbed against her. Before she knew it, he had her flipped onto her back and pinned beneath him with her arms above her head. During these times, he was so far removed from the broken man she'd discovered after his nightmare that she could almost believe there were no barriers between them.

"So easy to distract," he murmured as he traced her lips with his fingers.

"Only by you," she replied, arching beneath him when he clasped hold of her breast. Her heart pounded in her chest as she watched him. She could spend an eternity with this man and never grow tired of him or the way he made her feel.

His gaze latched onto the fresh bite marks on her neck, *his* marks. He'd never get enough of seeing them on her flesh and looked forward to leaving them there for an eternity. Footsteps from somewhere outside the gym had him rolling off her and pulling her to her feet. He adjusted himself in his sweats before turning to face whoever approached. Before he stepped into the doorway, he'd known it would be Lucien.

"Ronan would like to speak with you," Lucien said.

Abby's hand tightened in his.

"I'll be right there," Brian told him. Turning to her, he kissed her forehead. "Why don't you find Vicky and Aiden," he suggested. "I'll join you when this is over."

She glanced nervously at Lucien. Brian could feel her apprehension vibrating through the bond connecting them. "Okay," she relented.

Reluctantly, she released his hand and watched as he grabbed his hoodie from the bench, tugged it on, and zipped it up. He walked down the hall toward where Lucien waited in the shadows. She waved her hands before her to ease the tremor in them, but she couldn't shake the bad feeling settling in the pit of her stomach.

Turning on her heel, she grabbed her towel from the bench and wiped the sweat from her face before wrapping it around her shoulders and walking toward the front door. She exited the building and jogged across the grass toward the back of the massive main house made of gray brick. The brisk, early November air brushed over her skin, cooling the sweat on it as she moved. She slipped in through the back door of the house and made her way to the kitchen that was only used to store bags of blood within the massive, industrial-sized fridge.

On her way out, she passed one of the turned vampire recruits. "Hey, Vicky," he greeted.

She didn't bother to correct him. She liked that Vicky was looking healthy enough that others had started to mistake them again. The only way most of the others had learned to tell them apart was Brian was usually by her side. Without him now, they just assumed she was her sister.

"Hey," she replied and strode down the hall toward the only room with a TV in it. The TV in Vicky's room had already been removed and put back in storage as soon as she'd been well enough to spend more time out of bed than in it.

Ronan's order took the training going on in this place extremely serious. The single TV and a small library of books were the only sources of distraction or mindlessness in the whole place, and most of the books in the library were on fighting techniques. There wasn't one book for leisure in there.

She didn't know how Aiden, king of reality TV, PlayStation, and anything sports related was surviving in this place, but he appeared to be thriving. She found Vicky sprawled on the sofa, remote in hand as she flicked through the stations. With the size of this place and the obvious wealth here, Abby would have expected every channel known to man, but there were only ten.

"What are you doing?" Abby inquired as she plopped into the love seat next to the sofa.

"Trying to find something other than the news and exercise programs. Seriously, how do these guys survive in this place?" Vicky demanded.

"I don't know."

She'd never been a huge TV watcher, but she really missed her Netflix, and she knew Sam and Dean were getting into some kind of trouble on Supernatural. She also missed music, but she'd discovered her phone got zero reception here, including internet. But then, she had the best distraction of all in Brian. She'd happily give up Netflix and her phone for more days and weeks to stay ensconced here with him.

"Ugh." Vicky tossed away the remote after she settled on CNN. "Guess we'll watch more of the human population killing themselves and each other."

"Vampires are doing the same."

"True. Guess both species are stupid."

Abby couldn't argue with that. "Where's Aiden and David?"

"David's with Mia." They'd come to learn the woman they'd freed after Vicky in the warehouse was named Mia. She was the only other rescued vampire from the warehouse who was still here. She had no family and wasn't ready to travel to the safe place Ronan's order had organized for her.

"They've been together a lot lately," Abby commented.

"They have," Vicky replied. "I think he likes her."

Abby's eyebrows shot up at her statement. "Do you think it's possible one of The Stooges has been taken down?" she inquired.

Vicky grinned mischievously at her. "I don't know, but how funny would that be?"

"Pretty entertaining," Abby agreed, considering her uncles had often griped and rolled their eyes over the actions of her mated family members, but they'd all embraced the family instead of moving on over the years. "And really sweet. Can you just imagine him finally finding someone?"

"There you go again," Vicky said. "You'd make Cupid gag sometimes."

Abby scowled at her. "It could be good for him."

"Or bad. In case you haven't noticed, our family members never have an easy go of it with their mates in the beginning."

Abby shrugged; her mating wasn't everything she'd dreamed it would be, but she was happy or at least comfortable with the way things were between her and Brian.

"Maybe David will be different," she said.

"I think you're getting ahead of yourself on this one."

"You're probably right. I mean, seriously, one of The Stooges?" Abby said, and she and Vicky giggled at the idea. "Where's Aiden?"

"He started talking his Zen bull again, and I tuned him out. I think he's meditating in the garden or something."

The garden was the only other distraction around this place. Not that it was much to look at right now, but she imagined it was spectacular in the spring and summer. Now, it was just dormant roses and perennials lining the border of the maze, which consisted of rows of hedges winding their way through at least six acres of the property. The maze alone was a thing of beauty. She'd only had one opportunity to explore it for an hour with Vicky and Aiden, but it had been a lot of fun. They'd never found the center that Brian had promised her was a worthy enough reason to solve the maze, but she hoped to try for it again.

"I still can't believe Aiden meditates," Abby said.

"He said it helps him keep his mind clear. I told him I thought his mind was pretty empty already."

Abby snorted with laughter and draped her legs over the arm of the chair so she faced her sister. Vicky had filled out again over the week, and the hideous bite marks on her were gone. A steady supply of blood had replenished the weight she'd lost, and rest had diminished the circles under her eyes. Though she looked better physically, Abby would still catch her staring into space with tears in her eyes every once in a while. She knew it would be a while before Vicky completely recovered, if ever, but Vicky was stronger than most gave her credit for.

"How are you doing?" she inquired.

"Better today." Vicky unwaveringly met and held her gaze. "Really, I am. Eager to get out there and get after Duke. I can't wait to stomp that douchebag into the ground." Red flamed around Vicky's eyes as she said this.

"Soon," Abby assured her.

"Yeah, I know, but I don't get the point of all this training. I only want to kill *one* vampire not become the military vamp Aiden has. I have to admit, I am liking the new definition of these guns though," she said as she held up her arms and flexed her biceps.

Abby laughed when Vicky kissed the small bulge the movement created. "Wonder Woman, look out."

Vicky grinned at her and dropped her arm. "Damn right."

Vicky's eyes drifted to the fresh bite on Abby's neck. She jerked her gaze away and toward her wrists, but not before Abby saw the apprehension in her eyes. Sadness swelled within her for her sister. She didn't know if Vicky and Duke had exchanged blood or not, but she knew a vampire bite now represented pain to her sister.

Abby's gaze fell to Vicky's wrists when she rubbed them together. The skin around Vicky's wrists was still darker in color from the cuffs that had once encircled them. The rest of her injuries had faded, but those shadows stubbornly remained.

"Vicky—"

"How are things going between you two?" Vicky interrupted her.

Abby sighed and swung her legs back and forth. Vicky didn't want to talk about what she'd endured, and Abby knew better than to push her. Her sister opened up when she was ready, often in small bits and pieces, but it was better than nothing. "They're good."

Vicky smiled at her and propped her head in her hands. "You've yet to dish on how things are in the bedroom."

Abby chuckled. "And I'm not going to."

"Oh, come on." Vicky bolted upright on the couch. "I had to share an egg, a womb, and a room with you all those years. I deserve some of the good stuff now that you're *finally* getting laid."

"Vicky."

"Abby," she replied in the same exasperated tone Abby had used on her. "There are so few options for me here, and I'm not sure I'm hard up enough to jump into bed with one of these military types. However, that Lucien is yummy." Abby couldn't argue with that. "Let me live vicariously through you while I'm enduring the celibacy enforced on me by being here."

"It's really…" Abby had to pause to think of a word to describe how it was with Brian. *Mind-blowing, unexplainable, better than I ever imagined.* She found those things froze on her tongue and what came out was, "Nice."

"Boring!" Vicky cried with a roll of her eyes. "Give me the juicy tidbits."

"It's not that I don't want to tell you. It's that it's Brian. I can't stand *any*one else thinking of him in such a way. He's *mine*."

"You're such a goner, but fair enough and understandable. Answer me this at least, how many times have your eyes rolled back in your head?"

"Too many to count."

Vicky laughed and threw herself back onto the couch. "I'm happy for you, Abs. I really am."

Abby rose to her feet and walked over to sit beside her sister on the couch. She didn't tell her Ronan had called for Brian or that there had been no declarations of love between them, or that even through the bond connecting them, she hadn't felt his love for her. Vicky may be trying to act like her old self, but she wasn't there yet. She may never be there again. She had enough to contend with without Abby adding to it, and Vicky would worry about her; it was inevitable.

Abby had also come to realize there were things Brian kept locked away from her. Before it had all been so new with him that she hadn't detected the block, but she now felt it every time they were together. Then again, she'd been keeping parts of herself locked carefully away too, especially her growing feelings for him. It was difficult to keep it from him when she was in his arms, but she couldn't let him take that last piece of her, not yet anyway.

Draping her arms around her sister, she hugged her close. Vicky's hands encircled her arms as she leaned into Abby's embrace. "I don't know what I'd do without you," Vicky said.

"Fortunately, you'll never have to know."

Brian froze when he stepped into the doorway of the TV room, and his heart swelled as he watched the sisters holding each other close. The bond between he and Abby was intense, unshakeable, but this one was nearly as deep. Their love and need for each other radiated from them. He'd wanted to kill Vicky for what she'd put Abby through; now he would do anything to keep Vicky safe and Abby happy.

Sensing his presence, Abby lifted her head from her sister's shoulder and smiled at him. He smiled back at her. *We'll talk later,* he told her through their bond and slipped away before Abby could stop him.

It must not be too bad then, Abby decided as she turned her attention back to Vicky. Reluctantly, she allowed her sister to start braiding her hair.

CHAPTER TWENTY-EIGHT

"WHAT ARE YOU DOING?" Abby inquired when she stepped into their bedroom an hour later. He turned in the act of tossing his shirt into a duffle bag. His eyebrows shot up when he spotted the braids Vicky had elaborately interwoven through her hair.

"Like the look," he said and placed a shirt in the bag.

Panic slid through her as she glanced between him and the bag. "Where are you going?"

Brian winced at the distress radiating from her. Leaving her here was tearing him apart inside as it was, but knowing how badly it would affect her only made it worse. Pulling the zipper closed, he set the bag on the floor before turning to face her. "I have to meet with Ronan. He thinks he's discovered who the vampire imprisoning purebloods is."

Abby tried to control the frantic beat of her heart as she watched him. "Who is it?" she inquired.

"Drake Wilston. He's a pureblood who gave into his thirst for blood and death long ago. He fled the country years ago, but there are rumors he's back."

"He's a pureblood?" Her stomach twisted sickly at the possibility of one of their own torturing her sister in such a way.

"Yes. Apparently, human and turned vamp blood is no longer satisfying him. It's only a matter of time before he decides to start killing the purebloods too. He'll go through them fast once he does."

"My family."

"Is safe. I've already called Stefan. They're prepared, and no one knows where they are. They'll be fine."

"I should go home. They may need the extra protection I can offer."

"Not until I get back," he replied. "You're safe here."

"Brian—"

"No!" he barked, his eyes blazing red. "On this I will *not* budge. You are safest here, and I have to know that while I'm gone." Her eyes narrowed as her hands fisted. She was preparing for a battle when he spoke again. "Vicky isn't ready to leave here and face your family yet either. She knows they can smell the difference in her and realize she's killed a human. Are you willing to leave her behind?"

"That was low," she grated through her teeth, "and I can come back for her when this is settled. As you said, I will be safe here and so will she."

"I swear to God, Abby, if you try to leave this place, I will chain you to the bed. You will do as I say on this."

She could feel his apprehension and exasperation beating against her, but everything in her rebelled against being ordered about in such a way. "I won't be the obedient little woman you'd prefer!"

A muscle jumped in his cheek when he spoke. "I wouldn't prefer that at all, but you have to listen to me when it is best for you, for *us*. Worrying about you could get me killed."

That knocked some of her anger away as her original panic for him rushed back to the forefront. "That was even lower," she murmured.

He stalked across the room toward her, his large muscles flexing with his strides. She was torn between kicking him in the nuts again and throwing herself into his arms. "How long will you be gone?" she asked.

"I don't know."

He didn't give her a chance to say anything more before he took hold of her cheeks and bent his head to take firm possession of her mouth. Need and desperation clamored hotly through her body as his tongue thrust demandingly against hers. She was helpless to resist him. She didn't know when she'd see him again. He'd be going out there to try and find the monster who was responsible for hurting her sister, and he would be leaving her behind.

She broke away, panting for air. "Let me come with you."

The red in his eyes flared as he looked at her. "No. There is much of what I am that I would prefer to keep you from, and this is part of it."

"I've seen you kill, seen what you can do. Don't leave me behind to worry."

He bent his head to kiss her again, his tongue delving into her mouth in deliberate thrusts that had her scrambling to remember what she'd been saying. Her knees knocked together to the point she feared her legs were going to give out. Her fingers curled into the flesh of his arms, drawing blood. The scent of it on the air only fanned her fevered need for him.

He'd been sliding his hands down to take her shirt off. Now, he grabbed hold of the front of it and tore it open. Abby gasped as the material fell away to allow cooler air to flow over her heated skin.

His hands ran over her hungrily, squeezing and kneading her breasts as he ran his thumb and forefinger over her puckered nipple. *Hate this bra.* The words blazed from his head and into hers, seconds before he ripped it from her body and flung it away.

Abby arched her back and nearly screamed when his fangs sank into her breast and his tongue slid over her hardened nipple. She bucked against him, tearing at the clothing keeping him from being exposed to her. His shirt fell away in tatters, but she barely noticed it as his arms locked around her and he lifted her up.

Carrying her to the bed, he released her breast to settle her on the mattress. He slid her yoga pants down her legs and threw them aside. The ravenous look in his eyes as he sat back to survey her caused her body to rise invitingly toward his. He rose and tossed away his own pants so swiftly that she barely saw him move.

He knelt between her legs again; his tongue licked over his lips as he hungrily stared at her already wet sex. His erection throbbed, but he knew if he thrust into her now, it would be over soon, and he didn't want that. *Regain control. Slow it down.*

She lifted her hips again, but he still managed to keep himself restrained from seizing hold of them and driving himself into her. Grabbing hold of her hand, he brought it to his chest before bringing her fingers to his mouth and drawing them in one by one. Her eyes darkened as she watched him, her breath coming in faster inhalations as her pulse quickened.

He brought her hand down. Instead of wrapping it around his aching member, he rested it against her wetness. Her eyes widened, and she went to pull her hand away, but he kept it there as he slid her finger into her.

"Let me watch you, Abby," he said as he leaned down to kiss her lips. "Let me see what thoughts of me drove you to do all those many years when I wasn't there to satisfy you." Just like he wouldn't be there for her soon, but he'd be back. He'd always come back for her.

Abby remained unmoving beneath him, hesitant to do this in front of him, but then he pushed her finger into her again and groaned above her. She was helpless against him. She'd yet to deny him anything he asked for in bed and she wouldn't deny him this.

Leaning back again, he kept his palm against her and his eyes latched onto their hands. This time, she didn't need him to guide her but slid her finger into her herself. His cock jumped, and an enticing bead of liquid formed on the head of it as he released her hand. He never tore his eyes away from her hand as he reclaimed possession of her breasts with his large palms.

Abby's legs fell further open as coiling tension built within her. Bending low, he closed his mouth over her other nipple and bit down. Abby screamed as his fangs pierced her flesh and her body fractured apart. She was panting when he grabbed hold of her waist and lifted her up.

She didn't have time to gather her scattered thoughts or stop her legs from shaking before he spread his knees on the bed and thrust her onto him. Tremors from her first orgasm still wracked her when the full feeling of him inside of her caused another one to rock through her.

"I'm going to fuck you for hours," he murmured against her ear. "You'll scream my name so loud the entire house will hear it."

She had no doubt about that, but sadness filled her when she realized he would not be taking her with him.

~

ABBY KNEW he was gone the minute she awoke. The emptiness of the bed and the absence of his mind brushing against hers caused her to curl into a ball. She shoved her knuckles into her mouth to stifle her sobs. She hadn't realized how much his mind had been intertwining with hers since the bond had been completed between them, until now. He'd become a constant, welcoming, comforting presence to her.

She could still feel him at the edges of her mind, but not as strongly as she had these past couple of weeks. Maybe distance had somehow dimmed the connection between them, or maybe he was shutting her further out. She suspected it was the latter, and he was trying to keep her protected from what he was doing.

She lay for an hour before finally forcing herself from the bed and into the shower. Lying around crying wasn't going to help any.

Climbing from the shower, she dressed before returning to their room. Her eyes fell on the letter propped against the lamp on the bedside table. She'd been too out of it with misery to notice it earlier.

She practically flew across the room to pull it off the stand. Her hands trembled as she unfolded it. *Don't worry about me, dove. I'll be back in no time and you can yell at me then for not saying a proper good-bye.*

She hastily wiped away her tears when someone knocked on her door. She knew it was Vicky before her sister opened the door and poked her head in. "Oh, Abby," she said when she spotted the tears in Abby's eyes.

"I'm fine," she hurriedly assured her. "Really."

"No, you're not." Vicky shut the door and walked into the room. She plopped onto the bed beside Abby and threw her arm around her shoulders.

"I am," Abby insisted, unwilling to unleash her burdens on her sister.

"Stop saying that. I'm not going to break, come on, lean on me too, like you always used to."

"You've been through so much—"

"And so have you. I know what you went through to find me, know how difficult it can be when a mate is discovered. Being chained to a wall might actually be preferable to the experience."

Abby snorted then sniffled and wiped at her nose. "It might be."

"Seriously, Abs, treating me like I'm going to break is getting old. I'm not going to fall apart, I promise. I'm going to be stronger than I ever was, and I'll have better taste in men.

Abby couldn't help but laugh. "No, you won't."

"No, I won't," Vicky admitted. "But I may go all 'hit it and quit it' with them, so they have no shot of discovering I'm a purebred, or maybe I'll stick with humans. They're malleable and easier to beat up."

"Solid plan."

"It is. Now lay it on me. What has the awful ass done?"

Leaning against her side, Abby told Vicky everything she'd been holding back for the past six years. From the first time she'd seen Brian, to all the clunky attempts at other men in her life, to his dead wife and children, even sharing the fact that he didn't want children now and was taking care to make sure it didn't happen.

Once the dam broke, it unleashed a torrent that was unwilling to be stemmed. Brian may not like her talking about these things with someone else, but Vicky was her sister, and she so badly needed someone to talk to. When she was done, Vicky frowned as she stared at the far wall and swung her legs back and forth.

"I think we're both better off being single," Vicky finally said.

Abby chuckled and swung her legs in rhythm with her sister. "Maybe."

"He cares about you, Abby. It's so clear in the way he watches you. Half the time he looks completely awed by you; the other half makes even *me* blush."

Abby laughed and leaned against her. "I love him."

"No shit," Vicky replied. "Have you told him that?"

"No, it's the first time I've actually admitted it to myself."

"You were always the romantic in the family. Always dreaming of finding your mate and thinking it was so great when Isabelle found Stefan, even when it looked like it might destroy her."

"Don't remind me."

"But daydreams and fantasies aren't real. You have to work at real life, and you can't expect him to be the first one to say he loves you or to realize it. He's already lost one family; I'm sure the idea of losing another one terrifies him enough that he's going to keep his heart protected as much as he can. He's also been alone for a long time, and with you, he's getting one big-ass family. That can't be easy to accept."

Abby bit her bottom lip as she pondered Vicky's words. "When did you become so wise?"

"Every once in a while I have a good idea. Don't get used to it."

"Never," Abby promised.

"Why didn't you try to find Brian sooner? When we were kids, all you talked about was finding your mate. If you suspected he was yours, why did you wait so many years before contacting him?"

"I was afraid I was wrong, and he would reject me, or I was right, and he really was as awful as everyone said. I believed it would be better to stay away, until I was older."

"And what would have happened when you were older?"

"I have no idea," Abby admitted. "Maybe I would have been better able to handle him."

"I think you could live to a thousand and still not know how to handle that man."

"I think you're right. What happened to him before, what he lost, what do I do if he never changes his mind about children? I never wanted the brood Mom and Dad have, but I would like to have at least one or two."

"That I don't know," Vicky said. "You're going to have to work that out with him, but it doesn't have to be right now."

"No, it doesn't."

Vicky released her and leapt to her feet. "Come on, let's see if we can solve the maze, or go punch something; that's always a good time. Then we'll go swimming. You can't sit here and wallow. I won't allow it."

Abby smiled at her as she shoved herself to her feet. Vicky looped her arm through hers and propelled her toward the door.

CHAPTER TWENTY-NINE

THE WIND BLEW his hair back and chilled the exposed skin of his face and hands as he looked up and down the busy street before turning right. This wasn't the normal hustle and bustle of a city; this was the movement of people and vampires who skulked through the shadows, studiously trying to avoid the law or death.

"Hey, baby," a woman with a red-painted mouth and blue eyes greeted him as he walked by. "Fifteen dollars and I'll make you forget all other women."

Brian's skin crawled at the idea of touching the woman, let alone in a sexual way. "Fifteen dollars, and she'll make you holler," Declan quipped from behind him.

Brian shot a look at the vampire over his shoulder. In the dim radiance filtering from the few unbroken streetlights, the red in Declan's dark auburn hair shone like blood. His strange, almost silver, gray eyes twinkled as he winked at the woman who had been trying to pick up Brian.

The woman grinned at him and stuck out a bony hip. "I'll make you holler for free, baby," she offered.

"I bet you would," Declan replied. The woman grinned at him enough to reveal her blackened and missing teeth.

"That is enough to make any man holler," Brian said before taking a left into another back alley.

Two humans in the middle of going at it didn't look up as they walked by. All he wanted was to get back to Abby, but before he touched her again, he was going to scrub his skin for an hour. He couldn't allow her to be exposed to any of this. Right now, he kept her mostly blocked from his mind; he didn't want her to accidentally glimpse or sense something she shouldn't.

These two humans and the woman back there were the best of it. In the shadows, he could hear others having sex or fighting. The rancid stench of death emanated from something far larger than a rat or stray dog between the brick walls of the alley. Music played from somewhere, but the bricks surrounding him distorted the noise and made it sound as if it came from everywhere at once.

At the end of the alley, he made a right as he followed the call of a soul he'd only encountered once before, and it was before the man had taken a turn for the worst. It had been fifty years since he'd seen Drake, but he clearly recalled what Drake looked like; there were few as ugly as he was.

Stopping before a warehouse, Brian crossed his arms over his chest as he leaned against the wall. They weren't in the main part of the city, but a large suburb about a half an hour outside of it. It had been possible for him to track Drake to the winding streets of this forsaken town, but he was still struggling to keep a hold on him.

"What is it?" Killean demanded gruffly from behind him.

Brian glanced back at the other vamp, his gaze remaining steady on Killean's golden eyes. Many often glanced nervously away from those eyes, if not because of the feral gleam in them, then because of the mask of indifference Killean often wore. The scar that marred his face also caused some to turn away from him. The scar sliced straight down Killean's right eye from his deep brown hairline to the center of his cheek.

How he hadn't lost his eye was a mystery to Brian, one he'd most likely never know the answer to. Killean hadn't been fully mature when the scar was obtained, but it still should have healed and faded away. However, the blow had been deep enough to leave him marked for the centuries of his life. He wasn't about to ask Killean how he'd gotten it. Killean had the warmth of a tomb, and conversation was often a lost art on him. Besides, Brian didn't overly care. Many wore scars no one would ever see, including himself.

Brian turned away from him. "Drake's moved."

He stood for a minute, searching through the sickly souls in the area. Some of them were still vibrant; he assumed those belonged to the well-fed vampires feeding off the humans and vamps who weren't as powerful as them.

"Where?" Killean demanded.

"This way," Brian said with a jerk of his head and led them through a series of more rat-infested alleys. He'd scrub himself for two hours before touching Abby again. He'd never allow her soul to be tarnished by the hideousness of this place.

Stopping in the alley, he stared across the street to a club with a sign that read, *Vampyre* in dripping red blood. "Humans are so stupid sometimes," Declan said as he watched a couple hurry down the stairs.

"Not going to argue with that," Brian replied. "He's in there."

Killean cracked his knuckles, the only enthusiasm he showed over finally locating Drake. "Call Ronan."

Declan already had his phone out and pressed to his ear. He shook his head before sliding it into his pocket. "Voicemail. He and Saxon must still be taking care of that nest of Drake's men."

"Sounds like Drake is all ours then," Killean said and stepped from the shadows. He strolled across the street toward the club.

Brian glanced at Declan who shrugged. "Ronan's got his own fun right now; we'll take ours." Declan grinned as he slapped Brian on the shoulder. "You'll be back with your mate in no time."

"Let's get this over with then."

Brian walked beside him across the street as Killean descended the stairs. About the only thing Killean did get excited about was killing, but then, so did he. Brian followed him down the stairs and stepped into the poorly lit club. Declan and Killean fanned out, their gazes sliding over the crowd as they searched for Drake in the crush of humans grinding against each other to the rhythm of the sensual music flowing from the speakers beside the stage.

On the stage was a band of vampires with their faces painted white and streaks of blood trickling from the corners of their mouths. The blood was real, but the humans didn't care or notice as the lead singer swayed back and forth with his microphone. The band members behind him played a keyboard and guitar.

Humans danced on the stage amongst them, swirling to the flow of the changing lights and the beat. A human woman with her face painted white and fake fangs hanging over her bottom lip held out her wrist to the guitar player. She cried out in ecstasy when he sank his fangs into her. Brian had heard about clubs where people pretended to be vampires, and he realized that was exactly what these people believed was happening here.

"*Really* stupid," Declan muttered.

"This way," Brian said and shoved his way through the bodies.

Fury ate at his gut as he tried to remain focused on Drake's soul, but it was difficult to stay locked on him in this crowd of vamps and humans. The asshole was not only risking exposure with this place, but he was also targeting vampires like Abby. If it were the last thing he did, he would make sure Drake died this night.

Walking along the back wall, he continued to search the crowd, but his ability kept pulling him to the center of the wall. He stood before it, frowning as he studied its smooth black surface. "What are you doing?" Killean demanded from beside him.

Brian rested his fingers against the wall, searching for something that would explain why he was drawn here. "There's something here."

"A wall," Killean said slowly.

"My ability has never failed me before. It may not be able to pinpoint someone every time, but it's never misled me. Right now, it wants behind this wall."

"Interesting," Declan murmured and stepped beside him. His gaze ran over the wall then to the end of it. "This way."

He turned and led them down a hallway with bathrooms and a few backrooms off of it. Drawn to the first backroom, Brian turned the knob and stepped inside. No one was within the room of cleaning supplies, but he instinctively knew there was more to it. Walking around, he searched the shelves and walls for anything that would somehow get them behind the wall.

He was about to go and find a sledgehammer or dynamite when he heard a click. Killean stepped away from the wall that swung open. Dim light, from the room they were in, spilled into the hall beyond the door. Killean reached into his black trench coat and pulled out two stakes. Declan swung a crossbow out from underneath his coat, and Brian pulled his own stakes free.

Adrenaline pulsed through his veins, and his fangs tingled in anticipation. He'd told himself he'd kept Abby shut out because he didn't want her to experience the places he did, but he knew it was because of *this*. She couldn't know how much he enjoyed and thrived on the rush of the kill, no matter how deserving that death may be.

He stepped into the once hidden hallway with the others. As soon as they moved past a certain point, the door began to swing shut behind them. He glanced up in search of cameras but saw none in the hall. The door must close on a sensor or timer. Declan took a step toward it and reached out to stop it from shutting.

"Leave it," Killean murmured.

Declan's hand fell to his side as the door clicked shut. Brian didn't bother to look back; he'd tear this place apart with his bare hands if it became necessary to escape. Voices floated from behind the closed door at the end of the hall. The closed rooms they passed on their way toward the voices all held the faded scent of someone within them, but he detected no heartbeats behind the closed doors. All of the known vampire purebloods had been accounted for as of this morning, so it wasn't their scents he detected.

Killean was actually smiling by the time they arrived at the end of the hall. Declan's face had become unreadable as his eyes remained fixed on the door before them. Brian's pulse thrummed in his ears. He grabbed hold of the handle and looked to the others. At Declan's brisk nod, he jerked the door open.

The dozen or so vampires within didn't immediately react when they glanced up from the cards in their hands. One actually lifted his hand in greeting before the smile froze on his face. Before they could react, Declan released a bolt from his crossbow that went straight through the closest vamp's heart. Startled shouts finally erupted in the room as the vamps leapt to their feet. The card table they'd been sitting around was flung into the air, chips and cards scattered around the room as they charged forward.

Brian swung out, driving his stake into the chest of the one who leapt at him before spinning away to grab another's head. He yanked back with so much force that the vamp's spine tore from his body before he collapsed at Brian's feet. Palming the vamp's head in his hand, he smashed it against the next vampire who charged at him.

The vamp flew across the room and crashed into the wall across from him. Through the pulse of blood pounding in his ears, he heard the door behind him close.

Where's Drake? The thought had just crossed his mind when a thick gas began to flow into the room. Brian's eyes darted up to the vents he hadn't noticed at the top of the wall when they'd first entered. He stepped to the side to avoid the next lunging vamp and slammed his foot into the man's back when he fell to the floor. The crack of the spine beneath his foot sounded as more gas spilled into the room.

The vampire wailed beneath him. Raising his foot, he planted his boot into the back of the vamp's head, driving it into the floor. His throat burned, and his eyes watered as the gray gas filled the room like smoke from a fire. He had no idea what was being pumped into the room, but he could feel a strange lethargy starting to take him over as his head spun.

"We have to get out of here," Declan choked out and stepped toward the door.

Brian held his breath as he lunged for the handle of the door. He yanked at it as another vampire staggered toward him through the smoke. Before the vamp could reach him, his eyes rolled back in his head and he collapsed on the floor. His fallen form was promptly swallowed by the gas permeating the room. Brian jerked on the door handle again. From the other side of the door, a loud click echoed.

Killean elbowed him out of the way and seized hold of the handle. His eyes blazed a fiery red, as the handle remained unmoving in his grasp. All around them, the remaining vamps collapsed to the floor.

Brian's vision blurred, and he tightened his grip on his stakes as darkness beckoned invitingly to him. He stumbled into the wall, leaning heavily against it as he tried to keep his rubbery legs under him. He had to stay awake; he'd never wake again if he went under now. Declan fell beside him, his crossbow clattering against the tile floor as it skittered away. Killean slumped against the door then sank to his knees as the gas took hold of him.

Unable to withstand the burning of his lungs anymore, Brian sucked in a greedy gulp of air then coughed against the gas searing his lungs. He'd promised Abby he'd return for her. He realized now, he wouldn't.

Abby, her name was a blaze of agony across his mind as his legs gave out. He'd failed to protect his family again, and now she would lose her life too.

∼

Abby bolted upright in bed. Sweat coated her body and her nightgown was tangled around her legs as cold dread slid down her spine. She'd dreamt of Brian the past three nights he'd been gone, but they'd been dreams of longing. This had been a nightmare the likes of which she couldn't escape. He'd been choking on something, unable to breathe, her name the last thing on his mind before he was dragged away from her.

He was in trouble. She knew it as surely as she knew she was right-handed. Throwing back the sheets, she almost toppled off the massive bed in her rush to get out of it. She snatched at her phone on the nightstand and hit his number. The ceaseless ringing set her teeth on edge. She'd spoken with him earlier and he'd been fine, but she couldn't shake the certainty he needed help.

She didn't bother with her robe as she rushed toward the door and flung it open. She ran down the hall, but she had no idea where she was going. No idea which room was Lucien's.

Finally, she gave up and started shouting his name. "Lucien! Lucien!"

She ran down another hall, her heart thumping more wildly with every passing second. "Lucien!" Her screams were becoming shriller, her voice raw from her cries. "Lucien!"

"Abby? What are you doing?" she turned to find Vicky rushing toward her.

"Where is Lucien?"

"Right here." Abby spun to find Lucien standing behind her. She had no idea where he'd come from, and she didn't care. His sandy hair stood up in tussled spikes, and his sweats hung low on his waist. His pale chest was bared as he hadn't bothered to put a shirt on. His sleep-swollen eyes focused on her. "And not at all pleased about being woken at this hour."

Abby didn't give a shit what pleased him. "Brian's in danger."

Lucien rolled his eyes. Abby almost punched him in the face for the reaction, but managed to keep herself restrained. "You probably had a bad dream."

"It wasn't a bad dream!" she snapped at him. "I have to find him!"

"Abby—"

She shrugged off the hand Vicky rested on her shoulder. "I'm not screwing with you," she snarled at Lucien. "You have to call one of your friends, *now*."

"I don't take orders from anyone except Ronan."

He was a good eight inches taller than she was, but they were standing toe to toe as she glowered at him. "Then call Ronan because I am going after him."

"You're not going anywhere."

Spinning away from him, she ignored the startled looks of the other recruits who had joined them in the hall as she rushed by them. She shook off Vicky's hands again and put her shoulder down to shove her way past Aiden and David when they stepped together to block her way.

"Abigail!" Aiden shouted as she broke through them, adrenaline and panic enhancing her strength.

"Get back to your rooms!" Lucien barked behind her. There were some scurrying sounds followed by the thumps of doors closing and the ringing of a phone.

Abby flew back into her room and raced around it as she tugged clothes on. She didn't care about her things, but running out of here half-naked in search of Brian wouldn't do her any good if he were in the city. She didn't have his ability, but she *would* find him. She didn't let herself doubt that; she may lose her mind if she did.

She snagged two stakes and a crossbow from where Brian had

stashed them in their room just in case. A shadow fell over the doorway while she was shoving her feet into her hiking boots. "I'll kill you if you try to stop me," she spat at Lucien without glancing up at him.

"I'm looking at her right now." She spun toward him, crossbow raised. She was prepared to fight to the death to get free of this place. He calmly lifted a hand to forestall her trigger finger while he listened to whoever was speaking through the phone. "We'll be there soon."

He hung up the phone and slipped it into his pocket. "Ronan wants to see you, now."

"Where is Brian?" she demanded.

"Brian, Declan, and Killean have vanished. He's hoping you can help find Brian."

Abby's heart sank. She'd known something was wrong, but the confirmation of it was a knife to her soul. *Not dead, missing. If he were dead, I would know it. I'd be dying too.*

"Let's go," she said brusquely and threw the crossbow onto her back.

"Can I get dressed first?" he inquired.

"No."

CHAPTER THIRTY

In the end, Abby had to wait as Lucien, Vicky, Aiden, and David all dressed. She'd paced ceaselessly back and forth, fighting the urge to scream as the five minutes had dragged endlessly on. She'd practically ripped the door off the Range Rover Lucien pulled in front of her, earning her another glare from him. She ignored it as she dove into the passenger seat.

"Blindfolds," he said and gave her a warning look when she heaved an exasperated sigh. The others all pulled theirs on, except for Aiden who silently urged her to do so with his eyes.

"I can run from here," she said. "And probably get there faster."

"You'll never make it beyond the gates on foot. Put it on or I'll sit right here all night."

She almost pointed out that would probably only piss off Ronan, but she was wasting time. Reluctantly, she pulled the blindfold over her eyes and sat back in the seat. Her foot tapped against the floor. Not being able to see did nothing to ease her growing anxiety.

Still alive. Still alive.

It was all she kept telling herself as she listened to the gates rattling closed behind them and the vehicle descending a hill. The others tried to draw her into conversation, but she was having none of it as the tires hummed on the road and she sensed the flashing of headlights washing over them through the blindfold.

Her fingers dug into her palms as the sounds around them changed. Blood welled forth beneath her nails, but she couldn't stop herself from tearing at her skin. "You can take them off now," Lucien said.

Abby tore hers off and flung it aside as she drank in the sights around them. They weren't in the city, but what looked like a large, run-down town that progress had forgotten as they passed empty businesses and crumbling, boarded-up homes. There was a fair amount of people on the streets and wandering through what businesses remained open at this hour, mostly bars and strip clubs.

Lucien pulled the Rover to the side of the road behind a sleek, black Mercedes. Abby jumped out of the passenger side of the SUV before he came to a complete stop. Her gaze flashed around the area, and her nose wrinkled at the scents assaulting it. Exhaust, decay, sewage, and body odor all combined into a mix the likes of which she hoped to never encounter again.

She barely glanced at the Mercedes when the driver and passenger doors opened. From what she'd heard about Ronan, she assumed it was he who emerged from the driver's side due to his reddish-brown eyes, sable hair, and the air of authority he emitted in waves. The other vampire with him had dark-blond hair that hung in curls to his collar and vivid hazel eyes.

Her attention was drawn across the street when a loud squeal of laughter pierced the air. *Ignore it all. Ignore them. Focus on Brian. You can find him.*

Abby forced herself to smell past the hideous odors burning her nose and to open her mind to the pathways connecting her and Brian. The bond between them was more sealed off than it had ever been before, but she could still feel the tremulous thread of it calling to her and connecting them.

"I brought you here because, as his mate, I believe you can track Brian, and hopefully find my men."

Abby didn't glance back as these words were spoken just behind her. The depth of the power washing over skin told her it was Ronan without having to look. Abby closed her eyes as the cool breeze drifted over her face. She scented the air again, but it wasn't a smell that drew her onward. It was something else, something within her blood.

She didn't look back at the others as she fled heedlessly down an alley.

~

"I suppose you're curious as to why you're still alive," a voice said from somewhere within the white room Brian had awoken to find himself in.

The effects of the drug still pulled at his eyes, and his head pounded as he strained against the bindings holding him to the table. He tried to look down, but found he couldn't move his head. His forehead was also locked down with a metal binding, the same as the ones strapped over his limbs and torso. Metal bit into his flesh and broke his skin when he flexed his muscles. He gritted his teeth and pulled against the holds as violently as his drugged body would allow him to.

"Enough of that," the voice chided. "We'll have to give you another dose if you can't behave."

He fell limply against the table, shaking as he inhaled a breath. The small burst of strength had left him weakened. He tried to hide the tremor in his muscles, but he was aware the voice had seen them when he heard a chuckle.

"Might just keep you alive," the voice purred.

Why am I still alive?

He blinked against the harsh glow, but he couldn't lift his head to look at who was speaking to him. "Oh, forgive me. I forgot you can't move."

The rays of the lamp positioned beside him lit the vamp who stepped forward with a halo that burned Brian's irises when he tried to focus on him. Closing his eyes, he counted to five before opening them again. A sneer curved his lip when he recognized Drake illuminated by the light. Brian lunged against the restraints, a snarl escaping him when the movement failed to gain more than a couple centimeters of space between him and the table.

"I'm going to rip your throat out and bathe in your blood!" he spat at Drake.

Drake's thin lips quirked into a twisted smile that caused the grotesque right side of his face to pull back awkwardly. Judging by the left side of his face, Drake had once been handsome enough with his jade green eye and refined features. An accident as a child had left the right side a sunken mass of twisted scars and flesh. He had no ear on that side, his eye was a socket, and the hole in his cheek revealed his teeth and tongue beyond.

In public, Drake usually wore a mask to shield the ruined side of his face, but Brian had already seen him without it and wasn't shocked by his appearance now. He kept his face impassive as Drake moved his tongue within the hole, purposely playing with his teeth on that side.

"What a colorful image you paint," Drake replied and folded his hands before him. "Unfortunately, I don't think you're going to get the opportunity."

Brian stared relentlessly at him. "Where are Declan and Killean?"

"Safely locked away. Their blood is what I need."

"And what do you want from me?" he demanded.

That hideous smile tugged at his face again. "You're going to bring me the prize I seek."

A sick feeling, which had nothing to do with the gas he'd inhaled, twisted in his stomach. "I'm not bringing you shit."

"Oh, but I believe you already are." Drake stepped forward and leaned over him to inhale deeply. A sigh escaped him, and his tongue clicked against his exposed teeth. "One of my men was hidden in the warehouse. He saw you leave with the twins; I want them back. One alone made me a lot of money, but *two* of those pretty little darlings will draw a lot more vamps here and fetch me a high price. Judging by your scent, you're mated to the one I didn't possess. The fresh blood so to speak. She'll come for you; I'm sure of it. She *will* find you through the bond. I could never forget what her sister smelled or tasted like, and I can't wait to find out how your little darling tastes too."

Brian howled and jerked against the bindings holding him. The effects of the gas were wearing off as his muscles strained against the restraints and adrenaline coursed through him. The veins in his arms stood out starkly as he thrashed against the bonds. At first Drake watched him in idle amusement, but when something popped and a few bolts gave way, Drake took a hurried step back and left the room.

Gas began to fill the room when Brian tore his right arm free of the restraints. "I'm going to kill you!" he roared as the effects of the gas seeped into his system once more.

~

ABBY STOOD across the street from the club, her heart racing as her blood pulsed through her body. She took a step into the street, but Ronan grabbed hold of her arm and pulled her back. "You will stay out here," he commanded brusquely.

"No, I won't," she replied.

His reddish eyes narrowed on her. Aiden stepped forward and

rested his hand on her shoulder. She resisted his grip when he tried to draw her away. "Abby—"

"I'm not arguing," she cut Aiden off. "I'm simply stating a fact. I won't stay out here. I… I can't."

Ronan's nostrils flared, and the power emanating from him increased, but he bowed his head in acquiescence. "If that is what you want."

"It is."

"I don't think it's a good idea," Aiden said.

"He is her mate. She will die if he does. She has a right to defend her life and his, if she can," Ronan replied.

Her brother opened his mouth to protest further, but Ronan turned away from him. Aiden took a deep breath. "Stay close to me," he told her.

"I'm stronger than I look," she retorted.

"Maybe so, but I'd prefer to have you where I can see you."

Abby wasn't going to spend the time arguing with him over it. "I'm coming too," Vicky said. "No way I'm staying behind if Abby and Aiden are in there."

"Stay out of the way," Ronan said and stepped into the street.

Lucien and the other vampire walked by Ronan's side while David, Vicky, and Aiden stayed near hers. Abby kept her gaze focused on the club as she tried to contain her excitement and dread. He was in there. She knew he was, but would they be able to get him out? Were Ronan's men in there with him, or were they somewhere else?

She swiftly descended the steps, nearly colliding with Ronan's back when he stopped abruptly outside the door at the bottom. He gave her a look that caused the others to take a step back. She had to fight the urge to shove him out of her way and plunge into the club.

Ronan thrust the door open and wrapped his arm around her shoulders. He pinned her firmly against his side as they stepped into the shadowed interior. After club Dracul, she was pretty much prepared for anything. She barely noticed the people and vampires grinding against each other as she frantically searched the crowd.

She went to step away from Ronan, but he pulled her back. "I agreed you could come, but you will not run off on your own or draw unnecessary attention to us."

She opened her mouth to protest, but the look he gave her silenced her. He was being benevolent right now, that wouldn't last if she pushed him. Clamping her lips together, she gave a brisk nod. He kept his hand firmly on her shoulder as they walked through the crowd.

Abby followed the pull of her bond with Brian to the back wall. She stood, staring at it in helplessness and frustration. "I don't understand," she murmured. "He's here, I know he is."

Ronan gazed over the wall before turning to the vampire who had arrived with him in the Mercedes. "Saxon, Lucien, see if you can find something."

They both faded away into the crowd. Still holding her shoulder, Ronan maneuvered her to face the dance floor as he leaned against the wall. Abby glanced behind her again before looking at the powerful vamp holding her. His eyes surveyed the room with a casual air that belied the tension she felt in the rigid body beside her.

"What is going to happen if they can't find something?" Abby asked Ronan.

"Then I will find a way to get these humans out of here and tear this wall down with my bare hands if necessary."

"I like the way you think."

She itched to do the same thing herself. She was half-tempted to start killing the humans in order to get them to scatter. Humans had never bothered her before. She'd always liked them and their world, but their presence here grated against her skin. She had to fight the urge to scream at them that they were a bunch of idiots for being here. Closing her eyes, she took a deep breath to steady her mounting impatience.

"They are my men," Ronan said, drawing her attention back to him. "I will do whatever it takes to get them back."

"Brian's not one of your men."

Those strangely colored eyes slid to her. "He may not have gone through the training, or be a pureblood, but he *is* one of us. He will not be left behind."

Abby almost sobbed with relief. She bit her lower lip to keep it from quivering as his eyes burned into hers. He didn't come across as the hugging type, but Abby almost threw her arms around him. Saxon and Lucien saved her from the impulse when they reappeared.

"I think we've got something," Lucien said and jerked his head toward a back hallway.

Ronan's hand on her shoulder kept her restrained. "It will do him no good if we find him, only to lose you. Remain calm or I will have Lucien drag you out of here."

Lucien gave her a smirk that made her realize he would enjoy doing just that. Abby glowered at him. "Stay here and keep watch behind us," Ronan said to David as they stepped into the hall.

David's eyes shot between her, Vicky, and Aiden but he took up a protective stance at the beginning of the hall. Ronan turned to Vicky next. "You're to stay with him."

"But—" she started to protest.

"There are no buts," Ronan interrupted firmly. "Stay with him."

Abby recognized the fighting expression on Vicky's face as she thrust out her chin. Aiden grabbed hold of her arm and turned her around before she could gear up for an argument. "Stay here," Aiden commanded her.

"I can help!" Vicky protested.

"Being here is as important as being with us. We'll need a warning if someone tries to come at us from behind."

Vicky sulked as she folded her arms over her chest. She relented when David grabbed hold of her shoulder and pulled her closer against his side. "This sucks," Abby heard Vicky mutter before

Lucien all but shoved her into a room full of cleaning supplies and various extras from the bar.

She glared at Lucien when he brushed by her to press against something on the wall. Abby stepped back as the wall swung inward to reveal a long, dimly lit hallway.

"That looks about as welcoming as the closet in *Poltergeist*," Aiden said.

Abby shuddered at the comparison and wondered if something would slither out to grab hold of them. "I don't like this," Saxon said.

Ronan's gaze ran over the walls of the hall before them. "Neither do I."

As they stood there, the door started to swing closed again. Ronan thrust his hand out, his muscles bulging as he strained against the door. Abby realized it was made of a foot-thick steel. The metal beneath his hand bent in. With a low creak, the door stopped moving and ground to a halt. A bolt fell from somewhere and clattered against the floor before rolling away into the shadows.

Abby almost laughed out loud at the realization he'd literally busted the springs out of the door but managed to keep it suppressed.

She barely kept her jaw from gaping when he released the door to reveal his handprint dented into the steel. He hadn't even broken a sweat. The vast amount of power that had taken rattled her. Thankfully he was on *her* side. She hadn't felt overly confident they'd all get out of here alive; now she knew this man really could tear this place down with his bare hands, probably in a matter of minutes.

They remained in the doorway, peering down the hall. Ronan stepped inside first. He didn't bother to pull weapons free like the rest of them did, but she realized now *he* was his biggest weapon. Abby had believed they would creep down the hall. No, Ronan and his men stalked down it as if they owned it.

She glanced at Aiden who nudged her arm before stepping inside. Was he really going to become one of these men? Was he really going to do this for the rest of his existence? It seemed so at odds and out of place with the easygoing brother she'd always known. Right now though, his leaf-colored eyes were as steely as the door Ronan had just dented.

"Come on, Abs," he said.

She walked by his side down the hall. Focusing inwardly, she sought Brian through the connection binding them. The call of him drew her onward, but his mind remained blocked to hers.

The scent of drying blood wafted to her before they stepped into the small room littered with dead bodies, cards and poker chips. *None of them are Brian.* She knew that, but her gaze still darted around as she sought to reassure herself none of the dead bodies were his.

"They came through here," Lucien said as he kicked aside a head with the spine still attached.

A queasy feeling assaulted her and sweat broke out across her upper lip when the head thudded across the floor before settling against the wall. Saxon bent to examine another vamp with arrows protruding from his chest. "Definitely Declan's bolts."

"What is that smell?" Aiden asked as he sniffed the air from the doorway.

"I don't know," Ronan replied.

The door began to close behind him when Aiden stepped the rest of the way into the room.

CHAPTER THIRTY-ONE

"Ah, they're here," Drake purred from beside him.

The effects of the last round of gas made it so Brian could barely get his eyes open to look at the monitor one of Drake's men had wheeled in while he'd still been struggling to wake up. There were at least twenty separate pictures on the large screen, each showing a different space or viewpoint. Most of them were focused on empty halls and rooms.

On one of the screens, he spotted Declan restlessly pacing behind the wall of a glass cell. Killean sat on a bed in a separate cell with one of his knees drawn up and his arm draped over it. Whereas Declan looked about ready to start beating on the glass and shouting, Killean appeared bored.

Drake's head tilted to the side as he studied the monitor. "Only one twin though."

Brian closed his eyes when his vision blurred. He forced them open again before Abby stepped into view on the monitor. His heart lurched into his throat as the camera angle showed her walking down the same hall he'd first traversed. Ronan strode down the hall before her with Lucien and Saxon flanking her sides and Aiden at her back.

From the angle of the camera, he could tell it was located within the room he'd been captured in earlier. They were only a few feet away from that room.

He strained forward against his restraints to discover his freed hand had been re-bolted to the table. More metal crossed over his chest and arms than before he'd passed out.

Drake cast him a negligent glance. "Had them reinforced while you were sleeping."

Sweat slid down his face when he fell back against the table. Tremors rattled his body as it worked to shed itself of the rest of the effects of the gas. "Ronan's confidence will get him killed," Drake said as he tapped the remote against his good cheek. "I won't be keeping him alive. He would fetch a fortune on the market, but he's too risky. With as old as he is, we don't know what he could be capable of, you know?"

Brian's heart raced when they stepped into the room where he'd been taken. *Abigail, go back!* She showed no reaction to the message he tried to send directly into her mind on the monitor. The gas had somehow managed to dim whatever it was in his mind that opened into hers.

Fisting his hands, he pulled against the metal binding him. His muscles bulged and his veins swelled, but there was no screeching of metal against his burst of strength. "No!" he bellowed.

Not Abby, he would not allow Abby to be chained to a wall and feasted upon by greedy, ravenous vampires. Her radiant soul shone through the black and white of the TV. The idea of it being dimmed in any way caused savagery to surge within him. *No* one would ever touch his mate in such a way.

Drake glanced back at him, his one eyebrow lifting as his mouth quirked in amusement. "My, the mate bond does make one persistent, doesn't it," he murmured. A keen light came into his eyes as his gaze raked over Brian. "I was going to kill you right away, but I think I'd like to see how and what this bond does to a vampire. It shall be fun!" he declared and threw his hands into the air.

"I am going to shove your intestines down your throat before I kill you," Brian vowed.

"How dramatic." *Snap, snap* went Drake's fingers above his head with a dramatic flair.

Brian bared his fangs at the man, but Drake turned his back on him again. Brian's gaze was drawn back to the monitor as the door started to close and gas released into the room. "Abby!" he shouted.

Ronan moved so fast Brian didn't see him until the door was torn from its hinges and crashed into the wall across the way. Lucien pushed the others back out of the room as the gas continued to fill it. Ronan remained behind, his eyes now entirely red as he surveyed the room. Then his head tilted back, and his gaze latched onto the camera.

His glistening fangs were revealed by the smile curving his mouth. Walking across the room, he climbed the bodies to grab the camera. His red eyes filled the lens before he tore it from the wall and the screen became nothing but static.

"Interesting," Drake murmured as he tapped the remote against his cheek again.

~

Gas slid down the hallway past them, floating in waves that made the hall smoky. Abby held her breath and tugged her black sweater over her nose. At least now she knew what the smell in the room had been as the acrid smoke made her eyes water.

"It should be safe. It's dispersing in the open space," Lucien said to her.

She still hesitated before pulling her sweater away from her mouth. "I've found a door," Ronan said from inside the room.

Abby stepped back into the room and surveyed the bodies. "This is where they were taken from?"

"Most likely," Ronan replied from where he stood with his hand wrapped around the edge of a door on the other side of the room.

Beyond the door was a set of stairs. Lucien moved to go down them first, but Ronan held him back. "Keep an eye out for cameras."

Lucien nodded before descending the stairs. Ronan gestured for Saxon to follow, then her and Aiden. Abby's nose wrinkled when the scent of mildew and the decaying aroma of death and garbage hit her like a punch in the face when she began to climb down. Lucien and Saxon exchanged a look as they stopped at the bottom of the stairs. Above her, she heard the grating sound of another door being broken.

Looking back, she saw dim rays of light around the door's edge from where it had been propped at an angle. Aiden pressed closer against her back when Ronan climbed down to join them and moved forward to stand at the front of the group. Out of instinct, she took hold of her brother's hand and grasped it within hers. He glanced at her before squeezing her hand and releasing it.

"There," Lucien said and pointed at something in the hall.

Before she could blink, Ronan vanished. She heard a wrenching sound and then he reappeared and dropped a camera at the foot of the stairs. He stomped it beneath his boot and gestured down the hall.

He tore more cameras from the walls as they moved beneath the earth. The stench of death and garbage grew with every step she took through the old sewage or water system winding beneath the surface of the town above them. She forced herself not to inhale as she followed the pull of Brian within the convoluted tunnels, leading them unflinchingly onward when they came across a branch within the concrete walls surrounding them.

She'd expected the concrete to be cool to the touch, but the circular tunnels kept the heat pressed against her. Sweat trickled down her brow and back as she walked. Little illumination pierced the confines, and most of it came from the holes the tree roots had created when they'd broken through from the surface above.

Arriving at another door, her heart beat faster as her hands rested against its smooth surface. Brian was close, so close she could almost feel him beneath her fingers again, almost smell his woodsy, evergreen scent. Her hands frantically searched for a way to open it as frustration swelled within her.

A hand rested on her shoulder. Feeling out of control with her desperation to get to him, she snapped her fangs at it. "Easy," Ronan cautioned and nudged her away from the door. "I'll find the entrance."

Abby couldn't stop shaking as she waited impatiently for him to search the door. A click sounded before it began to swing open. "What did you do?" she asked.

"Nothing," he replied. "Be prepared."

Aiden grabbed hold of her shoulders and pulled her back when something rushed at them from the shadows.

~

Brian jerked and thrashed against his bonds; Drake laughed as he watched the horde of twenty or so vampires descend on Abby and the others. It was the first chance he'd gotten to see her again since she'd left the gas room. He'd caught only a glimpse of her before she was swallowed beneath the rush of vampires.

"Abby!" he bellowed as fresh terror and strength streamed through him.

Drake glanced back at him when metal squeaked and bent, before turning away as if nothing more would happen. A fresh wave of dizziness assailed him, causing him to pant for air as he fell back against the table. He had no idea what they'd given him, but he couldn't shake its lasting effects.

In their cells, Declan stopped pacing, and Killean tilted his head to listen. Declan approached the thick glass wall of his cell and rested his hands on it.

On the video of Abby and the others, three of the vampires from the initial rush flew back into the hallway, all three of them missing their hearts. A handful more followed behind them.

From beneath the crush, he caught a glimpse of Abby's blonde hair as she wrestled against the vampires grasping and tearing at her. A punch connected with her cheek and she staggered backward. One of Brian's metal bindings popped open when he lunged forward. They'd hurt her; they *were* hurting her. He wouldn't allow it.

Straining to break free, another restraint popped open. Drake waved a hand absently at him as if trying to shush him while his gaze remained locked on the screen. "You know," he murmured, "I didn't find the other twin overly appealing, but there's something about yours... She's such a little fighter. The things I'll do..." Drake's voice trailed off as he licked his lips.

"*Fuck you!*" Brian thundered.

"You mean *I* will fuck *her*."

One of the bonds on his thigh gave way beneath the swell of blood and power rushing through him. Not his sweet Abigail, not the woman he loved more than he'd ever dreamed possible.

The realization hit him harder than a punch in the nose. He'd never thought he could be capable of loving someone again. He'd believed the ability to love had been destroyed with his family, but she'd made him capable of it again with her determination, strength, and the life she radiated. Somehow, through all the depravity and death within him, she made him so much more. She made him better. She accepted him for what he was, and she *wanted* him despite everything he'd done in his long, bloody existence.

Though there had been none so far, he expected guilt to swell forth with the realization of his love for her, but it remained buried. The guilt and hatred that had driven him every day of his vampire years had been drowned out by Abby's tender touches, her soft kisses, and her passionate spirit.

Looking back, he questioned if he'd still been in love with Vivian all these years or consumed by his guilt and self-hatred over his failure to keep his family safe. Sometime over the decades, he'd begun to move on from his love for her without realizing it. He'd been a fool for not seeing his love for Abby sooner, for not acknowledging everything she'd come to mean to him, and now they could die without her ever knowing it.

"So much spirit," Drake murmured when Abby plunged her stake into the chest of a vampire and grabbed another by his hair. Jerking his head back, she sank her fangs into his neck and tore his throat out.

His sweet, determined, seductress was as savage as she was loving. She'd believed she was as capable as he was of violence, and she was. *And she's capable of it for me.*

Abby kicked her victim away as the crush of vamps pushed them from the hallway and into the room from where the vampires had originally sprung. Abby was buried beneath the horde again. The loss of her sent a fresh burst of adrenaline rushing through him.

"Guards!" Drake didn't bother to look away from the monitor as another clamp broke away from Brian's thigh. "I would drug you again, but I want you to watch everything I do to her." Maliciousness gleamed in his eyes when he glanced at Brian. "I think it will be fun."

Two guards stormed into the room as Brian heaved against the bonds again. "Hold him," Drake commanded.

He bared his fangs at the men who seized hold of his shoulders and slammed him against the table. His muscles swelled as he thrashed against the table.

"That's it, love," Drake murmured.

Brian's eyes shot to the monitor as Abby broke free of the pack and staggered into the massive room that opened up behind her. Five vampires circled her as she edged around the sofa in the sitting room someone had established in the middle of the tunnel system. She grabbed hold of a small lamp and threw it at one vampire, who ducked to avoid the blow. Using his distraction, she leapt onto the couch and over the back of it.

The vampire nearly collapsed beneath her when she landed on his back, but he managed to keep himself upright. Before he could react, Abby used her fangs to tear a gash across his neck. Blood sprayed the room and her as she jumped away from him. One of the other vamps grabbed her wrist. She spun and smashed her fist into his chest, tearing his heart from him and stomping on it.

That's my girl. Pride and fear for her swelled within him; he renewed his battle against his captors when Abby leapt back over the couch. He realized one of the vamp's had a crossbow seconds before the bolt hit her shoulder. Brian roared with fury. He managed to knock away one of the hands holding him as he flailed wildly. Another restraint gave way beneath his flexing forearms.

Abby stumbled back, her eyes latching onto the crossbow before she turned and fled down the hall. "Here she comes," Drake said excitedly.

"Abby, no!" Brian shouted.

CHAPTER THIRTY-TWO

Abby tore the bolt from her shoulder as she raced down the winding tunnels. The slap of her pursuer's feet echoed around her as she ran. She kept her hand pressed against the wound to staunch the flow of blood soaking her sweater.

Behind her, she could hear the others still battling against the vampires. She had no idea how to get back to help them, and she didn't much feel like coming up against a crossbow again. She was following Brian's pull through the tunnels when a bellow reverberated over the concrete surrounding her. "Abby, no!"

The sound of Brian's voice caused her heart to leap. It didn't matter that he was telling her not to continue, all that mattered was seeing him again. Her hand fell away from her shoulder, the pain of it forgotten as she poured on the speed. Rounding another curve, the tunnel widened before her.

A door opened to reveal a sterile white room. Her eyes latched onto Brian, strapped to a table raised so she could see him and tilted so he was almost upright. Blood trickled from his forehead and other places across his body as he strained against the holds on him. His muscles grew larger before her eyes as his veins throbbed with the blood filling them.

The sight of him, covered in bruises and blood, caused something to emerge within her. She'd been angry and determined before, but now she was *enraged*. A ruthless snarl tore from her as she plunged heedlessly onward.

Brian lifted his head. His eyes widened on Abby as she ran toward him with far more speed than he'd considered possible for her age. Her eyes glowed red, illuminating the darkness surrounding her.

"No!" he shouted at her. "Don't come in here!"

She'd never obeyed him before; he hadn't expected her to do so now. She plunged into the room, oblivious to Drake standing by the monitor. Drake's head tilted to the side as he watched her. He adjusted himself in his pants and groaned as he stroked himself. As his hand fell away, he licked his lips.

"Get out of here!" Brian hissed at Abby when her hands fell on the metal clasps holding him in place.

It was too late though as the three who had been chasing her stepped through the door. "Close it," Drake commanded.

Abby's gaze shot to Drake, her eyes burning hotter as her nostrils flared. A pureblood scenting out another pureblood, but Drake was far older than she was. Brian thrashed against the bonds again when Drake sniffed the air and moaned. Abby's lips curled when he reached down to fondle himself once more.

"Your blood smells like heaven," Drake murmured. "I'm betting your body will feel like it too."

A ripple of shock radiated from Abby and into him. The effects of the drug were fading; he could feel a thin thread connecting them again and pulsing to life between them. He tried to probe her mind, but found he was still shut out from her.

"I've decided to keep you for myself," Drake said to her. "We'll let him watch, of course." He flicked his fingers at Brian as he moved closer to her, circling her from the other side of the table. "It will be more fun that way."

Abby took in the other vampires in the room before landing on the one holding the crossbow now aimed at Brian's heart. "Move that," she spat at him.

"Not until you come to me, love," the hideous looking vamp across from her replied.

She had no idea what had happened to him to leave such destruction on his face, and she didn't care. "I'm guessing you're Drake," she said.

He gave an elegant bow with a wave of his hand. "My reputation precedes me, I see."

Abby glanced at the two vamp's still holding Brian. Their gazes were focused on her, but the look in their eyes said they were prepared to kill Brian if it became necessary. She grasped the metal band wrapped around his bicep as she prepared to wrench it free.

"Tsk tsk, love," Drake said. "Those are to stay in place."

Brian kept his eyes on Drake as he continued to close in on Abby. There was nowhere for her to go. If she moved away from him, she would be within reach of the three vamps who had chased her in here or the two who stood just behind him.

Her fingers caressed the flesh of his arm before she released him and took a step away. Brian gritted his teeth and attempted to lunge for her, needing her back, needing to protect her as she edged closer to the other three.

One of them snickered at her and altered his stance as he prepared to grab hold of her. Her reddened eyes met his. Within their ruby depths, he saw what he'd always seen with his Abby, a refusal to back down and admit defeat. He had to help her.

One of the vamp's jerked him back against the table and punched him in the temple when he tried to surge forward. Lights burst before his eyes as he fought against the darkness threatening to drag him under. He couldn't pass out now, not when she needed him so badly.

"Don't hurt him!" Abby cried.

"He doesn't have to experience anymore pain, just come to me," Drake said with a beckoning wave of his hands. "Otherwise…" he gave a nod at the vamp's holding Brian.

Before he knew what they intended, one of them grabbed hold of his right hand and jerked all of his fingers back. Brian clamped his teeth against the shout that almost escaped him when his fingers were ripped back and bone burst through his skin. Sweat beaded across his forehead and slid down his body. He could feel blood dripping from where one of his bones had pierced the skin of his palm.

"No!" Abby screamed.

She lunged toward him, but froze when the other guard grabbed hold of his left hand. "Do it!" Brian sneered at him. "What I'll do to you will be much worse. You have no idea who you're fucking with."

The guard's hand trembled on Brian's when he bared his fangs at him and snapped his teeth. "Don't," Abby pleaded. "Don't hurt him anymore."

"Then come, I've a present for you." Drake slid his hand over his erection again.

His one eye rolled in his head as he licked the side of his face that still had lips. He was the most hideous man Abby had ever encountered, and that hideousness had little to do with his looks. The rot within him made him truly disgusting. She'd never smelled anything worse than the way Drake smelled. The main source of the decaying stench they'd been following through the tunnels had been coming from *him*.

Her gaze slid to the asshole with the crossbow again. She could get to him, take him and maybe the two next to him out, but the two still holding Brian were a problem. Then there was Drake. She could feel the power oozing off him. He was another pureblood, capable of anything. She looked to Brian again, coated in blood, with sweat beading across his brow and his fingers bent in a way they were never meant to go.

His reddened eyes held hers, his fangs shining in the light beating on him. There had been no spoken words of love between them, but she *did* love him. She would die for him and she would die without him. Even if there was no love on his part, she knew he cared for her. She could hand herself over to Drake now and wait for an opportunity to escape. It may destroy something within both of them, but they would find a chance to break free, and they could be with each other again once they did.

They may be different afterward, but they would survive it. Everyone was changed by life at some point in time. If they weren't changed, then they weren't living.

Brian watched the emotions flickering over Abby's face. When her gaze slid to Drake, then back to him, he sensed a wavering within her. *No, Abby, don't ever give into him.* Tears swam in her eyes as he finally succeeded in penetrating the haze that had been enshrouding his mind to communicate with her.

The guard's hand tightened on his. "Don't," Abby said to him. "Don't. You win."

Brian's heart pounded against his ribs. He strained against the bonds as Abby held her hands up and took a step closer to the three who had chased her in here. Closing her eyes, she took a deep breath before opening them again. Resolve and something more glistened in her eyes when they met his. The lethal look in her gaze caused his heart to stop for a minute.

Then, the guard released his hand and bashed his fist against Brian's face again. Blood exploded from his mouth, and he snarled at the guard who smiled back at him. "I'm not fucking with much," the guard said with a dismissive glance over Brian's body.

The fresh scent of Brian's blood on the air and the sight of his torn skin caused something to swell within her. He was *her* mate, and they were abusing him. His hand, his *bones*... Her fangs pricked and extended. Saliva dripped from the ends of them when her lips skimmed back. She'd heard about bloodlust, but she'd never truly experienced it, not until now.

Now she could feel it thrumming through her veins, pulsing throughout her body. Red shaded her vision and her fingers curled as the room around her became strangely serene. No one moved, even the heartbeats faded away until there was nothing but stillness and her need to kill. Then a single drop of Brian's blood landed on the ground with a plop that unleashed the growing frenzy within her.

When one of the vamp's stepped toward her, she spun so swiftly that Brian never saw her move before blood was spurting from where the vamp's throat had been. The vamp holding the crossbow fired a round a split second after the crossbow was jerked up in his grasp. The breeze the bolt created blew against Brian's ear and sliced his flesh when he twisted his head to the side in order to avoid taking it in the face. It hit one of the guards behind him in the shoulder, knocking him back.

Abby reloaded, spun and fired the crossbow at one of the guards trying to hold him down. Clawing at his chest, the guard fell back as he struggled to tear the bolt free. Brian surged forward against the bonds. Metal pings reverberated around the room when more bolts gave way. Jerking his right wrist free, Brian tore at the bonds holding his other wrist as the two other vamps who had chased Abby into the room ran for the door. He felt the movement of air from her passing more than saw her as Abby leapt onto the back of one and sank her fangs into his throat.

She jerked back with all her might. Brian's fingers froze in the act of trying to tear the metal from his forehead when she tore the vamp's head from his body. The one who had been holding the crossbow screamed and threw himself against the door when she dragged him down. Blood coated her, but beneath it, he also saw the subtle shift in hue on her skin.

The change of skin color happened amongst the pureblood males when they'd been pushed to the edge, or when their mate was threatened. Usually, they were also much older. When Ethan and Ian had exhibited the trait at such a young age, it had been surprising. To see Abby doing it now was astounding. It was extremely rare for a female to exhibit the turning, but before his eyes, Abby's skin was darkening and her eyes were becoming redder. She wrenched the head from the vamp's shoulders as easily as if she'd plucked a flower from the garden.

Brian tore the band from his forehead as she spun toward him. The last bonds gave way against his feet as the guard who had punched him tried to run past. Brian snagged hold of him and sank his fangs into his neck. He welcomed the hot wave of blood as it replenished the blood he'd lost and washed away the remaining effects of the gas. The guard thrashed in his grasp, trying to fight him off. Brian grabbed hold of his chin and wrenched his head to the side, ceasing anymore of the man's struggles.

"I told you I'd make you pay," Brian snarled at him before throwing the drained vamp away from him.

Abby bolted past him again. There was only one vamp left in the room for her to go for; one who was far more powerful than she was. He spun in time to see her vanishing through a door he hadn't known was behind him. Instead of staying to fight, Drake had fled like the coward he was, drawing Abby into his convoluted tunnels.

Leaping off the table, Brian fled down the hall after her. "Abby!" he shouted, but she didn't slow as she ran heedlessly around the corners. He knew that she was consumed by bloodlust and all she could focus on right now was the fact that Drake must die. She wouldn't stop to think that Drake could be luring her into a trap.

CHAPTER THIRTY-THREE

ABBY WAS nothing but a blur before him, one he was determined to catch as he poured on the speed after her. She had the strength of her pureblood and so did he. He drew on the flow of her within his veins, the flow of the *many* lives and power he'd harvested over the years. Never had he needed that strength as badly as he did now.

He felt his muscles swell with it as he began to take her over. Wrapping his arms around her waist, he lifted her up and spun her away when Drake turned and charged at them. Abby's displeasure beat against his mind as he set her on her feet beside him. Everything in him screamed at him to stand before her, to protect her, but she could hold her own, and standing behind him was not where she would be throughout the rest of his life.

No, she would stand at his side from here on out.

Panicked, Drake's eye was red as he barreled toward them. Brian braced his legs apart; a smile spread across his face as he thought of everything he was going to do to this bastard. Before he reached them, Drake dashed to the left and toward a tunnel Brian hadn't noticed in his urgency to get to Abby.

"No!" Abby shouted and dove at the tunnel. Rolling across the ground, she popped up in front of it just as Drake hit her with the force of a Mac truck. Something in her shoulder gave way with a loud pop that echoed throughout the room. The fingers of her right hand went numb, but she swung up with her left hand and punched him in the temple.

His fingers tore at the flesh of her arms when he snatched hold of her and threw her back. Unable to keep her balance, Abby stumbled and fell onto the concrete floor. Drake loomed over her, his fangs dripping as he glowered at her.

She'd believed the roar in her head was from the blood pounding against her temples. She realized now it was coming from Brian as he leapt onto Drake's back and clutched his head. Drake squealed like a rat. He reeled away from her and started to beat at Brian over his back. Abby scrambled to her feet as Brian sank his fangs into Drake's throat.

Drake squealed again and spun in rapid circles that became a blur to her eyes. Brian hung onto him, refusing to relinquish his hold. Trying to differentiate one from the other, Abby threw out her leg. She somehow managed to time it right enough to trip Drake with her foot. He stumbled forward before his legs gave out and his knees hit the concrete.

Brian's pleasure and assurance of victory beat against her as he grabbed hold of the back of Drake's head and smashed it into the floor. The man's arms and legs jerked out as his forehead caved from the force of the blow.

Turning Drake over, Brian grinned down at his one good eye. "I made you a promise," he said as his hands dug at the vulnerable flesh of Drake's belly.

Abby took a step forward, drawing his attention to her before he could tear Drake open and shove his intestines down his throat. Brian's hands stilled as he warred with his more vicious nature and stared into her reddened eyes. It didn't matter how badly he wanted to torture Drake, didn't matter he knew she would never turn away from him, or that she was more than capable of brutality. He simply couldn't be that kind of a monster in front of her.

Releasing his stomach, Brian drove his fist into Drake's chest. Flesh and bone gave way beneath his hand. He winked at Drake as his hand wrapped around his pulsating heart and tore it from the man's chest. Gurgling sounds escaped the vamp. Blood shot from his lips as he coughed and choked it up. Brian threw the heart aside and wiped his hands on his jeans as he rose to his feet.

Abby ran to him and threw herself into his arms. He wrapped his arms around her, inhaling her sweet scent and savoring the feel of her body against his. She slid her legs around his waist as he pulled her head back to claim her mouth. A whimper escaped her when his tongue traced over her lips before greedily slipping inside to take in the taste of her. He couldn't stop the shaking rattling him as she pressed closer, the hand on her good arm desperately grabbing him. He ignored the pains in the mending bones of his hand as he clung to her.

Tears streaked through the blood coating her face when she pulled away to look at him. "You're okay!"

"I'm okay," he said as he brushed her hair back from her face. Her eyes gradually returned to their beautiful emerald color as she gazed at him with a wonder that rattled him.

"I love you," she whispered.

His heart jumped in his chest and a lump lodged in his throat at those humbling words. His hand stilled on her face, cupping her cheek.

"You have to know that. I thought I was going to lose you..." her voice broke on a sob. "You don't have to say it back. I understand if you don't feel it too. I know you love your wife—"

"I did," he interrupted. "Very much, but not as much as I love you."

She drew her bottom lip into her mouth as she stared at him with hope shimmering in her eyes. "Really?"

He grinned at her, pulling her head down so her forehead rested against his. "Truly."

More tears spilled from her as she threw her good arm around him. Her fangs scraped against his neck as she snuggled closer. "Feed, Abby."

"No, you're wounded."

"So are you. I need this."

So did she. Unwilling to argue with him, her lips skimmed back, and she sank her fangs into his neck. A mewl escaped her when his powerful blood filled her mouth. The fingers of her good hand dug into his shoulder as his love for her pulsed against her through the bond.

The walls he'd erected between them crumpled, and he allowed his self-hatred, his anger, and the thrill he got from killing to pour over her. She'd known he was a killer, she'd accepted this, but she'd never realized how much he enjoyed destroying those who deserved it. He'd been afraid, if she'd known how much pleasure he took in it, she would turn away from him. Instead, she found herself loving him more. No matter what, he was her vampire, her mate, and she was never going to let him go.

Brian's good hand dug into Abby's waist as he turned his head into her neck and nuzzled the hair back from her skin. He scraped his fangs over her flesh before biting deep. Her acceptance of everything he was swept over him as she allowed him to feel the love she'd been keeping locked away in order to keep her heart protected from him.

Releasing his bite on her, he lifted his lips to her ear. "I will never break your heart, Abby. I treasure it above all else." Tears wet the collar of his shirt as they slid down her face. "Shh, dove," he whispered.

He wanted to stand here and hold her forever, but that would have to wait until later. He had no idea how many of Drake's men may still be wandering these tunnels. "We have to go," he said.

Disappointment filled him when she reluctantly retracted her fangs from his neck, but the bond between them remained open. Her mind brushed against his as she kissed him tenderly. Then, she bolted upright in his arms as she completely recalled where they were.

"Aiden!" she gasped.

She went to squirm out of his arms, but he held her in place. "No, not yet," he groaned. "I just got you back."

Abby stopped moving and dropped her head to his shoulder again. She was in no rush to be free of his arms yet either. He kept her close against him as he strolled through the tunnels, moving with single-minded determination as he was drawn forth by the essence of their friends and family.

"Almost there," he murmured.

Turning a corner, he stopped and waited until Ronan came around the next bend in the tunnel. The older vampire stopped when he spotted them. Ronan's eyes ran over the two of them before settling on Abby and widening when she turned in Brian's arms to look at him. Brian set her on her feet when her brother appeared behind him.

"Aiden!" she cried and ran toward him.

He lifted her and hugged her close before settling her on her feet. "Are you injured?" he demanded as his eyes ran over the blood drenching her.

"It's only my arm," she replied. "I'll be fine."

"Well now, that's unusual for a woman pureblood," Declan said when he spotted Abby's still mottled skin tone.

Abby glanced down at her strangely colored arms and managed to raise her good shoulder in a shrug. "Don't fuck with my mate," she replied.

Declan laughed and folded his arms over his chest. "Apparently not."

"Drake?" Ronan asked Brian.

"Dead."

"Good."

"I say we get out of this place," Declan said. "I have beers and babes waiting for me somewhere I'm sure."

Walking over, Brian gently took hold of Abby's dislocated shoulder. "I can put it back in place, but it's going to hurt."

She bit her bottom lip and gave a brisk nod. "Do it."

Brian's hand remained on her shoulder, but he found he couldn't bring himself to do it. Ronan stepped forward and brushed his hand aside. "Allow me," Ronan said. Brian moved reluctantly out of the way. "Don't attack me or I'll knock you out, and then your mate here is going to get all pissed off."

"I won't." Brian's teeth ground together as he fought to keep himself restrained. Declan and Lucien stepped in front of him when Ronan took hold of Abby's shoulder.

"Count to three," Ronan told her.

"One, two…" Snap.

Abby barely kept herself from screaming when he shoved her shoulder back into place. Declan and Lucien grabbed hold of Brian, holding him back when he jumped forward. His eyes burned with the fires of Hell once more.

Abby slid between the two men and toward Brian. He wrapped her up in his arms once more, holding her close against him as he sent a scathing glare at Ronan. She rested her hand against his cheek. "I'm fine."

His eyes bled back to their beautiful, ice-blue color as he kissed the tip of her nose and lifted her. She wrapped her arms around his neck and nestled closer to him.

CHAPTER THIRTY-FOUR

"You should go home, Abby." Vicky swung her legs back and forth while sitting on the edge of the back porch swing. It had been a week since the events occurred in the tunnels, and the first time Vicky had brought up the idea of home to her. "The others should meet Brian."

"They have met him," Abby reminded her with a nudge of her elbow against Vicky's side.

"Let them see him as he is with you. It will go a long way to melting the rest of their reservations about him. It has with me."

"They'll meet him again, eventually." Abby's eyes scanned over the massive bushes of the maze before them. She still hadn't made it to the center of the maze, something she'd become determined to do. "And they understand that I prefer to stay with you right now."

"And what does your mate prefer?"

"Do you honestly think Brian is eager to plunge into the Byrne clan?" she asked with a smile. "You know how someone's not a people person? Well, he's not exactly a vampire vamp."

Vicky laughed and swung her feet out again. "He's *really* not. I would like to be there when he is engulfed by that horde. I guarantee it will cause some good laughs."

"It will," Abby agreed. "But you're not ready to go home yet."

"I'm not."

"The family will understand you didn't mean to kill her. The Stooges and Mom and Dad won't even be able to smell it on you."

"It's more than that." Vicky took a deep breath as she lifted her head to study the gardens. "I want Duke dead first, and I can't go back there when killing him is all I can think about. I'm not ready for family loving when all I feel is hate for him."

Abby rested her hand on top of Vicky's. Over the past week, many of the vampires who had been involved in Drake's operation, including Garth, had been taken out by Ronan, Brian, and the others. Brian had happily been the one to destroy the vampire who had killed Marissa and set Abby up to be captured.

Brian had informed her that, while undergoing questioning, Garth had admitted he'd known Vicky was in the warehouse. When Abby had called him claiming to be Vicky, and then sent her picture, Garth had realized he'd be able to capture her too. They'd been prepared for Abby's arrival that night. They hadn't been prepared for all of them.

Though most everyone had been destroyed, Duke was still out there. Brian had offered to help find him when Vicky was ready, but her normally impatient sister had decided to spend more time training here before going after Duke. Abby suspected it was because she was more scared of what was out there than she was letting on, but Vicky would never admit that.

"I understand how you feel and I'm staying with you until you're ready," Abby assured her. "We'll go back together. We can use Brian as a distraction and some entertainment when we do."

"You two are evil." Abby turned at Aiden's words as he stepped beside her and grinned down at them. "But it really is going to be entertaining. You know those kids are going to swamp him just because they'll find it fun to torment him."

Vicky and Abby laughed as they pushed back on the swing again. "Looks like you're going to be stuck with us for a bit," Abby told him.

He pulled one of the other chairs forward and settled into it. "I'm okay with that. Have you talked to Mom and Dad?" he asked Vicky.

"A few days ago," she replied, her eyes darting to the side.

It had been a short conversation, consisting mainly of Vicky insisting she was fine and that they should stay with the others. When Vicky had grown tired of the conversation, she'd thrust the phone at Abby and walked away. It had been up to her afterward to keep their parents from jumping into the car and driving around New York in search of the training compound. She'd promised to let them know if anything changed, but she believed it was only a matter of time before she got the call saying they were in New York and insisting on seeing Vicky.

The sun was hanging lower over the maze when Brian stepped onto the porch. "Come with me," he said and stretched his hand out to her. He helped her to her feet. "Don't expect her back anytime soon," he said to Vicky and Aiden over his shoulder.

Vicky gave a small wave while Aiden shook his head and folded his arms over his chest. Brian led her down the steps and toward the maze entrance. "Are you finally going to show me how to get through it?" she inquired.

The wicked smile he sent her melted her heart and curled her toes in her boots. "I'll show you anything you want."

"I'm going to hold you to that."

The way his eyes hungrily ran over her caused her voice to come out huskier as they stepped into the entranceway carved between the ten-foot-tall, thick, green hedges. He led her unerringly forward, taking turns that left her confused and uncertain of where they were.

By now, she would have come across at least ten dead ends, but he never encountered a wall.

"Did you use your ability to get to the center?" she inquired suspiciously.

He tugged her against his side. "Nope, I'm naturally good at everything I do."

"You're not very good at being humble."

"I've never tried it before, but I'm sure if I did, I'd be fucking fantastic at it."

Abby laughed as she leaned against his side. "I'm sure you would too."

She searched the hedges as they strolled through the maze together. She couldn't tell if she'd already been in this area before or not. After ten minutes, the pathway widened and they stepped into a large clearing in the center of the maze. Abby's mouth fell open when she finally discovered the secret the maze had been hiding.

She didn't know where to look first as her gaze flitted over the large glass building before them. There was a fountain inside the building with vines twisting over the sides of it. Roses climbed a trellis, their thick red and yellow blooms dangling over the top of it. Stepping forward, Brian pulled open the door to the large greenhouse and gestured for her to enter with a small bow.

Her gaze continued to run over the assorted plants and flowers blooming within the building. All around her were hundreds of roses, orchids, hydrangeas, and lilies. Spongy plants sank beneath the weight of her hiking boots when she stepped onto them. The setting sun lit the glass surrounding them with pinks, yellows, and oranges as it dipped toward the horizon.

"This is amazing," she breathed.

"Not as amazing as you," Brian replied as he watched the delight dance across her face while she moved through the greenhouse.

The warmth of the humid air within the building felt good against her chilled skin. She turned as she gazed at everything, trying to take it all in. Brian stood by the fountain; his eyes locked on her while she inspected the plants and inhaled their sweet scents. He didn't move as he watched her with a predatory hunger. She smiled as she walked back toward him; her fingers itching with the impulse to touch him. Her skin became electrified with her need for him.

When she was only a foot away from him, he pulled something from his pocket and went down onto one knee before her. Abby froze, and her hand flew to her mouth as he opened the box to reveal the large diamond within. Tears burned in her eyes as the fading sun lit his hair and eyes and caressed his chiseled body.

"I don't know how long I'll have to work with Ronan, but I can promise you that when it's done, I will take you everywhere you ask to go and live out every one of your dreams with you. I will love you every second of every day for the rest of our lives, and I will protect and cherish our children with everything I am."

Her head shot up at those words. They'd yet to discuss the idea of children since the first time. She hadn't been able to bring herself to risk ruining the bubble of bliss that had been surrounding them this past week by bringing it up again. He'd still been pulling out of her when they made love, so she had no reason to suspect he'd changed his mind.

"You want children... with me?" she asked in a hitching voice.

"I want everything with you. As soon as my time with Ronan is over, and you've done everything you want to do, I would love to see our babe growing within you."

A sob escaped her at his words, and he took hold of her hand. "I never thought I'd meet someone like you, Abigail Byrne. You've turned a desolate life into one of promise and love when I never believed there would be again. Will you marry me?"

Unable to speak, Abby could only manage a nod as tears spilled down her cheeks. The radiant smile on his face caused her heart to swell to near bursting when he slid the ring onto her finger. She didn't get a chance to look at it before he was rising to his feet and wrapping his arms around her. She cried out in joy when he spun her around before claiming her mouth with his.

Abby's hands slid into his hair, and she pulled him closer as the swelling evidence of his arousal pressed against her belly. She'd once wondered which side of him was more dominant, the brutal one or the tender one. She knew now they were both intricately woven together to create this enticing, frustrating, amazing vampire who was completely hers, and she wouldn't have it any other way.

She'd never been happier in her life than when he laid her down on the spongy plants and took possession of her. With him was where she would always belong.

The End.

Fractured **(Vampire Awakenings, Book 6)**
is now available on Amazon:
brendakdavies.com/Frppbk

Read on for an excerpt from book 1 in Brenda's The Road to Hell Series—now available!

Stay in touch on updates and new releases from the author by joining the mailing list!

Mailing list for Brenda K. Davies and Erica Stevens Updates:
brendakdavies.com/ESBKDNews

GOOD INTENTIONS

River,

It has been thirteen years since the war started, the bombs were dropped, and the central states became a thing of the past. When the war ended, a wall was erected to divide the surviving states from those destroyed. I never expected to go beyond the wall but unlike all the others who volunteered to go, I wasn't given a choice.

With a dim knowledge of what I could do, the soldiers came for me. They took me beyond the wall where I learned that the truth is far more terrifying than I'd ever dreamed. Alone, with humans and demons seeking to learn what it is I can do, I find myself irresistibly drawn to the one man I should be avoiding most. One who intrigues and infuriates me. One who is not even a man, not really.

Kobal,

My entire life, I've had only one mission, reclaim my throne from Lucifer and put right everything that was torn apart when he was cast from Heaven. It's a mission I haven't wavered from, not even when the humans tore open the gates and unleashed Hell on earth.

Now, I've never been closer to obtaining my goal yet I find

myself risking it all because I cannot stay away from her, a human who may be the key to it all.

This Series will follow Kobal and River throughout. Not all things will be resolved in this book. Due to graphic language, violence and sexual content this book is recommended for readers 18+ years of age.

Sneak Peak

River

I was nine when the first of the fighter planes flew over thirteen years ago. I remember tilting my head back to stare at them as they moved over us in a V formation. Excitement buzzed through me, but I felt no fear. The planes had been a more common sight before the military base closed last year; despite that status, planes still occasionally flew over our town.

When the planes vanished from view, I turned my attention back to the game of hopscotch I was playing with my friend, Lisa. I was about to beat her, and I wanted to finish before Mother woke from her nap and called me away. Lisa stared at the sky for a minute more before turning her attention back to me. She bent to pick up the rock on the ground as four more planes flew over us in a tight formation. They left white streaks in the sky as their engines roared over us.

The rock Lisa had picked up slid from her fingers and clattered onto the asphalt. Together, we watched as the second wave of planes disappeared from view. I don't know why the initial wave of planes hadn't bothered me, but the second wave caused a cold sweat to trickle down my neck.

Following the noise of the planes, the world around us took on an unusual hush for a Saturday afternoon in July. Normally there were shouts from kids playing up and down the street. The rumble of cars driving down the highway, heading toward the beach, was a near constant background noise now that tourist season was in full swing.

Turning my attention back to Lisa, I waited for her to pick her rock up again and continue, but she remained staring at the sky. The planes had unnerved me, but what did I really know? At that point in my young life, my biggest problem was napping in the house a hundred feet away from me. I hoped the planes hadn't woken Mother; grouchy was a permanent state for her, but when she was woken from a nap, she could be a real bear.

I glanced over at my one-year-old brother, Gage. My heart melted at the sight of his disheveled blond hair sticking up in spikes and his warm brown eyes staring at the sky. He lifted a fist and waved at the planes fading from view. His coloring was completely different from my raven hair and violet eyes, due to our different fathers. Mine had taken off before I was born; Gage's father had at least stuck around to see his birth before leaving our mother in the dust.

Turning his attention away from the sky, Gage held his arms toward me before shoving a hand into his mouth. Unable to resist him, I walked over and lifted him off the ground. I cradled his warm body in my arms. I always brought him with me during Mother's naps so he wouldn't wake her, and because I couldn't stand him being alone in the house while she slept. I'd been alone so many times before he'd come along that I refused to let him be too.

Gage wrapped his chubby arms around my neck, pressing his sweaty body against mine. Lisa wiped the sweat from her brow and brushed aside the strands of brown hair sticking to her face. Waves of heat wafted from the cooking asphalt, but I barely felt it. I'd always preferred summer to winter and tolerated the heat better than most others.

Six more planes swept overhead, leaving a loud, reverberating boom in their wake as they sped by. Car alarms up and down the street blared loudly, horns honking in quick succession, and headlights flashing had all the dogs in the neighborhood barking. The relatively peaceful day had become chaotic in the blink of an eye.

Along the road, doors opened and beeps sounded as people turned off their alarms. Shouts for the dogs to be quiet could be heard over the alarms that continued to wail loudly. Some people ran out of their homes and toward the squealing cars to try and turn off the alarms that wouldn't be silenced.

Gage's arm tightened around my neck to the point of near choking. I didn't try to pull him away; instead I held him closer when he began to shake. Then just as rapidly as the rush of noise had erupted on the street, everything went completely still. Even the dogs, sensing something was off, became almost simultaneously silent. The few birds that had been chirping stopped their song; they seemed to be holding their breath with the rest of the world.

I remember Lisa stepping closer to me. Years later, I can still feel her warm arm against mine in a moment of much needed solidarity. "What's going on, River?" she asked me.

"I don't know."

Then, from inside some of the nearby homes, screams and cries erupted, breaking the near silence. Exchanging a look with Lisa, we turned as one and ran toward her house. We clambered up the steps, jostling against each other in our rush to see what was going on. We'd scarcely entered the cool shadows of her screened-in porch when I heard the sobs of her mother.

We both froze, uncertain of what to do. Tears streaked Gage's cheeks and wet my shirt when he buried his face in my neck. He may have only been a baby, but he still sensed something was completely wrong.

Instinctively knowing we would be shut out of whatever was going on if we alerted them to our presence, it had to be grown-up stuff after all, we'd edged carefully over to the windows, looking in on the living room. Peering in the windows, I spotted Lisa's mom on the couch, her head in her hands as she wept openly. Lisa's father stood before the TV, the remote dangling from his fingertips as he gaped at the screen.

My eyes were drawn to the TV; my brow creased in curious wonder at the mushroom cloud I saw rising from the earth. A black cloud of rolling fire and smoke covered the entire horizon on the screen.

Beneath the cloud, words ran across the bottom of the screen. *The U.S. is under attack. Nuclear bomb dropped on Kansas. Possible terrorist attack. Possible attack from China or Russia. Numerous areas of reported violence erupting.*

"It's World War III," Lisa's father said as the remote fell from his hand and her mother sobbed harder.

My heart raced in my chest, and my throat went dry as I struggled to grasp what was going on. I knew something awful had occurred, but I still couldn't understand what. How could I? I was a child. My time on this earth had been spent trying to avoid my mother as much as possible. It had also been filled with taking care of my brother, friends, TV, books, school, and the endless days of summer, that until then, I'd been so looking forward to.

I hugged Gage as I vowed to do anything I could to keep him safe from whatever was about to unfold.

Standing there with Lisa, I may not have completely understood what was happening, but I knew nothing would ever be the same again. The only world I'd ever known was now entirely different.

The cries and shouts in the neighborhood increased in intensity when more planes flew overhead with a loud whoosh that rattled the glass in the windows before us and set off some of the alarms again. Turning, I glanced back at the street to find some people running back and forth, hugging each other before running toward another house. Some got in their cars and drove away with a squeal of tires. Much like a chicken with its head cut off, they were unsure of where to go or what to do.

What could anyone possibly do? Were we next for the bombs? The hair on my nape rose.

I turned back to the TV and watched as the cloud continued to rise. More words flashed by on the bottom of the screen, but I barely saw them. I became so focused on the TV, I never heard my mother enter the porch until one of her hands fell on my shoulder.

Tilting my head back to look at her, I realized it must be worse than I ever could have imagined if *she* was touching *me*. It was the first time she'd touched me in a comforting way in years. It would be the last, that wasn't by accident or in anger, for all the years following.

"What is happening?" Lisa inquired in a tremulous whisper.

"The end," Mother replied.

I wouldn't know how right she was until years later.

Available now.

Good Intentions **on Amazon:**
brendakdavies.com/GIambk

FIND THE AUTHOR

Erica Stevens/Brenda K. Davies Mailing List:
brendakdavies.com/ESBKDNews

Facebook page: brendakdavies.com/BKDfb
Facebook friend: ericastevensauthor.com/EASfb

Erica Stevens/Brenda K. Davies Book Club:
brendakdavies.com/ESBKDBookClub

Instagram: brendakdavies.com/BKDInsta
Twitter: brendakdavies.com/BKDTweet
Website: www.brendakdavies.com
Blog: ericastevensauthor.com/ESblog

ALSO FROM THE AUTHOR

BRENDA K. DAVIES PEN NAME:

The Vampire Awakenings Series

Awakened (Book 1)

Destined (Book 2)

Untamed (Book 3)

Enraptured (Book 4)

Undone (Book 5)

Fractured (Book 6)

Ravaged (Book 7)

Consumed (Book 8)

Unforeseen (Book 9)

Coming 2019

The Alliance Series
Vampire Awakenings Spinoff

Eternally Bound (Book 1)

Bound by Vengeance (Book 2)

Bound by Darkness (Book 3)

Bound by Passion (Book 4)

Coming 2019

The Road to Hell Series

Good Intentions (Book 1)

Carved (Book 2)

The Road (Book 3)

Into Hell (Book 4)

Hell on Earth Series

Road to Hell Spinoff

Hell on Earth (Book 1)

Into the Abyss (Book 2)

Kiss of Death (Book 3)

Coming 2019

Historical Romance

A Stolen Heart

ERICA STEVENS PEN NAME:

The Coven Series

Nightmares (Book 1)

The Maze (Book 2)

Dream Walker (Book 3)

Coming June 2019

The Captive Series

Captured (Book 1)

Renegade (Book 2)

Refugee (Book 3)

Salvation (Book 4)

Redemption (Book 5)

Broken (The Captive Series Prequel)

Vengeance (Book 6)

Unbound (Book 7)

The Kindred Series

Kindred (Book 1)

Ashes (Book 2)

Kindled (Book 3)

Inferno (Book 4)

Phoenix Rising (Book 5)

The Fire & Ice Series

Frost Burn (Book 1)

Arctic Fire (Book 2)

Scorched Ice (Book 3)

The Ravening Series

Ravenous (Book 1)

Taken Over (Book 2)

Reclamation (Book 3)

The Survivor Chronicles

Book 1: The Upheaval

Book 2: The Divide

Book 3: The Forsaken

Book 4: The Risen

ABOUT THE AUTHOR

Brenda K. Davies is the USA Today Bestselling author of the Vampire Awakening Series, Alliance Series, Road to Hell Series, Hell on Earth Series, and historical romantic fiction. She also writes under the pen name, Erica Stevens. When not out with friends and family, she can be found at home with her husband, son, dog, and horse.

Printed in Great Britain
by Amazon